ALL SHE HAD BEEN MISSING

❖

"Would ye be able to trust a mother who gave ye up?"

"Depends."

"On what?"

"On why. How. And if she was really, deep down in her heart, sorry."

"Sorry canno' change the past, Mitch."

"Neither does bitterness. That particular insidious little poison can eat up your heart, if you aren't careful."

"Ye sounds as if ye know what ye're talkin' about."

"What I know about, Glenna, is regret, truckloads full. And I can tell you, it's the same poison. I'd hate to see you have them if you and Mrs. Wescott didn't find some common ground to at least try and begin healin'. Don't be bound up by your bitterness. It can destroy you if you don't take care."

DIANE HAEGER

PIECES OF APRIL

HarperPaperbacks
A Division of HarperCollins*Publishers*

HarperPaperbacks

A Division of HarperCollins*Publishers*
10 East 53rd Street, New York, N.Y. 10022-5299

This is a work of fiction. The characters, incidents, and
dialogues are products of the author's imagination and are not to
be construed as real. Any resemblance to actual events or
persons, living or dead, is entirely coincidental.

ISBN 0-06-101192-4

Cover illustration by John Ennis

Cover photograph copyright © by Chris Close/Image Bank

First printing: July 1997

Printed in the United States of America

Visit HarperPaperbacks on the World Wide Web at
http://www.harpercollins.com/paperbacks

❖ 10 9 8 7 6 5 4 3 2 1

For my children, Elizabeth and Alexander,
with the greatest love.

This book has been a three-year labor of love in so many respects, mostly because it has taught me the value of patience, persistence, and an unswerving belief in pursuing, first, the stories that come from my heart. There have been so many people who have supported me to that end, but foremost, I owe a debt of gratitude to J.R., which I can never repay, for graciously gifting me with hours and hours of information, advice, and friendship—and for giving me a selfless glimpse into the mind and heart of a Catholic priest, without which I could never have brought Stephen Donnelly to life.

And to my Scottish contingent—Ray "the Highlander" Shields, Ian Smith, Scottish novelist Harriet Smart, and the people of the lovely village of Glenfinnan—for all of the wonderful details about their extraordinary country.

To Gary Hoff, M.D., for his help with understanding the intricacies and nuances of advanced diabetes.

To my husband, Ken, who has been there every step of this wild ride with me, for helping with endless hours of research on yet another journey, and for giving me encouragement beyond the pale.

To Meg Fried, the greatest (and most merciless!) editorial assistant a writer could ever hope to have, for all of the hours she has put in on this book.

To Dick Hanke, as always, for his encouragement.

To my editors, Carolyn Marino and Jessica Lichtenstein, who are the embodiment of professionalism, for their insight and their vision for this book.

And last, but by no means least, thank you to the many kind readers who continue to write to me with their many wonderful comments. It is a joy and a privilege to hear from each of them.

So faith, hope, love, these three;
but the greatest of these is love.
—I Corinthians 13:13

PROLOGUE

Glasgow, Scotland, 1958

"No, Don't take her! God, I'm begging you, please, don't take her from me!"

Ross Maguire turned away from the tortured expression on his daughter's sweat-drenched face and the bare, milk white forearms extended up to him in pleading. Isabelle's anguished cry across the vaulted mahogany bedroom was piercing, but he was glad at least that it drowned out the faint mewling of the newborn baby girl he had torn away from her breast.

"It's for the best, Isabelle."

"She's crying for me! Please, Daddy! Oh, I can't stand it!"

It was all planned. Decided. His voice was a monotone of conviction in the shadowy darkness. "She'll be well cared for. I'll see to it."

"But she needs *me!* She needs her mother!"

He heard the haunting echo of Isabelle's pleading even through the barrage of street noise as he settled back and the taxi, a big ebony-colored cab, began to chug its way through the traffic steadily down toward Mansion Street. He was still shaking as he held the newborn child in his arms, wrapped only in a pale blue blanket the midwife had brought. He hadn't even taken time to properly wash her, fearing that he would lose his nerve altogether.

This must be done, he told himself. *I'll not let you raise a bastard. A priest's child, for the love of God!* he had told Isabelle. *The sin that was begun here will be left here.*

And it was better this way. Isabelle would get over this in time. She would have other children. Legitimate children. He hoped they would be with that promising young politician, Frank Wescott. And, also in time, she would see that

I

he had been right. What he had done had been for her own good. For the good of the family.

Ross Maguire, a tall man with a commanding presence and a shock of copper hair set off against his dark black overcoat, closed his eyes for a moment. The old taxicab still smelled of a woman's cheap perfume. He could still feel her warmth on the seat beneath his thighs. It made him a little sick, the aroma of gardenia mixed with the smell of dried blood still on the child, exhaust fumes as well.

As the cab slowed in traffic on Bridge Street, guilt began again to gnaw at the corners of his conscious mind like a vicious animal, even as he did his best to rationalize what he was about to do. It had been slowly eating at him every day since he and his daughter had left Sunny and Alice alone out in the Highlands at Willowbrae. As they had settled in Glasgow to await this day. Until now, he'd managed to be so methodical. Practical. He'd paid a small fortune to rent a fashionable townhouse on the Landsdowne Crescent with a little back garden so that Isabelle would not need to go out publicly. Would not need to be seen in her condition.

He took a deep breath and then another, trying to still this sudden and annoying tremble. He hadn't let Isabelle know, until tonight, that he meant to give away her child.

Damn. Should have had that glass of Scotch, he thought. But he hadn't been able to bear the sound of Isabelle's sobbing another moment.

The child in his arms was quiet now. Probably sleeping, at last. Thank the Lord for small mercies. He closed his eyes for a moment and laid his head against the back of the torn leather seat. When he opened his eyes again he pulled the blanket away from the tiny face for the first time. Safe enough now, he thought, to look upon her at least once so long as she was asleep. He gazed in at a crop of fuzzy dark hair and a sweet rosebud mouth, slightly parted. But then his heart lurched, and it was like a clap of thunder rolling through him, when he saw that pair of piercing blue eyes, like little buttons, so innocent and trusting, and they were open and gazing up at him.

Holy hell! She's the very image of Stephen Donnelly! What divine retribution that is!

His Scots blood boiled at the mere thought of Stephen with Isabelle, what they had done together to beget this child. Dear God Almighty, how he'd trusted that boy! Helped him at every turn and, in the process, practically served up Isabelle to him on a silver platter!

What had happened between them was a sin: He was a boy who had chosen the priesthood and now wanted Isabelle. As her father, the shepherd of his young, Ross was ultimately responsible. This baby who seemed so serene and contented just now in his arms, those blue eyes cutting at his heart like tiny jagged sapphires, would forever remind him of that.

"Carmelite Convent, sir," the cabby called out in a thick, working-class burr as he cranked down his window and spit into the street. The cab then slowed and inched toward the curb beneath the arc of young oak trees lining the road.

It was very dark. Almost nine o'clock. The building before him was poorly lit, but he could see the imposing salmon-colored stone, in the Romanesque style, set very close to the street. Extended around it on the other three sides was an imposing high stone wall. Another shiver crawled up his spine as he paid for the ride and opened the car door.

Lord, give me the strength. . . . he thought as his heart began to thump so wildly that now, suddenly, he almost could not breathe. *I cannot take her back to the States as my grandchild. It would ruin everything. I know You don't expect me to suffer that. I've been generous to the Church. Very generous, they tell me. That ought to count for something with You, shouldn't it? Give me a marker or two I can call in now?*

Rationalizing did not still his heart. It was pounding so like a drum that he could hear little else. There was hot blood rushing into his face and he had begun to perspire. Was this what it felt like in the moments before you had a heart attack? he wondered. The tightening in his heart squeezed until it became a fearsome ache. He moved up the tree-lined walkway with the tiny bundle squirming in his arms, almost as if she knew what was about to happen. Could she possibly? Of course he was being ridiculous. A baby wasn't really a person, thank God. Not yet. He had covered the little pink face over again with the corner of the blanket, unable any longer to look upon her for the way his conscience slammed at him when he did.

The urge to turn around and run off into the night with this child, take her back to Isabelle, and to deal with the consequences, slowly grew very strong within him. Ross actually began to wonder, as his heels clicked against the stone steps, if it wasn't actually the hand of God tapping very firmly on his shoulder, telling him that this was wrong.

You're being ridiculous, Maguire. He shook his head and took yet another steadying breath. *Do it and be done with it.* Just a few more minutes and it would be over and he could go across the Great Western Road for a couple of drams of good Scotch. He certainly couldn't go back to Isabelle, her tears and her pleading. Not sober.

Besides, it was all arranged. The abbess knew of a childless Catholic couple who had longed for more than ten years to have a child. And didn't this little soul deserve a proper baptism and then a family like that? People who could love her unconditionally? People who would not be forever reminded of her very conception as he would? He ran a finger along her smooth tiny cheek. *God forgive me,* he thought, *but we Maguires cannot be asked to bear a cross like that. . . .*

He pressed the tarnished buzzer beside the door. Then he waited.

"Believe me, it's better this way," he glanced down and whispered to the warm little bundle, so snug in his arms.

Better for you, his conscience murmured back. But he refused to listen to that.

Suddenly the small oak window in the heavy grand door

snapped back with a little click and a pair of gray eyes in gold-rimmed glasses peered out at him. "Yes?"

His throat tightened but he forced the words out anyway. "I am Ross Maguire. The abbess is expecting me."

The little window closed again.

As he waited, the baby's fussing escalated and became a cry, and Ross found himself softly swaying and settling her against his chest, in that gentle way he had done with his own two daughters.

"There, there, little one. You'll be happy soon," he whispered, glad this would not go on much longer. Glad Sunny didn't begrudge him his decision. He couldn't have faced seeing that look of betrayal he'd seen on Isabelle's face coming from his wife too.

The thick old wooden door swung back with a sound like a cat's cry, and he was finally ushered into a vast shadowy stone room with two small stained glass windows. But the nun who had answered the door had already disappeared. He had been only this far into the dank, musty cloister one other time. Then it had been daylight. Tonight this sacred dwelling smelled very like a tomb.

Two weeks ago he had come here to arrange to give away his grandchild and had waited for an audience with the abbess in this room, along with other people making donations to the order of cloistered nuns who did not interact directly with the outside world. The old and dented turnstile before him was the place where he had watched a stoop-shouldered old man leave a donation of groceries. He had placed the bag on the turnstile with much effort and then waited while the sisters within turned the mechanism, swiveling it around to receive the offering. After that, a middle-aged woman had come to ask the sisters to pray for an ill child. She had left a fistful of flowers. Another man before him had asked them to pray that he receive a job. Ross Maguire had listened to the Glaswegians dispassionately that day.

But now the turn was his.

And he was about to surrender a good deal more than groceries.

"It's time, Mr. Maguire," came another woman's voice, this one thin and slightly warbling, from the other side of a small window covered over with opaque fabric that further separated the Carmelite sisters.

Ross glanced down at the turnstile half of a painted metal drum. "Here?" he asked in surprise. And with the question he heard his own voice quiver.

"Yes, there."

Wracked now by a trembling he could no longer still, Ross Maguire bent over the cold and sterile receptacle on which he had seen groceries and flowers placed. Objects. Offerings . . . The child was crying again and squirming in his arms. Her tiny wail was a haunting sound echoing across the silent and very dank stone chamber.

"Hail, Mary, full of grace, the Lord is with thee," he found himself softly reciting as he finally placed the squalling infant on the cold, carved wood, still covered only in that soiled blue blanket in which he had so quickly taken her away. "Holy Mary, Mother of God, pray for us sinners . . . now and at the hour of our death. . . .

"God be with you, Mr. Maguire," the same warbling voice came back to him from the darkened other side. But now suddenly the words sounded hollow. Insincere. In them, he certainly heard no empathy. No hint of understanding.

But perhaps he didn't deserve any.

The images splintered like broken glass across his mind. Isabelle's pleading. Stephen's remorse. Those damn blue eyes . . .

Could he actually do this? How many lives was he about to change if he did not stop this now? As the turnstile began slowly to turn away, pulling the still-squalling infant steadily out of his sight, Ross Maguire's heart began once again to beat very fast. Hard and fast. Until it was slamming against his rib cage. Life was full of choices. None of them were without consequence.

Tears started in the back of his eyes and he sagged against the stone sidewall, knowing that he would not, could not, change this, and yet feeling that he might well have just made the most awful mistake of his life. A bit of remorse came to him just as the little child, his first grandchild, very slowly, and forever, disappeared from his sight.

But, even so, "May God forgive me . . ." was all that he whispered.

Love is a circle that doth restless move.

—Robert Herrick

CHAPTER

I

Glenna

Arrochar, Scotland, 1994

The scent was like nothing else in the world.

Glenna turned the steering wheel slightly, and the car veered slowly down the next slim, twisting road, more like a well-worn path, through a grove of moss-furred beech and oak trees. A long succession of bends and curves and then there it was. That seductive blend of heather and broom with a subtle hint of sage, made more intense, more sweet somehow, just as it always was after a rain.

It was only drizzling now, but by the flooding in the places where the road dipped, it appeared there had been quite a storm while she was away. But it didn't matter, not the mud on the newly washed car. Not the slower-than-normal pace she needed to take. Nothing mattered now that she was back from London.

Home again.

She unrolled the sticky window of her old black Range Rover with a little grunt from the strain, not caring that the cool drizzle spattered in on her face and neck. The autumn rain sprinkled the celery-colored collar of her best Saint Laurent suit, the one she took out of the bag at the back of her closet once a year when she went down to London.

The rain tossed along with it the added scent of chimney smoke from the low-lying cottages around her. She breathed deeply and smiled.

God, how she had come to love it, all of it.

There was nothing like Arrochar in the autumn. Nothing in the world. And London, choked with all of its cars, fat red buses, cabs, and sirens, well, the Londoners could have it.

She was happy that the surgeons' convention only came once a year. Then, after a dreary three days of overblown speeches, too much drinking, and an exhaustive round of glad-handing, she could return here, to the simple life in the place her heart always would be. To Aengus and their daughter. To Kate.

The Range Rover trudged up a brilliant green hill, belching a thin little stream of white smoke, past an ancient stone wall leaning against the old rowan trees with the last of the summer roses joining them all like old friends. The road dipped and rose again beneath the pewter sky, and she was nearly there.

Glenna felt her heart quicken as it always did. As it always would.

She imagined the cottage before she saw it, graceful in its simplicity, old white stone, the two charming dormer windows, the gray slate roof. That old stone wall with the wooden gate slung back, waiting for her.

She could not imagine a greater sense of peace in the life that had become hers in Arrochar—until she turned the corner and the road widened. When she saw them standing there, a ring of people around the cottage. They were talking, clutching one another, and trying to peer inside the open red front door.

Glenna switched off the motor, and her heart began to pound. *Oh, God . . .*

She bolted from the car and tromped through the mud-sodden courtyard, forgetting her expensive pumps. Before her was a sea of faces. They were faces she knew, all of them frozen with concern. Worry. Some even with what looked to her like anguish. There was such a sudden roaring in her ears that she wasn't certain if she had cried out.

Kate, she thought wildly. *My child! My Lord, no!*

Glenna dashed across the threshold and inside the cottage, pushing past old, slack-shouldered Donny Mackay and his grandson, Kevin, who were standing near the door. She heard the moaning and the low rumble of well-meaning voices.

A fire was lit in the old hearth and she could see the feet of someone lying on the long oak refectory dining table. They were circling it, leaning over it. But the moaning did not come from a young girl. It was the anguished sound of a man . . . Aengus.

She saw him spread out on the table, eyes rolled back in his head, his red-gray curls brushed back flat, away from his face. Jenny Mackay, Donny's white-haired wife, was tending to him, and she could see that he was wrapped in blankets.

Kate was holding his hand to her chest and silently weeping.

"What's happened?" Glenna breathed, the words not coming fully across her tongue.

"Oh, thank the Lord ye've come back home, Glenna!" Jenny said in a panic. "We've been tryin' for hours but could no' reach ye at your hotel!"

She pushed her way up to Aengus, lying lifeless and pale, so deathly pale, his sweet, square face drained of life and color. She looked up at her adolescent daughter, but Kate was too distraught to give her any answers.

By instinct, and years of training, she reached down, unwrapped his arm from the tightly wound blankets, then took up his limp, liver-spotted wrist to check the pulse. "What happened? Why've ye got him down here?"

"We thought 'twas best to leave him be," Jenny said as kindly as she could manage. "Not move him again. His condition seemed too grave to risk it."

His breathing was very rapid. His pulse was rapid as well. Her heart lurched until she felt a sharp jolt of pain. Diabetic coma. It had to be. What she had feared and fought against for almost ten years now. Bloody hell! He hadn't taken his insulin again! She had left it out for him herself. Lectured him like a child about taking it before she left.

"Damn ye, Aengus McDowell," she murmured, completely overcome for a moment by concern and by love. Now, at this moment in time, she was not a doctor, but a wife whose husband she had left laughing and waving in the front garden only a few days before. Who appeared to her now very near death.

"Someone has got to tell me what happened!"

"He'd gone out walkin' again, Glenna," Donny said carefully.

"Like the last time, he was no' himself," Aengus's sister Janet concurred.

Kate only sobbed, hands steepled over her face.

"He was gone all last night," Janet explained. "We only just found him at dawn. Still stormin' it was, and he with the bluest lips ye'd ever seen. Your Katie was a champion, though, I'll tell ye. We could no' get him up the stairs so she told us to lay him here. She gave him his injection, lit the fire, and covered him over, tight as a babe, with blankets till he warmed."

Glenna's face was stricken as the story unfolded, but the cool reserve of a doctor was returning. It was likely that he had suffered hypothermia from the prolonged exposure, she deduced as she listened. Kate knew a bit about that, watching her mother with patients through the years, and having asked questions. Her daughter had done correctly, she thought.

And yet the shot of insulin Kate had given her father had been too little, too late, Glenna surmised, looking down at her husband now who did not even stir. But it was not her fault. When Aengus got it in his mind to do something, like going out and gathering wood, or not to do something, as in helping himself to extra cake and not taking his insulin, there was simply no stopping him.

That stubborn pride of his was the first thing Glenna had come to love about him. It was that which had helped to rescue her from an existence that had been slowly killing her. Now, it appeared to be, rather more quickly, doing him in.

"What else have ye done for him?" she asked evenly.

"Only given him a bit o' whiskey to try to warm him inside as well."

"He spat most o' that back out."

There was no use in telling them how quickly that would

have turned to sugar in his bloodstream. How that quite likely had complicated things all the more. "Did no one think to get him to the hospital over in Glasgow? Or at least to call Dr. Maxwell before now?"

"Ye're no' thinkin', lass," Janet said, resting a careful hand on Glenna's trembling arm. "That's an hour's drive, and the storm last night was verra fierce. Phones were down and the roads are still flooded now."

"Was there nothin' else ye could think to do to get him out o' here?" she asked, trying hard to keep that little note of hysteria from creeping back into her voice. "Ye see, he's very ill now!"

But even as she spoke the question, Glenna knew the answer.

The people of Arrochar did not trust doctors or hospitals too far away, no matter the consequences. Glenna McDowell was an exception because she was Aengus's wife. Because she was one of them now.

Beyond that, it might as well have been 1894 in Arrochar as 1994. Little changed in a town the size of a bump in the road. Life went on as it had for centuries. The Highlanders were born. They lived a simple life, they worked and loved their families, protected them. And they died. Sometimes prematurely, if the good Lord willed it. All with little interference from outsiders. Even Glenna had had to prove herself, having come from a town fifty-five miles away. Distance was like time; anything but the here and now was too long. Too far away.

When the widowed Aengus McDowell brought home a stranger as his new bride, people in town turned a suspicious eye to the girl young enough to be his daughter. Pretty enough to have been someone's city mistress. And not too many years after they married and had a child, Glenna was leaving them five days a week, going to live in Edinburgh to go to medical school! Poor Aengus, they whispered. How long can a thing like that last?

But they stayed married. Glenna came back a doctor. The

McDowells settled down. So did everyone else. The gossip slowly died away. The people of Arrochar had a doctor, their own doctor, and soon people trickled in to see her with this pain and that. The occasional baby was even born, and after a while, "Doc McDowell" became one of the most important threads in the fabric of their small and tightly knit community.

Kate held her sides, as if that alone could hold in the fear and frustration, as she watched her mother once again become doctor. Healer. It seemed to her as if a switch went on when it happened. She had seen it so many times before. She watched as her mother checked his pulse, lifted his limp wrist, look at her watch. She saw her mother's face tense. Those blue eyes of hers narrowed, the blue intensified. *Blue like an August sky.*

He might have been anyone. A stranger. A friend for the way her mother cared for him so calmly. But he wasn't just anyone. He was her *da*. The man who had taught her to fish for salmon and how to catch a rainbow.

He was older than everyone else's father and impossibly past it. But he was kind and sweet, and she wasn't at all ready for him to die. He had been sick like this before. It seemed as if he had been sick nearly all of her life. And his refusing to believe that he was only made things worse.

"Bring me his insulin, will ye, Katie?"

The question had been asked with expectation. Without the need to turn around. And still neither the syringe nor the insulin came. As her mother finally retrieved what she needed herself, and prepared the injection, Kate's mind ran only to escape. She had been in this room too long, with these people too impossibly prepared for him to die. She had done all that she could for him.

After she had caused all of this in the first place.

If her father was going to die this time, she was not going to be there to watch the whole miserable process. All of the weeping and shaking of heads. The guilt she felt now, as it was, was choking her.

When Glenna turned around to the hand that had always been there to help her, to fetch her instruments when she asked, Glenna saw her daughter instead turning away from her and heading for the door. "Katherine Mary! Ye're no' to leave me now! I need ye!"

"I've got to go, Ma."

"Where?"

Kate turned back around briefly, hand on the knob, tears raining down her cheeks, the sloppy leather bag she insisted on using now for a purse slung over her shoulder. Her expression, when she looked back at her mother, was still stricken, and her face was puffy and red from crying. "I don't know, Ma. I just canno' stay here right now and watch him die!"

"Katherine Mary McDowell! I will no' have that sort o' talk here around your da! Not when he needs both of us!"

"But it's the truth, isn't it? He's dyin', isn't he?"

"We don't know that yet!"

"Well, I don't want to watch you discover that it's true! I canno'!"

She pushed past their neighbors and her aunt, who still ringed the door with their well-meaning expressions of concern, before Glenna could object any further. And she ran as fast as she could away from that, and the truth of her own guilt. And as far. She knew that her legs would take her to Mary's house, where there would be comfort. A trusted ear. And another of those little white pills. If she wanted them.

Damn ye for not doin' as ye'd promised!

Damn ye for getttin' old when life is just startin' to get so good!

Glenna tried to clear her mind of thoughts like that as she worked over Aengus, assessing his condition with every bit of skill and calm she could enlist. And she tried not to be any more hard on herself than she could be on Kate. After all, people could see this as her own fault for leaving an aging husband with a recurring illness in the first place. Selfishly pursuing her career by going to a conference.

Glenna could see it that way herself if she thought too long about it.

She had worried about going to London even as she set foot on the plane three days ago. Even though Aengus had encouraged her actively for weeks.

"Ye've got to go, Glenna Rose," he'd told her. " 'Tis what ye do. 'Tis what ye love."

"What I love is you."

"And I'll be here, as sure as the sunrise in the mornin', waitin' for ye to come home."

But he'd been forgetting things lately. He'd gone out without his hat and shoes only the week before, and Kevin Mackay, on his way home from school, had found him sitting on a stump on Old Kirklee Road.

His condition at this moment was dire at best. It took her little to see that. Aengus needed to be in a hospital. This she could not mend alone. His breathing was still rapid, the mucous membranes were dry and his pulse was very rapid. He had been without his medication too long. Yes, dear God, it was a diabetic coma. She only hoped it had not already been too long to reverse.

"Is the phone in workin' order again?"

Janet, tall and rangy with her brother's coils of red hair, was wary. "Why would ye be wantin' to make a call just now?"

"Bring me the phone, Janet. I've got to order a helicopter and get him to a hospital. Your brother's verra ill."

"Ye know how he'd feel about it, Glenna."

She looked at him head on. "Your brother could die from this, Janet."

"Then he'd want to die here, in his own house, his wife beside him, not with a lot o' doctors and nurses he didn't know buzzin' around him, and tubes stickin' out everywhere."

She knew it was true. She knew Aengus. He would be angry as a hornet if she took him away from Arrochar. If he survived this.

She picked up the receiver. "Well, on this one occasion, I'm afraid Aengus is about to be overruled."

"I won't be lettin' ye, Glenna." Janet's freckled hand was over hers, pressing the receiver firmly back onto the phone.

"Don't be a fool. He needs a hospital!"

"His wife's a doctor. 'Tis close enough."

She cast off her hand with a fierce jerk, her eyes were blazing. "For the love o' God, are ye wantin' him to die?"

"I want ye to respect his wishes. . . . And for ye to see him made well yourself."

"Ye don't know what ye're askin'! 'Tis no' a simple thing to see him from this!"

"I've seen ye cure dozens o' people in this very house. Are ye sayin', then, ye cannno' do the same for yer own husband now?"

Frustration welled inside her and then began to spill, hot and vile, from every pore in her body. Glenna wanted to strangle Janet for her naïveté. She meant well, but Aengus's sister may just be about to cost him his life. She should call for a helicopter. Push her authority here. Aengus could be at Saint Mary's over in Glasgow in less than an hour. In an ICU. With the most sophisticated equipment. And they would save him. She was not so certain that, alone, she could do the same.

And yet something stopped her from insisting, even through the anger. As she glanced down at her husband, so pale and limp, what stopped her was Aengus himself. Her mind skipped back, like a stone across water, to something he'd said last year after a particularly bad bout of influenza, when they'd almost lost him then.

"Tell me that when 'tis my time, Glenna, you'll let me die here in this house," he'd said.

"What are ye talkin' such foolishness, Aengus McDowell? There'll no' be dyin' in this house by any McDowells for a good many years yet."

"Still, promise me."

She had seen his eyes, the shade of moss, desperation spiking there.

"'Tis no' the lot for a man like me to be pincushion to a sour-faced stranger in a white coat, poked at and prodded, trapped inside four grim walls of a hospital and made to listen to some machine beepin' away at ye until ye're beggin' for the grave. . . ."

She had wanted to laugh at the way he said it, that thick Scottish burr so endearing from a man whose entire life had been spent in another era. But knowing how serious he had been, how deeply rooted in the soul of Arrochar his wishes were, she had only smiled her softest smile and taken his hand in her own.

"If I'm to die, I want the last thing I smell to be the heather, and the last thing I see to be your lovely face against the moors outside. . . ."

"If it ever happens, and it's not goin' to, mind ye, but if it ever did," Glenna had said, "I'll remember."

She looked down at him now, so pale, so deathly pale, his scrambled red curls shot with gray and smoothed back away from his square, proud face. And those wonderful shaggy red-gray brows over eyes that could not see her.

Another image swooped down on her, cold and dark and very vivid. She thought of the hospital in London where she had trained. Doctors and nurses, strangers all, swarming like flies around patients. Charts. Tubes. Needles. So many wires taped here and there. And that monitor Aengus had so despised, recording every endless heartbeat with a blip as if it were about to be the last.

She glanced around their home now, crushed with cozy old furniture and family photographs. The low, beamed ceiling and the soot-stained fireplace that had always been like a protective shell to them. A place to which she had escaped the adoptive father who had abused her. A place into which Aengus had welcomed her and made her feel like the queen of his own charming little castle. A modest home that was his birthright. And he wanted nothing so much as to share it with her.

Janet was right. Come what may, Aengus especially belonged here. If he was going to survive this, she was going to have to save him herself.

This was not the world the way it was down in London, nor even in Glasgow. Things were different here. Loyalty and tradition were valued above all else.

And he would not die from this, no matter how desperate

it looked, she tried to tell herself. Death would be unthinkable. Twenty years ago, he had been the only one in the world to make her want to go on living.

His patience and kindness had taught her that there were other things in this world besides retribution and penance. The penance had always been the most difficult part for Glenna. Paying for sins she did not understand. Sins she had no idea she had committed.

But her father had been undeterred. She had evil inside of her, he had said.

Aengus had said *the devil* to all of that. He had been a such big, important-looking man to a desperately lonely young girl back then. And he had taken her away with him to Arrochar and never let her look back.

He had always been more father than husband. More friend than lover. He had been a savior, taking her from the misery of an adoptive father who had punished her in some way every day of her life for not really being his. . . . There were just so many years between Aengus and herself. But they had made a life, nonetheless. And then Kate had come. The joy of his heart. And of hers.

"Aengus McDowell, you fight this," she whispered through her tears so that only he might hear. "I'm no' ready just yet to give you over to the good Lord. No, He'll have to fight me tooth and nail if He wants to take ye from me now."

She touched his forehead.

"All right, Janet, you win this time," she said finally to her husband's only sister, but in a low tone that said she did not feel at all confident about what she had decided. "I'll do for him what I can."

Mary seemed glad to see her even though it was a surprise.

She was already dressed for going out in faded blue jeans, an old evergreen sweatshirt with *Glasgow University* slashed across the front, and worn brown boots, ankle high, that looked meant for hiking, not a night on the town.

Dressed up, are ye? Kate thought with a hint of a smile, looking over at her friend, a girl who was older, dangerous. Fun simply because her parents so vehemently disapproved. *I canno' imagine what's the occasion.*

Mary's parents were sitting in their cramped living room with the faded rose wallpaper, the matching blue ginger jar lamps and the old 1950s camelback brown sofa with a strip of lace that once had been white tossed over the hump. A touristy collection of cups and saucers, from places like the Tower of London and Brighton Beach, were the highlight of the drab room, set neatly in a mahogany china closet and lit like something valuable by a forty-watt light bulb.

The old television, low to the ground with legs, had been turned on, the rabbit ears rammed stiffly into a perfect V, and a droning laugh track crashed through the silence predictably every few seconds. But neither of them were watching.

Mrs. Keith, a stout, short-haired brick of a woman, was knitting something in crimson wool with loose cable stitches, but Kate couldn't make out even what it was meant to become. Mary's father had the evening paper held up in front of his face and a beer bottle half-empty on the table between them. Tonight he didn't even grunt at her. Only Mary's mother looked up briefly to nod a greeting.

"Super, ye're just in time."

"Time for what?"

"Goin' into Glasgow for a poetry readin'."

So that was the big event, Kate thought. *I knew it had to be something for her to break out the "good" denim.* Wisely, she kept her snide thought to herself as she set down her floppy brown handbag on a chair by the door. "Ye're kiddin', right?"

"I'm no'. The man's as famous as they come. Stephen Drake's his name. The library's full of his books."

"I don't much fancy poems, Mary."

Tonight she could not have cared about anything less. Her father was probably dying. Maybe he was already dead. Her heart clenched in her chest at the mere thought. But if Kate had come for consolation about that, she had come to the wrong place. Mary was a party girl. Having a good time was how she defined her life, how she freed herself from this mediocre life and the harsh gray world which, they both knew, one day would swallow her back up, no matter how she tried to fight it.

"Are ye up for chummin' me, then?"

Kate's mind traveled quickly back to the alternative. The little, low-ceilinged cottage a village away. By now, everyone would be crying, hugging her mother. Everyone offering what a good man Aengus McDowell had been. If only he hadn't eaten more than that one slice of cake. If only he hadn't been left alone to go out in the rain. To get lost . . .

Kate had known the danger of his going without insulin for an extended period. It was not an excuse. She had heard her parents arguing across the hall about it more than once. And her father was such a stubborn, such a prideful man.

"I tell ye I don't need drugs, Glenna!" she'd heard her father shout. "And I'll eat what I like when I like it! What's a man's life if he canno' have a bit o' cake, now and again?"

"Ye do need them, damn you! This is serious, Aengus, I mean it! I canno' be here with ye every minute o' the day. Ye've got to care for yourself, as well!"

Kate flinched at the memory, which cut like a knife wound across her heart. Very sharp. Piercing. It was her fault. All of it. God, why had she done it—given in to his pleading?

Just one wee slice more o' that lovely cake, darlin'? Just a wee slice. 'Twill be our secret, he'd pleaded, those hazel eyes of his wide and watery now with age, and so sad when he wanted them to be. Like a basset hound's. She'd held her ground at first, but in the end he'd won her over as if, somehow, her mother did not discover it, there could be no real harm done.

They'd sat together at the kitchen table, that old trestle thing Glenna so loved, the fire warming the little room, turning it all shadowy and golden against the grayness outside. And it was like when she was a little girl, laughing, sipping tea, and eating the spice cake she'd made for her mother's return.

Stupid, stupid fool, making a cake in the first place when Ma's no' around to watch him! Tempting Da that way, as if things could ever be as they were when you were a child! You're not a child, and your da is not the same man! What were you thinking, Katherine Mary? She did not need her mother's chiding, or worse yet, that look of disappointment in her eyes. Her own conscience was like a giant stone pressing the breath out of her as it was.

And when they'd found him, at last, unconscious, and brought him back to the house, he'd looked like a corpse already, all soaking wet, his face the color of wet flour, lips swollen and blue, parted slightly. He didn't look anything like her da. That wasn't him. But she'd given him his insulin anyway, with hands trembling so fiercely she could barely point the needle. And Aunt Janet, her father's sister, and Mrs. Mackay looking on, both of them shaking their heads, holding each other steady, and whispering to each other unanswerable questions about how this could have happened.

And then they'd all waited as it rained.

The phone lines down. The storm growing more fearsome each hour that her mother was away. It beat against the windows, rattling them, thundering down, like angry gods, against the slate roof. If they were angry, whatever gods were up there, they were certainly angry at her.

And so she had sat with him all day while the rain came, holding his hand, talking softly to him, waiting for the insulin to work, willing him to open his eyes and look up at her. But it had not happened. Nothing had happened. The last time she'd seen someone in her house so close to death, it was old Mrs. Ramsay. And she had died there.

Kate just couldn't go back to that. Not yet. Besides, her ma had Aunt Janet and Mrs. Mackay to hold her up.

She'd go back tonight, when the worst of it was over.

Coward! Leavin' your ma to try and fix what ye've done!

She's a doctor. He's in far better hands with her than with me!

Her mind waged the silent battle as she stood waiting for Mary.

So, ye did no' want to be perfect anyway really, did ye? Like your ma. Selfless. Committed. Ye've been tryin' to heave that stone from your chest for quite a while now. Doin' all that ye could to be bad. Well, foolish girl, it looks as if ye've finally got your wish now, doesn't it? Bad in the first degree . . . But I'll bet ye never guessed it'd be your da who'd pay the price!

"So, will ye go to the readin' or no'?"

The voices snapped off. She was young for coffeehouses. Not quite sixteen, with a friend here who was nearly twenty. But then she was too young for a lot of things she'd been doing lately. "Why no'?" Kate said in defiance as she stood in the doorway to Mary's small bedroom, where clothes were draped over everything. A dirty dinner plate was still on the bureau.

Mary's smile was wide and a little dark from all the tea she drank. "That's the spirit! 'Tis bound to be great. There's quite the mystery about Stephen Drake, ye know."

"How d'ye mean?"

"Even now, with how famous he is, no one really knows much about his past. He came out o' nowhere, it seems. My English teacher told us that. Romantic, in a mysterious sort o' way."

"I never figured ye for the sort who'd fancy poetry."

That same blithe smile she always had bloomed now on Mary's little cherry of a mouth. "Oh, I'm fair full o' surprises, Kate McDowell!"

That was true enough. The world she'd shown to Kate was a world of casual drugs and city boys ruled by their hormones. And what she considered good times. It was a world that Kate had never for a moment even imagined when she'd decided she wanted to stop being good. So far it had done nothing for her but get her caught up in a web of self-abuse.

Turning back now no longer seemed an option. She was too far away from Katie McDowell, Aengus's little girl. Too far from the good, hardworking life her mother had modeled for her. The one Glenna had made for herself—a woman who had overcome abusive adoptive parents to go through medical school, who went against the odds of her life to actually become a doctor.

And the thought had occurred to Kate that if she were waiting for someone to turn her life around for her, she would probably be waiting a very long time indeed. Kate was not here tonight just because of what had happened with her father. She was here because of who she had become.

"So do ye want to check in at home before we go? 'Twill be late when ye get back."

Home . . . The twinge was very sharp before she answered. "I won't be needin' to ask tonight."

Kate did not feel like telling Mary the truth just now—that she had made a mistake that her oh-so-perfect mother never would have made. So dedicated, Glenna. So levelheaded. Working constantly, helping the sick. Seeing poor patients, day after day, even when they couldn't afford to pay her. Night after night, selflessly caring for an increasingly ailing husband. Asking nothing for herself. Doing all of it quietly. Perfectly. Enviably.

Kate couldn't tell Mary that those shoes were simply too big even to try to fill. What was the point of trying to tell her any of that, after all? They weren't that sort of friends. And what happened with her da was her own private hell to face, whatever happened to him, when she returned to Arrochar.

"I was plannin' on takin' the last train back, unless we can bag a ride."

"I could do with a bit o' fun just now," Kate decided, blocking out the truth and the image of her father's kind face. The image of him spread out, like a corpse, on the dining table.

"And, who knows, ye might even fancy the poems."

"True enough." Kate tried to smile, but it was more of a grimace. "What could it hurt?"

CHAPTER

2

❖ Kate

Kate and Mary took a table near the beer-spattered bar, then ordered coffee.

The Bull & Bear was almost full already, and people were still streaming up the outside stairs and in through the door behind them. It wasn't every day that a cult hero like Stephen Drake read his poetry, or even came out publicly, for that matter.

It was a warm and close place with the blazing inglenook fireplace next to the little stage that had been set up. The dark wood paneling and low ceiling made the place seem even smaller. Kate suddenly wished she'd worn something cooler, something less tasteful than the Burberry tweed jacket she had grabbed off the peg at the last desperate moment. She seemed to be the only person in the place under thirty-five who was not wearing blue jeans or black leather. The expensive jacket would give her away, she realized now, if the calf-high Italian boots did not. For someone who was trying to be bad, Kate McDowell wasn't doing a very spectacular job of it.

The Bull & Bear was in an old whitewashed building, the second floor of an old coaching inn, still with the original ring trusses downstairs. The spotlight and empty stool seemed strangely out of place, Kate thought, as Mary lit a cigarette and leaned back in the hard wood chair to see who else interesting might have come in.

There were photographs and small pictures on the walls, mostly of Robert Burns, Scotland's most beloved and famous poet. And there were the black-and-white images of another man whom Kate assumed was Stephen Drake, the poet who was synonymous with Glasgow. This was a big event, even by the standards of a city the size of Glasgow, she thought. Even the cabbie had been talking about it.

The coffee came finally in big clay mugs stamped with a lion's crest, carried by a potbellied, red-bearded man in a long white apron. She took a swallow of the thick scalding liquid as Mary waved across the room to two young men slouched in their chairs, both in blue jeans and black leather jackets.

"Do ye fancy us wavin' them over?" Mary asked with an eager smile.

Kate glanced at them. If Mary was interested, the two were trouble. The sort of trouble that in Mary's company she usually welcomed, just for the pleasure of being bad. But not tonight. Right now Kate felt that vulnerable part of herself, something she had not felt for a very long time, pushing back in on her. It was the little girl inside, the one she should have been, pressing her to go home, to be with a da she adored.

"Oh, lord." Kate rolled her blue eyes, eyes she had gotten from her mother, as she tried to ignore the sensation.

"Now, what'd be the harm? We're out for a night on the town, right? And the one I know, there on the left, is fair gorgeous."

"Then why'd ye ask me?"

Kate let the question lie, and Mary did not answer it. She didn't want to sound too perturbed, since Mary Keith had insisted on paying the five pounds it took to get inside. Not to mention how she had flirted and sweet-talked the doorman into letting them up to the front of the very long line.

She was like that—big and bold and immovable as an ox. But it seemed natural for Mary. She was also taller than most girls her age, with dark straight hair, straight bangs that stopped at the midpoint of her eyes. Voluptuous, the magazines called girls like Mary. A good time, the few friends they so far had in common called her.

She was everything Kate wasn't. Kate had tried very hard

for the past year to be bad. As bad as Mary Keith. But so far, she hadn't been too successful.

Still, their friendship had given Kate a reason and a way to get out of a stifling town the size of Arrochar. Curiosity and boredom. That was how it had begun. Kate, the good child, had begun to rebel. She had been the good child all of her life. High marks at school, never late, and certainly never a disappointment to her parents, a kindhearted, aging father and a mother who worked too much and never seemed to enjoy herself.

Kate had tried smoking, but she never could quite tolerate how it burned her lungs, and you simply did have to inhale to look like you knew what you were doing. And she had tried running away, usually only here to Glasgow, staying with some friend of Mary's just long enough to drive her mother wild.

Mary suddenly motioned with a wave to the boys across the room. Kate saw, with relief, that only one acknowledged her. He was out of his chair and heading toward them like a shot. He was small and wiry, his hair that same soft nutmeg shade as so many Scots boys, and he had freckles. He compensated for those softer features by wearing a heavy black leather jacket and by chain-smoking rancid-smelling British cigarettes. He was like a welterweight fighter coming toward them, Kate thought. A toughened-up city lad.

"How are ye, Terry?"

"Hey, Mary! What's up?" the fighter asked as he kissed her cheek.

"I'm takin' all suggestions." Her eyes widened. Then she laughed.

She was always talking like that. Suggestive. Everyone laughed with her. Even Kate, because she knew it was the thing to do when you were with a girl like Mary Keith.

"There's to be a party on High Street after this. If ye'd fancy goin', I could see ye inside."

Mary looked to Kate hopefully. Kate bought herself a moment by taking another swallow of coffee as the boy pulled at his black jacket and withdrew a small silver flask. It glinted in the room's low, smoky light. He poured some into his own coffee and then offered it to Kate.

"No, but thanks."

"Aw, come on. Just somethin' to warm ye up a wee bit."

"Go on," Mary coaxed, still smiling as she moved her chair closer to the boy.

A little reluctantly, she agreed as people pressed against them, squeezing into the tables all around. "Okay, then. But just a bit."

The boy called Terry poured a liberal splash into her mug, then into Mary's. Kate sipped her spiked coffee and actually found herself getting anxious for the reading to begin. She didn't like boys much. She certainly didn't think much of this one. He looked just like all of the others she had met, figuratively stripping off her clothes with his wide eyes full of expectation and ready to follow suit with his hands at the first hint of approval.

But still, relief washed over her like a wave when Mary, very brazenly, reached across the table and took his stubby fingers into her own hand. A moment later, they were huddling like lovers. Kate knew, because she knew her friend, that if they weren't lovers already, they would be after tonight. For Mary Keith, it was all about quantity and adventure. A big game.

The house lights were suddenly dimmed before she was ready, bringing her back to the moment. People's voices and their laughter slowly began to fade. Someone in the back began to clap alone until everyone followed, and it rose to a crescendo, sounding suddenly like a clap of thunder.

She recognized Stephen Drake from his photos on the wall as he walked through the crowd and up to the little stage. He hadn't changed that much since they were taken, Kate thought. A little more silver in the hair, perhaps. But little else. He was still tall and stately, impeccably dressed.

He took the stage without acknowledging the audience beyond a small nod as he seated himself quietly on the stool. There was a table beside it holding a book of his poetry and a cup of tea with a spiral of steam rising from it. Stephen

Drake took a swallow and picked up the volume that was covered in crimson leather as the room fell to a sudden hush.

It was all so odd.

The way Kate felt watching this man, hearing him read, it was as if she knew him, or should know him. Something. The hair on the back of her neck was standing up as he spoke, and she didn't have the slightest idea why.

What she did know was that hearing him made her uncomfortable; the way he touched her with his softly spoken, heartfelt words. And something more. A great sadness had swept over her as she listened to his deep, evocative voice.

> *In the darkness of the night, you were mine again,*
> *where all dreams were possible,*
> *when our past; those moments in Glenfinnan . . .*
> *circumstance,*
> *could no longer take you away.*

More poems. More discomfort and a tremendous need to crawl out of her skin. Then the end. A break in the reading. *Mercifully.* Kate felt an overwhelming rush of relief when at last he took a break from reading. She shook her head, always such an unbelievable sap for things like mournful poetry and old movies with happy endings, she reasoned. That was it. That must be it. Tonight, with her father near death back in Arrochar, and she beginning to feel the strain of unbearable guilt for leaving, this burst of strange emotion was the very last thing she needed. It was so strong that she'd almost forgotten about Mary, her wild friend Terry, and the party they were planning to find after this. What on earth was happening? She despised poetry.

"Do ye fancy another coffee before he starts up again?" Mary asked her. "I'll get us another round."

"I think I'd like to leave."

Mary was surprised. Her wide eyes grew wider and she set down her cup. "He's no' finished with the readin' yet."

"I don't fancy hearin' any more."

"But he's so famous," her friend Terry remarked, huddled over Mary like a scruffy bear coat and as surprised as Mary that she wished to leave.

"Aye," Mary said. "I had to read his poems at school last term."

Kate was insistent. "Then ye've likely heard them all before anyway."

"'Tis no' like ye, Kate," Mary said, trying to speak beneath her breath as the stage filled with what appeared to be the poet's handlers, several representatives and a few of the more aggressive fans seeking autographs. "Ye've always been up for a good time. And this is once in a lifetime. They say Stephen Drake's a real recluse, and still quite handsome he is. A readin' like this out in public is a rare thing indeed."

Kate stood and began to collect her purse and jacket. "I don't care. I want to leave."

Stephen Drake was sitting back down after the break, taking a sip from a mug of tea. He was alone again on the little wooden stage beneath a soft blue spotlight. Kate was the only other person standing. Quite suddenly and strangely, their blue eyes met.

When a moment before she had been poised to flee the room, now she felt suddenly rooted to that very spot on the floor. For that single moment in time, it was as if everything stopped. The sound of glasses clinking. People murmuring, others laughing.

Mary was right, he really was a handsome, self-assured looking older gentleman, she thought in the splintered moment of thoughts and emotions that rushed through her. He was far more like some mature matinee idol, with his thick silver hair and piercingly deep blue eyes, than like an avant-garde poet who had found fame, along with Kerouac and Ginsberg, in the 1960s. She looked a little more closely.

He was dressed impeccably in a navy blazer, gray sweater vest and slacks and a blue silk scarf knotted at his neck. His eyes were the same color as the scarf. Beneath the lights, both seemed to shimmer. Yes, they certainly reminded her of her mother's eyes; that incredible lustrous blue.

But unlike her mother's eyes, Stephen Drake's bore the most incredible sadness Kate had ever seen in her life. It was as if those eyes alone said that everything else about him, the image of great wealth and success, everything, was a lie.

What was it about this man—someone she had never seen before—that had touched her so unexpectedly? That had made her want to run and yet to stay near him at the very same time? Yes, his poetry was poignant and hauntingly real.

And still it was something more.

Kate felt a little numb as she tried to search herself for an answer, then as suddenly and unexpectedly as every other emotion she had felt this evening, she changed again. A great wave of guilt hit her, once and then twice, until she felt as if she were drowning in it.

She felt utterly sorry for having left Arrochar and her father in so dire a condition. That man on stage before her had brought out something she had come all the way to Glasgow to get away from. Damn him! Now the guilt, no longer ignored but acknowledged, smacked her squarely. A hint of the old Katie McDowell, young and sweet, pressed through the facade again. What on earth could she have been thinking? Trying to be like Mary. Trying to feel like Mary. Tonight of all nights.

She loved her father more than anything on earth, and she had behaved selfishly by leaving when he and mother needed her most. She felt her stomach twist until she was sick. He had always said that sometimes life was hard. But she had never known that the mere thought of losing someone you loved so much could ever be this hard.

Kate reached down onto the little round table, through a blue haze of cigarette smoke, to swallow the rest of her coffee as Mary and Terry openly kissed. She didn't really want more coffee, but it seemed like the simplest way to break eye contact with a man who had now entirely unnerved her. A moment later, she moved backward slightly and knocked over the stool she'd been sitting in.

As she picked it up nervously, she saw from the corner of her eye that there was someone else on the stage again with Stephen Drake, whispering in his ear. He looked up at the young man and smiled, then took the pen and paper for another autograph. The moment was over. Kate was relieved. And actually a little sorry.

"'Tisn't a problem, me stayin' if ye catch the train back yourself, is it?"

Mary had spoken the words as a question, but meant it rhetorically. She had no intention of leaving the Bull & Bear before the reading was through—before she had negotiated the rest of her evening with this boy she barely knew.

"No," Kate lied. "'Tisn't a problem."

"Ring ye up tomorrow?"

"Sure."

Just as she turned, Mary called her back. "Want to take a little somethin' with ye for the ride?" she asked, holding out what Kate knew to be one of her little white pills.

Kate smiled and took it from her. You never knew when something to soothe your nerves might come in handy. Especially when your father was quite likely near death and your mother would be furious (and worse than that, disappointed) at your leaving.

She turned away again and when she reached the door, not knowing why but unable to stop herself just the same, she turned back one last time. Stephen Drake had begun to read again. The words came as they had before, across the chasm and the cigarette smoke and past the sea of attentive faces. They were low and practiced, his voice silky.

> She is the summer, the child of my heart.
> Warmth and sunlight.
> Well-worn memories,
> Like the jeans she wears.
> In her bright blue eyes, there is forever,
> and a way to begin again.

Kate was surprised that his voice trembled slightly. He seemed too practiced, too polished for that. This poem meant something great to him.

She stood at the open door, her hand on the doorjamb, watching him read, hearing how the words came, not from the page, but up from his soul. The back of her neck went numb with gooseflesh.

> Leaning against my car, as if she
> doesn't quite belong,
> and me knowing better than anyone
> that she does . . . my Glenna . . . my Glenna Rose . . .

After that she turned away, no longer seeing his face, the brightness in his eyes, for the sound of a name in a line of poetry whose familiarity was as unnerving as it was rare. "I've got to get out of here," she said to herself.

But even then she was thinking that if tomorrow everything turned out all right with her da, she would go to Mill & Evan's bookshop in town and look for a volume of Stephen Drake's poetry.

Glenna sat in the shadows beside Aengus as the little carriage clock on the mantle ticked. With the exception of Janet, who sat dozing in a chair near the door, everyone else had gone home. For over five hours, no one had heard anything from Kate. But she hadn't been able to think about that. Aengus was her first concern, and now she had done all that she could. At least for the moment. But there would be a very long night ahead.

She'd seen to his insulin. Then, after each dose, she'd carefully monitored his blood sugar and other blood chemistries. The sugars were still very, very high—1200 the last time she'd checked—and his blood was acidotic, with a pH nearly through the floor. It wasn't good. She was giving him saline solution from a bag hung over the makeshift bed she'd made by moving him to the sofa, and intravenous sodium bicarbonate to neutralize the excess acid in the blood.

She had catheterized his bladder to drain it and measure the amount of urine to tell if the rehydration was successful. So far it wasn't. And he hadn't moved at all, not a single muscle, since she had first returned.

"Come on, McDowell, wake up so that I can curse ye to your face for frightenin' me like this," she muttered, knowing there would be no response but needing to do it anyway.

Life without the kindness of this man before her was impossible to comprehend. He'd always made everything all right for her and now, when he needed her most, she might not be able to do the same for him. He might actually die without her having one last chance to tell him what he had meant to her.

No. She slammed the door fiercely on that thought. There was so much ahead of them yet. First, before he could even think about dying, they had to see Kate through this adolescent crisis of hers together. Lord, how had that come upon them so suddenly? Hadn't she just been born yesterday? Hadn't she just been holding that sweet child in her arms, nursing her, rocking her to sleep?

Glenna could still remember, equally clearly, the night their only child had been conceived. They'd gone into Edinburgh for an anniversary trip. She'd wanted to show Aengus a bit of the city. She had fully intended that night to make love to him with as much passion as he deserved.

At first it had been the pressure of her father, Andrew Ferguson, always ringing them up about money after he'd had too much to drink and telling her that the Bible demanded charity. Then it was the uncertainty of whether the townspeople in Arrochar would ever stop staring when she went out and whether they would really ever accept that such a young woman who'd married Aengus could truly love him. They were the excuses that Glenna had made so many times when he came across the bed to her in the dark of night, taking his pale, already sagging body only when he would not be put off any longer.

Feeling him heaving over her, sweating and moaning like a man in pain, wasn't how she had ever imagined it was supposed to be. He had been such a good and decent older man who had wooed her with kindness and then whisked her away from the nightmare life she had lived in Coatbridge that she really hadn't thought enough about her obligations.

The marriage bed.

But after what he'd done for her, the grand gift of freedom he'd given her, Aengus deserved better than he'd gotten in return. So she had rented a grand room at the Balmoral, planned everything down to the smallest details. A bottle of his favorite Scotch had been waiting on the bureau. Pink roses in a crystal vase were in the powder room in case they should like to take a bath. They would go to a movie, then order a light supper from room service when they returned. And then, after champagne . . .

But it hadn't happened at all the way she had planned it. They had never made it to the movie or even the bath that night. Dear Aengus had been so overcome with surprise and love for his young wife, that she would have done this for them, for their marriage, that he had pressed her down onto the elegant Brussels carpet before they were barely inside the door.

Back then he'd still had a bit of the brawn left, and that night he had used it to press her smaller body against the floor as he ran his tongue behind her ear, softly moaning.

"'Tis no one in the world like ye, Glenna Rose McDowell. No one. . . ."

Why couldn't she feel what he felt? He kissed her so sweetly, so lovingly, and even then she could not help wanting to pull away. But then suddenly his body was so tense, his mouth so hot over hers and he was driving into her, pushing all other thoughts away.

I do love him, she had thought as he had groaned one last time, dug his short, firm fingertips into her shoulder and then shivered against her. *And one day I will even be in love with him . . . I will. I want that more than anything in the world, and I know that I can make it happen. . . .*

Finding out she was pregnant several weeks later had drawn them even closer together. Aengus had long before given up on the hope of ever becoming a father, and he intended to treat his wife like fine china until the day the baby came.

It had made things easier between them sexually, because he resolved quite stubbornly not to touch her in that way. The life of this child inside her was too important to risk. *Besides,* he had smiled, his chest bowed out proudly, *there'll be a lifetime left for that!*

And, although they'd gotten the most magnificent baby girl nine months later, things had never been revived in an intimate way between them. Not as either of them secretly had hoped. There was colic. Then a year became two. Kate was teething. Molars. And then there was medical school. A dozen well-worn excuses slipping into place between them as comfortably as a favorite old sweater.

As Kate began school they made love rarely, celebrating it when they did, almost like an anniversary, promising not to go so long. And then there was the advancing diabetes.

Aengus felt less of a man, *Me needin' medicine every day like an invalid,* he had grumbled. Bouts of impotence followed. *'Tisn't fair. 'Tis no' how it's supposed to be.*

And so here they were now. Her dear sweet Aengus lying before her, close to death, and Glenna wishing, just praying silently, as she'd done as a child with the Fergusons, that she could make everything all right. Where in heaven was Kate just now? Now when she needed her so much. Good Lord, had she failed her only child too?

Glenna summoned all of her strength not to torture herself about that as well. She'd certainly have plenty of time for that later.

If Aengus survived.

It was after midnight.

Glenna saw the taxicab lights, like two giant yellow bug

eyes, moving into the drive, heard the crunch of gravel and the rattle of the old motor as it arced around near the front door. She stood beside the makeshift bed on the sofa on which Aengus now lay and drew back the curtains with two fingers. It was Kate. She knew that it would be. This was not the first evening that her daughter had come home late smelling of ale and cigarette smoke. Her stomach turned over at the thought of her precious child, their little Katie with so little faith in herself.

Glenna had tried to understand her willful daughter. She wanted desperately to be for Kate what her own mother had never been for her—open, caring, a loving figure on whom she could unconditionally depend. But the truth was that she and Kate seemed to be drifting as far apart as she and her own mother (her adoptive mother, she reminded herself when the hurt was at its greatest) ever had been. And she felt powerless to stop it.

Kate seemed so torn, fighting the village life in Arrochar, hoping that something might signal the right course out of town. Never looking inward for the confidence or the direction that would give her peace. And try as she might, Glenna simply couldn't help her child any more than she already had.

And it was so difficult to understand, to relate to, since Glenna had always remained the good child, trying desperately, for as long as she could recall, to please parents who were not to be pleased. Parents who had made the great sacrifice, they said, of taking her on at birth from a woman without a husband. A bastard. That's what she was, and Jean and Andrew Ferguson never seemed to want her to forget it. No matter what she did or said, no matter how she pleaded in every way possible for their love.

Just be a little cuter. A little smarter. A little less demanding, certainly pray more to that exalted Catholic God who never seems to hear, and maybe, just maybe, they will love me the way other children's parents love them.

She had uttered enough mea culpas for her sins of imperfection to choke to death. For the daughter she had never been. Could never be, to them. Pick whichever set she liked, both options were close to pitiful—parents who abandoned her, or parents who behaved, all of her life, as if they wished they could.

It was why she had at first wanted to go to medical school. Become a doctor. Make her parents proud . . . But Jean and Andrew were not her parents. Not really. As a teenager she had finally accepted that. Somewhere out in the world there were two strangers, one who had given seed to her, the other who had given her life. Both of whom had abandoned her, left her to the Fergusons and their punitive, pious brand of religion, as if somehow it was she who was responsible for her birth parents' great sin.

Eventually, the drive to become a doctor had become, in part, a way to get away, to make herself independent. She hated them, God, how she hated them, whoever they were, for leaving her behind like yesterday's newspaper. Leaving her with the Fergusons. And she hated the Fergusons for having been so incredibly righteous and selfless for having martyred themselves. For having deigned to take someone else's unwanted child into their Christian home.

Glenna always felt ashamed for having such unholy thoughts so regularly. But she could never quite bring herself to admit them in confession. *Bless me, Father, for I have sinned. I hate my parents. I despise all four of them. I wish they were dead. I wish the Fergusons would give me to someone, any- one else. Even to Protestants. . . . So I wouldn't have to try so hard all of the time just to fit in. To be loved. Even liked. I would settle for that. Not to carry so much hate in my heart . . . and despising my birth parents most of all . . .*

She blinked to clear away the memory but still, she could almost hear Father Buchanan's gagging cough of surprise echo out of the dark confessional and across the dim, dank chasm of Saint Patrick's Church. Imagining his reaction alone had been enough to deter her from the soul-cleansing act of confessing that particular little sin of pure hate.

So Glenna had spent years trying to blot the evil thoughts

from her own mind. Trying to be good. Very, very good. Without God's help. Without His understanding. Without the comfort of endless Hail Marys and Our Fathers.

Marrying Aengus had been her only break with a life bent on striving for perfection, cloaked in self-recrimination. It was an act of defiance for which the Fergusons had never forgiven her. Well, nearly hadn't. They had surprised her by paying for her medical school when she hadn't thought they'd ever had a penny. And that, at least, was something.

"I've been savin' the money for years for ye, Glenna," Andrew Ferguson had said with a foreign note of generosity. He had never, ever given her anything. "We might no' approve o' the man you're marryin', but the money is still yours."

But how strange that still seemed, that suddenly, out of the blue like that, they would have wanted to help her. She hadn't spoken to them since that day before her wedding. She hadn't missed them, either. And when they were killed in a car wreck on the way to Deeside, almost a year ago now, she had not gone to the funeral. Glenna had simply phoned Father Buchanan and had the house locked up. Then she put away thoughts of them again, feeling strangely little but relief at their passing. That same hatred and pure, sweet relief.

She never wanted her own daughter to feel those raw sorts of emotions. *If only Kate could tell me what she needs, what it is that makes her so unhappy with the bright, beautiful spirit that she is.*

She hadn't raised her daughter to be a Catholic, nor anything else. It was certainly easier not to go against the grain in a small town with a grand cathedral at its center. But it was also because of the bitter pill the Church had been for her. Glenna had begun to regret that now when a faith might have been just the thing to rescue Kate when it seemed that nothing else, and no one else, could.

Aengus said, "Let her be. 'Tis only a stage. She's young. 'Twill pass." But he had been saying that for over a year. Through the battling. The tears. The yelling. And the continual running away. Glenna wasn't certain if she were more angry now or relieved when her daughter emerged from the cab that sat idling out in front of the cottage. Maybe they wouldn't argue this time. Say things they didn't mean. Maybe she wouldn't run away, but stay here, at home. Where she was loved. Wanted. A part of a real family.

Yes, even now, there was always hope.

Please don't let this lead to another shouting match. More anger. Glenna was just so worried about Aengus. He needed to be her first concern. Not a willful child who, tonight, had very clearly put her own needs over those of her father.

"I'm glad ye've come back."

It was a good start. Glenna was happy to have said that.

Kate tossed her big brown leather bag and blazer onto the hall tree. "How is he?"

Her eyes weren't red. And Glenna couldn't smell any liquor. She glanced back at her husband lying on the sofa near the warm, crackling fire. He seemed to be resting comfortably. She had given him insulin and fluids. There was little else now. But he certainly looked peaceful enough, like when he was sleeping. It made her feel less of the anger she had felt when Kate had walked out on them both earlier that afternoon.

"The next few hours'll tell."

Kate ran her hand back through the tumble of copper hair. As her hand moved through, it cascaded back onto her shoulders. "What time is it?"

"Past midnight."

Kate's taut, defensive expression fell. Her full, pale lips parted into a soft O as she looked down at her father, a man for whom she and her mother were the entire world. "I didn't realize I'd been gone that long."

Steady. Steady. Say only what you won't regret. "Did ye no' think to ask the time?"

"Truthfully, no. I was wanderin' around for a while, just thinkin'. It got away from me, is all."

Kate lowered her eyes, but not before Glenna saw the flash

of guilt where normally there was such lovely brightness. She moved a step nearer to her father as Glenna rose from the small cane chair where she had sat unmoving since sunset.

"Can I . . . do anythin' to help?"

She had spoken the question in a voice that was softer, more gentle than the one Glenna had grown accustomed to hearing. It sounded almost like the old Kate, the dear child of her heart. Sweet Kate. Kind, sensitive girl whose birth had been such an incredible blessing to this house and to their lives.

Kate had always hated to see anyone suffer. She hated that her mother was a doctor and that, for as long as she could remember, their small cottage had been so often filled with the moaning cries of broken people, injured, ill. Sometimes dead.

Glenna remembered her as a wee child. To be like her mother, to conquer her fear of sickness and death, Kate had taken it upon herself to tend sick animals she found around Arrochar. There was not a crow or a rat too insignificant or too small.

Once, she had found an injured and maggot-infested owl down by the river that had been shot but not killed by a man hunting grouse. The poor thing's eyes were so wide, so fixed, she'd been certain the bird had been looking at her, asking her to save it.

Kate had stolen a bottle of her mother's hydrogen peroxide to clean the wound and had stayed up until dawn with a flashlight and a pair of tweezers trying to rid the poor doomed animal of the maggots. And she had cried and cried into her father's open arms as her mother had gently and humanely injected the poor creature with a sedative until it "went to sleep." It was a hint of that child Glenna saw now beside her, such a welcome stranger in a home that had been too long without her.

"Are ye all right, darlin'?" Glenna softly asked, and this time the words had no trouble finding their way up from her heart. "If ye're wantin' to talk about it, where ye were, I mean, I'd be pleased to listen."

The thought moved across Kate's mind that she might tell her mother about tonight, the unsettling impression it had made on her, listening to the famous Stephen Drake. That the experience had unsettled her so that she really had wandered alone around the quiet streets of Glasgow for more than two hours before she'd thought to find the train station.

But she had strayed too far from that warmth and understanding. Cruelly, she had often accused her mother lately of having no vision for her own life, having settled for a lackluster existence in a small town when she could have gone anywhere, been a famous surgeon. Maybe even down in London. How could a mother like that understand the drive she had, the curiosity for something more?

"It does no' matter," Kate finally said. "Nothin' matters but Da."

Glenna wrapped an arm around her daughter and drew her near.

"Would ye mind . . . if I sit with ye then? And wait for Da to wake?"

Glenna said a tiny, silent prayer of thanks. At least for now, for tonight, in the face of all the rest of it with Aengus, she had her daughter back.

That night, Glenna dreamed about her father.

It surprised her, because the mere thought of him could make her so savagely angry. When he did cross her mind, betrayal and anger oozed up from her like some thick, black poison that only she was there to choke on. She saw his face, a distortion of it, like an image in a sideshow mirror, twisted, laughing. Taunting her with Scripture, with her duty to her father. And all the while, that foul liquor on his breath . . .

Honor thy father.

But the ugly memories were natural, really, considering how tired she was as the sky began slowly to lighten, preparing for morning. In the same chair, she had finally relented and for a few brief moments, closed her eyes. She was always most vulnerable then.

And the dream had come after she had watched Kate with Aengus. The tenderness, that concern between father and daughter was something she couldn't begin to conceive of for herself, yet it was something she had watched here with the greatest pride.

Aengus was a splendid father. She told herself every day of her life how right she had been to marry him. She hadn't loved him, not in that passionate way a woman loves a man. But, still and all, he had been the best thing to ever happen to Glenna. And love, deep and enduring, like a fine silk thread, had woven itself from that.

Glenna had let Kate administer the last dose of insulin and change the cool cloth on his forehead. It had made her feel a part of things. It had made Glenna feel that they were a family again.

As she watched her daughter, a memory formed. Glenna remembered that once when she herself was eight years old, she had tried to run away from home. She had meant to go anywhere but back to Coatbridge. Andrew Ferguson was not going to beat her again. Not in the name of God or anyone else. And she certainly wasn't going to let him touch her, recite the Twenty-third Psalm, and call beating righteous.

As she had walked along the dirt lane, hung low with the branches of an elm, her head lowered, scuffing dirt with the tip of her loafer, a car had slowed beside her. It was long and shiny, and there had been a driver. Like something out of the movies.

She had been curious and yet afraid at first, even thought of outrunning it in case there was danger. Until he had lowered that dark back window, his face slowly coming into view. Not until she had seen the startling kindness on that face, a face she had never seen before or since, did her pace begin to slow.

"Are you lost?" he had asked.

And yet he was the one who didn't seem to belong. Didn't

speak as a Scotsman would. He was an American. And she remembered thinking that he was the most handsome man she'd ever seen, dark hair, strong square jaw, if not for that marked sadness in his crystal blue eyes.

"I'm no' lost," she had answered, still walking slowly, the tires rolling along beside her, crunching dirt and rock and gravel.

And he was awkward too. She remembered that because he seemed to want to say something more. To keep the connection alive, as if they knew each other, but he wasn't sure what to say. Glenna had never known a grown-up like that, one at a loss for words.

"May I offer you a lift somewhere?"

"That'd be difficult."

"Why's that?"

"Because I don't have the slightest idea where I'm goin'."

Why had that answer seemed to matter to him? She would never know. But he had ordered the driver in front of him to turn off the ignition anyway. He had come outside with her and leaned against the shiny car, glistening like a freshly polished silver service. He was dressed in a heavy Aran sweater and slacks. He reminded her of that new young American actor, Warren Beatty, only his hair was a good deal darker. He didn't seem to belong to that car nor to this place.

In the silence, he picked up a stone and tossed it casually into the trees, then leaned back against the car again and crossed one leg over the other casually. "Had a fight with your parents?"

"How d'ye know that?"

"Lucky guess."

He smiled so kindly at her. He was a stranger and yet she knew she was safe with him. He would not hurt her. He did not seem capable of it. Not the way her father did. He did not have the same glazed, icy stare that said when he drank, *I'd just as soon kill ye as look at ye! Another man's bastard your ma insisted on takin' in . . .* He didn't need to put that into words. The expression in his eyes when he looked at her said quite enough indeed.

"So then, are you running away?"

"I'm no' certain. I think 'tis some sort o' sin not to honor your father."

The man picked up another stone and tossed it. "That depends."

"On what?"

"Why you'd be leaving him."

And she had almost told him the truth that day too, felt the words of confession pushing their way forward on her tongue, aching to be heard. Crying for a safe haven. A place just to be Glenna, and eight, without a father who loathed her.

But kind eyes or not, he was still a stranger. Glenna had decided in that split second, between his statement and the need for her to offer a reply, that the risk was too great. If somehow this man knew her father, or even her mother, and told them, her life on this earth would be more of a hell than it had already been. If that were even remotely possible.

"I'll likely go back."

The words had actually burned her mouth, acquiescence sliding forward, tasting like acid. But she was only a child. Where would she go? Who on this earth would care for her if she didn't go back?

Faced with such hopelessness at home and such gentleness from a stranger, Glenna suddenly wanted very much to cry. She felt the tears sting her eyes and yet they hung there, glistening.

"I know a little something about feeling like you don't belong."

She tipped her head. "Ye do?"

"I spent a big part of my life in the wrong place with the wrong people, trying to tell myself it was the right thing to do."

"But ye're no' there now."

"No, you're right. I left. I had friends, and somewhere else to go. It was a great gift when I needed it. Everyone should feel that they have at least that."

She watched him draw something from his pocket. A calling card.

"I'd like you to do me a favor," he said in a voice that was as strong and certain as it was gentle. It was like a warm cloak wrapping steadily around her. "This has my telephone number in Glasgow. If you ever find that you've nowhere else to go in the world, if you need a friend, I'd like you to feel that you can call me."

She glanced down at the plain white card with the simple black name embossed simply beside a number. *Stephen Drake.* The strange thing was that it didn't seem at all odd to her that he should offer it. There really must be kind people out there in the world after all, and this stranger must actually be one.

"'Tis fair kind o' ye, Mr. Drake."

He didn't seem to want to know her name, though, she had remembered thinking. It didn't seem to her as if he needed to. As it had been from the moment he stepped from the car, it seemed as if he already knew her. Knew everything about her. As if he could actually read her mind simply by looking into her eyes, see how strange it was that they hadn't had a proper exchange, he then said, "But of course we haven't been properly introduced."

He liked it when she smiled because he smiled too. "I'm Glenna Rose . . . Glenna Rose Ferguson." Suddenly she felt awkward. She felt her face warm with a blush.

"What is it?" he asked.

". . . Only that I've never told anyone that before. My full name, I mean." She lowered her eyes. "I've always hated the Rose part."

"Oh, I think it's very poetic."

She looked up again. Tipped her head slightly. "You do?"

"I certainly do. And I wouldn't be at all surprised, if I were you, Miss Glenna Rose Ferguson, if one day your lovely name didn't end up precisely that way. In a poem . . . Glenna Rose," he said in a lyrical tone, gazing up at the clouds.

"'Tis most kind o' you to say."

"Not kind at all. Simply the truth." He extended his hand. "It's a pleasure to meet you formally, Miss Glenna Rose Ferguson."

He had squeezed her hand, almost too hard. There was a hint of desperation in it. As if they were the best of friends, and not saying hello but good-bye forever. "Aye. 'Tis the same pleasure to meet you," she said awkwardly, keenly aware that although she did not feel it, he was still a stranger.

But even in her confusion at this very curious encounter, she felt herself smiling, and Glenna realized that it was the first time in weeks she'd felt anything close to happiness.

"I'd like you to think you have a friend out there in the world, Glenna."

"'Tis a pleasant enough thought."

"Quentin here is my driver, and a dear friend," he had said, introducing the tall, balding man with round, horned-rimmed glasses and a snowy clipped beard. "If you ever call that number and I'm not in, you can ask for Quentin and he will help you. I trust him with my life, and so can you."

"I do thank ye."

"And now, if I could ask another small favor of you."

She had tipped her head warily. He watched her.

"It's all right if you would rather not."

"No. What is it then?"

"I was going to ask if you'd object to my man Quentin here taking a photograph of you. I've just gotten a new camera and I'd like to be certain that it works properly."

She had wanted to ask him why a complete stranger who just happened upon her on an old country road, far too far from America, should want to take her photograph, even as a test, when he could just as easily take a photograph of his friend beside him.

But it had seemed somehow inappropriate to ask at that moment. Perhaps he was lonely himself, she had reasoned with the naïveté of a child.

And so she had given him what he had asked for. A single photograph, she leaning against the door of his car, gazing up, wide-eyed, trying very, very hard to smile . . .

Glenna ran a hand across her weary, bloodshot eyes, wishing she had at least dozed on the plane up from London.

Wished she hadn't stayed out so late the night before. Her mind was playing tricks on her now, taunting her with memories of longing to be rescued by a handsome prince in a shiny car.

Memories of a prince who had never come again.

Glenna sat up and glanced over at Kate, who was curled on a chair by the fire. She had refused to go up to bed, wanting to stay near her father in case anything changed.

Glenna stood and checked his pulse. Stable. That was some improvement. Aengus was as still as if he had died, but his skin was warm, even though his breathing was still shallow. She touched his weathered cheek with the back of her hand.

"I'm no' a handsome man, Glenna," he had said that night at the Rose and Thistle, when he had proposed. "A face like a leather strap is that which'll greet ye every mornin' of your life. But beneath will beat a heart as pure and full o' love for ye as ever a man could love his wife."

Her lips turned up now in a slight, nostalgic smile. Aengus had been a man of his word. He had been a grand husband and with him she had had a good life. A safe life. And, after all, could a woman really hope for more than that?

There was a tiny voice in the back of her mind then that said, *What about really falling head over heels in love, just once in your life?*

But Glenna was too stubborn, and too full of loyalty to Aengus, to listen to that.

The worst was finally over.

By the second day, Aengus had finally improved enough to be moved to his own bed upstairs. He had eaten a bit and was even talking. Glenna and Kate, both still exhausted, sat at the trestle table in the midmorning, sipping thick black coffee as a heavy rain pelted the cottage and slid across the windowpanes.

They hadn't spoken about much except Aengus's condition since Kate had come home. Instead, they found themselves just going on with one another, perhaps a little softer. Certainly a little kinder.

When there was the crunch of gravel in the drive outside, they both looked up from their cups. It was still raining.

Kate lifted her neck to see out the window. A car she didn't recognize had stopped with an uncertain little jerk in front of their cottage, the wipers slapping furiously at the windshield.

"Who might that be comin' out here in this weather, do ye suppose?" Kate asked.

Glenna stood up and shoved her hands into her front pockets, wondering. She wore black knit slacks and an old plaid shirt of her husband's, with a red turtleneck sweater beneath. Her hair had been pulled away from her face into a tortoiseshell clip very early that morning, but two small wisps had pulled away in the time since, and spilled now onto her ruddy cheeks. Her face was clean, and she wore no makeup at all. But she didn't need any.

Kate stood too and opened the front door as they watched a tall stranger with a briefcase pull a jacket over his head and dash toward her through the rain. She moved back as Glenna drew near. They hadn't been expecting anyone. Especially a handsome stranger with tanned skin and cropped hair the color of butterscotch topping.

"I'm lookin' for Glenna Ferguson." The accent and clothing were American. So was the man.

"Glenna McDowell, she's called now. 'Tis my mother ye're after."

"Is she at home?"

Kate turned to Glenna. "Ye're lookin' at her there."

The stranger wiped his feet on the doormat as he came inside. "Name's Mitch Greyson, ma'am," he said in a deep Southern drawl, nodding to her and then reaching out to shake her hand. He was solidly built, and to call him "great-looking" would not be an overstatement. Glenna could see that his eyes were wide, a tawny shade of brown, with remarkably long lashes. He had a strong, square face framing them and a good-natured smile that seemed difficult for him to hide. He moved forward in jeans, a crisp white shirt, and an expensive camel-hair blazer. She came toward him in an unexpected silence that seemed to go on forever.

He seemed to be studying her face, looking at her intensely. As if he knew her. And when she glanced down she realized that he was still holding her hand. He realized it too and pulled slowly away.

In the charged silence, he moved a few steps to set his briefcase down, then flicked the brass tabs to open it. Glenna watched him carefully. Yes, he was thoroughly American. What, she wondered, could a man like that want with her?

Glenna's voice was stiff. "What might I be doin' for ye, then, Mr. Greyson?"

He glanced over at Kate. "I'd like to speak with you in private, if I might, ma'am," he said, and his voice came tinged with a surprising Southern gentility. There was a small pause before he continued. "It's kind of an awkward matter. I've traveled quite a long way about it."

So the man was a stranger. And he had come about business. The sound of a door closing upstairs spilled into the sudden silence, startling her, reminding her of reality apart from the strange intensity of the moment. She tipped up her chin and frowned slightly hoping to still her heart. "Well, I have no' got any secrets from my daughter."

"If it's all the same to you, ma'am," he said in that same deep voice, though this time the words came with a hint of warning, "you'd be wise to make that decision *after* we speak."

Kate had watched carefully the exchange between her mother and this man, a strange unmistakable spark of something she knew she didn't like—and she had missed none of it. *I may still be a child,* she thought, *but I see how he is looking at her. How she is looking at him.* Her stomach churned.

"Never mind," Kate said in a short, flippant tone. "I'm goin' to the kitchen."

◆　　　◆　　　◆

Glenna was speechless. It was the very last thing she had expected to hear from this man. She leaned on the dining table for support, but there was nothing in the world that could help her bear the shock of what she saw on the ivory sheet of paper she held in her hands.

"Where . . . did ye get this letter?"

"As I've said, Mrs. McDowell, it was written by your birth mother, a woman named Isabelle Wescott."

Glenna sank into one of the chairs, her face suddenly ashen. Thoughts were bumping into one another inside her mind. Dark, incomprehensible thoughts. She had always known she was adopted, but it had been years since those thoughts had turned to curiosity about the parents who, so long ago, had given her up. Unknown people who had never looked back to a child they'd left behind.

The taste in her mouth, when she tried to speak again, was corrosive, like acid. "If this is some kind of joke, Mr. Greyson, I can assure ye 'tis in poor taste."

"It's no joke, ma'am. Now, I'm sure this must have come as somewhat of a shock to you after—"

She sprang to her feet, dropping the letter onto the table. "*Somewhat*, Mr. Greyson? *Somewhat*? Perhaps ye should try an *unbelievable* shock. A *devastatin'* shock."

"Should I call your daughter for you, ma'am? Ask her to get somethin' for you?"

"No!" She drew in a breath, exhaled, trying to steady herself. "'Tis no' a concern o' hers. . . . No' yet." *Kate has dealt with enough lately,* she was thinking. *She does not need this sort of shock now to set her off again.*

They were silent at the table as a car engine starting up was heard down on the road below the house. Finally, Glenna looked up at Mitch. Every part of her felt hyperalert.

"So what could she possibly want from me after all this time?"

"I'm told that her letter speaks for itself. But I believe Mrs. Wescott desires an opportunity to know you."

"'Tis impossible, what she's askin'!"

He saw the shock on her face, stopped, then began again. It was that pure vulnerability masked so well by fury that reminded him of Livi. The sensation was unsettling. He had not expected to be reminded of his late wife coming here this morning.

"Mrs. Wescott thought that when the time was right you might agree to meet with her." When Glenna made no response, Mitch put his hand gently over hers. "Maybe you should take some time to think this through. I don't need—"

"No! She must have had a thousand chances since the day she gave me up." Glenna's voice was tinged with bitterness. And with an unexpected hint of pain for what her early life had become without a mother to really love her. "Chances to come here. Even just to write. Times I needed someone, anyone to help me. Well, I do no' need her now, 'tis certain. No' anymore."

She stood and walked slowly back toward the fire, arms folded across her chest. Mitch Greyson watched her. Close up, he was relieved to see that she looked different from the photograph he had snapped to send back to the agency for their client. In the daylight, he could see that even she had her imperfections—the little bump on the bridge of her small, freckled nose, and eyes that even in their blue brilliance were not quite even. Thank goodness, he thought, she is not the absolute perfection the camera had captured yesterday as he had taken that secret photograph of her returning from a trip.

"When are ye to report back to the woman, Mr. Greyson?"

"I was hopin' to be able to call Mrs. Wescott back in the U.S. with a report this evenin'."

Glenna whirled back around, the shock squeezing her heart, blocking out the sudden connection to this stranger she at first had felt. "She's American?"

"Yes. She's recently widowed. Her husband was a United States senator for many years. Quite an important figure in American politics."

"But I was born here . . . I thought that I was born here, in Glasgow."

"That was the information I found when I was trying to locate you. You were born in Glasgow, ma'am. But your birth mother is from San Francisco."

"San Francisco? But that's . . . 'tis no' possible."

"I'm afraid it is."

"And my . . . father?" Her mouth was dry. So unbelievably dry. "Is he, at least, a Scot?"

He felt something catch in his throat as he tried to answer her. He was heartsick seeing how stunned she was. "I'm sorry, Mrs. McDowell. I have no information on your . . . birth father."

Suddenly she was charging back at him, her blue eyes glittering in the dim, gray morning light. The pain grew, twisted and pushed inside her. "But you must have seen a name! Ye saw my birth certificate, did ye no'?"

"I did, yes."

"Well, what name was listed as belongin' to my father?"

Damn, he hated this part of the job. Mitch Greyson took a deep breath. "It was unknown, Mrs. McDowell. . . . Your father was listed as unknown."

Glenna gripped the oak banister after Mitch Greyson had gone. Her dark, sleek hair, released from its tortoiseshell clip, fell forward onto her cheeks, an onyx cascade. Her hands were shaking so badly that she couldn't still them. Isabelle Wescott's words came to her like an echo moving up through her thoughts. *My daughter, How to begin a letter like this has haunted me for more years than you can imagine. . . .* The harder she pushed them out of her mind, the more insistent the bits and pieces of that letter became. *I can say only that I was a child myself. I had not the power nor wisdom to fight the forces against me. . . .*

It wasn't possible. How, why, was this happening *now*? It was too late to make a connection. Too late to make amends. She didn't want a mother now, didn't want an excuse for the past she had suffered. For parents she had despised.

I don't want to know they were real people, Glenna was thinking as she wrapped her arms around herself, feeling icy suddenly and very alone. *I don't wish to know that there might have been a love story between the two that gave me life . . . and a good reason for everything that happened to me.*

3

 Mitch

Glenna was walking alone in the meadow beside her house late the next afternoon when she saw the same car make the turn by the market and come down the lane toward her. She looked back at the house where Aengus and Kate were still asleep, then up ahead again at a car that she knew carried Mitch Greyson.

She held her breath as he pulled to a stop in the drive, got out and walked in long even strides toward her. "How are you this mornin', Dr. McDowell?"

She tipped her head, surprised. "How'd ye discover that I was a doctor?"

"The men at the inn where I'm stayin' are a vocal lot. Why didn't you correct me?"

"It didn't seem all that important yesterday."

He conceded the point with a small, gentle smile that made dimples emerge just above his square jaw. "I've come back to see if you might have changed your mind, that things might look different to you this morning."

Her color rose a little. "Believe me, there is nothin' that can change the past I have lived, Mr. Greyson, nor my feelin's about it now."

Mitch looked at her solemnly. Her blue eyes met his defiantly as if she were daring him to push something he could not possibly understand. "I'm sorry."

"Aye. I am, as well."

In the silence that followed there was an intensity, that same intensity between them as yesterday. Before he had told her why he'd come. Very carefully, Mitch placed a hand at the base of her arm just above the elbow and guided her away from her house out into the meadow. The wind was blowing and the morning air was bitingly cold. Her hair, dark and unbound, was raking back away from her face like a sail.

"Ye've come an awfully long way to do a disagreeable job like this," Glenna remarked as they sloshed in an even pace through the damp grass and finally came to the stone fence that circled the McDowell property. She rested her arms on top of the barrier and looked out at the empty road ahead before he answered.

"Maybe so. But it pays the bills. And I've always wanted to see Scotland." He smiled again. The dimples reemerged as his gaze met hers. They were standing close and Glenna's heart was suddenly beating very fast. "All in all, I'm not sorry I came."

It was a lazy smile he had given her and a blithe reply, but the confident way he carried himself, the well-schooled tone in which he spoke (in spite of that wonderful earthy accent) told her unmistakably that this was no ordinary private investigator from across the miles. This Mitch Greyson had led a very privileged life in America.

What, Glenna wondered, had really led him so very far from home?

"'Twas kind o' ye to come all the way back here to try again. 'Tis no' your fault, the answer."

"I wish things could have been different for you, Doctor," he drawled deeply.

"I wish a fair lot o' things, myself, Mr. Greyson."

Her mouth was impossibly dry. She wasn't accustomed to being with men. Not men who looked at her the way Mitch Greyson did. "I should go back in."

"Before you do, there was somethin' I meant to give you yesterday." He reached into his jacket pocket and withdrew a business card. He gave it to Glenna.

"What's this for?" she asked, glancing at his name beneath the imprint Tremont & Associates, Private Investigators.

"In case you change your mind."

For a moment she wasn't certain what he meant. There was something in his tone. Then, of course, she knew he had meant about Mrs. Wescott. "I will no' be doin' that," Glenna said.

She offered the card back to him but his hand closed over hers and he pressed it gently back to her. "Just the same. I'd feel better if you had it."

Glenna looked at him and felt a shiver. "I must go in."

Mitch glanced at his watch. It was surprisingly expensive, she could see. Patek Phillipe. What a jumble of contradictions he was, she thought fleetingly as he stood, tall and athletic before her in his expensive boots, cashmere blazer, and Western turquoise belt buckle that glinted in the pale morning sun. There was something a little mysterious about him.

"Yes. Perhaps you should go," Mitch said evenly, without taking his eyes from her even as she turned and walked back across the tall grass to the little stone house.

With her father upstairs still asleep and her mother outside alone with that man, Kate felt the fury, confusion, and the curiosity inside her mingle and begin to build as she watched Glenna and Mitch from the kitchen window. Especially since her mother believed she was still asleep. She sat alone at the table, holding the letter. She was thinking about trying to call the States, and a complete stranger, one who also happened to be her grandmother.

Ma would be livid if she knew. Glenna had made that perfectly clear last evening when she told her daughter everything. About having been adopted. About her birth mother being American. Wanting to find her. Now. Kate had seen the strain on her face. The betrayal.

"And I have no wish to discuss it any further, do ye understand?" Glenna had said firmly. "Your father and I simply thought ye had a right to know."

Kate couldn't begin to imagine what it would be like to have been given away as a helpless baby, with absolutely no say in the matter. Not to know the people who had given you life. To feel, perhaps, that you had done something to cause them to give you up.

But last evening, long after the private investigator had gone, Kate had been tempted by that envelope lying on the kitchen table. A creamy vellum, it was the stationery of someone very important. She had known that it had been the one sent by her grandmother. Inside lay perhaps an explanation of what had gone wrong all those years ago. Her mother had read it, obviously. So had her father. And yet Glenna was firm in her resolve not to respond in any way. Kate, however, was brimming with curiosity. Especially after her mother's unbelievable story.

So when she'd found an opportunity for a bit of privacy, after they had gone to bed, Kate had read the letter herself. And even now she felt the surprise at those words. How could a cruel, selfish woman—a woman who had given away her child—have written something like that, so full of passion and contrition? What on earth had happened to Isabelle Wescott, her grandmother, to have made her give away her child?

Perhaps it was selfish, but she wanted to know her. She wanted Isabelle to know them. A daughter and a grand-daughter, two women with whom she shared the same bloodline. The same ancestry. Did she have other children? Other grandchildren there, in America? She looked down at the words again,

> *My Daughter,*
> How to begin a letter like this has haunted me for more years than you could imagine. I am your mother. Yet everything I can think of by way of explanation for that seems so impossible now. I can say only that I was a child myself, and I had not the power nor the wisdom to fight the forces against me. And for that I will pay the highest price for the rest of my life; the loss of the most precious gift I was ever given, you, my sweet, sweet firstborn child.

But how was she ever going to gather the courage to try to call San Francisco? And more than that, what would she say if, my God, she actually managed to reach her? Kate had no idea at all how to bring her mother and grandmother together for a meeting that might well change both their lives. After all, it wasn't as if Isabelle Wescott was just down the road in the next town.

Kate glanced down at the letter and then over at the phone. Then at the letter again. And how badly could the conversation go if she did get through? Mrs. Wescott wanted to know her daughter. She had gone to the trouble and expense of hiring a private detective to locate her. Presumably she would be receptive to her daughter's child. Presumably.

Kate lifted the receiver and began to dial the country code. Her fingers were shaking. She was openly defying her mother, a mother she had once adored. But a mother who now seemed dull and driven. A workaholic who was walking out in the paddock with a man a lot younger and a lot more handsome than her da.

She dialed the city code and then began to dial the number.

"Blast!"

Kate slammed the receiver back onto the cradle. She sprang to her feet and began to pace back and forth across the cozy, low-ceilinged room, ringing her hands and trying her level best to mount her courage. *Courage.* It was what her father had always called his precious Scotch whiskey.

"I do believe I'll be takin' a wee drop o' courage before I'll be forcin' myself to do that!" he used to say. Or, "There's nothin' like a wee drop o' courage to bolster a body, now and again."

Kate moved slowly into the kitchen and reached up into one of the tall pine cupboards that squealed as she opened it. A bottle of Glenlivet, long untouched, sat, bright, shiny label out, as if it had been waiting for her all along. Her father didn't drink it anymore. At least not regularly, not with the diabetes. So it was just going to sit here. Untouched and unappreciated. Perhaps she'd have just a drop, at that, of her father's courage before she phoned. Just a drop.

She took out a cup and poured. The strong, grainy smell swirled up into her nostrils. Before it could overwhelm her, Kate took a long swallow. And then another. She felt the slow burn in her throat, the warmth wash over her. Courage was a good word for it, she thought.

When the conviction she had longed for did not come, Kate reached into the black leather pocket of her jacket, still slung on the back of the kitchen chair. The little white pill she set on the table glistened in the morning light. She really did want to call Isabelle Wescott now, while she had the privacy. And why shouldn't she take a little something that would make that a bit easier? And what could it hurt? She'd taken this kind of pill once before. All they did was relax her.

"Well, no time like the present, I expect."

Kate washed one pill down with a swallow of Scotch, then she picked up the telephone receiver again, hoping something brilliant would come to her when the time came. She glanced up at the staircase, then back at the front door one last time as she pressed her finger into the number 1 of the old black rotary dial telephone. Kate wasn't certain if the pill was already taking effect, or it was the Scotch. Or both. But she was calmer suddenly about calling.

She dialed the number and waited for it to connect. *Ring* . . . The false courage was dissolving slowly as the phone rang a third time. *Ring.* . . . And then there was her heart thumping like a dull base drum against her rib cage.

Click.

Someone had picked up.

Kate fought not to slam down the receiver in response. This was it. This was her chance. Maybe it was even a way out of Arrochar. A moment later, there was a connection and she heard a woman's voice from a distance, as though she were drawing the phone to her ear and muttering.

"All right, all right, hold your horses!" An irritated sigh was followed by an uncomfortably long pause. "Yes, hello?"

Kate felt like she might faint. She forced the sound from her own mouth. ". . . Mrs. Wescott? Isabelle Wescott?"

There was a great deal of static on the line. "No. This is her housekeeper. And, for that matter, have you any idea what time it is to be calling? It's the middle of the night!"

Disappointment was as heavy inside her as a stone. "I'm sorry, I did no' think o' that."

"Well, now that the damage is done, I'll take your message."

"I'll just call back."

"Mrs. Wescott likes to know who has called."

"'Twould be better if I called back."

The woman was perturbed. "Might I at least tell her your name?"

"I'd prefer to tell Mrs. Wescott that myself, if ye don't mind," Kate said. "It's bound to come as a bit of a shock to her. But I do thank ye just the same."

Suddenly, Kate felt a hand heavy on her shoulder, fingers pressing angrily into her skin. She spun around and saw her mother, who had pushed down the little button in the receiver cradle, cutting them off. She had heard enough to know that Kate had been trying to phone Isabelle Wescott.

"Ma, I—"

"What am I to say to ye, Katherine Mary? What in the name o' heaven would make ye do somethin' like this so against me?"

Kate saw her mother's face, white with an expression that made her look as if she had just been kicked in the stomach.

"Well, don't ye have a thing to say for yourself?"

"I thought I had a right to know her."

It was a weak defense, considering how brief a time it had been since Glenna had even discovered this woman's existence, and Kate knew that her mother could hear that in her tone.

"I trusted ye with somethin' painful by leavin' that letter for ye to read."

Why was it, heaven forbid, that now, at this precise

moment in time Kate suddenly felt a giggle forcing its way up from the pit of her stomach like a bubble of air? She should have been moved to tears by the guilt and by her mother's pained expression. God, she was drunk, drunker than she'd ever been. That had to be it, her father's Scotch making her feel giddy, like a child at a birthday party when all of the presents were for her.

"Are ye purposely tryin' to hurt me, Katie? Is that it, then?"

"Why does this only have to be about you?"

"Because I'm the one 'twas given up! And no' only by one set o' parents!"

"Well your real ma wants to know ye now!"

"My 'real ma' saw me given over to hell with the Fergusons, Katie."

"Och! Why d'ye always have to be so rigid? Things change, ye know!"

"Not this."

The more stony her mother's tone, the more that giggle crept up its inevitable passageway along her throat. Completely unwarranted. Entirely inevitable. Kate bit her lip as hard as she could battling to regain her self control. "I b'lieve I'll just . . . go back up to bed for a bit."

"Ye'll be goin' back to bed when I say ye'll go to bed!"

Her masterful tone was Kate's final undoing. The laugh exploded past her pursed lips and she gripped her sides, doubling over in a high-pitched fit of uncontrollable laughter.

Then, like a sack of flour, she quite promptly fell from her chair straight onto the floor.

"What is it's the matter with ye? Have ye taken somethin', Kate? Hold your head still. Let me see your eyes. . . . Good God almighty, they're like pins! What have ye taken?"

Her mother was gripping her shoulders and shouting at her as Kate erupted in a new fit of giggles. "I'm . . . I'm sorry, Ma. Truly." She covered her mouth with her hand. "'Tis no' funny. . . . I know it. I just . . ."

Glenna leveled her blue eyes on Kate. "Ye've taken somethin' with that Scotch, haven't ye, Katherine Mary? Haven't ye?"

Her tongue was thick. Dry. Her mind was spinning. "Don't make a fuss, Ma. I'm fine."

She struggled to stand, only to realize that it felt as if all of the bones in her body were gone and what remained of her was a bag filled with sand.

"Maybe I just need a bit o' tea."

"What ye're *needin'* is your stomach pumped! Did Mary Keith give ye some sort o' drug, Katherine? Answer me!"

Kate's knees buckled again as her mother's arm wrapped firmly around her waist. "I just need a wee bit o' sleep, that's all. . . . Just a bit o' sleep . . ." she slurred and giggled as they stumbled toward the stairs.

"This is no' over, Katherine Mary," her mother said stonily. "We're goin' to discuss this tomorrow, I can tell ye that!"

She was glad she couldn't see her mother's face from behind. She really had begun to feel a little sick, and all she wanted to do was sleep. Disappointment. Apprehension. Fear. Even exhilaration. And now stomach-churning sickness. Kate had felt each one of those things this morning. But what she must try to remember was that she had made the connection. She had pushed past everything to reach her grandmother. Isabelle Wescott.

She knew it wasn't going to be easy tomorrow to explain to her mother what she felt and why she'd done it. Why she'd had to do it. It was as if some force greater than herself was urging her on, pressing her toward something inevitable. Something even she did not quite understand. At least not yet. And how on earth did you explain something like that to a mother who was as serious and inflexible as Glenna McDowell?

The boys. Drinking. Running away. And now, it appeared, she had begun to flirt with drug use as well. It was still so hard to believe of their little Katie lass. Glenna sat at Aengus's bedside in the coppery lamplight, but not addressing what had happened earlier. Not until it was nearly dusk and he could not manage to sleep any longer.

"I just don't know what to do for her," Glenna said, the first to break the silence between them. She rubbed a hand over her weary eyes and breathed another sigh. "'Twas no' what I was trained for; how to be a parent . . . how to deal with this."

"I don't expect there's anyone of us who's trained for it, darlin'. Learnin' this is strictly trainin' on-the-job."

"But she's no' our little girl anymore, ye know? And the worst part is, I don't even know when it started to happen, or why. 'Tis like when she was a wee bairn and we took her down to England on that holiday trip. She was so young, but she galloped right up to that great big slide at Watermouth Castle anyway, do ye remember that?"

"How could I forget?" Aengus smiled grimly, looking worn and tired again.

"She insisted on goin' up. She was always such a brave wee thing, and she could no' have been more than three. Just when she got to the top though, and looked at how far it was to the bottom, I could see the fright on her face. She wanted to come back down to us. But by then there was another group of children blockin' the way behind her. She could no' turn back . . ." Tears swam in Glenna's eyes at the recollection. "That sweet wee girl of ours stayed on that huge slide and started goin' down because she didn't know how to get off . . . and there was nothin' we could do . . . no way that we could help her."

Glenna took a piece of tissue from her skirt pocket and wiped her eyes. "She's like that wee child again, Aengus, goin' down so fast, and we're powerless against whatever it is that's drawin' her."

"She's told me that she's bored here. She wants more out o' life than what Arrochar can give her."

"A good home. People who love her? There was a time when I would have sold my soul for what she has here with us!"

There was a little silence before he gently said, "Maybe 'tis time ye dealt with that, yourself, Glenna."

"Dealt with what?"

"How ye feel about the Fergusons."

"They're dead. I feel nothin'."

"'Tis why, sometimes, ye still cry out in your sleep? . . . 'Tis no' possible no' to feel somethin', sweet Glenna, after what ye were made to go through as their child."

She couldn't look at him for a moment. It was an old defense. "I don't want to talk about them. They're no' the issue."

"Is it no' all part o' the same issue all woven together like a grand rug—what it was that became o' the wee bairn ye were, after ye were given up? And the way ye worry so now about Katie."

"'Tis over. They canno' hurt me anymore. They're dead," she said again, as if she were trying to convince herself more than Aengus.

But he loved her. And understood her. Because he had known her back then. "Maybe this comin' up now with your real mother is a good thing really; a signal for ye to sort out all o' the threads o' your life, finally. I know well ye have no' wanted to talk about it since the Fergusons' passin', but—"

"And I'm no' wantin' to now."

"Let me be sayin' my piece, Glenna, please."

Aengus took the business card Glenna had shown him earlier off the bedside table, the card with Mitchell B. Greyson's name on it, then twisted it absently between his fingers. When she didn't object further, he finally continued, but carefully. "I've always thought that the Fergusons would stay demons in your mind if ye did no' go home to Coatbridge and finally face their deaths and what ye left behind there. . . ." He looked at her squarely. Strongly. He was, in that moment, the very man she had married. The dream, the hope of a secure life, when nothing else had mattered more. ". . . 'Tis time, my Glenna."

Glenna's blue eyes swiftly darkened. "Ye ask too much o'

me, since what ye really want me to arrive at by doin' this is to face Isabelle Wescott."

"Don't ye think ye should find out a few things before ye're decidin' to despise her?"

"She gave me away! I was a helpless babe, and yet she went and handed me over to strangers as if I were no better than yesterday's news!"

Aengus was still calm. His kind gaze was weary but still steady. He reached across the bedcovers and pressed his large liver-spotted hand atop hers. His voice went lower. "Now, ye don't truly know that, dear heart, do ye? Ye don't know anythin' about what really happened all those years ago. Times were different then."

"Givin' away a child is givin' away a child."

"People do all sorts o' things for reasons o' their own. Reasons not everyone else would understand . . . like why ye married me."

She stiffened defensively. "I loved ye, Aengus McDowell. Pure and simple."

"And I've been the most blessed man on this earth because ye made yourself b'lieve so." He squeezed her hand. "But after all o' these years between us, good years, surely ye can admit that there was a wee bit more to it than that."

"Don't go talkin' such foolishness. Ye're just tired, 'tis all that is."

"Yes, I am tired. And I'm old. But I've no' lost my senses. At least no' yet. Glenna, my darlin' lass, ye needed to get away from Andrew Ferguson, and I was just old enough and flattered enough by a beautiful and desperate young woman to oblige ye. It has no' been so long that ye don't recall how it was back then, has it?"

"'Twas different, and ye well know it."

"Ye mean because your life was complicated? Because ye did somethin' ye might no' otherwise have done if ye were no' desperate?"

"I did not marry you out o' desperation! And I do resent the suggestion otherwise!"

"Ye did the best ye could for yourself at the time. I know that."

In spite of what he was suggesting, Aengus was not accusing her. His eyes were so full of pure love that it made Glenna weep. She covered her face with her hands, entirely overcome, as Aengus braced a hand on her shoulder. "'Tis no' to say that ye have no' been the finest wife a man could ever ask for, because ye have, and I don't regret a single wakin' hour I've had with ye. I'm only askin', for your own sake, my sweet Glenna, that ye think about it. Perhaps, at a place in time, all those years ago, there was someone else who did the best she could with the hand that ol' fate dealt her."

"So what if she did? It's too late now for there to be anythin' besides blood between us."

"Are ye so certain o' that?" He glanced down at the crisp ecru business card printed in black. "Why don't we have another talk with this Greyson lad here and see if we canno' at least use him as a bridge back to your real mother when ye're ready?"

"No."

"As much as it pains me to say it, I'm no' goin' to live forever, my dear heart, and when I'm gone, who will you and Katie have but one another?"

As fast as Glenna brushed the tears away they came again. "That's enough. Besides, I don't want to hear ye talkin' such foolishness. Ye're no' goin' anywhere, Aengus McDowell."

"Perhaps no' today nor even tomorrow. But I'm no' well. We both know that, don't we?"

"Ye are gettin' better."

He leveled his eyes on hers again. "No, darlin', I'm no'."

There was such honesty out now that she couldn't insult him by laying a lie between them. "Well, ye could go on like this for a good long time. A lot of diabetics do."

"Aye, perhaps that much is true. But in the meantime, ye've go' so much to learn about yourself, where ye've come from, and maybe even another family out there to love ye. A mother, and maybe even brothers and sisters to help ye put the pieces of your life together, at long last."

"And father *unknown?*" The word hung in the air, thick and taut, for a moment. "After everythin' Andrew Ferguson dealt me in my youth, now I've come to find out that I really am a bastard child too! What does that make my mother, this woman ye're thinkin' now I should give a chance with my heart?"

"Sweet Glenna, darlin'," he said as lovingly as any words he had ever spoken to her, "what it makes Isabelle Wescott, like the rest of us, is human. Only human."

Aengus took her into his arms after that and held her while she sobbed. It was not like Glenna to weep, but this profound loss came from a place so deep inside her that even she had not realized before now that it was there.

"Will ye at least think about it? Do that much for yourself and for Katie?"

"The answer will still be no . . . I canno'."

"Come to bed with me, hmm?" he whispered as he stroked her hair. "Let me hold ye in my arms until ye fall asleep like I used to when I first took ye for my wife."

And Glenna fell deeper into his safe embrace. They had not made love for such a long time, with Aengus's condition steadily worsening. His old Scots pride forbade him any more even to try. And it would be no different tonight. But tonight she could think of nothing she wanted or needed more than the tender assurance of this man, a man who had become father, husband, and friend. The only certain thing she had ever had in this life.

The only thing besides their sweet Kate.

I had not the power nor the wisdom to fight the forces against me . . .

Glenna absently tossed a loaf of bread into the red hand-basket inside McGregor's Market without looking at it, just as she'd done with the milk, the cheese, and the canned ham.

There were still too many thoughts like that, rushing at her. And others. Kate . . . Isabelle Wescott . . . the Fergusons . . .

An increasingly defiant daughter. A mother she did not want. And dear, dear Aengus, closer to death than she wanted to believe. Glenna squeezed her eyes. Her life seemed quite suddenly to be coming apart at the seams.

But could Aengus actually be right about how to begin putting it right again? He usually was right about things when she stopped arguing long enough to think about it. But go back to Coatbridge? Face that sealed tomb of memories now when she'd put them aside so successfully for almost a year? Aengus had called them demons, but he didn't know the half of it, did he?

Did he really think that going back there, going through the Fergusons' personal effects, would be cathartic? That she could get past the hatred somehow just because they were dead?

On the other hand, perhaps at least it was time to think about selling the old place. She'd avoided it long enough, and Father Buchanan had phoned her twice to say that there was a couple who had made inquiries about it. It would be good to be rid of it once and for all. Rid of the memories and the responsibility. The darkness. But even if she did decide to go, a trip was not going to work any miracles, change how she felt about the notion of Isabelle Wescott. It was simply too late for that.

"Well, this must be what they call fate."

Glenna turned around suddenly, the familiar deep drawl jolting her back to the moment. Mitch Greyson had made the declaration smoothly, and it unnerved her, standing here in the dimly lit isle between the canned soup and canned meat. She looked up into eyes that shone with unmasked admiration.

"Now that you're here, I have a confession to make, Doctor."

Glenna glanced around nervously. Finally she looked back up at him.

"I didn't go back to your house yesterday entirely for Mrs. Wescott's sake, even though I told you I did."

"No?"

"That first time, I sought you out on Miz Wescott's behalf. It was my job. But yesterday mornin', that was for me." A thickly set old woman moved past them. Mitch smiled and nodded. "I was worried about you," he said deeply once they were alone again. "I never had to deal that kind of blow to anybody."

"I take it ye have no' been doin' this kind of work for long, then."

"You could say that."

Glenna paid for her things first, then waited awkwardly outside the front door as Mitch paid for a carton of orange juice and a packaged scone. He hadn't asked her to wait, but their conversation had been cut off as they drew inevitably toward Doreen Drummond in her faded coral smock, sitting on her stool in front of the cash register with a judgmental expression slashed across her thick, ruddy-cheeked face.

Outside it was easier. Glenna walked with him, both of them holding bags, as they moved steadily toward his rental car. The mist that had been falling all morning turned just then to rain. Glenna and Mitch dashed back under the eaves of the market.

"Let me give you a lift back home," he said to her then, and it surprised Glenna that it had come out more as a statement than a question. There seemed a certain inevitability about them, about how they had seen one another again. About the intimacy that had so strangely connected them through his announcement about Isabelle Wescott. Still, Glenna felt herself frown slightly, feeling that it probably wasn't right, and yet knowing somehow that she was going to do it anyway.

Without either of them saying anything else, Mitch then opened the passenger door, took her bag of groceries from her and helped her inside. They pulled out onto the muddy road, windshield wipers slapping against the glass, and

Glenna settled back against the seat. It was strange, but she already felt entirely comfortable with this man. She didn't want to question that, didn't want to know what it meant.

"So what did ye do back in the States?" she asked. "Before ye started huntin' people down and tryin' to patch up the past?"

This time she wasn't looking through him as the question came. There was none of that same perfunctory tone to what she asked as there had been on the day they'd met. Mitch could tell she truly wanted to know something about him. Her blue eyes were wide and focused directly up at him. So he smiled that same smile that had always won people over since he was no more than a boy. And then, quite abruptly, his smile faded. She deserved better than the cliché of his trying to charm her. But he really had no idea how to answer her.

Telling her the truth, of course, was impossible. So was lying. As he had known he would be from the moment he had developed that photograph, Mitch felt totally disarmed by Glenna—by the long sweep of her neck, the intelligence and the depth in those blue eyes, framed by long dark lashes. He had long ago given up hope that there could ever be another woman who could make him feel that same lack of self-possession Livi had.

Prison had battered all of the youthful softness out of him and reduced him, inside those walls, to an animal whose greatest aim and desire was for survival. Or so he'd thought.

Until now.

"Oh, I did a little of everything, Doctor. Nothin' to write home about, I'm afraid."

"Call me Glenna, if ye like."

His smile deepened to something warm and sincere that he hadn't felt for years. "Yes, I'd like that," Mitch said. "I'd like that quite a lot."

They were both silent as they came to the place in the road where they would have turned to the right, taking them back down to her home. To Aengus and Kate. But there was a barrier there and a road crew in dirty royal blue jumpsuits. The area was flooded. "We'll have to be goin' the long way round," Glenna said. "'Tis a fair bit longer, I'm afraid." Mitch did not respond, and after that the only sound there was between them was that same steady slap, slap of the windshield wipers. "Ye really could have let me walk."

"I would not be much of a gentleman if I'd done that, now would I?"

He looked over at her and smiled again as they turned the corner and began to climb up the twisted incline of King's Road. Glenna looked out the side window at a scene, like a watercolor painting. They passed a long cluster of trees near the road and a crumbling white stone fence. He turned on the radio to a station when he recognized an old Bobby Darin song playing.

"Pretty words, don't you think?" Mitch asked her as he reached across to turn up the volume.

"What's that?"

"The song. I've always like the idea that somewhere out there, there is a whole world waiting for each of us. We just have to find it."

"Hmm." She smiled over at him, a shaft of sunlight in through the windshield highlighting her face. "I never thought much about it."

"Take me, for example. Here I am, at this very moment, half a world away from everything I know, driving down a road I've never been on before with a very beautiful woman who doesn't know me from Adam, one I've only just met. And to tell you the truth, I've never felt a whole lot more at ease in my life."

Glenna looked at him again, her head tipped a little. "An American who fancies sentimental songs and rescues housewives who did no' think enough to bring a brolly. Ye are fair full o' surprises, aren't ye, Mr. Greyson?"

A car came at them. "I'll take that as a compliment."

There was another little pause as they both listened to the rest of the song. Mitch was softly singing along with the words. He took his eyes from the road for a moment and met hers. He didn't see the curve ahead until it was too late. Suddenly, he was gripping the steering wheel like a lifeline, eyes wide as saucers. He rammed his foot onto the brake, and Glenna stiffened in response, her feet jammed up against the floorboard, as if she somehow could stop them.

"Oh, my God!"

The squeal was very loud as the car began to spin like a top and they were flooded with the smell of burning rubber. And then there was no sound. No sound at all. A moment in time. Frozen. Only the car spinning, crashing through a guardrail, then thumping into an empty field as black and endless as the sea.

"Are we dead?"

They were both breathing very hard. Panting.

Then suddenly, Glenna was laughing nervously at what Mitch had asked, as if she wasn't quite sure herself. She saw something on his forehead and reached up with a trembling hand to touch it. "Dear Lord, ye're bleedin'!"

"I think I hit the steering wheel. But it's just a scratch."

"I'm the doctor here, let me have a look."

"Are *you* all right?" he asked her as she blotted the bloody wound on his forehead with a piece of tissue from her purse.

"Aye . . . I think so. What happened?"

"I'm not really sure. I drive all the time at home and I've never had an accident. Of course, over there, I drive on the proper side of the damn road."

She tipped her head. "Ye've never driven a car like this, with the steering wheel on the right, have ye?"

"I wouldn't exactly say never."

"What *would* ye say then?"

"Hardly ever. Once . . . Yesterday."

Glenna smiled, feeling more relieved than angry that at least neither of them was seriously hurt. "Are ye wantin' me to see if I can get us out of here and back up to the road?"

"I got us down here and I'll get us back out, thank you," he said with mock pride.

Glenna settled back against the passenger seat and brushed the hair from her eyes. Her heart was still pounding. The car started up easily, but when Mitch put his foot on the accelerator, the engine began to whir. The wheels were stuck in the wet soil.

"Blast!" she murmured. She was thinking of Aengus now and feeling guilty.

"Do you suppose we should hitch a ride?"

She thought about it for a moment as he looked at her. His gaze was disconcerting. *I can do this,* she thought. *I can be here with him and keep control. Just like always.* "We should probably wait with your rental car. Someone is bound to see us down here before long. Besides, 'tis comin' down in buckets out there now. . . . How's your head?"

"Feels like I just went five rounds with George Foreman. And I lost by the first."

Glenna laughed suddenly, not loudly, but enough to make him smile in return. He loved the sound of her laughter. The sweet, lyrical tone of it.

"Ye're the first person in a long while to make me laugh," she said.

"And *you* are darned pretty when you do."

He'd known the risk of saying that to a married woman, when the sincerity behind his words could so easily creep in and betray him. But he didn't care. It was as true as anything he'd ever said in his life. It was not just the way she looked. Or spoke. Or laughed. It was all of that. And more.

Quite to his surprise, Glenna didn't stiffen in the face of his compliment or become indignant. Instead, she just leveled her eyes on him. Her smile lengthened. He wanted to tell her the rest, that he had surreptitiously taken her photograph days ago for his client in San Francisco and become enchanted by her then. That a photograph was nothing compared to the reality, the flesh-and-blood woman actually sitting now before him. Of course, he couldn't say a word of the truth. She was married, he reminded himself. Here in Scotland, she had a life. And he was still trying to make sense out of the shambles that was left of his own back in the States.

Neither of them said anything for a few moments after that. The car was getting cold with the steady stream of rain that was battering them, and Glenna had begun to shiver. She wrapped her arms around herself and looked back up to the road, but there were no other cars coming.

"I'd put my arm around you, to warm you up," Mitch said gently when he saw her shaking. "But I wouldn't want you to think I was bein' forward."

"And of course because ye know that I'm married."

"Of course," Mitch said, but they both knew by the tone of his voice that he wished very much that she weren't.

Glenna looked away from him, out into a culvert that was all weeds and tall grass, then glanced down at her watch. She would be late, and not only did she need to check on Aengus, but there were patients in town to see. "Suddenly, so many things are comin' at me," she softly said.

"There's still time to change your mind as far as Mrs. Wescott goes."

"I don't feel anything for her but a lot of anger."

His reply came after a moment. "Relationships like that take time."

"And they take trust."

"Which you don't have?"

Glenna looked up at him suddenly. Her eyes were so blue and bright just then, so full of pain and betrayal, and the desire to be loved, that they took his breath away. "Would you, Mr. Greyson?"

"Now, you really have got to start callin' me Mitch or I'm gonna feel positively prehistoric here."

She laughed at that, then her face softened again. "Ye did no' answer my question."

"Ah." He looked up thoughtfully, considering it. "Would I be able to trust someone who had disappointed me . . ."

"Would ye be able to trust a mother who gave ye away?"

"Depends."

"On what?"

"On why. How. And if she was really, deep down in her heart, sorry."

"Sorry canno' change the past, Mitch."

"Neither does bitterness. That particular insidious little poison can eat up your heart, if you aren't careful."

"Ye sound as if ye know what ye're talkin' about."

"What I know about, Glenna, is regret, truckloads full. And I can tell you, it's the same poison. I'd hate to see you have them if you and Mrs. Wescott didn't find some common ground to at least try and begin a healin'." He touched her chin with a finger, then stilled it there for only a moment as he softly said, "Trust me, Glenna McDowell. Don't be bound up by your bitterness. It can destroy you if you don't take care."

"I'll try to remember that."

Suddenly two men were getting out of a truck up above on the road and coming toward them. Instinctively, Glenna moved to the far side of the seat. Away from Mitch. Away from the moment. "Well, I think we've been rescued," he said deeply, his eyes playing over her face for what they both knew would be the last time.

Glenna looked away then and watched two figures make their way toward them down the little hill. She was not just going to remember that, as she had told him, Glenna would remember all of this, the intensity of what she had missed sharing with a man. And specifically Mitch Greyson. Yes, him she would remember, she knew already, for the rest of her life.

Glenna closed the door and sagged against it, unable to catch her breath. Her heart was pounding like one of those great Highland thunderstorms. In her entire life, no one had ever looked at her like Mitch: full of a pure, carnal desire, veiled only slightly behind laughter and clever banter that, when it was all mixed together and offered up to her for an entire afternoon, had completely overwhelmed her.

Yet it was more than all of that, or even the way that combination of new and exciting things had made her feel. Beneath that glib, carefree cowboy exterior of his was something more, something rich and very complex. There was an inner depth that radiated outward, finding her. It had pulled her for an instant this morning away from herself. Away from the reality of her life.

Even though he had behaved like a perfect gentleman, she could feel all of that as surely as heat rising off an open flame. Good Lord Almighty, did he have to be so fit—so devilishly handsome? And so tender? Did he have to speak so cleverly and make her feel just like a schoolgirl again? All the things that Aengus had never been, and had never been able to give her. All the things she had read about, which she had known existed, but which she had never experienced for herself.

Glenna thought sometimes, in her weaker moments, that she was very like a child pressing her nose against the glass barrier of an ice cream counter where everyone else was getting their favorite flavor. And she didn't even have the luxury of knowing how it tasted.

Ungrateful harlot! Aengus saved your life! Can true affection no' be enough for ye?

She pressed her hands to her ears, certain that the voice inside her head, just then, had belonged to Andrew Ferguson. That alone was certainly punishment enough for what she had begun to feel.

And it wasn't like she'd never felt anything, making love with Aengus. Her dear husband's passion, back when they'd been intimate, had been carnal, but in a rough, unpracticed way. A groping, panting sort of thing, she thought now. Never entirely pleasurable for her, but seeing how happy it made him had given her a kind of satisfaction.

Aengus McDowell truly loved her. He was the first person to come into her life who ever had. That was what she had been telling herself for twenty years. And now this morning, heaven help her, she began to wonder if it had been that way only because she had never found the courage to look beyond the safety of him.

Kate's head was pounding.

The shrill sound of the phone ringing downstairs didn't help. Even her eyes hurt when she opened them to the hazy sun filtering in through her gauzy white bedroom curtains. The darkness was still clinging to the corners of her mind when she heard her mother's voice downstairs. Glenna was on the phone.

"Well, thank ye indeed for your kindness, and for ringin' me back. I'm sorry I've taken so long to call, Father Buchanan, and I'll see ye tomorrow. Aengus has made me realize that it's high time I return to Coatbridge."

Kate's mind cleared a bit more. And then she remembered. All of it. It wasn't a nightmare or a hallucination. Every bit of it had happened, from the phone call to the Glenlivet, to the little white pill. And she had no one to blame for this splitting headache but herself.

"Are ye awake then?" Glenna asked a few moments later after Kate had heard the click of the receiver and the creaking floorboards as her mother came upstairs.

"Oh, leave me to die in peace, would ye?"

"I've brought some good strong tea," Glenna offered a little more gently.

Thoughts went skittering across Kate's mind. Images. All of it dark, seeming like blackbirds startled suddenly into a gray winter sky. The voice of the woman at Isabelle Wescott's house. Her ma's face, so full of hurt after that. Her father's wide, kind eyes so full of question about his dear sweet Katie when she had gone up to see him. *How could ye have done this to your ma? She trusted you.*

She pulled the pillow up, rolled onto her back and pressed it on top of her head, but all that it blocked out was the light. The thoughts and the images were still there, in living color. How, indeed?

"Here, drink this. 'Twill do ye good."

Kate sat up and realized that she had slept in her clothes. She took the steaming cup from her mother and tried to drink a bit of the tea. She took another sip. Her throat, which had felt as long-sealed as a tomb when she woke, began to clear and her mind emerged ever so slowly from that heavy, Scotch-laden fog to which she had surrendered it. The pounding dulled a little. She took another swallow. "Thank ye for this," she said, gesturing with the cup.

"I'd like us to try to talk about what happened," Glenna finally said.

"I don't know if I'm quite up to that."

Her mother persisted. "Knowin' how I'd feel about somethin' so painful, why would ye defy my wishes like that, Kate?" Glenna asked, seeking through her own layer of anger to understand a daughter she didn't know anymore. "Please, my girl. I'd truly like to understand."

Kate looked up, her round face alive with what looked too much like contempt. "Same reason *you* let that man from America pursue you: curiosity mostly. And at least in my case what I did was no' considered a sin."

"Kate!"

"I saw ye alone with him, Ma. Then Mary rung me this mornin' early to say she saw ye get into a car with him in town! I saw him look at ye that first day, and you lookin' at *him!*"

"Ye saw nothin'!"

"Lie to yourself, then, but don't bother tryin' it with me! I know what I saw."

Glenna sank onto the edge of the bed, silenced by her daughter's accusation and by the truth in it. She watched as Kate rose quickly, still in her blue jeans and old ivory Aran sweater, her room grainy with the early morning light in through thin gauzy curtains.

"'Tis no' about me, Katherine Mary," Glenna shot to her

feet again and watched helplessly as Kate laced up a pair of worn black boots. "'Tis about your open defiance of everything—all the things your da and I dreamed for ye!"

"That's just it! 'Tis what *you* dreamed! What you think is best! Well, ye don't know what I want, Ma! I'll tell ye, I don't want to be like you and I certainly don't want your kind o' life! Workin' yourself to death in a small town so ye aren't havin' to look at the life ye've made with a husband old enough to be *your* father! And your eyes still filled with the reflection of all the things ye should have done but didn't!"

Glenna's mouth felt frozen. For a moment the words in her throat would not come. There was a coldness gripping her heart. "Ye don't know what ye're talkin' about," she whispered.

"Maybe not. But I *do* know I canno' stay here just now." She moved toward the door.

"Where do ye think you're goin'?"

"I'm goin' out for a walk. The air in here is full o' too many o' your secrets, and it's startin' to feel like poison."

Thinking of the other times this past year Kate had run away, Glenna jerked toward her and grasped her arm, but Kate wrenched it back. "Katherine Mary McDowell, don't ye dare to walk out o' that door! Not again!"

"Ye canno' control me, Ma!" She pivoted back around defiantly, her wide eyes blazing. "I'm fifteen! I'll no' do as ye ask! I'm no' wantin' to be sorry one day for the things *I* did no' do with my life!" One heartbeat, then two. "Now, I'm goin' out to get some air."

A moment later, the echo of the front door downstairs slamming shut shattered the tense silence of the little stone house.

An hour later, after Glenna had found the biscuit jar in the kitchen emptied of the thousand pounds cash Aengus kept there, she sank onto her child's unmade bed and surrendered her face defeatedly to her hands. Kate had not gone for a walk. She had run away. Again. This was the fourth time this year. The police wouldn't even try to look for her for forty-eight hours. And there was nothing else Glenna could do. Keeping hold of Kate these days was like trying to hold on to a cyclone.

Part 2

I so often wonder what you remember
of those pieces of April,
moments more precious than jewels. . . .

—Stephen Drake

CHAPTER
4

 Isabelle

San Francisco, 1994

"They've found her, Alice."

There was silence after that, and with it a long, tangled vine of memories. Promises. Secrets. Isabelle stood in the silence with her hands on the back of one of the matching bergère chairs as the soft sun of late afternoon fell over the salon. Alice was at the grand bay window, with its draperies of apricot silk. Isabelle's declaration lay suspended, thick and taut, between the sisters. Both of them were pretending to see the sunset and the garden spilling over with pale clematis and fat mauve roses. The splash of color from the daylilies. The ancient urns full of marigolds. And beyond the black wrought-iron gate, the parade of cars trapped in five o'clock traffic out on fashionable Fillmore Avenue.

This was a small room, but it was Isabelle's favorite place in the old Victorian house. Depending on the time of day, the flood of comforting light either brightened or mellowed the blue-papered walls and the chintz- and tapestry-covered furniture, and warmed the overly high ceilings. Isabelle still spent most of her time these past few years surrounded by the silver-framed photographs of her grandchildren and her three grown sons displayed on the small accent tables and on top of the baby grand piano. The rest of the furniture was old but good. The fabric on much of it here in the salon had begun to fade, but she had trouble discarding even the most insignificant things.

And so it had become their ritual every afternoon these past two weeks since her Frank had died. Two middle-aged sisters talking together here, as they sipped their sweet

Spanish sherry and watched the sun set, a pink and orange burst over the mist-shrouded San Francisco Bay.

"I got the call from Scotland this morning."

"Are you sure you really want to go through with this?"

"How can you even ask me that? She's my daughter, my *child!*"

"I just think it could be grief moving you and not logic. Frank's only been gone such a short time. Why didn't you give yourself a few more days, a month before you pursued something so—"

Tears stood in her sea green eyes, making them glitter. "I've waited a lifetime for this chance, Alice."

"I don't know what good can come of it," Alice said as she turned her glass of sherry contemplatively between two fingers.

Seeing how much pain it still brought her sister after all these years, Alice felt her heart catch. She wished her words would come more softly. But it was not in her to equivocate. Not with Isabelle.

Not with what might be at stake if she went through with this.

"She'd be a grown woman now, and you've your own family to think of."

Isabelle's hands tightened on the tapestry-covered chair, and Alice saw that her words sent a new wrench of pain through her sister. The tears Isabelle was trying not to cry began to stream down her still-smooth cheeks. Finally she found her voice again. "A family of which she should have been a part if I had known how to fight them."

"My God, what more could you have done?"

Silence fell deeply between them then. And, in that silence, they remembered. The vine unfolded, untangled itself before them, the leaves, each a chapter of their lives. The years since their father had been called to Scotland seemed little more than yesterday. The secret they had carried, the sacrifice one had been forced to make there, had bound them more tightly than blood.

They made an odd complement to one another, these sisters. Isabelle was slim and small, with her neat copper hair, which she wore pulled away from her face, only partially streaked with strands of gray. Her pale green eyes were fringed with long copper lashes.

Her face was a perfect oval on a long slender neck wreathed with a small gold chain and locket. She wore a navy cashmere cardigan, an Hermès scarf wrapped across her shoulders, and a navy skirt to her knees. Her shoes were sensible but expensive low-heeled navy and cream Adolfo spectators. She was still called beautiful in certain circles, but the image she had long presented to most of the world was *classic*. Rich and elegant, Isabelle looked like the perfect politician's wife she wanted the world to see.

Beside her, Alice seemed blatant, her tall, ample body stuffed into an azure St. John Knit spring suit a size too small. Her own oval face, unmarred and unlined, was accentuated by hair that had been colored just a shade too auburn for a woman her age. The liberal application of tangerine lip paint only pushed the image closer toward garish. But then that was sweet Alice, a woman completely without subtlety and fond of the impression she made.

"I am well aware of the odds against making her understand or accept me," Isabelle finally said, as she took a handkerchief from her pocket and daubed her eyes. "Nor do I expect her to forgive me. Not when I can not even begin to forgive myself. But with dear Frank gone, there was no longer any reason for me to keep my search a secret."

"You did a noble thing in that, Belle. Frank had important work in the Senate."

"I had no other choice. I knew that. But now I do, and I so badly want to see her just once again in this lifetime, Alice, to look upon those eyes I saw for only a moment . . ." Isabelle swallowed hard against the rising ache swelling up from her heart. The wound there lay open again and raw with remembering. "You are the only one who knows how much I have always wanted that."

"What on earth will you tell the boys?"

"The truth."

"Oh, Isabelle, you cannot possibly be serious! What about the public? Have you thought about what Arthur's constituents will think? Your son hasn't quite reached Frank's political zenith, nor his security. And there are your friends, the board members of the Maguire Foundation—"

"I don't give a damn about anyone else, Alice! I've spent too many years doing that," Isabelle shot back, her chin quivering as she struggled against a new wave of tears. "She was my child, every bit as much as my sons. Nothing else beyond the emptiness in my heart matters in the slightest."

Then the silence came again, heavy and dark, a shroud of things spoken and things not. Both women sat without moving in the tasteful salon filled with remembrances of the successful life Isabelle had made after Glenfinnan. It was strange how things could look so ordered on the outside, Isabelle thought, and yet how they could be so tumultuous if you were able, even for a moment, to pull back the shade and really look inside.

"I tried so hard to find her," she whispered, each syllable attached now to another excruciating memory.

Her mind crisscrossed back, touching on all of the times through the years she had tried to find her little girl. Each recollection was like touching a hot stove, the searing memory of following leads, of praying God for just one small break. Finding dead end after dead end, trails gone cold with time. Chances taken that had risked her husband's hard-won Senate seat. And hadn't she gotten close, excruciatingly close, that once, when one of the Carmelite nuns had almost taken pity on her, believing that she had never intended to give away her child—only, in the end, to have the abbess refuse her?

And there were other chances she'd taken after that that had risked even the very foundation of her marriage because Frank Wescott, God rest his soul, never knew.

She had wanted to tell him. Meant to tell him. Kind Frank.

Understanding Frank. Over their many years together, the man she had been forced to marry became a man she grew to love. Never like Stephen . . . No, no one was ever like that. But different. Safer.

How, through the years, she had ached to tell Frank. It was the greatest single part of herself that he didn't know. And so, she came to realize as she laid him to rest, he never really had known her.

But if he'd known about the child, Frank would have risked everything to help her. As a senator's wife, she had learned quickly that when it came to politics, some ambitious reporter would uncover the truth. And Isabelle could never quite bring herself to dash Frank's hopes and dreams. Even to save her own. She could still wince now at the imaginary headlines: *Senator's wife had love child with Catholic priest.* . . .

His career, just beginning in 1959, could never have survived a scandal like that.

No, she could balance it all herself, she had decided. Her youthful zeal and her love for a child she had seen only once had convinced her. She could keep her husband's career intact and she could find her child. If anyone could, she could.

How many times through the years, had she had gone back to Scotland on her own? Trips too numerous to count, when her husband had believed she had gone for pleasure or to check on Willowbrae, her family's estate. As she had searched alone and cried alone, shaking her fist at the heavens, as the trail to that child of her heart grew cold.

There had even been a time when desperation had broken her down and she had almost sent a letter to Stephen himself, through the rectory in Chicago, only to have her father, an invalid after a serious stroke, widowed, and living with them here on Nob Hill, intercept it and then threaten her.

Send that letter and I will tell Frank everything! I swear I will. And if it comes out he'll lose it all! Do you want that on your conscience along with everything else?

That last time, when the dream had slipped away yet

again, had nearly killed her. From then on, Isabelle felt, behind the mask of money, parties, fund-raisers, and even the other children, that she was very slowly falling apart, eroding like some great intricate sand castle, being slowly swept out to sea. And what was killing her was the ocean of pain and the memories that no one in the world could help her fight.

But even so, she would never give up searching, longing, struggling to find her child.

That truly would have been the death of her.

Tangled in her thoughts now, Isabelle at first did not hear her sister's kind proposal. "Perhaps you should come out to the vineyard with David and me for a few days," Alice offered, reaching down to the small rosewood table for the last sip of sherry that lay in a tawny ring at the bottom of her Waterford crystal goblet. "Being alone so much really isn't at all good for you."

The corners of Isabelle's pale lips tightened, lifting in a grim smile as she wiped again at her tears. "What you mean, my dear sister, I believe, is that reflection isn't at all good for me."

"Perhaps that, too. You haven't spoken to me about the . . ." Alice's voice caught in midsentence, and she seemed not to know suddenly what word to use. That surprised Isabelle, since Alice—funnier, older, always more confident—was rarely at a loss for words. "You haven't spoken about the child, for years," Alice forced herself to say.

"I should have found her."

"Daddy made that impossible from the very beginning. You know that."

Alice could not stop those last few words from tumbling out, opening more of the ancient wound than she had meant to. She silently cursed herself for that annoying habit of always speaking before she thought. She watched her sister's hands tighten again on the back of the chair so that her knuckles were large and white, accentuating lavender veins in her slim hands. Alice saw the weight she had lost, too much for someone who was already so thin.

Isabelle sank into the slightly worn ginger silk-covered chair, exhausted. "God, how I hated our father for what he did."

Isabelle's housekeeper, Willa Robbins, a big, square woman, parted the doors and came into the salon in her no-nonsense, thick support hose, with heavy-footed strides. Willa bore a clattering silver tray of fresh scones and two crystal dishes, one brimming with raspberries, the other with cream. Today Isabelle found the fragrance sickeningly sweet.

"Well, I hope *you* can get her to eat something." Willa, who was as overweight as Isabelle was thin, with a great double chin, full patchy-red cheeks and a pink bulb of a nose, huffed as she set the tray down near Alice and put her hands on her ample hips. Eyeglasses dangled from a silver chain across her chest.

"*Et tu, Brute?*" Isabelle daubed at her eyes again then gave Willa a crooked little smile.

"Perhaps she won't tell you, but I will. Mrs. Wescott hasn't taken more than a few bites of food in over a week."

Willa was homely and kind, in her crisp white blouse, its bow tied at the neck, tartan skirt, and stout bricklike lace-up shoes. She had always reminded both the sisters of dear Maureen Donnelly, their parents' housekeeper, *Stephen's mother*. Isabelle tolerated Willa's well-meaning intrusions out of nostalgia. The past had long had a hold over her.

Isabelle sank farther into the chair and laid her head back against it. She closed her eyes and waited for Willa to leave them alone again. When she did, the silence returned and there was nothing for several minutes but the sound of her own beating heart.

"Do you know, I don't believe I ever told you this before," Isabelle said softly. "But sometimes when I try to sleep, I close my eyes and I can actually still see her. So tiny and pink, crying out to me. I can remember touching her for that single moment the good Lord let me have with her. . . . the softness of her skin . . ."

"Don't do this to yourself, Belle."

"It wasn't the same way any of my boys felt, you know.

I've never touched anything so exquisite, before or since. . . ." She was sobbing softly as she spoke those last words, her heart aching almost as much as it had on that horrid night in Glasgow. Why did some memories remain so vivid, she wondered, when others just simply died away?

Alice reached across the rosewood table between their two chairs and pressed her hand onto her sister's. She had known there was something wrong with Isabelle that went even beyond Frank's sudden death. She had sensed her uneasiness, seen the decline in her health. But never once had she suspected this.

"It was all such a long time ago, Belle."

Her voice quivered with emotion. "In my mind, and my heart, it was only yesterday."

"I am worried for you," Alice said softly. Urgently. "I'm afraid there'll be so much heartache in this for you."

"No more than I have borne all these years with this vast, empty space inside of me. . . ." A motorcycle passed beyond the gate, a monstrous thing, revving its engine all the way and tearing brutally into the delicate silence.

Then it was quiet again. "So what do you know so far?"

"Nothing much yet. Only that the detective has met with her. I hired Tremont & Associates, the best there is. If anyone can present my case in a kind and gentle way, they can."

Alice Hart stiffened in her own chair and carefully set down her empty glass. Even though they were middle-aged, the intimacy of their conversation had actually made her feel as if they were adolescent again. She might not have taken the time to show it back then, but she loved Isabelle more than anyone in the world. More even than her own husband. But it was a different kind of emotion, loving a sister. Even now, she still had that overwhelming urge to protect her.

And she had always known that what had happened in Glenfinnan was partly her fault. Oh, the guilt! The knowledge of the part she'd played drove the final nail into the coffin of regret she'd been living with all of these years. She had been young herself then. Still unmarried at twenty-four,

Alice had been exceedingly self-absorbed. Making a good match for herself had consumed both herself and her parents to the exclusion of all else.

If only they'd seen what was happening with Isabelle and Stephen Donnelly—good God, by then *Father Donnelly*—right beneath their noses! But they had all been too taken up with considering Alice's marriage prospects, her offers, from the deliciously convenient distance of Scotland.

It had all seemed to matter so much back then. Connections, finances, appearances. And oh, what a price her sister had paid for all of that! And Alice wasn't even Vanguard's wife any longer. The marital coup of the season had lasted only slightly longer than the honeymoon.

The black oak grandfather clock, a Maguire family heirloom, chimed a quarter past five, catapulting Alice back to the present.

"What if she doesn't want to hear from you?"

"I am not going to think of that," Isabelle said stubbornly, lifting her chin a fraction, and making Alice remember the sister who had never been afraid of anything or anyone. A sister who, before she went to Scotland, had fought fiercely for what she wanted. And yet who had gone on to lose the two things she had wanted most.

The man she loved. And their child.

They linked hands in the sun-filled salon that still smelled of sherry, rich clotted cream, and pastry. Alice's tone was gentle not so much because she believed it was the right thing to do but because her sister needed her. "Waiting is the hardest thing in the world, I think."

"I've had a lifetime of it," Isabelle said.

After she'd said good-bye to Alice, Isabelle went back inside and into the kitchen.

She desperately wanted a sherry, but she wisely settled on tea.

Her head was spinning already. She put her water on the

stove with a shaky hand and turned on the flame. Isabelle liked this old kitchen. She had always felt comfortable here, from that first afternoon when Frank had brought her here as a new bride. It was a kitchen full of the comfort of wonderful smells, with warm red brick walls, copper pots and baskets hanging in clusters from the ceiling.

She reached into one of the tall walnut cupboards, with its beautiful stained glass panes, for the white pottery jar brimming with loose Earl Grey tea. Just as she had known it would, a light rain began to fall. She heard it against the windowpanes, tiny drops at first, then heavy sheets of water pressing against the glass. No, she thought with a little smile, her bones never lied.

As she leaned against the worn sideboard, she could see Stephen's face. It was the first time in a very long time. Isabelle took in a breath to steady her heart, then exhaled. The water rose to a boil and the kettle whistled. It became a high, shrieking sound before Isabelle heard it. She was listening to the rain. Remembering little things.

As she took the tray up the drafty, creaking back stairs and into her bedroom, her mother's Sheffield teapot with the delicate pink roses rattled against one of the matching cups. Her hands were still trembling. She hadn't realized until then that her entire body was trembling, too.

The rain came, faster now, beating out a rhythm against the windowpanes, and her mind wound around the image like a strand of her mother's precious pearls, seeing him again. *Stephen.* The housekeeper's son. Her very dearest childhood friend. *And so very much more.* She remembered the scent of incense. The aroma of smoke from the votive candles. Aging, rich beeswax layered on old pews. The cool feel of holy water on her fingertips. Stephen's lips on her skin. The musky, purely male scent of him. She closed her eyes. Squeezed them shut.

Had anything ever felt like that again? Had anything with Frank ever come close? But the answer had been burned across her soul, branded there, a long time ago. Being held by Stephen. Touched by him. The way they had made love, breathlessly, desperately. Their bare bodies warm and wet, joined beneath that old gray flannel blanket. His fingers wound in her hair. Lips moist and tender on the column of her neck. So much hunger there. Hidden away like that from the world. Trying to outrun fate and a God who would punish them for this.

For the forbidden.

Their words whispered to one another that night in Glenfinnan would be with her forever. Just waiting, like now, to be remembered.

Go home, Isabelle. Please.

Touch me, Stephen. Touch me once, and if you still can say that you want me to leave then . . . I will do it.

The images and the echo of voices in her mind skittered around and around like little gray mice inside a maze. Never quite able to escape. Always heading for that same trap her heart had set so many years ago. *If only . . .*

She sank onto the dressing table stool, covered over with a needlepoint rose. Her eyes moved beyond the bottles of rosemilk, her collection of unopened bottles of cologne and eau de toilette from well-meaning sons who hadn't a clue what fragrance she liked. A jar of hairpins. And then, behind them, a small old-style bottle of perfume with a square black cap and a worn silver label.

The old bottle had sat in that very spot on her dressing table for decades, becoming part of a collection of other incidentals that crowded the glass-topped table. She had not touched it or given it more than a cursory glance for a very long time. It hurt too deeply. But neither could she bear to part with it. That bottle was a little piece of Stephen, the way they had been as children.

Amid a burst of steel gray thunder coming through the tall French windows, she pressed her fingers around the old bottle of My Sin. Her heart quickened as memories flooded her like a rushing river. Brilliant, cold, and very fast.

Isabelle could laugh now at that particular irony. My Sin.

As if, somehow, Stephen's giving it to her all those years ago, the day before he'd left for the seminary in Chicago, had been a foreshadowing in some bad Greek tragedy. And it was a tragedy, what had become of them after that. So beautiful, bittersweet. Never quite meant to be.

The memory of that long-ago afternoon, even long before Glenfinnan, reared up again in her mind. She saw it. Saw him . . . Suddenly it was like yesterday, and they were standing alone in the old garage, half in shadow, half in light, their fit young bodies slashed with gentle beams of sunlight that flared between the old rotting wall boards.

This was their secret place, away from the rest of the world. Even among the cobwebs and the dust, the old rusted hubcaps, spark plugs, and antique chests. Where they had smoked their first cigarette and laughed so hard both of them had begun to choke. . . . Where they had shared so many other childhood rites of passage. But Stephen was not a child anymore, he was a man, really, and he was taking the train to Chicago that night, leaving their world forever. Leaving for the seminary.

"I'll buy you all the vestments and incense you want, if that's what it is," she'd told him.

"This is no joke, Slugger."

"All right, then. Tell me why you're doing it."

Watching the hurt expression suddenly in her eyes, Stephen took a breath. "Oh, don't look at me like that. I do have my doubts about going, all right? Even if it does mean a free college education. But it's something my mom wants for me and can't afford. And I'll have time to decide about actually becoming a priest, if that's what you're worried about. They won't take me and I sure won't be ordained unless I'm sure."

"You're not priest material, Stephen. You know what you want to be. . . . all that you've ever really wanted to be."

"Oh, sure," he said, raking a hand through his full, dark hair, suddenly looking a little desperate and hating the fact that, even though she was so much younger than he, she knew him so well. "Like I'd be able to help my mom quit working with a way-out career like that. No one does that these days."

"There are some! . . . A few!"

"Oh, come on, Slugger. Be serious."

"I am. I believe you could do it if you wanted to. Besides, I don't want you to go," she admitted as the tears swam in her eyes and then cascaded down onto her full, pale cheeks.

"Aw, don't go and start blubbering now, and make me feel doubly worse than I do. Not when I have to leave. Come here, you silly goose," he said and pulled her to his chest very quickly.

She may have been thin and shapeless, with bony little limbs, and features she had not quite grown into. And he may have been years older. But no one in the world was ever going to believe in him like she did. Hadn't he always known that?

Stephen had reached across to his red and white letter jacket, flung casually over the car's fender. He took a small package wrapped in blue foil out of his jacket pocket. "I almost forgot."

"What's this?"

"It's a going-away present for my best pal."

He watched the small box of My Sin tremble in her hand. "I smelled it at Wembley's the other day," he said, "and I thought, now that you're growing up, you might want to wear perfume sometimes. Guys love that stuff. And I'm sure while I'm away there'll be a lot of those around here."

"No there won't."

He moved to the door. "Don't give up on the whole male species, hmm?" He smiled that million-dollar smile. "Remember, we're not all bad. Now, give me one last smile to send me off?"

"Don't go!"

She ran after him, across the garage, but he simply opened the door, turned and smiled at her one last time, in those soft streamers of sunlight. Then he went out the door.

"No, please!" she cried, sinking down onto the dusty, cold slab floor, arms clutching her waist. "Don't go," she said, a quiet keening sound. "You'll never come back to me. . . . Never . . ."

The windows rattled as the rain beat against them, coming now in long icy sheets against the glass. Isabelle squeezed her eyes, closing out the girl she had been, and set the old bottle back in its place on her dressing table. Her fingers were still trembling.

After a moment, with one hand on the dressing table top for support, Isabelle moved slowly in her long ivory night-dress toward her elegant Windsor bed. She felt the familiar ache returning. It came from deep inside her heart, as painful as the memories of what she had so briefly shared with Stephen later. In Scotland.

Oh, Stephen . . . Whatever did become of you? Of us after Glenfinnan?

The memories and images kept returning. There was an old, crumbling stone wall ahead, a fine mist turning steadily into rain as the muddy road curved beneath a heavy bow of oak trees. She could see it all so vividly. The rented Jaguar, all of them huddled inside up from Glasgow, Mother, Daddy and Alice. All of them young again and full of life, and peering out the car windows at the majesty of the Scottish Highlands. And then before them, as they rounded the corner, there it was quite suddenly, almost like a mirage, there was Willowbrae. . . .

CHAPTER
5

⬥ Isabelle and Stephen

Glenfinnan, Scotland, April 1957

"So how long do we have to stay all the way out here in the middle of nowhere?" Alice droned as the car curved along the old single-lane road beneath a lush bow of trees.

"Can't you ever say anything nice about anything?" Isabelle snapped.

"Hush! Both of you!" Sunny Maguire scolded them from the front seat of the sleek Jaguar they'd leased, sitting properly erect in her new beige suit, gloves, and smart pillbox hat as if she was heading for tea at the Ritz, not venturing out into the rural Highlands. "This is your father's ancestral home, and his grandmother has just died! Show a bit of respect!"

Alice slumped back, fanned out her gray felt skirt, propped her black stiletto heels against the back of the front seat, and went back to filing her fingernails with a silver nail file.

Ross Maguire, who loved grand cars and speed, showed no mercy as they neared Glenfinnan, taking the rutted old road like a local, and they all did their best to hold fast to the polished brown leather seats. Then one last turn of the steering wheel, and the boughs of trees opened up like two grand emerald fans. The house before them, shrouded in mist, was not a house at all but a mossy stone castle that looked to Isabelle very like something out of a fairytale.

"Holy cow!" she gasped, two fingers pressed to her lips.

"Somebody actually lives there?" Alice asked, duly impressed by a house far bigger, more grand, and more magnificent than their own back in San Francisco.

"Your grandmother and grandfather Maguire lived in this

house all of their lives," Ross said, looking up at the formidable white brick dwelling surrounded by a forest of trees, which he had not seen since he was a boy. "Before that, an extremely long line of Maguires have inhabited this place. It's been our ancestral home for over four hundred years."

They all climbed out of the car and stood in the gravel drive looking up at a building that had three stories, a turret, and more parapets and old-fashioned leaded windows than they could count. To one side was a forest of birch trees and bog myrtle, and on the other lay undeveloped land rising up to a rugged vista of pewter hills.

"Loch Eilt is down there beyond the trees, beautiful and blue as wet ink. I remember that much," Ross explained with a satisfied smile as he surveyed the property.

"What's a loch?" Isabelle asked.

"A grand lake, my girl, and the Maguires have always fancied Loch Eilt their own."

"Holy cow," Isabelle echoed.

Inside, Willowbrae was every bit as impressive as it had been at first glance. A magnificent double oak door carved with the Maguire family crest opened into an expansive two storied foyer with a sweeping oak staircase carpeted in crimson. There were ancient paintings on the paneled walls and a suit of armor standing guard in a niche. Upon closer inspection, Isabelle saw the banister layered with dust and spiderwebs in the iron chandelier. Ross Maguire's eyes followed his daughter's.

"Looks like quite awhile since Grandmother Maguire had anyone attend this place properly," he said, his voice echoing into the cavernous expanse.

"Gee, by the time they finished, it'd be time to start all over again." Isabelle shook her head incredulously, breathing in the musty smell of the ages.

Alice giggled at that, and the two girls exchanged a glance filled with amazement. "Can we look around, Daddy?" Alice asked, sounding suddenly almost like a child.

"I don't see why not." He smiled proudly. "Willowbrae will be our home until I've finished my business here."

"Maybe it won't be so bad to stay here for a little while, after all," Alice amended. "I'll bet the people around here will think we're royalty or something."

"Isn't that just like you." Isabelle rolled her eyes. "It's not enough that you're the belle of San Francisco. Now you want to conquer Scotland too."

"Not such a bad idea."

"All right, both of you," Ross interceded.

The two girls giggled and dashed up the staircase, racing each other to the top. "I get to choose the first bedroom," Alice declared excitedly as they sprinted down the crimson-carpeted corridor into a bank of sealed oak doors on both sides. Alice opened one door, but the room was shuttered and very dark. She slammed the door shut and leaned against it, looking as if she were suddenly out of breath.

"What's wrong?" Isabelle asked.

"I don't know. I just got this awful chill. I think maybe this place is haunted."

"Oh, don't be ridiculous." Isabelle rolled her eyes again.

"Maybe I'll change my mind about choosing the first bedroom. Do you want to share?"

"With *you?*"

"Gosh, in this place I'm sure there's one big enough for both of us."

"Alice, you're grown up already. The only reason Mother and Daddy brought you on this trip in the first place was to put a little fire under Henry Vanguard's kettle to see if they can make him whistle. They really want him to propose."

"My, aren't we the snide one today."

"Well, it's true, isn't it?"

"All right, I guess they do, and I'm not going to have a thing to say about it! Gee, I don't like him very much, much less love him!"

Isabelle put an arm around her, feeling a sudden and rare burst of sisterly affection. "Oh, come on. Let's find ourselves the most splendid bedroom in the place to share."

And they did find it after surveying three others. It was a

huge, paneled room with a beamed ceiling and an ancient black oak four-poster bed draped in elegant red and blue tapestry. There was an old sea chest at the end of the bed and a grand leaded window that looked over the trees and all the way out across Loch Eilt, glittering in a pale shaft of sunlight like a magnificent sapphire.

"Isn't it grand, Belle?" Alice asked breathlessly, pulling back the two window panels and leaning out to catch the air.

"That it is."

"No wonder Maureen said Stephen didn't sound in his last letter as if he minded being sent here."

"Did you ever find out from her exactly why the diocese had sent him to Protestant Scotland, of all the places on earth?"

"Well, we're Catholic, and it didn't stop our ancestors from planting roots here for generations."

"You know what I mean."

"No, if she knows she didn't tell me. Only that he was to take a six-month leave and would be considered a visiting priest here during his time."

"I can't wait to see him. It'll be nice to see a familiar face here, I think."

Stephen and Isabelle hadn't spoken to one another since that incident in Ross Maguire's shadowy garage when he'd given her the bottle of perfume. Somehow after that, after the things he had made her feel, the desperation at his leaving, it seemed a sin even to think about him. *For I the Lord am a jealous God*—she remembered reading that in Exodus, and Isabelle wasn't certain she was prepared to go up against the good Lord Almighty.

"Girls!" their mother called to them in her singsong soprano. "Girls? Where are you?"

"In here," Alice answered, lying on the grand bed, her arms crossed behind her head.

The sisters exchanged a complicitous little glance, saying silently that they knew Mother would ruin all of their fun. She wasn't a bad mother, Isabelle often thought as she grew older. In fact, Sunny Maguire adored her daughters, sometimes to a fault. She was always worrying about their grades and helping them with their homework, caring about their friends and making sure that they had the perfect party dress to create an impression.

The problem was that physical involvement often took the place of a real emotional connection to her growing daughters—that final link that might have made their mother-daughter bond something truly extraordinary.

But it was the way it had been with Sunny's mother before her. Sunny Maguire had always had money. For her, it was not a privilege but a birthright. And with that, there was a certain order to things. A certain distance maintained. Even with one's own children.

Sunny breezed into the cavernous room just then, still wearing her hat and gloves. "Isn't this marvelous?" she asked, surveying the room and looking as fresh as she had when their day's journey began. "Goodness, if I had known, I would have made your father bring me here ages ago."

Isabelle and Alice smiled and stole another glance when she turned her back.

"My, what a view!" she sighed. "But I'd love to get a closer look at it all. Would you girls like to take a little walk with me down by the lake?"

"Loch, Mother," Isabelle corrected her.

"Sounds lovely," Alice said. "You know, I actually think I could learn to like it here."

"Is Daddy going to join us?"

"No, girls," she said with a regal smile, as she clasped her gloved hands before her. "He's gone on ahead for a walk into town. A bit of nostalgia, I suppose. And to find the presbytery so that he can ask Stephen Donnelly to join us for supper."

After they all had rested, freshened up, and changed clothes, they went downstairs for supper. While there wasn't much in the way of a proper staff at Willowbrae, there was an aged Highland couple called the McNultys. Both of them lived, along with their adult son Ian, in the little stone cottage out near the gate. In Mrs. Maguire's latter years, they had functioned as caretakers and housekeepers, and Mrs. McNulty was a fairly decent cook.

The grand dining hall, with its blazing fire, dark paneling, and vaulted ceiling, actually looked warm and inviting. Ross and Sunny stood in the corner with Alice, sipping gin martinis.

Isabelle was racing down the staircase, knowing she would be late and that her father despised tardiness. Especially from his own family. Just as she reached the bottom, the sound of the brass knocker against the solid old door echoed through the vaulted foyer. Isabelle glanced around for staff, or someone to answer it. She knew it would be Stephen. Her heart gave a little thump of anticipation. It had been almost five years. Would he notice how much she had changed? What would he remember now about that last afternoon?

When no one came to answer the door, Isabelle pressed away the questions and reluctantly turned the tarnished brass knob herself. And then there he was, standing before her, his blue eyes rooted on her. Eyes she knew, that knew her. He smiled. She did so in return. But they did not embrace like the old friends they were. Instead, Isabelle simply stepped back from the door, her heart pounding very fast.

"It's wonderful to see you, Stephen."

"How are you, Isabelle?" he asked, and his smile was contained.

Isabelle suddenly felt like a stranger with him for the first time in her life, she in her new topaz straight skirt, gauzy white blouse, and heels. Nearly a grown woman now. And he was in a long black cassock that matched the color of his hair. But what she focused on was that collar, white as a dove's wings. A Roman collar. Forever the symbol of the clergy. The reality of it hadn't hit her—really hit her—until

that moment, seeing him for herself. This boy she once
secretly had thought she might actually be in love with, her
Stephen, was, now and forever, a real Catholic priest.

In the swirl of anticipation and memories, Isabelle hadn't
noticed that there was someone standing behind Stephen
until he stepped forward. It was another priest in the same
dark cassock and white collar, only he was short and stout
and nearly bald.

"Father Lewis, may I present Isabelle Maguire." Stephen
turned toward Isabelle, his tone more formal. "Father Lewis
is pastor at Saint Finan's."

"Father," Isabelle nodded politely and extended her hand,
which he took and shook in that rough, friendly way that
country people have.

"'Tis indeed a pleasure, lass."

"Please, come in," she said, a little embarrassed by the
need for such formality with Stephen.

"Gosh, I hadn't thought," she said in a low, awkward tone
as they walked toward the dining hall, her new black patent
leather heels clicking across the bare parquet flooring, the
old priest a few steps in front of them. "Maybe I should be
calling you *Father* Stephen now."

He did not look directly at her, but she could see his eyes
crinkle in the corners with what seemed like a hint of amuse-
ment. That was something familiar, she thought, drawing in
a little breath of relief. A spark of the old friend.

"Just Stephen is still all right."

"Good."

Time away from one another, and growing up, had
changed them both. But he had changed the more, she
thought. Stephen looked tired. He was certainly thinner. His
dark curls had been tamed back with a close haircut, but his
eyes were still as brilliantly blue as ever. Perhaps more so,
now that his hair no longer framed his face to soften them.
Whatever had caused him to be sent all this way had made
an impact on him. That was for certain. Eventually, he would
tell her what it was, she knew. No matter what, they were

still friends. A Roman collar couldn't change that much between them.

Ross Maguire smiled broadly when they all came into the dining hall. He, Sunny, and Alice had been standing beneath a leopard head trophy with their cocktails in hand, and he came forward swiftly. A scratchy version of a Glen Miller tune played in the corner on an old Victrola. Isabelle swallowed a little lump of embarrassment at her father's suit, all of it entirely blue and green tartan (good Lord, the vest too!), ornamented with a stand-out red bowtie.

It reminded her of the time when they were children, that first winter Sunday when Stephen had become an altar boy, and her parents had just come back from a holiday in Honolulu. To Alice and Isabelle's complete horror, their father, dressed in a white dress suit and shirt, had waited until the very moment when the church was full, then, with that flaming red hair, his face bronzed by the Hawaiian sun, he had slowly, leisurely strolled toward the front of the church where they were seated with their mother.

She still cringed at the memory of the audible gasps as he had nodded, smiled, and greeted people all the way to the front pew. Ross Maguire was not only a captain of industry, she had learned for certain that day, but a master of self-promotion. There wasn't a single soul in Saint Francis' church that Sunday, including poor Father Keough, so dependent upon the generous Maguire donations, who wasn't made aware that Ross was the most influential member of the parish.

But there were reasons for everything. Isabelle's father had not been born to wealth as her mother had been. A Scots immigrant whose family had more faded European lineage than money, he'd made his fortune by struggling in the import business. Chinese goods in San Francisco were a gold mine. But he'd begun by licking labels and hauling crates as someone else's hired help. The one thing he could not buy, with a background like that, was a position in society nor the respectability that came with it. Sunny had given him that,

and a sense of direction. They quickly became a team, working together (she, throwing parties and wooing investors) to
make Wescott Limited the most powerful import company
on the West Coast. Surprising or not to San Francisco's elite,
their affection for one another was real and enduring.

For their twentieth anniversary, Ross had given her a key
to his heart, made of twenty-four karat gold and studded
with diamonds. In front of everyone, he'd wept openly as
he'd called her the woman of his dreams. Isabelle felt a little
tug of affection for her father, remembering that.

"Ah, Stephen!" Ross said now with a broad smile, his
straight white teeth sparkling like piano keys. "Good to see
you, my boy. And you must be Father Lewis. My grandmother spoke often of you."

"Pleased to meet ye, Mr. Maguire. Your grandmother was
a lovely, pious woman. She's sorely missed here in
Glenfinnan already."

"Thank you. . . . Well. It was good of you both to come."

"Good of you to invite us, sir," Stephen said.

Ross slapped him across the back. "No need for formality,
Stephen. So far from home like this, and you being
Maureen's boy, you're almost a part of the family."

Isabelle stifled a smile. This was the same Stephen
Donnelly who had never once been invited to eat at their
table ("It just isn't done, Puppet. . . . Not with the help,") but
was relegated even in the later years to taking his meals in
the kitchen with Maureen. And now suddenly he was family?
There was an ulterior motive, as bold as a hungry cat, lurking not far behind. She was certain.

"That's very kind of you to say, sir."

"Besides, what a great honor it is to have an actual priest
among us. Mrs. Maguire and I haven't yet had an opportunity to congratulate you on your ordination."

Bingo! There it was. Of course. Church connections. In
Ross Maguire's case, one could never have too many. A mal-
leable young priest who was indebted to him might one day
actually come in handy. . . .

"Thank you, Mr. Maguire." Stephen nodded as Alice brought him a gin martini like the rest of them were drinking.

"Well, if I don't need to call you 'Father,' you certainly don't need to stand on ceremony. You're welcome to call me Ross."

Isabelle cringed.

"I haven't had an opportunity to thank you yet for the good word you put in that I be sent here."

"Your dear mother is a loyal employee," Ross said, rocking back on his heels in his tidal wave of tartan. "And she is a fine woman. I was only too glad to do it. Although I'm still not quite certain I understand what necessitated your being sent away from the States so soon in the first place."

"A bit of time for reflection," Stephen equivocated smoothly. "Something most new and anxious men of the cloth, I am told by my superiors, can benefit from having."

"Yes," Father Lewis interjected in his gravelly Scottish burr. "And the dear boy has done nothin' but work like a veritable Trojan for me since he arrived. He's been my right arm, in truth, and I do no' have a clue what I'll be doin' when he leaves us."

Father Lewis resembled a stout little leprechaun, Isabelle thought, fighting a smile. His face was craggy and red with age, and probably drinking, but his expression was terminally impish. That alone made him instantly likable.

They all sat down in their polished Windsor chairs at a table draped in lovely white Scottish linen and covered with steaming china dishes filled with salmon, venison casserole, and, for the first course, a curiously titled Scottish soup called cock-a-leekie. Two grand candelabra blazed, one at each end of the table, as they ate.

"Ooh, that smells lovely," Alice said as Mr. McNulty bent first over her shoulder with a steaming silver platter. His son, Ian, an overgrown man whose face still resembled a boy's in its full shape and pale tone, cleared away the soup bowls clumsily. "What is it?"

"'Tis called haggis, miss."

"I smell onions. What else is in it?"

He looked at her with a spark of pleased surprise that she had asked. "A sheep's stomach is filled with chopped heart, lungs, kidney, Miss Maguire, and then mixed with a wee bit of oats and some spices."

Alice's lips twisted sourly as she backed firmly away. "I think I shall pass on the haggis, Mr. McNulty."

"'Tis somethin' of a national dish, miss, and not all that easy to arrange. My wife spent the better part o' the mornin' puttin' it together as a welcome."

"It's really quite good if you can get it past the sound of it," Stephen offered, fighting a smile.

"It would be polite at least to try it," Sunny Maguire leveled her gaze upon her eldest daughter.

"But, Mother, I—"

"Alice," Ross's voice boomed across the table with that steely tone that had always kept those near him in line, "try a bit of the haggis, dear. Your mother is right. It's polite."

"I don't see any of you very quick to try it," she scowled.

As she lifted her silver fork reluctantly, Alice's thin lips twisted as though she had just tasted a bitter lemon at the mere notion of putting it in her mouth. Sunny pressed the white linen napkin to her mouth so that no one would see her smile. Ross's copper brows merged in a disapproving frown when he saw her. And suddenly an awkward silence fell over the table as the McNultys stood off to the side, waiting for someone to eat.

"Oh, for heaven's sake," Isabelle said with her best superior smile. Then, quite ceremoniously, she lifted her fork full of the steaming pie and, with everyone's eyes suddenly rooted on her, she very bravely pressed a huge bite into her mouth.

The breath her mother drew inward was audible. Ross shot his wife another reproving glare just as Alice groaned in open disgust.

"It's lovely, Mrs. McNulty," Isabelle pronounced after

she'd swallowed and taken a sip of wine. "I especially love the slight taste of cinnamon."

The old cook beamed, her broad chest bowing slightly. "Why, thank ye, Miss Maguire. Thank ye indeed."

As husband and wife moved out of the dining hall, her whispered words echoed back. "See there, Raymond, I told ye at least one o' them'd have enough pluck to try it."

"Aye, but who'd have thought 'twould be the youngest lass!"

The conspiratorial laughter of the diners filled the vaulted hall once the McNulty's had gone. The formality was suddenly lifted and Ross poured more wine for everyone, then lifted his glass to his youngest daughter.

"Who would have thought so, indeed," he concurred with an approving smile.

After that, they heard stories about Constance Maguire, Ross's magnificently eccentric grandmother who had stayed a Catholic and supported her church here in Glenfinnan in spite of the enormous pressure from the Protestants. "Heretics," she had called them, right up the day of her death. When Ross excused himself to the game room for a cigar and Father Lewis consented to join him if the cigar was accompanied by a dram of Connie's twenty-year-old Scotch, Sunny Maguire leaned nearer to Alice.

"So, then. Has there been any word at all from Henry Vanguard yet?"

"You would certainly know before me if there had been, Mother."

"Well, I cannot imagine why this all should be taking so long. The boy is either going to propose or he's not," Sunny said, drinking the rest of her burgundy in a ladylike sip and then lighting a cigarette. The smoke rose in a white plume as she leaned back in her chair and exhaled. "There's simply got to be a way to make him propose—and believe me, I'll think of it."

"I've had a call every day since we arrived in Glasgow from Willie Amsley. Doesn't that count for something in all of this? After all, Daddy says he's still in the running."

Instead of answering, Sunny Maguire simply patted her

daughter on the back of the hand and smiled. "Oh, let's shoot for the stars a little while longer, while they're still within our reach, hmm?"

Stephen and Isabelle exchanged a glance. Suddenly, it all seemed very funny. Miserably funny. Her father dressed up like a Scottish circus clown. Her mother matchmaking for all she was worth. Isabelle put a finger to her lips, fighting a pressing urge to giggle. The urge was contagious, and she saw that Stephen was biting his cheek and averting his eyes to keep from doing the same thing.

And there it was.

All of a sudden. Another hint, just the slightest spark of the old Stephen. An ache for the old days quickly filled Isabelle, days when their conspiratorial laughter had filled the house on Nob Hill. Days when they were free to be themselves, when they had understood without words just what each other was thinking. . . . And when, God forgive her (she hated even thinking it, looking at that collar) she had slept with his picture beneath her pillow. Isabelle hadn't realized until now how much she missed the way it used to be, having Stephen in her life.

"Well, I, for one, need to get some air," Isabelle said, thrusting back her chair and straightening her skirt.

The McNultys had begun to clear the table amid a great clatter of dishes and silver, and Alice and Sunny were still debating the merits of certain suitors. "I do believe I'll join you," Stephen said, smiling as he pushed his own chair back from the table.

There was a grand stone terrace outside at the end of the dining hall with a view of the loch. Isabelle leaned against the railing and drew in a breath, and the cold night made her shiver. As she wrapped her arms around her waist, Stephen came and stood beside her.

"It's nice to know some things haven't changed," he said, with a calm smile. "Your father still hasn't found a new tailor, and your mother is still trying to marry off Alice."

"Yes, and she and Daddy still think everyone is beneath her. They've gone through nearly everyone in the San

Francisco social register. It's kind of like watching ducks in a shooting gallery. As of a week ago, the only two left floating were Henry Vanguard and William Amsley."

"Lovely choices. *Old* money or *more* money."

"And now you've seen which one mother is rooting for."

They both began to laugh, as they always had when they were young. For a moment only, they were without the wall the priesthood had placed so powerfully between them.

The cool evening breeze was tossing her hair as they stood close together, still chuckling. A tangle of copper caught on her eyelash and Stephen reached up to brush it away. Then his hand froze in midair, and she felt an ache of anticipation. He looked like a priest, but he smelled like a man, raw and purely male.

Suddenly Isabelle felt her face flush, and she was as warm as if it were the middle of summer. It was an awkward sensation, this closeness, now, and it was made more awkward still when Stephen made no move to back away. But there was still that collar. Stiff, white, and forbidding. After another moment, he casually lowered his hand.

"That really was brave of you," he said, and she saw a muscle flex in his jaw as if he were trying to rein in words he was not quite ready to say.

"What was?"

"Going first with the haggis like that. I'm glad to see that you're still as bold and as brave a girl as ever."

"Well, you were right. If you don't think about it, it doesn't really taste all that bad."

"You always were a brave girl, weren't you?" he smiled. "Right from the start."

And she had been that. Neither of them had ever forgotten their meeting. When she wasn't yet eight, a girl in pale copper pigtails and a powder blue pinafore, and he was almost thirteen, the new housekeeper's son.

They both laughed now as they stood on the balcony remembering, until Stephen finally looked away from her, out across the dark, unending horizon, the hills still touched with the last bit of rose glow from the sun. The air was sweet and heavy with the profusion of wildflowers, primrose, milk-wort, and wood anemones, carpeting the glen below as it sloped down in the misty darkness to the water's edge. "I do miss San Francisco," he sighed.

"Well, it misses you. So does your mom."

Stephen looked back at her. "How was she before you left?"

"A little slower these days, truthfully. But she still insists on doing everything herself. That house of ours is still her total domain."

"Mother is sure you Maguires could never get along without her."

Isabelle softly chuckled. "She's right, you know."

"She certainly did find a place to belong."

"And you, Stephen?" Isabelle asked, turning to look at him again, her smooth ivory face as perfect as a cameo in the shadows the lamplight cast out from the dining room. "Have you found that place to belong, as well?"

He looked out across the darkness. Because she knew him Isabelle could see that he was trying very carefully to gauge his words. She saw that same little muscle flinch again in his jaw, his eyes narrow ever so slightly.

"There are times when I think it is the most right thing I have ever done in my life."

"And the other times?"

"It is like any other new marriage, I suppose. There are disappointments, too."

"I think Father Keough would be so proud of you."

She saw a little flicker of pain pass across his smooth, tanned face—one only she could have recognized. Isabelle touched his hand gently, and very quickly the years slipped away.

"I think about him so often," he said in a low voice. "And God, I miss him."

His history with old Father Keough was a long and complex one. It had begun when Stephen's mother, Maureen, had finally won the issue of his becoming an altar boy. He hadn't wanted to at first, but from there, Stephen had been quickly rewarded with doing special services. And to an impressionable boy it steadily became much more. There was never a time when Father Keough was not available to talk things over. When Stephen had finally made varsity basketball his junior year, Father Keough had even come to several of his games and stood in the stands rooting as loudly as any of the other fathers. And Isabelle, who had been there too, had never missed the upturn of Stephen's chin nor the spark of pride in his eye when he'd glanced up in the bleachers and seen the old priest there beside his mother.

"Did you ever think . . . I don't know, that maybe you did this for him, because he was so much like a father to you?" she asked, deliberately turning away from the stark white-against-black of his collar, feeling as if their childhood connection still gave her the right to ask. But even so, she was near enough to feel him stiffen in response. As he faced her again, a shadow fell over his expression.

"I became a priest because I love God, Isabelle. One day you'll love a man like that, and then you'll understand."

Isabelle felt as if she'd been dashed with icy water. He had pulled away from her emotionally, and she wrapped her arms around herself again as a defense against it. But what else could she have expected of him? No matter what she had wanted to believe an hour ago, Stephen had changed.

"Father Keough was a good man," she said carefully, watching the light go out of his beautiful blue eyes.

"The best."

"I'm so sorry."

"You know, I still can't quite make myself believe that he's actually gone."

Something shifted again between them as a spark of their past closeness flared up. One moment there had been that strange antagonism and then suddenly there was something raw and very powerful lurching between them. When tears stood in Stephen's eyes, Isabelle wrapped her arms around him. Consolation, she was thinking. It wasn't strange any longer, but the most natural thing in the world to do.

In response, he reached up, his fingers curling around the slim column of her neck. They were suddenly twined like new spring vines, something she had longed for, dreamed of—before he had become a priest. Her small breasts in the gauzy blouse pressed against his black wool cassock.

Neither of them moved away, and their eyes still met. In this moment of grief, Stephen looked as if he was actually about to draw her nearer. His gaze had already done so. . . . *But was that possible?*

The sound of the French door squealing as it swung back blotted out the question, sending a dagger of guilt down Isabelle's spine. Alice's lovely brown eyes narrowed slightly, seeing her. Seeing them. In the silence her lips tightened.

"Well, what on earth are the two of you doing out here? It's positively freezing and it's so dark you can't see a thing."

"I just wanted a breath of air."

"Where are the others?" Stephen asked, moving a step away from Isabelle.

"They're still in the game room staring up at more of those poor animal trophies. Father Lewis is explaining, in excruciatingly vivid detail, how and where our great-grandfather killed each and every one of them."

"Well, if you'll excuse me," Isabelle said to Stephen and her sister, wanting suddenly to be away from all of them, but most of all from Stephen, "I think I've had enough Scottish air for one evening."

And, by herself, she went very quickly back into the house.

"Well, 'twas a grand evenin' indeed," Father Lewis said with a grin as he looked at Ross, "and I do thank ye again quite kindly for the hospitality."

They were all standing at the open front door, the cold, misty night air rushing in at them as Stephen and Father Lewis said good-bye. Isabelle hung back, clinging to the mahogany banister a few steps away.

"And since ye've seen so little of this part o' the country," the little cleric went on, "tomorrow, after mass, Father Stephen and I should like very much to invite ye all out for a wee bit o' sight-seein'."

"Oh, we couldn't possibly impose like that, with all that you must have to do." Isabelle's mother clutched her pearls, managing to sound suddenly a little too much like a poor imitation of Scarlett O'Hara.

"I have no' nearly the schedule to keep to that I once had, Mrs. Maguire, now with Father Stephen at my side. My sermons for the next two weeks are already prepared. And stirrin' ones they are indeed!"

"Well, darling," Sunny said, turning to her slightly drunken husband for confirmation, "that would be lovely, to see a bit of the countryside. . . . Don't you agree?"

Alice and Isabelle lay together in the huge old mahogany poster bed with its heavy draperies tied back at each corner. It was very dark in this grand old room, and the stillness of the countryside seemed deafening to two girls who had grown up surrounded by the noise and bustle of city life.

"I was surprised at Stephen tonight, weren't you?" Alice said into the darkness.

Isabelle turned onto her side and pulled up the covers. "How do you mean?"

"I don't know. He had an edge, or something. I'm not sure what it was, but I don't remember ever seeing it before."

"He seemed the same to me," Isabelle lied.

"He's still handsome, that's for sure. . . . Brother, what a waste."

"Because he became a priest?"

"With that face and that body, I'll bet he could have been like Marlon Brando or even James Dean if he'd wanted to."

"I think that's sacrilegious when you're talking about a man of the cloth."

"Maybe . . . but it's the truth. He totally missed his calling."

"You say."

"Yes, I say."

"Well, he seems happy to me."

Alice sat up and switched on the lamp beside the bed. The room filled with a pale yellow glow. "I don't think he seems happy at all. He reminds me of those guys during the war who joined the army just because they thought they should."

Isabelle rolled onto her back and looked over at her sister. "You really think Stephen became a priest out of some sort of misguided sense of duty?"

"Well, Maureen and Father Keough certainly pushed him hard enough to make him confuse desire with duty. For almost a year before he went into the seminary, Maureen was after him. 'Think about it, Stephen,' I'd hear her say to him. 'Just consider it. What more noble, what more extraordinary life could there be?' I love her to death, but she really was shameless about it. Then Father Keough! I actually think he came to believe he was Stephen's real father after a while, taking him everywhere the way he did. Showing up at ball games. Sitting right along side Maureen . . . And what father doesn't want a son to follow in his footsteps?"

Isabelle neatly folded down the covers over her chest as the question hung in the air between them. "Believe me, Alice," she finally said with a yawn that made her words sound convincingly disinterested. "Before he was ordained, I used to wonder the same thing. But if he became a priest it was because it was the life he wanted."

"Spoken like someone whose crush on him is entirely a thing of the past."

Isabelle's eyes snapped open. She sat up and looked over at Alice. It was something they hadn't spoken about in years.

"So, does Stephen know you're still carrying a torch for him?"

Isabelle raised her head defiantly. "I'm not carrying a torch!"

"I saw you looking at him out on the terrace, and that seemed pretty hot to me."

"You're disgusting."

"You're out of your league."

"It's late," Isabelle said, turning away again, not wanting to think of him like that. "Let's go to sleep."

"So are you saying you don't still have a crush on Stephen Donnelly?"

"I'm saying I'm going to sleep."

The next day, all huddled together in Father Lewis's chugging, cocoa brown Morris Traveler, a boxy old British car with wood-paneled sides, they had driven for over an hour along a narrow winding road, laughing and singing Scottish folk songs. The tunes and their laughter echoed across the vast loch on one side and into the mist-laden, heather-clad moors on the other. Beyond, the magnificent mauve mountains rose up into the clouds, dwarfing the lone car as it made its way southward.

The ruins at Kilchurn were of an old red stone fortress set on a marshy outcrop extending out Loch Awe. It had once been quite grand, the seat of the powerful Campbells, but now Kilchurn Castle was little more than a few towers and scattered stones swept and battered by cold rainy wind and by time. Still, in its remains there were a few ancient hints of how majestic it once had been.

"Ooh, let's go in!" Isabelle said excitedly as the car approached the castle, so stark against the cloudless azure sky.

"It's no' thought safe, lass," Father Lewis warned as he turned off the ignition.

Isabelle leaned forward, bracing her arms on the back of the front seat. "Oh, nonsense. It's survived since Mary Queen of Scots was here, hasn't it? It'll certainly bear a little more weight from me. Someone else is going to come along, aren't they? Mother? Alice?"

"Don't look at me," her sister shook her head. "It's freezing out there with all of that wind. Besides, what'll the elusive Henry Vanguard say if I break my leg now? Or worse yet, my slim little neck!"

"Mother?" Isabelle asked, turning the other way.

Sunny Maguire fingered her pearls. "Not me, darling. The drive is lovely, but it's not the least bit ladylike to go tramping through a bunch of puddles and rushes into the cobwebs. Especially in one's good shoes."

"Oh, all right. If ye're really wantin' to go up, I'll join ye, lass, as I'm the one that brought ye," Father Lewis acquiesced, rolling his eyes in the rearview mirror. Then, smiling again, he turned to Ross Maguire. "Join us, will ye?"

"I think I'll just stay and keep the ladies entertained while you have your look around."

"Well, at least you'll come, Stephen," Father Lewis said.

There was a little silence before he answered. "Sure," he said. "Why not?"

The wind came in frigid gusts up off the water, and although the sky above them was still crystal blue and cloudless, the air was very cold. Isabelle ran across a field of blowing grass carpeted with bluebells to the steps leading up to the old red stone ruins. Stephen and Father Lewis came along more slowly behind her, walking down an old dirt path in their black cassocks and white collars, which were stark against all the pastel colors of very early spring.

Stephen watched Isabelle up ahead of them, feeling a strange ache well up inside him and begin to spread as she moved so freely, her loose copper hair and the hem of her skirt blowing out like a sail against the breeze. The sensation was foreign and a little unsettling as he watched her near the old stone archway where once there had been some sort of grand door. *Her legs are so much longer than I remember. . . . and she looks so graceful all of a sudden. . . .*

Stephen felt the odd sensation like a hand moving up his chest to clutch at his throat. *Stop it*, he thought.

Father Lewis was telling him something about the history of the castle. ". . . and if memory serves, that happened round 1440. . . . Then in 1746 . . ."

But Stephen hadn't heard anything beyond that. *I wonder*

*when she stopped wearing her hair pulled back. . . . It's so lovely
this way, long and soft around her face. . . .*

Still several steps ahead of them, Isabelle ducked inside
the arched entrance and made her way up a narrow, crumbling stone staircase. It was very dark and low, built for people from another time, obviously much smaller than she. The
stairwell grew darker still as she climbed and it wrapped
around an old turret. It felt as if she were on an adventure.

"Come on! I'll race you to the top!" she called out, but no
one answered.

It didn't matter. This was the most fun she'd had since
they'd gotten to Scotland. A week in dreary industrial
Glasgow didn't count. If her mother wasn't whining on to
Alice about Henry Vanguard, her father was making endless
business calls to the States or seeing to the arrangements for
his grandmother's estate. Lost in all of it, and left on her own
most of the time, was Isabelle. Good little Isabelle. Certainly
too good to worry about, her father always joked.

The crumbling and seemingly endless staircase led finally
into a large, vaulted round room with a gutted fireplace
hearth that dominated an entire wall. Isabelle was struck by
the ancient, ruined grandeur. Her mind swam with imagined
images of graceful lords and ladies dancing as the turbulent
waters battered the rocky banks below.

She moved in further, almost able to hear the music, to
smell the venison roasting in the hearth across the room. She
curtsied to the imaginary lord before her, then twirled
around, holding up a make-believe ball gown of heavy velvet
encrusted with precious stones. She felt entirely taken up by
the magic of an ancient, mystical Scotland.

Stephen reached the top step, with Father Lewis a flight
behind, just as she had begun to dance. "Go on ahead,
lad. . . . These ol' legs prefer a more reflective pace. I'll be
right along," he had said.

Isabelle didn't see Stephen as he stood alone in the little
stone alcove, and something stopped him from calling to
her. She just looked so incredibly beautiful, carefree, dancing

amid the ruins of this once-majestic fortress. A memory crept up, one he hadn't thought of in years. Her freshman prom. She had still been so awkward back then, so vulnerable to Alice's ribbing.

"It's a shame you don't have a date for the dance," Alice had cruelly teased. "It sounds like it's going to be fun. I hear the guy who's gonna sing sounds just like Eddie Fisher."

He would never forget Isabelle's face, embarrassed, angry, hurt at not having been asked to the dance. And faced with Alice, who had more suitors than she could ever go out with.

"She has a date," Stephen said, standing between them in his argyle sweater, corduroys, and loafers.

"Oh sure." Alice rolled her eyes. "Like who?"

"Like me."

Her eyes widened. Her mouth dropped. It was wonderful, he thought, to see Alice Maguire speechless; it was such a rare occasion. "In fact, we were just finalizing things when you came in."

Alice's eyes had narrowed suspiciously. Then she started to chuckle. "Aren't you a little old for school dances now, Stephen?"

"Oh, come on, Alice," he said blithely. "No one is ever too old for a little fun."

"Except maybe you," Isabelle chimed in at last, empowered by this gallant knight who had ridden up so unsuspectingly to save her from a fate worse than death: torment by an older, prettier sister.

And they had gone to that dance, and he'd actually had fun, mostly because he saw how proud, how happy and awkward, pretty Isabelle was, stepping on his toes in her first pair of peau de soie shoes, and that pink organza party dress, the one with the white tea roses. But she had done him so many favors over their childhood years, she had been so kind to him, always listened, read his poetry, really cared what he thought. . . . In spite of their age difference and how out of place he had felt, he had owed her.

Stephen smiled as he leaned against a crumbling stone

wall, remembering that. Now Isabelle had grown into her looks and was quite uniquely beautiful. Not in the traditional way that Alice was, but she was developing a slim grace and elegance that he hadn't expected.

That same curious sensation washed over him again at that moment, and suddenly he was very warm, as if he'd worn too many clothes, and he knew she still hadn't seen him. It was sensual, an earthy sensation. It was something he was definitely not supposed to feel. He knew that. *Not for Isabelle. Good Lord, not for any woman. Besides, you idiot, she's just someone from your childhood. . . . It's memories and home-sickness you're feeling. . . . nothing more than that. . . .*

Sensing him standing there at last, she stopped and turned. Isabelle didn't know why, but her knees felt weak as he looked at her. She was certain that in all her life, he had never looked at her quite like that. His hands were at his sides, and his lips were slightly parted. She drew nearer, and suddenly the moment was extinguished as Isabelle forced away the feeling, passing it off with a winsome smile. Yes, she had loved him once. But she mustn't think of that. Not anymore.

"I was just being silly . . . imagining what it must have been like here."

Her voice, soft and a little embarrassed, broke the still-ness. Then they could hear Father Lewis's shoes slapping heavily onto each of the stone steps as he drew nearer. As they continued to look at one another, with the little chasm between them, her skin tightened oddly to gooseflesh. *What is this? What on earth is happening?*

Afraid to hear the answer, and closing off the question as if she were closing a door, Isabelle took another step forward. Then it happened so quickly that she had no time to break her fall. The rotting floorboards gave way beneath her with a groan and then a crack, like the sound of a whip. She went down, twisting her ankle, in a flash of dust and wet wood. "Isabelle!"

The instant hung in space. There was only that pained

expression on her face, the musty smell of rotting wood, and the far-off sound of seagulls screeching. Stephen lunged for her just as Father Lewis stepped, huffing and puffing, into the ancient room behind them.

"Silly of me. I should have been watching where I was going in an old place like this," Isabelle said weakly as Stephen scooped her up into his arms and helped her back to her feet. "I'm fine, really."

"Are you sure? Can you walk on it?"

They were looking at one another, both a little out of breath, and Stephen was still holding her. "Don't give it another thought," Isabelle said, trembling.

It was several days before anyone at Willowbrae saw Stephen again.

After the outing to Kilchurn Castle, the cold, rain-drenched days that followed were spent exclusively at the manor. The swelling in Isabelle's turned ankle slowly began to go down while Ross made continual phone calls to the States on Alice's behalf. During Alice's absence from the San Francisco society scene, the elusive Henry Vanguard had become more serious about requesting her hand in marriage, and the two prospective fathers-in-law spent countless hours discussing the terms of a prospective union. Everyone was so excited, especially Sunny, and it seemed to Isabelle as if no one had talked about anything else for days.

It had rained at home in San Francisco, but certainly nothing like this. The rain beat an incessant rhythm against the tall windows. After two days, she had explored all of the rooms in the old stone manor and had uncovered, she was certain, all of the secrets the place had hidden. After three days, Isabelle began to fear that she would completely lose her mind if the rain did not cease.

She tried hard not to resent her sister, but as more calls were made to the families of both Henry Vanguard and William Tyler Amsley, and as the merits of each blue-blooded suitor was discussed ad nauseam at breakfast, lunch, and dinner, Isabelle actually began to fantasize about ways to sabotage the telephone cable.

She opened the musty, leather-bound volume of *Gray's Anatomy* she'd found back in the States at a flea market, knowing that she was safe to read the chapter on the muscle groups in relative peace. So far, Sunny had refused to consider the idea of her attending medical school one day, fearing that her younger daughter would then never find a suitable husband. And without her sister's florid beauty, Isabelle was made to believe it was a dangerously real possibility.

In orange capri pants, a fuzzy yellow sweater, and saddle shoes, Isabelle sat alone, curled up on a red velvet sofa in the library. It was a dark, forbidding room with heavy oak paneling and endless shelves of books behind gold mesh, but it was one she liked for the cozy fireplace, which the McNultys always seemed to keep stoked. She also particularly liked the painting of her lovely, smiling great-grandmother, which was suspended over the hearth.

In a house filled to brimming with heavily framed ancient portraits of long-dead ancestors, all wearing powdered wigs and somber expressions, this place was a welcome haven. Try though she might to block out the world and all of its incessant rain, she could still hear her father and mother as they conferred over yet another transatlantic phone call.

"I'm simply not going to include that, Vanguard," her father shouted. He then whispered to his wife, "He wants me to pay for the Westerhout house for Alice and Henry on Nob Hill. Hell, I didn't make Nob Hill till I was damn near thirty, and I sure as the devil didn't get it from my father! Let *him* do it if he has to!"

"Shh!" Sunny urged him.

Suddenly Ross was yelling again. "Well, maybe *you* should consider what *you* would be losing!"

Isabelle set down the book yet again and stood. It was no use. She stretched her arms above her head and went over to the grand window that had a view of the loch. It wasn't even noon. What on earth was she supposed to do with the rest of the day?

She had tried for days to garner just a bit of someone's attention—perhaps to get her mother to play a few hands of cards, or to get her father to take a walk with her out alone and talk about the best schools for premed courses, since there wasn't much more time to apply. But everyone was so taken up, it seemed. With Alice. Always Alice.

"Why don't you be a good girl and go and put your feet up," Ross kept saying. "You've got to give that ankle a rest." But she knew what he really meant: *I'm busy. I haven't got the time.*

During all of it, Alice was no better company. She was like a cat caught in a tree. She stayed up in their room most of the time, pacing, smoking cigarettes she had stolen from their mother, and waiting for the phone to ring.

The scene beyond the grand bay window looked very like a painting by Maurice Utrillo, all those smudges and runny colors like a gray, rainy day in Paris. Only this wasn't Paris. It wasn't even Fresno. It was beautiful here and dull. Majestic and horribly dull.

Suddenly, she saw something move, but she was steaming up the window as she pressed her nose to the glass to try to make it out. Then it moved again. Something big and black and soggy. A dog. There was a huge dog out there, lurking beneath one of the hedges.

Isabelle dashed for the front door, limping slightly, and grabbed an umbrella from the brass stand beside it. The wind was very strong coming up off the water, but she held onto the open umbrella even as the rain sprayed her face. The large black canine, like an oversized rat, offered no resistance, not even so much as a growl, as Isabelle searched for a collar or some means of reining her in. "Well, look at you. You look just like the Loch Ness monster," she laughed. "Big and soggy! Come on, girl, let's get you in and dry you off," she said, taking her neck and leading her gently toward the kitchen at the back of the estate.

She twisted the knob, then opened the red painted door with a little nudge of her knee, since years of rain had warped the wood. Isabelle pushed inside the warm pine kitchen where the McNultys had a fire lit in the grand, ancient hearth beside the stove. "Are you hungry, girl, hmm?" she asked as she tried to pull her inside. But suddenly the mutt was immovable. She sat at the back door, dripping wet and completely unwilling to advance.

"Come on, it's all right. I live here. Really." She looked back at the dog, who sat stubbornly on her hindquarters, looking up at her. Not moving. "Well, if you don't like the accommodations, suit yourself, but I'll bet you'd still like something to eat. You wait here, then," she instructed, leaving the back door ajar as she moved quickly toward the refrigerator. There were bound to be leftovers from last night, another Scottish feast.

"You have to be firm with her," a voice said through the sound of the rain. "Inside . . . thatta girl. Good ol' girl . . ." The voice belonged to Stephen.

Isabelle spun around, looking up with surprise from a plate of cold salmon as the cold, wet black dog padded in and parked herself beside the blazing fire. "Since when are you so good with dogs?"

"We had one like her in Chicago. Sort of the rectory mascot. She just needed a firm hand. But I'll admit this one's more skittish. Where'd she come from?"

"I'm not sure," Isabelle smoothed the dog's wet ear. "I've never seen her before, but she was lurking out in the bushes just now rather forlornly. I'm think I'm going to call her Nessie."

"You don't mean you're going to keep her."

Isabelle tipped up her chin. "I most certainly do."

"What will your father have to say about that?"

"Nothing, I expect. He feels guilty as it is for neglecting me over here. My guess is that he'll be only too glad if he thinks all it takes is a dog to appease me."

Stephen chuckled and put his hands on his black-draped

hips. "She does kind of resemble the great monster, from what I've heard."

They looked at one another as the dog devoured her cold salmon lunch, and then they both sat down at the kitchen table. "So what are you doing here, Stephen?"

Isabelle could see him take a breath, then exhale. He looked uncomfortable. Suddenly out of place with her again. His elbows rested on his knees, his head hung slightly between his shoulders. The kitchen around them was full of the scent of wool from his damp cassock and the heady scent of the lamb stew Mrs. McNulty had left cooking on the stove.

"You asked me a question the other night, and you deserved a better answer than the one you got. I saw you come around back as I drove up, so I followed you."

She could tell that it was no longer easy for him to speak with her like this, but he seemed to need to do it. That strange, firm cord connecting them was still there.

"I owe you an apology, Slugger," he said haltingly, and Isabelle felt her heart lurch. It had been such a long time since he had called her that. A long time since she had felt that innocent childhood kind of intimacy with him.

She was off balance suddenly. "An apology for what?"

"For not telling you the whole truth. We were always honest with one another in the old days, and I miss that. The fact is, the diocese in Chicago called it a vacation, but they sent me away here to Glenfinnan as a veiled reprimand. They were going to send me to South America before your father intervened. It seems that I pressed too hard trying to expose a certain errant priest who is quite favored by the diocese, and the bishop was not amused. I learned the hard way that honesty is more easily expendable than the ability to elicit large contributions."

Isabelle smiled at him, that beautiful radiant smile. "Well, now I *know* you would have done Father Keough proud," she said softly.

"Sometimes I'm not so sure about that."

"Oh, come on," she said, leaning forward in quiet support.

"He never once walked away from the right path either. No matter what the consequences were."

The smile broke slowly across his face as they looked at one another. "Thanks," he said. "Believe it or not, at this point, that actually helps."

"I'm glad."

"Even about Father Keough. I can't really seem to talk about him with anyone but you. It's too close, you know?"

"Yes."

"And you were right. He did want the priesthood for me more than I wanted it for myself at first. And I wanted very much to please him. . . . especially after I knew he was dying. It seemed, back then, like a path of such honor, and my faith was already there. It felt like a natural progression and something I could give back for everything he'd done for me. I guess I just had no idea about the politics . . . the business of being a priest."

"I'm glad you told me, and about what happened in Chicago," she tentatively offered, not quite certain if she should say anything further.

They looked at one another for another moment. Then Stephen stood. "Well, I'd better be getting back. I just really wanted to clear the air between us."

"Thanks."

"I haven't liked feeling that we couldn't talk anymore."

"Maybe we still need my father's garage for that," Isabelle laughed.

She hadn't meant it the way it sounded, but the image shot up between them unexpectedly anyway, brightly like a flame. *The secret place . . .* Playing there so many times as children. Holding one another there that one afternoon years later. In friendship. And consolation. Feeling things neither of them had expected nor ever forgot.

"Stephen?" she asked as he put his hand on the knob and pulled the door back.

"What is it?"

"Have you been writing any poetry lately?"

He smiled. "Not for a long time."

"That's too bad. You really do have a talent."

"Who knows? Maybe I'll start again some day."

"I'd sure like to read it if you did."

Stephen chuckled, remembering all the years he had shared his most private words only with her, because he had trusted her. Years in which she had been his harshest critic and his biggest fan. "Now, who else would I show them to?" he asked.

A few days later, after taking a long walk with Nessie down beside the loch, Isabelle sat down at the breakfast table beside her father, who had his nose pressed into a three-day-old copy of *The Scotsman*. An old newspaper was better than no newspaper at all, he'd begun to say since they'd arrived in Scotland. Sunny Maguire, dressed in a beige A-line skirt and matching cashmere sweater, smiled as her younger daughter came into the room.

"Good morning, darling. Sleep well?"

"Fine, thanks. Where's Alice? She was awake before I went out for my walk."

Sunny smiled and took a delicate sip of tea. "Oh, you know your sister. She's feeling rather uninclined for company these days until all of the particulars are settled."

"So is she going to be given over to Henry Vanguard, then?"

"That's vulgar, Isabelle!" Her mother was not amused.

Ross put down his newspaper and pressed the black eyeglasses back up onto the bridge of his nose. "It's all settled, Puppet. On the first of September, your sister will become Mrs. Henry Vanguard the third."

He said it as if he'd just won the jackpot. And then Isabelle realized that was precisely what he had done. "I was up until almost three this morning finalizing the details with his father."

"You mean Alice doesn't know yet?"

"You're the first. Besides Mother, of course."

Ian McNulty emerged, just then, from the swinging door that led into the kitchen. He was holding a clear glass pitcher of orange juice and a fresh pot of tea. Isabelle looked up and smiled. "Morning, Ian."

She watched his pale skin flush at her acknowledgment. "Miss."

He wasn't ugly, she decided. Just overly big and simple. Isabelle didn't fear him, but something about him told her to keep her distance.

Mrs. McNulty followed her son, bringing in a fresh rack of toast and a steaming plate of kippers and eggs. The old woman huffed as she set them on the table. Isabelle took a slice of toast, set it on her plate, and then reached for the raspberry jam.

"Don't you think she had a right to have a hand in any of it, Daddy? After all, you're not marrying him. Alice is."

"Watch your tone with your father, Isabelle."

Ross Maguire simply smiled. She could tell that nothing was going to ruin his mood today. "I understand how you feel, Puppet, but one day when your sister is the most prominent woman on the West Coast, she'll thank me for all of my efforts, I promise you. And when your turn comes—"

"Oh, I'd prefer to choose my own husband, Daddy."

His laugh was big and loud and slightly boorish. "That's very funny, Puppet."

"I mean it. I'm not as interested in money as you and mother or even Alice is."

"You are different from your sister, that much is certain, and, actually, I do have something different in mind for you."

She took a bite of the toast, then wiped her lips on her napkin, trying hard not to seem even a little curious. "Like what?"

"Power."

"Daddy." She rolled her eyes and smiled at him, feeling now that it was all part of some great fantasy that Alice's betrothal had conjured. "So, how do you plan to get me something like that?"

"Frank Wescott."

She began to choke and had to take a huge swallow of juice before it stopped. "The congressman?"

"The senator by November, if I or my bank account have anything to say about it."

Good God, he was serious! Isabelle slumped back in her chair, her mouth agape. "You're serious."

"I'm always serious when it comes to my girls, Puppet."

"I don't even know the man, much less love him!"

"A highly overrated commodity in marriage, Isabelle," her mother calmly put in as she sipped her tea. "Better to have a good match, and friendship. Believe me," she smiled at her husband. "It'll hold you in far better stead than relying on passion."

"Not that you won't have any of that," Ross chuckled. "Wescott's a handsome devil. I'm sure you remember him, he's a big guy with sandy blond hair and broad shoulders. He used to play quarterback at Stanford back in his college days. Great for the image . . . The two of you met once, at that party last autumn in Pebble Beach. Apparently that was enough for him. He's quite serious about you, actually."

Her head was spinning. "You've talked to him about me?"

"Several times."

Isabelle pushed her chair back from the table. Her expression was incredulous. "Daddy, my God, I'm not ready yet!"

Sunny scowled at her daughter. "Isabelle, watch how you use the Lord's name."

"You'd be an ace for him in the campaign, Puppet," Ross said, blithely ignoring her incredulity, "and it's bound to be a tough battle for the election. He's fighting an incumbent."

"Daddy, I'm not interested in politics and I'm certainly not interested in Frank Wescott."

"Well," he said, smiling, as if his words were merely meant to soothe a petulant child, "we certainly don't have to decide anything now. Today we're celebrating Alice. But suffice it to say that with suitors like these presenting themselves, I have every hope of seeing both of my beautiful daughters very well married indeed."

It turned into a lovely day for April, unseasonably warm, they were told, for this part of Scotland, and so Isabelle's mother decided to host an impromptu luncheon on the lawn. She had invited Stephen, Father Lewis, and a few of the parishioners from Saint Finan's.

Once everyone had arrived, they gathered inside the house, which everyone in town had long wanted to see. Then they moved out to the back lawn and a long table draped with blue-and-white checkered linen and cobalt Highland stoneware that Ross's grandmother had spent a lifetime collecting.

"'Tis a grand home your granny had," Effie Gordon exclaimed to Ross as he wrapped his arm around her frail, bony one and led her down the sloping lawn to the table.

Effie was a widow who had lived her entire life in a stone-and-thatch cottage at Kinlocheil, twenty miles from Glenfinnan. At eighty-five, she could speak plainly of the days when nothing faster than horse carts were able to come this way. But her claim to fame in the region was the vividness with which she could tell the tale of how her ancestors had fought alongside Bonnie Prince Charlie and the Jacobites at the 1745 rising here.

Still fiercely independent and proud, the slim, silver-haired lady hooked her cane onto the edge of the picnic table, tipped up her chin, and smiled her wrinkled smile, as if Willowbrae was the most natural place in the world for her to be. Isabelle marveled at her traditional Scottish pride, watching the old woman in her best blue tweed skirt and tiny ruby-chip earrings, sitting beside her daughter and son-in-law, Roddie and Mairi Campbell.

"How romantic to think that royalty was actually here, and fought for the place," Sunny gasped, her smooth pink lips parted slightly, her hand pressed lightly to her chest.

"Our land is rich with history and legends such as that," Mairi affirmed.

"Well, we certainly are enjoying our time here, and when we get back to San Francisco, I'm going to tell all of my friends they should consider Scotland for their next holiday. It really is a lovely little fairytale land, isn't it?"

Isabelle looked away with a little grimace. Her mother sounded suddenly slightly crass. Sunny hadn't meant it, of course, but this was a gentle country of gentle people, and it seemed to belittle them to reduce it to a tourist destination.

Just then, from the corner of her eye, Isabelle saw Nessie coming toward them from a stand of rowan trees at the bottom of the lawn. She smiled and stood. She'd been looking for the dog all morning and was surprised when she hadn't come.

"I warned ye to get out o' here, ye mangy beastie!"

It all happened very quickly after that. Nessie dashed back into the trees and Ian McNulty, the housekeeper's son, was running suddenly out the back door of the kitchen, carrying a rusty shotgun. Everyone looked up from the table in confusion.

"Oh, God, no!" Isabelle shouted, toppling her chair and dashing after Ian.

"'Tis only a stray, lass," Ian's mother shouted as she ran off. "'Tis no' a real dog. That good-for-nothin' old beast has been tearin' up my vegetable garden for weeks!"

But Isabelle was screaming. "Ian, no! You don't understand, that's my—"

Boom! The sound was like cannon fire. *Boom! Boom!* Twice more. It echoed across the emerald green field behind Willowbrae, and Isabelle felt her heart stop. A shiver rippled up her spine as she dashed into the field after Ian, tears streaming down her cheeks just as everyone else rose from the table trying to figure out what all of the commotion was about.

"What on earth . . . ?" Sunny asked, still holding her white linen napkin in one hand and grasping at her ever-present strand of pearls with the other.

"Oh, nothin' to be worryin' yourself over, Mrs. Maguire. Ian's just shot a stray dog that's been loiterin' round here a wee bit too often."

Stephen's chest squeezed tight as if there were a thick leather strap across his heart. He knew how much Isabelle loved animals. Yes, children and animals. She always had, and he could only guess that she'd quickly become attached to this one as well. A memory swam up unexpectedly. She was only eight or nine, but Isabelle had stayed up all night nursing a stray tabby kitten that had been abandoned by its mother, patiently feeding it cow's milk from an eyedropper. She had cried for days, and stubbornly refused to sleep or eat, after the tiny thing had died in her arms.

Stephen pushed himself away from the table and bolted down the hill after her. He found Isabelle past a clump of trees, slumped over Nessie's dark, unmoving shape. The memory of that kitten so many years ago and the brave little girl Isabelle had been tumbled over and over inside Stephen's mind, clashing with the dynamic young woman she had become. And yet she was still so unbelievably vulnerable when she loved something. *Or someone.*

Stephen sank onto his knees beside a sobbing Isabelle as Ian McNulty stood over them, the rifle slack inside his great, rough hand. "'Twas only a stray beastie," he said like a repentant child. Stephen cradled Isabelle's head and gave the caretaker's son a menacing glare.

"What the devil are you looking at? Go on! Get out of here!"

But Ian didn't move. He only stood there, big and loping, until Stephen, churning with rage, sprang to his feet. He charged at Ian with fisted hands, beating at his chest and feeling as if he wanted to throttle the very life out of one who had hurt Isabelle. "I said, get out of here! Go on!"

He was pushing roughly at Ian now, venting his rage over a harmless creature who had been senselessly killed and how Isabelle was suffering for it. Until something, an invisible force, something celestial, clamped a steady hand on his shoulder. *That's enough, my boy,* a silent voice urged him until Stephen began to regain control. He looked back at Isabelle, melting at the forlorn sight of her.

"She was such a sweet dog," she sobbed. "She'd never have hurt anyone. . . ."

"I know, I know," Stephen said, sinking back beside her and stroking her hair, aching as he looked at her.

Then, it seemed like the most natural thing in the world to do, to take her in his arms, once they were alone, and comfort her like this. To touch each of her cheeks with the back of his hand then softly, slowly, to kiss the tears away from them. But, as it once had been in her father's garage, there was a spark. Only now it became a bright flame. And it was suddenly something far more between them than consolation.

Realizing it, Stephen jerked away from her, and he could see that Isabelle, eyes wide, her cheeks still tearstained, was as shaken and surprised by what was happening as he.

"I'm sorry," he said, his whispered words to her suddenly full of anguish and yet unmistakable desire. *God help me, how I want to go on holding you. . . . but I can't. . . .*

Ross, Sunny and Alice, and the McNultys had come through the trees and were running toward them now to see what had happened. Stephen sat back on his heels and Isabelle went back to cradling the dog's lifeless body, crying softly into her matted black hair.

"Oh, dear," Sunny said, standing beside her daughter when everyone realized what had happened. "Come back to the house, Isabelle, and Mrs. McNulty will make you a cup of tea."

"I don't want any tea."

"Well, you certainly can't stay out here."

"I've got to bury her."

"Let Ian do that," her father said.

"No! He's not to touch her!" The tears still glistened in her eyes and slid down her pale cheeks again as she looked up, angry and defiant. "He can get me a shovel! And then all of you can leave me alone! Just leave me the hell alone!"

Sunny Maguire stood back up. Remembering their childhood friendship and knowing the comfort he had always
been to her, she put her hand on Stephen's shoulder. "Can
you help her, Stephen?" she quietly bid him. "Say something? I've never seen her like this."

"I'm sorry, I can't. I really do have to leave."

"But you just got here. We haven't even had lunch!"

He tried not to scowl at how thoughtless she sounded. "I
don't feel much like eating, under the circumstances, Mrs.
Maguire, and frankly, I don't think Isabelle will either."

"Well, can't you at least say something to her before you
go? Good Lord, look at her!"

"I think it would be better coming from you," he lied,
because he did not dare to say anything close to the truth—

That, God forgive him, he was falling in love with her.

Her mother wanted to give her one of her sedatives, but
Isabelle had refused. At least if you were feeling pain, she
thought, you were feeling something. At dusk, she took a
walk down by the loch, but without Nessie it wasn't the
same. When she went back to the house, Isabelle sat unmoving on the gray stone bench at the front door near where she
had first found her. The gulls were screeching overhead and
the wind was blowing quite hard, but Isabelle didn't hear
any of it. All she felt was dazed. Off balance. And all she
could hear was the gun blast over and over again. An echo
right down to her heart. *Boom. Boom . . . boom.*

Right now she hated Ian McNulty. For his stupidity. For
not caring about a poor defenseless dog. She wanted desperately to be able to talk about all of it with someone. *Someone?
Who are you kidding? You want to talk with Stephen. . . . Just like
always. . . .* But he had left so quickly, hadn't he? Without
even saying good-bye. And she couldn't bring herself to go to
him. Not now. Not after the way he had touched her, the
way she had felt being touched by him.

Isabelle walked alone down the little path to the arbor,

overgrown with emerald vines, then sank onto a rusty wrought-iron bench. A sudden noise and a shadow made her turn around with a start.

They stood facing one another for a moment, both of them silent. Awkward. They were alone. "I had to come back," Stephen said tentatively. "To see how you were."

"You needn't worry about me, you know."

"A lifetime habit is hard to break."

"Didn't you learn anything when we were kids?" she said softly, trying her very best to smile. "I really can take care of myself."

"This was different, Isabelle."

"Well I'm fine," she lied.

He waited a moment, watching her. "Are you sure?"

"Why wouldn't I be?"

"For one thing, you've just lost something you cared about."

"It wouldn't be the first time."

Isabelle's eyes held his as the echo of her words hung between them, their meaning only too clear to them both. Time stopped in that moment. Everything else did too. She couldn't hear anything but the beating of her own heart now, and it was all that she could feel. After a moment, Isabelle reached out and ran a single finger down the length of his black wool cassock. She felt him stiffen; the unexpected connection was raw and charged between them.

Then he closed his eyes and stopped her hand with his own. "No," he said very softly.

When he opened his eyes, they met hers again, so bright and full of need. "Just hold me like you did this morning," she bade him. "Just one more time."

"I can't, Isabelle," he said, his voice breaking, ". . . you know that I can't."

And then, as he had done earlier, before he could say or do something else he could only regret, Stephen turned from her and forced himself to walk away.

◆   ◆   ◆

Stephen clenched the lapis rosary beads and pressed them to his heart.

Domine, exaudi orationem meam . . .

His mouth was dry as desert sand. How many times had he asked, "Lord, hear my prayer"? Stephen had lost count. It was late, somewhere probably near dawn he suspected, and Saint Finan's was empty, dark, and very cold. There was no sunlight coming in through the stained glass, and the only light came from a row of votive candles he'd lit, flickering red-gold flashes before a statue of the Virgin Mary. The little church was also hauntingly quiet but for the faint murmur of his continual whispered prayers drifting up from the wooden pew, the place in which he had spent the night. Most of that had been on his knees until the searing pain of the cold stone floor (not the padded kneeler, which he had refused to use) brought something like a dozen fiery needles shooting up through his back and neck.

Good. A little pain was good. And a lot of pain was better.

That was what this was about. Temptation. And discipline. He hadn't tried hard enough not to feel those things for Isabelle. A kind of spiritual toughening-up program, one of his teachers in Chicago had called a day and night spent like this. No food. No water. No comfort.

It was an attempt to inflict discomfort on his body, suppressing sinful reactions. And since a hair shirt didn't seem practical in 1957, this had been the next best thing. It mattered little that Stephen's feelings for Isabelle were far more than physical. He knew his Thomistic philosophy well. Feelings were simply a part of the "passions," something to be overcome so that one might more freely use reason.

And it was all very logical. It had made perfect sense to him in Chicago. Before he had seen Isabelle again. Before he had touched her on the back lawn behind Willowbrae and brought even that little bit more of her into his heart.

He lowered his head again and tried to keep praying. But somewhere along the way, the words had become like a mantra to him. Sounds without meaning . . . *Isabelle* . . .

Isabelle. The thought of her, and the images, came forward as if out a dark cave, pushing everything else away. So lovely. So alive. For all of his praying, he still wanted to lose himself in the world of sensation with her.

Stephen did not know what was going to happen next between them, but he was finally tired of thinking about it. After drawing in a breath and kissing the cross at the tip of his rosary, he finally stood. His body ached. His mind was throbbing. That was enough torture for one long night, he resolved. He needed to try to get at least an hour or two of sleep. Father Lewis had taken Effie Gordon and her daughter into Fort William to see her ill sister, and tomorrow Stephen had agreed to say his first morning mass here. And, tormented or not, he felt the parishioners of Saint Finan's deserved better than the half a priest Stephen Donnelly felt himself to be at that disturbing moment.

With a heavy heart, Stephen hung up the old black phone in Father Lewis's office the next morning. The baby was very ill, and the midwife with whom Stephen had just spoken had said it was unlikely that the child would survive longer than a few more days. Baptism had become an immediate concern to the distraught mother.

Stephen had never baptized an out-of-wedlock child. But he also knew that it was imperative. The child's mother was a devout member of Saint Finan's parish and, until the last month of her pregnancy, had made the twenty-mile ride nearly every day to pray at Father Lewis's old wooden altar.

With Father Lewis over in Fort William to see to Effie Gordon's sister, there was no choice but that Stephen would go and perform the baptism. The only question now, he thought, was who he would find to act as sponsor. The midwife had already told him she was a member of the Church of Scotland, and the young girl's widowed father, with whom she lived, was away down in Glasgow on business for several days.

The door to the rectory office opened just then and Stephen glanced up. It was Isabelle with Alice and Ross Maguire, and the expression on Ross's face was one Stephen knew well. There was no mistaking it.

He wanted something.

Ross Maguire wrapped an arm around Stephen's shoulder and walked him outside and down the little stone path that led to the water's edge of Loch Sheil. The church bell at Saint Finan's, the small gray stone church perched on a bluff overlooking the loch, clanged just then. The sound filled the valley as the inky blue water beyond Saint Finan's stood as still as glass. The Scottish pines surrounding the church whispered in the silence as the ringing faded away.

Stephen turned around to see Isabelle standing back up on the bluff beside the rectory, her hair blowing in the breeze as she waited for them to speak privately.

"Look, Stephen, I'll be blunt. I need you to help me out here. I've been just a bit too preoccupied since we've been here in Scotland, with work back home, trying to wrap up my grandmother's estate, and now all of this business with Alice's betrothal. Point is, my girls haven't had a real outing and they were looking to me to get them out for a drive. I rather promised Mrs. Maguire that I'd take them somewhere today to get Isabelle's mind off that mutt of hers. And my wife despises it when I break my promises."

Stephen's stomach began to churn with that vague jolt of recognition. Whatever Ross Maguire said next, he wasn't going to like it very much. Ross pulled Stephen a little closer until the stench of too much cologne began to make him feel sick. "I couldn't help overhearing your phone conversation and, listen, take the girls with you over to Kinlochiel for that baptism this morning, would you? You'd be doing me a huge favor with my daughters, and you'd be saving my hide with Mrs. Maguire as well."

"Oh, I don't think—"

Ross was undeterred by the sound of an oncoming objection. He cut Stephen off quickly, as he always did with people when he meant to get his way. "We both need some-thing here, right? Even if you didn't owe me, Stephen, my boy, Father Lewis has taken his car. You're in need of one. And, as luck would have it," he said, smiling victoriously, "I am only too happy to offer mine."

Luck! Blast! I hadn't even thought about a car! How in blazes was I going to get all the way over to Kinlochiel?

Stephen still hadn't settled on the issue of godparents for the little child. Perhaps having Isabelle and Alice do it wasn't the worst idea he'd ever heard. Canon law did not require particularly that godparents be a man and a woman, just devout Catholics. "Sure, why not?" he said. *Have I really any choice?* was what he wondered.

"Splendid. I knew you'd see it my way."

"Have you any objection to Isabelle and Alice acting as godparents for me, then?"

"To bring another little soul into our fold?" Ross smiled. "Not a one."

It wasn't that far to Kinlochiel, but the road wasn't good. Stephen drove slowly, with lacy rowan trees above shading their path, and the old one-lane road rising and dipping end-lessly through the glen. It took almost an hour to reach the turn in the road where the young woman lived. They could hear the new baby crying as he parked the car outside in the muddy front garden and they all got out. A moment later, the midwife, a stout middle-aged woman in a long plaid dress, with a scarf over her hair, came out to greet them.

"I do thank ye for comin', Father Donnelly. Fiona really has been beside herself about a baptism."

"How is the child?" he asked.

"'Tis most likely pneumonia that's set in now, Father. 'Tisn't much hope I hold for the poor wee thing."

"Have you called a doctor?"

"There isn't one near enough to come."

"Over in Fort William, perhaps?"

"Oh, she canno' afford to pay for someone to come a distance like that."

"*I* can!" Isabelle said firmly, surprising herself and everyone who looked up at her. "Well, you cannot just let a child die!"

"Perhaps we should go inside," Stephen said to her in a calm, measured tone she did not recognize.

Isabelle looked at Stephen again, then at Alice. "Well, we can't, can we?"

They walked to the gray stone house, festooned by emerald ivy and fronted by a gray stone fence. The young woman inside was sitting beside the fire next to a low wooden cradle that she was rocking steadily. She was pretty, with a round face, peachy skin, and fluffy long red hair. But the expression in her light blue eyes, as she looked up, was dazed.

"I'm Father Donnelly," Stephen said softly as he extended his hand.

She rose and came over to him with her own hand held out. "Bless ye, Father, for comin'."

Alice, Isabelle, and the midwife stayed by the door as Stephen and Fiona walked to the cradle. The baby looked pale and, even from across the room, they could hear the faint crackle in her tiny lungs as she tried to breathe. Isabelle felt a sharp pain slash across her heart at the sound. *How does anyone ever prepare to give up so precious a gift from God as that?* And then she remembered that the child had been born out of wedlock.

This wasn't, she hoped, some sort of punishment for that.

Stephen then put his arm around the child's mother. He was saying something to her as they faced the fire, a consolation, that they could not hear. Then they both hung their heads, and Isabelle knew that he was praying with her. After a moment, she saw the young woman's rigid shoulders slacken and she knew that Stephen's mere presence was a comfort to her.

Sudden tears stung the back of Isabelle's eyes, and when she glanced over at Alice she was surprised to see them there too. Baptism was supposed to be a happy, life-affirming ritual, Isabelle thought, numbed with disbelief. But she could see only too clearly that for Fiona, the baby's mother, this ritual was rather a desperate last attempt to have her child welcomed back into heaven. It wasn't supposed to be like this. Nothing about new life was ever supposed to be this tragic.

They all waited silently as Stephen went back out to the car to prepare. They were ringed somberly around the young mother and the cradle. All but Isabelle, who went to the wood-frame window with the dirty panes and looked out into a sky quickly darkened by thick gray, rain-sodden clouds.

She watched silently and a little in awe as he carefully put the white surplice over his black cassock. It was a private ritual for a priest, she knew, but she could not help herself. Not when the priest was Stephen Donnelly.

Next, he pulled the purple stole out and, holding it up, kissed it before placing it around his neck. Isabelle's skin prickled with gooseflesh and she looked down for a moment and ran her finger along the windowsill, feeling strangely invasive, as though she were looking through a curtain, seeing something she wasn't supposed to see.

When he finally stepped back into the cottage, Stephen told Alice that she was to hold the baby for baptism, and he gave Isabelle a candle to hold. Everyone watched quietly then as he placed a bowl of water, some salt (to be put in the baby's mouth, symbolizing wisdom), a ritual (a book with services in Latin and English), and two small containers of perfumed oil, one called the holy oil and the other the sacred chrism, out on the scarred oak table.

When everything was properly arranged and a candle was lit, Alice came forward with the child in her arms. Stephen then looked over at Isabelle. "Since the child cannot answer, I will address the baptismal vows to you. As godparent, you must reply for her."

Isabelle felt a strange sensation begin to crawl up her spine as Stephen spoke his next words in Latin, the ancient, holy sound filling the small, dim cottage as a steady rain began to beat down heavily on the thatch roof above them.

"*Pax vobiscum,*" he said in Latin, extending peace, and looked up. "*Quo nomine vocaris?*"

Isabelle fought the sick feeling surging up from inside her stomach again. With an entire Catholic education behind her, she understood the words. "Her name is to be Shona Mary," she said in response.

"And what do you ask of God's church?"

It was odd having Stephen speak to her in this tone and in this formal way, and she strained suddenly to push the word out. "Baptism."

The next thing he uttered felt like her undoing. "If then you wish to enter into life, keep the commandments. You shall love the Lord your God with your whole heart, with your whole soul, and with your whole mind. And your neighbor as yourself."

Commandments. Everything she had ever learned in church and catechism classes came back to her now. *Do not sin. Obey the commandments. Obey the church. Obey . . . obey . . .* Was this all simply just part of the baptism? Or was it something more, that she and Stephen should have to face one another in this way? She hadn't tried to feel anything for him. No, never tried. It had always just been there in some form or another, as familiar and comforting as that old afghan at the foot of her bed at home, and for nearly as long as she could remember. A memory sprang up, his voice as he taught her how to dance in that old garage.

Come on, Slugger, stop giggling. Watch your ankles. Concentrate. Concentrate!

Stephen was looking at her again, asking her another question. "And so I ask you now," he said. "Do you reject Satan?"

She tried to swallow, but the stone in her throat was growing. "I do."

"And all of his pomps?"

". . . I do."

Isabelle is going to her prom with me, Alice . . . She had just accepted my invitation before you came in.

"And all of his works?"

Aw, don't go and start crying now, and make me feel doubly worse than I do. Not when I have to leave to go all the way to Chicago. . . .

"And all of his works?" Stephen repeated.

Isabelle shuddered in the little silence when she knew she was supposed to respond. She could not make herself speak. As their eyes met, as his purple stole glittered in the light from the fire along with that lovely dark hair of his, the rain outside became a torrent, battering the little cottage. Wind pushed against the old door and rattled the windows as he looked at her.

"Isabelle?"

She was shaking now, her throat gone unbelievably tight, as if someone were suddenly choking her into holding back the words because they meant far more than an ill child's baptism. But Stephen was waiting, they all were.

Isabelle cut her eyes away from his. ". . . Yes," she said. "I do."

He then took the dish of water and moved it over the baby's head. *"Ego te baptizo in nomine Patris,"* he said pouring once, *"et Filii,"* pouring again, *"et Spiritus Sancti,"* pouring a third and final time.

After the baptism, when Stephen had put all of the sacred articles back in the car and dashed back through the frigid April downpour to the warmth of the little house, Isabelle met him with the child in her arms. The midwife was across the room giving instructions to Fiona, and Alice was dialing the telephone.

"What's going on?"

"Mrs. Wallace has to leave. There's another baby to deliver. But Alice is calling a doctor in Fort William." She lifted her chin. "I'm not going to let this one die, Stephen."

He was thinking of the midwife's prognosis. "I know how you feel, Isabelle, I do. But sometimes things like that are beyond our control."

"Don't you think at least we ought to try? Poor little child hasn't even been evaluated! With the proper medication, you don't have to die from pneumonia anymore."

A crooked smile spread slowly across his face. "I suppose you're right at that."

Her smile suddenly matched his. "Of course I am."

"A proper doctor really should be the final judge, if that's possible."

"Absolutely."

"Do you really think your father will give you the money on behalf of a complete stranger?"

"Oh, I'm sure I'll have to work on him a bit," she said with a smile, "but he feels badly about Nessie. I know I can handle him."

Yes, she probably could at that. "Well, then, I think it's wonderfully charitable of you."

Alice hung up the receiver and came across the room as Mrs. Wallace was putting on her coat. "It's all settled," she announced. "I've found a Dr. Randall in Fort William. I've explained things to him and he has agreed to come. He has a few things to tie up, and then he promised to be on his way."

Isabelle glanced out the window as the rain beat fiercely against the glass, rattling it and shaking the entire house. "In this weather it'll take him forever."

"Yes, he probably won't be here until late tonight. But that is better than nothing."

"I don't know, miss, quite how to thank ye," Fiona said tentatively as she took back her child and held the new baby close against her breast. "At least now if 'tis the Lord's will to claim my sweet bairn, I'll know 'twas no' for want of me doin' somethin'."

Isabelle smiled and pressed an arm onto her shoulder. "Believe me, Fiona, it's my pleasure. And even more so if it does some good."

Everyone stood for a moment, awkward and uncertain of what to say next. The storm that had been threatening since morning had turned into a deluge and if they did not leave now there was no telling when they would make it back to Glenfinnan. It was Saturday, and in Father Lewis's absence, Stephen had confessions to hear this evening. He had to get back.

"Look, Stephen, why don't I stay here with Fiona and you take Isabelle back to Willowbrae so she can talk to Dad about the money?" Alice suggested. "Fiona's father telephoned this morning and is already on his way back from Oban, so I won't be alone long. Then, after Belle has wrapped Daddy around her little finger, as we all have no doubt she will do, he can come here later tonight to pay the doctor."

Stephen cringed. She had made it sound so simple. If he said no, that he wasn't prepared to ride alone in a car with Isabelle, even for twenty miles, what would Alice think? He couldn't admit that. But he absolutely did need to get back to the parish, and Isabelle did need to get the money she'd promised for the doctor. There were people counting on them both. There simply was no choice. He had to ride back to Glenfinnan alone with Isabelle.

"I'm sure you're right," he finally relented. *It's only twenty miles. We'll be home in less than an hour.* "I'll get Isabelle home and your father can bring the money back later tonight."

"Great."

Alice, Stephen thought, sounded so certain of herself.

"Damn!" Stephen growled and thumped his fist against the steering wheel as they sat on the old road halfway back to Glenfinnan. "Damn! Damn!"

Isabelle softly smiled and pressed a hand to her chest as a torrent of rain thundered down around the car. "I didn't know priests were allowed to talk like that."

"It's flooded! The damn thing is flooded!"

They had tried to avoid one another and yet had been thrown together again and again. It seemed so ironic to

Isabelle, like some badly scripted B movie. All of a sudden, a bubble of nervous laughter worked its way up her throat.

Stephen frowned and shot her an icy stare. "It's not funny."

Isabelle shook her head, held up a hand, and tried vainly to swallow her laugh.

"I've got to get you home."

He tried the engine again, but all it did was chug and then groan until it died again.

"Doesn't look like we're going anywhere for a while. Old Mrs. Gordon's cottage is just over that crest, isn't it? Maybe we should make a run for it and wait the storm out there."

"That is not an option, Isabelle! She's over in Fort William with Father Lewis to tend to her sister. And besides, she doesn't have a phone. Your parents will be worried sick if I don't at least find a way to call and tell them we're all right."

"Maybe we should walk back," she innocently teased. "It's only eight or ten miles. We could probably make it by midnight."

"Very funny, Isabelle."

"What? You don't feel like a brisk bit of the outdoors?"

The rain was beating down onto the windshield so hard that it looked like snow.

Stephen slumped back and laid his head against the seat. "Damn!"

"Four times," she said with a smirk. "What on earth are you going to say as penance for that?"

"Isabelle, this is not a humorous situation."

"Why not?"

"I think you know why."

"No, I don't," she lied.

Stephen felt his heart begin to beat very fast. He raked a hand through his hair, feeling like a caged lion as he leaned forward and tried the ignition again, to no avail.

"What do I know, Stephen?" He wouldn't look at her. "Stephen?"

His heart was thundering in his ears now. His throat

seemed to seize up, but he forced the words out anyway. Somehow the urge to be honest with her was overwhelming. What was it that was driving him to let down the barrier he had so consciously and rightly constructed since she had come to Glenfinnan?

"You know that there is something between us."

Stephen watched a glimmer of surprise cross her face. *God, she is beautiful. Radiant, her head tipped back, that long smooth column of her neck. . . .*

"I knew that something had changed," she softly agreed, "but I did not dare to hope—"

"Don't hope! There is no hope, there can't be! And we can't be here now. Like this! I know what happened the other day after Nessie died, and what it might have made you think . . . but I need to get you back to Willowbrae!"

He was still gripping the steering wheel, fingers wrapped around it so tightly that his knuckles were white. Isabelle reached out and put her hand on his. She was sure now that he really had begun to care for her. "Is it the worst thing in the world to feel something for me?"

"I love God, Isabelle."

"And I have always loved *you*."

So there it was, out between them. The truth. What they both had felt, known, and fought against, since the first day she had come here. There was another little silence, except for the rain thundering against the windshield, as they looked at each other. It was so strange here, just the two of them, as if they were in their own cocoon. Safe. Free . . .

Almost free.

Isabelle broke the silence. "I know that you love the Lord, Stephen. So do I. But I see now that, really, I have loved you for what feels like just as long."

Stephen inhaled deeply, exhaled, then waited a moment. "I think somehow I knew that there was always something between us. I just wasn't willing to admit it to myself."

"Because I was the great Ross Maguire's daughter?"

"Because I was the housekeeper's son."

He hung his head. His shoulders slackened as he closed his eyes. He hadn't been prepared for this kind of honesty when they'd left Fiona's cottage. But now, somehow it had taken on a life of its own.

Her touch just then, gentle as a whisper, fell upon his neck, tentative fingers pressed against his skin. Her face so near and her sweet breath against his cheek were a sudden invitation. *God no*, he was thinking. *Not now . . . She—this . . . it is too much to bear. . . . it is too much to fight against.*

"I know I'm not supposed to feel this way, I've known it since we got to Scotland, but I still love you, Stephen," she said in a voice barely above a whisper. "And I don't care what the risks are as long as you love me too."

And as he turned to look at her, Isabelle ran her fingers over Stephen's face, tracing his profile, then she closed her eyes and gently, sweetly, pressed her lips against his. It felt so natural, so soft, that at first he felt himself begin to melt against her. Giving in. Wanting to more than anything. And then suddenly, like an icy wave, the truth came at him. *I am not Stephen. . . . I am Father Donnelly,* his mind said . . . *Now and forever. . . . In nomine Patris, Filii, Spiritus Sancti. . . .*

Isabelle felt his lips close against her and she pulled away to see that Stephen's eyes were open wide in shock, crystal blue before her. That collar so stark and white against his throat. His face was still flushed unmistakably with desire.

Realizing what she'd done by kissing him, seeing the enormity of what was between them mirrored in his incredulous gaze, Isabelle pressed a finger to her lips. But she could not undo what she had already done. Nor could she change what she felt.

She loved him. There was no going back.

"Isabelle, I . . ."

The words fell away. He made no attempt to regain them. The moment of silence, as they gazed at one another, was an eternity. The sound of the rain. Their breathing.

Then quietly, he turned away from her and switched the key again.

Embarrassed, humiliated, and completely overcome by what had almost happened between them, Isabelle snapped open the car door as she heard the ignition groan again. Then she bolted suddenly into the vast and heather-spotted field that lay before them.

"Wait, Isabelle! Please, you can't—" he started to say, but before the words left his lips she was gone. Something not right nor logical but very powerful drew him then. In a moment of not thinking, only feeling, Stephen pushed open his own car door and charged after her. The rain was heavy. It pelted him in long driving sheets, some of it sharp against his face. It was an icy blanket beating him back. Pressing him, like a firm hand, away from her.

"Isabelle, wait!" he called out, but his plea was lost to the driving wind and rain.

She was heading blindly up the hill, and her dress and hair were being pulled back like a battered sail. He knew where she was going. She was heading to Effie Gordon's cottage anyway. *She was trying to get away from him because he didn't want her. . . .*

"Isabelle! Please wait!"

He chased after her and caught her finally, past the crumbling stone wall, at the white cottage door. Both of them were breathing very hard and she was crying as he gripped her shoulders and turned her around. She shook off his hands but he grabbed her again.

"Leave me alone!"

"I can't do that. . . . You know that I can't do that!"

"You can't afford *not* to leave me alone, can you, *Father Donnelly?*"

Her tone was angry, defiant. Filled with hurt. Reining in his heart, and the way it lurched toward her like a wild horse, he gently nudged her beneath the eve over the door. "Come on, let's go inside. At least I'll build a fire and we'll wait here until the storm has passed."

Isabelle sat shivering on Effie Gordon's box bed with its faded blue cotton tiebacks as Stephen built a fire out of peat, then waited, crouched down beside the hearth, for it to build. When he finally turned around and saw her, something inside Stephen snapped. He knew that it was his willpower against hers.

She was sitting there, arms wrapped around her waist, her long, wet hair hanging in copper streamers around her face, and those bright green eyes shimmering up at him, still full of tears. Stephen felt her eyes upon him almost like a caress. But she did not seek to beckon or draw him.

"There now, that's better," he said as he came to Isabelle, trying not to let her see how undone he was by her. "Come on, now. We really do have to get you out of those wet things or you'll catch your death."

"I'm fine."

"You're not fine. You're soaking wet. And you're shivering."

"I am not."

Stephen knelt before her and carefully pulled off one of her black heels and then the other. He placed them by the hearth to dry beside his own shoes. The tiny cottage filled quickly with the warmth and the mingling aroma of wet thatch and burning peat as the rain still beat down thunderously above them.

"Here," he said, bringing her a white muslin nightdress. "I know she's not exactly your size, but I'm sure Miss Gordon won't mind if you put this on while your dress is drying. In fact, if she were here, I'm sure she would insist."

While she changed, laying her wet hose, bra, and dress on the back of the little chair next to the fire, Stephen turned his back. The cottage was small, just as the car had been, and they were close again, moving awkwardly beside one another, trying to ignore what they both felt. Stephen took off his cassock, rabat, and collar. In the silence, he put them on the back of one of the other chairs. When he turned back to face her in black trousers and T-shirt, his heart thundered in his chest as he saw her lingerie lined up, each piece neatly, innocently, laid one beside the other. Seeing those things that had been most intimately near to her was more than he could bear. He drew in a ragged breath. Their eyes met.

Silently, he moved a step nearer until their bodies were almost touching. Stephen reached up and gently brushed away the tears that lay in ribbons on her cheeks. Then he touched her neck, ran his fingers down the length of it. She leaned against his palm and held her breath as he touched her.

"God, you are so incredibly beautiful . . ."

The sound of the rain against the windows and the thatch was hypnotic. The old cottage, steeped in history and Highland magic, did not protest as Stephen took her small face into his hands and kissed her.

They were alone here, welcomed by this warm little place with the pine sideboard of chipped and mismatched stoneware, the oil lamps, and the simple box bed. Stephen did not speak and Isabelle was glad, as his kiss deepened and he wrapped his arms around her. This was a dream, all of it, and words were something else. Words would bring reason and doubt, would lift a barrier against something they both knew now had been meant to happen for a very long time.

Stephen's hands were at the small of her back pulling her closer as he kissed her, as his tongue parted her lips and pressed inside her mouth. Then he lifted her up and set her gently on the little bed. It creaked against their shared weight as he pressed back the white muslin nightgown and buried his face in her bare breasts.

Her nipples hardened as he tasted them, one and then the other, consumed now completely by the sensations. The desire. And then suddenly he cast off his own clothes and arched over her, kissing her again, so warm and hard and full of need that she could not catch her breath.

It was awkward between them, both innocent about acts of love. This act of love. But Stephen's body, and his lust for her, drove him to discover the places of her that would receive him; neck, mouth, breasts, and then finally the small curve and the little patch of hair where her thighs met.

Isabelle gasped, and a groan tore from Stephen's throat as

she felt the sudden pressure of his hardness. He pushed against her with the full weight of his body. But it was over before it had begun. Isabelle had felt only a slight pressure between her legs, not the pain her sister had always told her to expect. Then Stephen sagged against her. "God forgive me," she heard him whisper into the shadowy rain-darkened cottage. "Dear God forgive me. . . ."

Then he fell onto his back and squeezed his eyes.

It struck her then that Stephen never had done this before either. This was the first time for them both. Something special, now a sacred bond between them.

Knowing that, she reached over in consolation, running a hand along the side of his jaw. Still afraid to speak and yet wanting to be what she had always been for him, his greatest consolation, Isabelle kissed him, lightly at first, one cheek and then the other. And he tried to turn away, tried to stop it, but she quickly filled his blood again. The sensation of wanting rushed through him, racing back. He knew it was wrong, but he didn't care. He couldn't care. Not now that he had touched her.

She saw it building in his eyes, the white-hot hunger, as he arched over her again, pressing her into the cool cotton sheets and the worn old patchwork quilt. His mouth came down hard onto hers this time and he crushed her with his embrace. The musky smell of his skin was like a drug to Isabelle and, as he pressed inside her fully for the first time, she wrapped her legs around him, taking him with only a little spasm of pain.

"Oh, Stephen," she sobbed, burying her face against his throat. ". . . Stephen."

As the rain continued to fall, beating a thunderous rhythm against the old stone cottage, something forbidden yet irresistible had been opened between them. The spark that had been kindled since that moment in her father's garage, among the crates and the cobwebs, was now a bright and violent flame. It was all sensation to them both. Forbidden desire wound inextricably with giving, friendship, and history.

◆   ◆   ◆

"Dear God," he said quietly. "What have I done?"

Above the bed, in an old wooden frame, Stephen saw for the first time a framed needlepoint. Three words were stitched in faded blue thread.

Christ My Righteousness, it said.

At that moment, it felt to him like a message from God himself. The Lord to whom he had committed his life had brought Isabelle to him as a test of his faith. A test of his loyalty. It was a test he now had miserably failed.

Stephen swung his legs over the side of the old box bed and squeezed his eyes. He felt heavy as lead and very dazed. His head was pounding as if he were hung over. And yet he hadn't had anything to drink. He couldn't blame any of this on that. No, for what had happened this afternoon, he had only himself to blame.

Being with Isabelle was like being in quicksand. The harder he had struggled against her these past few weeks, the more deeply she had drawn him into a place from which he knew he would never escape.

But when it had ended and she had drifted to sleep in his arms, less than an hour ago, Stephen had known fully, consciously, who he was. What he had done. And it was then that he had caught a glimpse of it—the needlepoint motto framed above the bed.

He looked down at Isabelle now, as she slept, and reality marched back across his mind, bringing with it responsibility and the searing ache of guilt against a God who knew all. Saw all.

In the crimson light of the setting sun, now that the rain had stopped, and the cottage was very still, he was still a priest. A man of God. A man committed to something other than Isabelle.

The devastation came at him like a wave, completely carrying him up inside its dark hollow core. He had meant every word of his vow to the priesthood. But he had meant this with Isabelle too. *Christ My Righteousness* . . .

Isabelle opened her eyes then, cutting open a corner of his heart with their honesty and trust. "Hi," she said softly, tentatively. Locks of her hair, dry now, were splayed out across the white cotton pillowcase like fiery copper flames.

Stephen almost couldn't look at her. They were still so near to one another, both still naked, cutting out any possibility that this afternoon had been some sort of dream his heart had conjured. Lightly, chastely, and without speaking, Stephen placed a kiss on her forehead. Then he turned from her and stood to dress. Never in his life had he been naked with another human being, and the vulnerability of this moment was physically painful.

He could not think of what to say; his head was still swimming with too many things. Too many images. Her milky apricot flesh, so warm and soft. The power of her body beneath his. The Bible, his white surplice, and the purple silk stole with the tiny cross he had kissed earlier today, before he had kissed her, waiting for them on the front seat of Ross Maguire's car.

Christ My Righteousness . . .

He pulled on his black wool trousers, the long ebony cassock and then purposely, yet with trembling hands, attached the rabat and collar.

"Are you all right, my love?" he heard Isabelle say when his back was turned to her.

Stephen's heart squeezed. It was he who should have been asking that of her, and the realization of that brought with it a pain nearly as searing as that he felt for having betrayed God. She was young, an innocent, and he had forever taken that from her. Somehow in the shadowy cottage, with the rain beating down, he had been able to force away the reality and the consequences of that—block it out, as if he had simply to close a door to make it go away. But now that it was over, the reality of what they had done, and all that it implied, was excruciating.

He turned to her only when the barrier of his cassock and collar were firmly back in place between them. "Your parents will be really worried by now. We've got to get you back."

In the exquisite beauty of her nakedness, Isabelle stood and came to him then and wrapped her arms around his waist as if they had been lovers for a lifetime.

"Being here reminds me a little of being in my father's garage. . . . This old cottage feels like a haven where we're safe from the rest of the world," she softly whispered as she gazed up at him. "I'm afraid to leave this place, afraid the spell will be broken, you know?"

"Right now, all I know for certain is that I've got to get you home before your father calls out Scotland Yard."

For the first time in his life, Stephen had no idea what to say, besides that awful, sidestepping banality, to this sweet, funny girl, a woman now, who had so firmly wrapped herself around his heart. And she deserved better than that. He didn't know what to say to her because he couldn't begin to know what to tell himself. What he had done by breaking his priestly vows was a mortal sin. And yet how could something so wrong have felt so wonderful?

In the face of her questioning expression, and her sweet, trusting eyes shining up at him, the urge to pray was very strong within Stephen. To kneel down right here on this cold stone floor and beg God for his forgiveness. It was what he had been trained to do. Look to God, not to his own heart, for the answer.

And yet, almost as desperately, he wanted to hold her again, kiss her and wrap himself in her sweetness until he could make time stand still forever. It was every opposite in the world spinning inside him all at once. Sweet and sour. Hot and cold. Fire and ice . . . Good and evil.

As the thoughts and the guilt raced through his mind, Isabelle stood before him, unmoving, her bare ivory breasts pressed against the starched black wool of his cassock. She was waiting for him to respond to something. Anything. But what could he possibly say?

Finally Stephen reached over to the chair and took up her blouse and underthings, then handed them to her. He waited awkwardly while she struggled with the little silver clasps behind her bra. Next, her stockings. Then, with trembling hands and eyes that could not quite bear to seek her out, he began tenderly to fasten each of the little flat pearl buttons of her dress.

It began to rain again, gently at first. The wind-driven rain beat a slow rhythm against the cottage. Stephen sank back onto the bed in the silence as Isabelle found her shoes. *My God, my God* were the words racing through his head. He didn't realize for several moments that she was standing over him, watching him.

"I guess you're right. We'd better go before it starts up again," Isabelle said, not certain of what else to say at the moment, beyond that.

Ross and Sunny Maguire were waiting for them in the gravel drive, beneath a sky full of heavy gray clouds, when they arrived back at Willowbrae. When Isabelle stepped out of the car, her mother ran to embrace her.

"We were worried sick," Ross said coming up behind them. "We phoned your sister, but she said you'd left several hours ago."

Stephen stepped forward. "It was my fault, sir. We went through a huge rut in the road about ten miles from here and the car stalled. Isabelle wanted to walk, but it was raining quite hard."

"It was a deluge," Sunny agreed. "I thought the heavens had opened up."

A hint of God's wrath? Stephen pushed the question quickly from his mind, knowing what he now had to say. To protect Isabelle. "I convinced your daughter that it was better for us to wait until it let up, and she finally agreed."

"Wise, my boy," said Ross. "You both must be famished. Come on in. Mrs. McNulty is making a stew for supper that smells absolutely sinful."

Isabelle turned to Stephen, but he did not look at her. "I can't. I've got to get back to the rectory. But thank you."

"Oh, nonsense. Surely you can have a bite to eat first."

"I'm sorry but I have to get back. I have . . . confessions to hear for Father Lewis tonight," he said, stumbling on the words, his throat seizing up as he realized for the first time in all of this that if he performed any sacred rite at all before his own confession was heard, it would be a sacrilege.

Sunny Maguire poured herself a sherry as she watched her husband don his jacket and hat, preparing to drive over, retrieve Alice, and pay the doctor who had been called. Isabelle had said she wasn't feeling well and had already gone up to bed.

"You don't suppose anything happened this afternoon, do you?" Sunny asked, sitting down beside him on the brown leather sofa beneath the wall of animal trophies.

Ross turned to her, the car keys in his hand. "Like what?"

"I don't know, exactly. . . . They were just gone an awfully long time."

"Oh, for God's sake, Sunny, the boy has been ordained."

"He's also a man, and there's always been something special in that friendship between the two of them. You know that as well as I do."

Ross wrapped his arm around her and pulled her to him. "Oh, come on, honey. You know what old Father Keough always used to say, those chosen fellows are neither men or angels—they're only priests!"

Stephen stood alone on the balcony of the rectory that looked down on Saint Finan's and the loch beyond. It was dark. It had been dark for hours and he could see little of what lay before him but the bold dark outline of the church, all in silvery shadows cast down from a bright three-quarter moon. His chest was tight, his lungs constricted, and he had felt for hours as if he could not quite catch his breath. For the past eight hours since he'd taken Isabelle home, guilt had made it so.

He should have tried harder to avoid her. That was what Father Keough would have said. He should have prayed away the temptation. He remembered that even Father Lewis had counseled him about that. (Thank God that dear old man was still in Fort William tonight, or who knows what sorts of things he might have confessed!)

But he hadn't listened to Father Lewis. And he hadn't listened to his own conscience. Eight long hours ago exactly, he had faced temptation and failed miserably. Now tonight he still felt like two men: The one who loved God. *And the one who loved Isabelle.*

And in that, there was no way to win. He would need either to betray the Lord, to whom he had pledged himself forever, or to lose the woman he had cared about since childhood. A woman whom, God help him, he now knew he deeply loved. All of this was his fault entirely. That he loved her desperately seemed of little consequence. He had known better. He had understood the tenets of the priesthood. And yet it hadn't mattered.

It's like cheating on your wife, only much worse, his classmates at seminary had often joked about breaking the vow of chastity. But he was certain that they didn't know the half of it. Stephen flinched as he thought of the wooden cross above his bed and Isabelle lying naked beneath it. *Christ My Righteousness,* it might well have said.

And yet he still wanted her. Now. Again. Forever.

He shut his eyes, taking in the sharp pain of betrayal with each breath. It was right that he was leaving, even if being away from her was already tearing apart his heart. He needed to make amends. And he needed to be absolutely certain of what to do. It could not be a decision made in the dark haze of lust or guilt. Nor even love. Both God and Isabelle deserved better from him than that. As he stood very still, powerless any longer to rein in the tumult of his thoughts, Stephen's mind spiraled nearly out of control like a dam that had suddenly burst. Thoughts . . . feelings. Images. Seductive memories. Her lips so soft and slightly sweet to him, like the taste of honey.

Her body so firm and . . . so unimaginably welcoming . . . Touching her. Tasting her. Losing himself in her warm, welcoming depths.

Stephen despised himself already for wanting to do it again, and much more, with her. It was as if the ground had opened up beneath him this afternoon and had begun to draw him down into the darkness. But he wanted to go. He wanted that more, it seemed, than breathing. He was trapped by his heart and by temptation here in Glenfinnan. And there was no way to escape it. *Or his love for Isabelle.*

How ironic, he thought with a small, pained smile as he gripped the cold balcony railing gazing heavenward, that he had been sent here by the Church and somehow the head of that Church, God himself, meant to make him face now what he felt for her—what he probably always had.

"I still love you, my Lord," he said in an agonized whisper, "but, God help me . . . I love her more."

By midnight, the air in Glenfinnan was cold and bracing with the wind blowing great gusts up to the rectory off of the loch. Isabelle did her best to steady Ian McNulty's rusty red bicycle as she neared the rectory. She saw Stephen's tall, lanky silhouette, lit only by the moon, as he stood alone and unmoving up on the dark balcony. She knew that he did not see her.

As she propped the old bike against the front steps, Isabelle's stomach twisted, and she was a little afraid to go to him. He certainly had not asked her to come. But she had to trust what she knew. What she felt. And she could not leave things as they were.

Stephen didn't hear her come into the house at first.

"I'm glad you didn't say anything to my parents earlier. At least not yet," she said softly when he finally turned around and saw her standing there in a ring of soft lamplight, alone, beautiful, dressed in her muslin nightgown, shoes and coat. "Until we've had a chance to talk ourselves."

His voice in response was flat. "What are you doing here, Isabelle?"

"I came to see you."

"It's the middle of the night."

"I know."

"How on earth did you get here?"

"I borrowed Ian McNulty's bicycle. Everyone turned in hours ago, but I haven't been able to sleep . . . not at all since this afternoon."

His blue eyes narrowed. She could see him close off to her. "Go home, Isabelle."

"I just want to talk about this, work out where we stand, just like always. Remember?"

Stephen tried hard not to look at her. His mind had already been swimming with thoughts of her, *of them,* for too many hours and he felt now like a man who'd gone too long without air. "Isabelle, please, you've got to leave here."

"Even after today, you're still the best friend I have in the world, and I just need to know what you feel. . . . You don't have to touch me."

He closed his eyes. "Would that *that* were true. . . . Go home, Isabelle," he said again, and this time his smooth voice was filled with a tremor.

"I am home. With you."

"You can't stay here. This house belongs to God."

"The church is the house that belongs to God."

"All of it belongs to Him, Isabelle. As I do."

"I don't care."

"You don't mean that."

"Yes I do. You can belong to the Church, but after what happened between us, Stephen, I will always belong to you."

His head snapped up, eyes defiant and glistening. "I don't want you! Can't you see? I *can't* want you! What happened today was a sin, a mortal sin! And if I hadn't made the excuse of being ill and had heard confessions tonight as I was supposed to do, it would have been a sacrilege! Do you have any idea what that means to a priest?"

He could see her grimace slightly at his harshness, but she did not weep or throw herself at him anymore than she had today. She just stood there looking at him, and it only made him feel more torn.

In response, Stephen lunged at her, gripped her shoulders and drew her closer, pressing her against him desperately. "I'm sorry. . . . I *do* love you. . . . God help me, I realized today that I've probably loved you for a very long time."

"We both tried very hard not to. God knows that, don't you think?"

"But I still have to be away from you for a while." He drew in a breath that felt like he was swallowing glass. "I'm leaving Glenfinnan in the morning."

"Where are you going?"

"To Glasgow on an Ignatian retreat. I really need to think, and the Jesuits there will give me time to do that. I owe that much to God, Isabelle."

She felt the weight of disappointment pressing her down. But she refused to be undone by it. Not now that they had both admitted what they felt. There were men who left the priesthood. She knew that it was not impossible that on this retreat Stephen would make his peace with God and decide to do the same thing. "How long will you be gone?" she asked shakily.

"The retreat lasts for a month, sometimes longer."

Isabelle tried hard to pace herself, to slow her breathing and not to let him hear the panic that she felt at that length of separation. "Okay. Well, I can understand that. I mean, I know this isn't easy for you, Stephen. I know what the Church thinks about this sort of thing happening with priests. I haven't even thought about what my father will think when he finds out. . . . But it doesn't matter. In our case what happened was beautiful and right, and it wasn't anything close to a sin. . . . I know that in my heart—and I'll wait for as long as it takes until you believe it too."

"For now, go home, Isabelle. Please."

They were still close. She had framed his face with her

hands. Her voice when she spoke now was soft and more alluring than anything he had ever heard in his life. "Touch me, Stephen. Touch me once, and if you still can say that you want me to leave, then I will do it."

"I am a priest, Isabelle!"

"But you didn't mean it, not the way you're supposed to! You did it for Father Keough, and for your mother, because you were trying to be noble and grand, and because whatever you felt for me back then, you were still the housekeeper's son, you told me so yourself. Those weren't the right reasons."

"Whatever the reasons were at first, the result—"

"Touch me," Isabelle whispered again.

"I can't promise you that I'll be coming back to you."

"It doesn't matter. . . . I just want to be with you tonight before you go," she murmured as he buried his lips against her throat, at last, kissing her warm skin, tasting her. "And when you come back . . . I will accept whatever you decide."

After a moment, his face taut with desire, Stephen took her hand and she followed him into the dark bedroom off the kitchen. In moon-blue shadows, she saw a narrow bed and a high antique wardrobe. There was a lamp on the desk, but he made no move to turn it on.

Silently, he sat down beside her on the edge of the bed and pushed the loose coat back from her shoulders. Isabelle could feel him trembling as he slipped his hands up from her shoulders past the curve of her neck. Then, with his palms framing her small face, he drew her toward his mouth. The kiss between them was urgent, a sudden need, hot and sweet, as if that same Pandora's box they had opened up together earlier today was opening up now to engulf them both.

As he kissed her, touched her, and pressed her back into the bedding, Stephen drew her nightgown off and tossed it along with her coat onto the bare wood floor beside them. His own dark trousers and white shirt joined her coat, and when he was completely naked, he came back to her, kneeling over her on the bed, the moonlight casting shadows on his young, strong body—his broad back, firm thighs, and the dark hair coiled on his chest. When they had lain in that old box bed earlier that afternoon, beneath the worn old patchwork quilt, Isabelle had not seen him fully naked, nor his desire, like this. He seemed now to be saying, *Here I am, this is me . . . all of me.*

A shiver of excitement ran through her, and she drew him down on top of her, kissing him, running her fingers down his back and along the gentle rise of his buttocks, which pulsed as he pushed suddenly, forcefully, inside her.

Isabelle wrapped her arms around the small of his back, drawing him in deeper, crying out as his body tensed against hers, as he kissed her deeply in her throat. All of it coming at her faster, deeper, harder. She pressed her fingernails into his back, scratching him, tasting the sweat rolling off his broad, firm shoulder.

Then she saw the cross on the wall across the room, and Isabelle squinted, her body tingling, as the angles cast a prism of multicolored light that slowly seemed to envelop them. Pale red, blue, yellow, and green. Shades. Shapes. A swollen aching sensation. Stephen was moving against her more urgently now, and she squeezed her eyes hard, feeling as if she'd been pushed quite suddenly from a very high cliff, and she was falling, out of control. Straining. Grasping. Reaching . . . Suddenly, she began to shiver uncontrollably, feeling herself carried swiftly down into a place she had never been, an exquisite cradle of dark velvet where there was neither guilt nor fear. *Only her and Stephen.* And she clung to that, and to him, as tightly as he clung to her.

It was just after six when Isabelle tiptoed back through the grand carved doors of Willowbrae and up the wide oak stairs to the bedroom she shared with Alice. She missed Stephen already. The month, maybe more, would be torture until she saw him again. And it was all going to be so complicated until she knew how things were going to proceed. She had no idea what a man went through when he left the priest-hood, but she had no doubt after last night that he would. They were meant to be together.

Trying very hard not to wake Alice, Isabelle slipped between the cold sheets of her bed, then lay very still in the darkness staring up at the ceiling. She wanted to hold fast to the last trace of what had happened between them again. What she knew now would always happen when they came together. Nothing mattered beyond that. Not even the fact that he had walked her home without speaking. That the expression on his face as they had turned up the road toward Willowbrae had mirrored the torment she knew he felt in his heart.

It didn't matter because, regardless of how wrong it was, they loved one another deeply. And they had for a very long time. They had a history. Surely God could see that. Understand it. The good Lord, in all of his wisdom, couldn't possibly want to hold Stephen to a vow he hadn't meant . . . *could he?*

No, after today, she would never believe that. What had finally happened was like a covenant that would seal them—something that would bond their two lives together forever.

Isabelle waited, full of faith, for Stephen to return.

He did not call, nor did he write. But she had understood that he would not. He needed time, he had said, and she wanted to give him that. Soon, however, it was the middle of June, almost two months since he had gone to Glasgow, and still there was no word. Father Lewis would say only that an Ignatian retreat was a solemn thing. There was no mail. No phones. Simply a lot of reflection and prayer. Sometimes a priest was so at peace there that a stay was lengthened. That appeared to be the case with Father Donnelly.

Slowly, the heather and broom began to cover the hills around Glenfinnan like a colorful purple carpet, and still Isabelle waited. She took long walks through the glen in the

cool spring sunshine beneath the cloudless blue sky, thinking about Stephen and what life they might have together.
She read. She went to church to pray.

And she waited.

In the meantime, her father had finally concluded Alice's
marriage contract with Henry Vanguard and seen to his
grandmother's estate. He was at last making plans for the
family to return to San Francisco. Isabelle tried not to panic
when he told her that, but as each new day passed, she
began to face the very real fear that they would actually be
gone from Scotland when Stephen finally returned. It had
been ten weeks. And still no word. More days passed.
Weeks. The plane tickets were bought and sent by messen-
ger to Willowbrae. Their reservations had been made to fly
out of Glasgow at the end of the week. And then it began.

The horrid sickness that she had been fighting finally
erupted. She was ill every morning, vomiting until she felt
certain she was going to die. *And she wanted to die.* She told
Alice it was the flu, but that excuse had begun to wear very
thin.

As Isabelle clung to the last shred of hope for a future with
Stephen, she accepted as fact what she had not wanted to
face. She knew her biology. She knew her body. Reluctantly,
she took a ride into Oban with Effie's daughter Mairi. The
doctor there only confirmed what Isabelle already knew.

She sat on the cold, hard edge of the bathtub, weak and
trembling, one morning early in July as her father pounded
on the bathroom door. Isabelle had just heard from Mrs.
McNulty last night that the handsome young priest, Father
Donnelly, was finally back in Glenfinnan and that she was
certain he would be saying Mass on Sunday.

*Performing a solemn rite again as only a priest in good faith
could do.*

Mrs. McNulty was glad about that, because he was so
much more interesting to listen to than old Father Lewis,
she'd told Isabelle through her thick Scottish burr. Isabelle,
in her shock, had needed to run out of the kitchen to be ill.

Mrs. McNulty couldn't have gotten it wrong. It all made sense. He had made his decision. The fact that Stephen hadn't called or come to see her since he'd been back only confirmed her worst fears. He'd made his choice. He had chosen God.

"Isabelle! Are you sick again?" Her father's voice boomed beneath the door as she vomited and sobbed, slumped down on the bathroom floor. "What in hell is going on?"

Ross Maguire was holding Isabelle by the collar of her dress, fingers pressing into her flesh, and she was weeping as he burst through the door to the church office. *He knows something,* Stephen thought as his heart leapt very suddenly up into his throat. *Oh, dear God, so he knows about Isabelle and me before I've even had a chance to see her, to tell her . . .*

"Where is Father Lewis? She has got to confess her sins!"

"Daddy, please!"

Stephen glanced over at Isabelle, saw the chalk white terror on her small face, which somehow looked paler and more gaunt. Then he looked back at her father as she struggled to break free of him. Stephen was sure he had never seen anyone so savage, eyes hard and steely, and full of contempt. A spark of self-loathing surged through Stephen's body, for having let it go this long, for having needed to pray and seek counsel, waiting almost three months to see Isabelle again.

Stephen rose slowly from the desk and the pile of papers there, quelling hard the urge to intercede, to tear Isabelle from her father's arms and protect her from what appeared to be possible violence.

"Father Lewis has gone to a deanery meeting in Fort William. I expect him back in about—"

Ross's face was crimson with anger and he was breathing heavily, like someone who had just committed a murder. Or was about to. "Then you'll do it! We're not waiting! She has waited long enough with that sin across her soul, and she needs to be heard!"

"Oh, God, no, Daddy, not Stephen!"

"Under the new circumstances, Mr. Maguire, I cannot hear—"

"Now! She must be heard now! Here and now!"

Stephen stiffened. Something was very wrong. "Mr. Maguire, confession is a very private thing between a person and the Lord, I cannot simply—"

Ross interrupted him, and Stephen felt the sparks of his anger like something shooting out at him from a firecracker. "I want to hear her admit now what she's done!"

Tears were raining down Isabelle's face, and the sheer desolation there had begun to make Stephen feel sick. "Look. I understand that you are upset, but I cannot change the tenets of our faith simply to accommodate that. I will hear Isabelle's confession, if it is what she wants, but I will do it properly and privately, in the confessional, or I will not do it at all."

Stephen steadied himself. He could hear her sobbing on the other side of the screen, and the chink of metal as she pulled the crimson velvet drape across the rod, cloaking her in darkness. Stephen held onto his rosary tightly, feeling as if something was coming at him very fast and he could not stop it. In Latin, he murmured through the mesh, "May the Lord be in your heart and on your lips that you may worthily confess your sins." He made the sign of the cross. "In the name of the Father, the Son, and the Holy Ghost . . ."

And then he waited. She was still sobbing.

"Bless me, Father for I have . . . Oh, I can't do this." He could hear her shift, then move; rise back to her feet.

"I am the Lord's vessel," he said in a quiet voice. "Tell it to God, Isabelle."

"I'm sure he already knows."

He could hear her press away the curtain and then Ross push her back inside.

"Confess it, Isabelle!" Her father charged, his voice echoing through the church. Stephen felt his chest squeeze. He was doing his best to control his breathing. But that thick dark thing was still coming at him, hard and fast. He knew what a devout man Isabelle's father was. If Ross was forcing this now, in this way, it was to steady his own anger as much as to have God absolve her of her sins.

He wanted to rescue Isabelle from this. The urge was overwhelming. Whatever she had done in his absence, he knew that it was only out of longing for him, confusion about what was happening. And desperation. All of that was his fault, and he intended to spend the rest of his life making it up to her.

"Bless me, Father, for I have sinned. . . ." Isabelle started, then stopped again. "Since my last confession, I have . . . I have had sex with a man . . . and . . . and I am pregnant."

It fell on him with the weight of a hammer; truth and darkness. He was frozen by it. Somewhere in the silence outside the confessional he could hear whispering: life, someone else's, he thought blindly.

He'd known he should have gone to her the first moment he'd set foot back in Glenfinnan to tell her what he had decided. That he was leaving the priesthood. But not for her. Not *because* of what had happened with Isabelle. It was very important to him that he know that, and that he make her understand that, too. They couldn't begin to build a life that would last based on a circumstance. Nor something based on passion.

He had been lying to himself for years, and he had made a grand mistake. The priesthood had not been his calling, not so much as the nearness to men he respected and the eternal tie to those he had admired—Father Keough especially, just as Isabelle had always believed. And he had been made to realize that in Glasgow.

But even as he'd stepped off of the train, his heart thundering with anticipation and love, he'd known he needed to be careful. Until he received word back from Rome about officially leaving the Church, it was his duty to wear his cassock. He couldn't possibly go to Isabelle at Willowbrae like that and take her in his arms as he longed to do. No, he would have to see her privately and arrange a time to meet. Then Father Lewis had hugged him, welcomed him back, and asked him, at that unbelievably inopportune moment, to look after things at the rectory for a couple of hours. It hadn't seemed so long, after all of the kindnesses the old cleric had shown him, and so Stephen had agreed, having passed two excruciating hours waiting, wanting to see her. Now here they were, he had not told her anything. . . . And she was pregnant.

His lips had moved and sounds had come out, but Stephen had no idea what he had offered Isabelle as penance after that. His mind was a top spinning out of control. *Pregnant.* The very word was like a stone around his heart. That she had faced this alone, the fear, the uncertainty, believing by now that he did not mean to honor what they had felt for one another or what they had shared.

The sound of Ross Maguire's heavy breath brought him back quickly to the here and now. Ross plucked Isabelle from the confessional with a powerful arm and began to drag her back, by the back of the dress, through the church spotted with kneeling women.

The three of them moved out onto the steps of Saint Finan's. The wind was blowing off the loch and the sky was very dark again as they stood there together. Then suddenly, looking at Isabelle and Stephen, their stricken expressions, Ross knew the rest of it.

In the little silence, Ross's flushed face turned the color of a fresh beet, and the veins began to stand out in his neck. Stephen watched his eyes narrow to slits as understanding hit him hard. "You sonofabitch! You bloody sonofabitch! I'm gonna kill you! I swear I'm gonna kill you right here in front of God and everybody!"

Ross was wild with rage. He lunged across the steps, lashing out at Stephen with two hard, coiled fists. Stephen held up his forearms, but only in self-defense, as a thumping blow landed across the side of his face. Then, as blood from his nose dripped down along his cheek, he was struck again. But Stephen did not strike him back, he simply stood there facing Isabelle's angry father, letting him vent his rage.

"*You!* All the time I welcomed you into my home, treated you like a son!" Ross growled incredulously, his eyes glittering up at Stephen with pure hate. "Shared my food with you, my wine . . . and what you really wanted me to share, all along, was my daughter! What did you do, Stephen? Lie in wait for her when she was a child? Think all of that time how you were going to seduce her? And then when my trust was greatest, when you were a priest—"

"Stop it, Daddy! It was my choice too!"

"You're a child, Isabelle. He is a grown man! *He* made the choice to seduce you and then to hide behind a cleric's collar afterward!"

Ross landed another powerful blow on Stephen just as those final words left his mouth, this jab to the side of the jaw, and Isabelle lunged for her father's arm to draw it backward just as he was jerking toward him again. "For the love of God, Daddy, stop it!"

"He has a right to this, Isabelle," Stephen said evenly. He wiped a smear of blood from across his cheek, as she still held her father's rigid arm. Two very old, stoop-shouldered women coming out of the church stopped and whispered, but neither Ross nor Stephen noticed.

"I was wrong," Stephen finally said, with a grimace. "I was a priest . . . I should have known better, and I'll not stop you if you want to strike me again."

"Oh, I want to do more than that!" he snarled, saliva pooling at the corner of his mouth. "I want to kill you, you ruddy bastard! I want you to pay for this! And, believe me, you will! I swear to God almighty, you will pay!"

"I think if we just talk this out, Mr. Maguire, you will see that I have every intention of—"

"I don't give a rat's ass in hell what you intend, Donnelly!"

"Daddy, please! Hear him out!"

"Save it for the devil, you sonofabitch, because when I get through with you, Lucifer will be the only one left in this world who'll have a thing to do with you!"

Then he jerked Isabelle's arm, pulling her roughly down the three remaining church steps. She tried her best to pull away, but Ross was stronger. His fingers were gouging her arm, cutting off the blood and, as she looked back at Stephen, her eyes bore the stricken expression of a lamb being led to slaughter.

"Mr. Maguire, I understand how you feel, but I really do need to talk to your daughter!"

"Go to hell, Donnelly!"

Isabelle was twisting furiously to break free of her father and Stephen was following them as Ross dragged her toward the shiny blue Jaguar parked up on the road. Stephen's heart was thumping like a drum as Isabelle looked pleadingly back at him and tears rained down her face. "Isabelle, I have got to talk to you!"

Ross stopped suddenly and pivoted back around. The copper hair on his forehead was wet with sweat, and his eyes were like two small beads, filled with contempt. "When hell freezes over, Donnelly!"

He shoved Isabelle into the passenger seat of the car and locked the door. She pressed her nose against the glass as he went to the other side and climbed in. Stephen followed him, kicking the door back open with a shove of his foot.

"Now wait just a minute. I understand that this has been a terrible shock, that you need time to think, but you won't be able to get rid of me just by walking away."

Ross jerked the door back. "Watch me!"

"The child is mine, Mr. Maguire! It's mine and, like it or not, you're going to have to deal with me and Isabelle . . . and with *that!*"

In response, Ross gunned the engine, drowning him out, and the tires whirled dry dirt into a fine dust cloud that rained onto Stephen's black cassock. "I love your daughter and we are going to be together!" he yelled as the car pulled away in an even greater cloud of churning flying dust and he began to race after it.

◆   ◆   ◆

An hour passed by the time he got to Willowbrae.

Stephen pressed the brass knocker several times against the old oak door before anyone answered. To his surprise, it was not Ross Maguire he suddenly faced but Sunny. She looked very drawn and tired. Her mascara lay in slim black ribbons on her smooth, sculpted cheeks. Her nose was red. So were her eyes. For the first time in all the years that he had known her, Sunny Maguire looked far less than her impeccable best. But under the circumstances, he understood that.

"I need to speak with Isabelle."

Her voice was a soprano monotone. "She's not here, Stephen."

"Then I'll wait."

He moved to push his way inside but she held the door firmly. "She's gone."

"What do you mean, gone?"

Sunny took a very deep breath and then exhaled, as if just talking with him took every effort in the world. And then he realized, it probably did. "Her father and I thought everyone needed a cooling-down period. . . . He's taken her away from here."

Dark panic rose quickly inside him. "And away from me."

"It really is for the best. You have a life to get on with . . . and so does Isabelle."

Alice, standing behind her mother, pulled the door slightly wider. Her eyes narrowed as she was glaring at him. The friend who, in childhood, had needled him as if he were an older brother and had even double-dated with him back in high school, was gone. This was an opponent. Someone who despised him for what he had done to her younger sister.

Stephen ignored their hostility and spoke with total conviction anyway. "I'm leaving the priesthood, Mrs. Maguire. I've already begun the process, and when I'm free I am going to marry your daughter. I can't offer her a life like she's had with you, I know, but I know I can make her happy . . . and I *do* love her."

The condescending smile that slimmed Sunny's lips suddenly made him shiver. "Of course you do, dear. It's the least you could say to me, isn't it, after what you've done?"

"Oh, Isabelle isn't going to be shamed in this, I promise you. I mean," he stumbled, uncomfortable talking about this but determined to make her understand, "I'm sorry about the way it happened, but I have every intention, Mrs. Maguire, of marrying your daughter and giving our child my name."

"Give her some time, Stephen. Give us all that. Don't push. As you might imagine, she's very confused just now."

"I know that she loves me. I saw it in her eyes just this morning."

"Yes, I know all about this morning."

"I need to tell her that I'm leaving the priesthood. She doesn't even know that I've decided that. You've got to tell me where has she gone." Stephen could hear the panic steadily rising in his voice, the words quicken as he asked the question, but he didn't care. The only thing that mattered at all just now was Isabelle, and finding her before Ross Maguire filled her head with some unbelievable lie.

Alice moved up beside her mother. "She doesn't *have* to tell you anything, Stephen."

"I think I have a right to know where she's gone—please!"

"My husband doesn't believe you have any rights at all."

"All right, I'll tell you," Alice said, interceding with a deadly calm. "She's gone home, back to San Francisco."

He watched Sunny and her daughter exchange a tentative glance, as if too much had just been revealed, then both of them looked back at him like two sentries guarding a castle gate. There would be no more discussion. No more admissions.

"So there you have it," Isabelle's mother said in a cool-toned pronouncement. "Follow her if you must, but right now, I really can't bear to look at that collar and your hypocritical face a single moment longer."

◆   ◆   ◆

Three days later, Stephen sank onto Isabelle's canopy bed, the one with the pink ruffly spread she'd had since grade school. He was holding that old bottle of My Sin he'd given her and the class photograph of him that she'd left sitting beside it. Funny, even after all the time she'd been away, it still felt like Isabelle in this room. Outside, the sound of the cable car clacking up Nob Hill jarred him and he opened his eyes.

It had been a ruse.

He had spent the last of his savings on the plane ticket back to San Francisco. He had been traveling for almost two straight days, if you counted the painfully slow train back to Glasgow, then all of the airline connections, the waiting. But his mother was very firm. Neither Isabelle nor Ross Maguire had been here for several months. Didn't he know that the entire Maguire family was in Scotland?

A cool sea breeze blew in through the open window and ruffled the curtains as he surrendered his face to his hands. He had never felt so hopeless about anything in his life. This was not a coincidence. This had been planned, meticulously, like everything Ross did. Always with the aim of winning.

In his ferocious anger, Isabelle's influential father had vowed to make Stephen pay. And he knew now that he would be made to pay in the most cruel way possible. Ross had every intention in the world of keeping them apart. In that horrendous moment of realization Stephen sat there on her bed, surrounded by her things; in her scent, the very feel of her, he saw a searing glimpse of his own future. He would not be able to be there to help Isabelle through any of this. Nor would he be able to tell her that he loved her desperately and that he was giving up everything to make a life with her.

But worse than that, and excruciating even to contemplate, he knew now that Ross Maguire was determined that Stephen never again in this lifetime see Isabelle or know their child.

CHAPTER

6

⊰◈⊱ Isabelle and Alice

"Our man has just met with your daughter, Mrs. Wescott."

Nathan Greer was known by his colleagues as a man of few words, and that was no exception now as he stood in Isabelle Wescott's salon in a slightly rumpled herringbone blazer, putty-colored slacks, and coke-bottle eyeglasses.

Exactly twenty-four hours after she had confessed it all to Alice, Isabelle reached for the arm of one of her bergère chairs to guide herself as she sank into it. Alice stood behind her sister with a hand clamped supportively on Isabelle's shoulder.

Isabelle's memories stumbled over her hopes. A thousand questions fastened themselves firmly in her mind. But she pressed them back, refusing to ask them. After all these years, she was accustomed to waiting.

"What is her name?"

"Glenna, ma'am, Glenna Rose. Her married name is McDowell. She's a doctor with a small general practice in a little village near Glasgow called Arrochar."

Isabelle was very near the edge of desolation rather than joy, and it had come very suddenly. She hadn't expected to feel that when this day came.

She held onto the shreds of her composure as a drowning man might cling to a straw. "She's . . . a doctor?"

"Yes, ma'am. Educated in Edinburgh."

The shock was there, the surprise at finally knowing. Isabelle was shivering even though there was a fire blazing in the hearth a few feet away. The agony of so many years, so many missed opportunities, were flashing like picture postcards in her mind, disorienting her a little. How she had hoped, long ago, to become a doctor herself. Stephen. Glenfinnan. That tiny baby still calling out to her, as she had for so many years. Glenna Rose. What a lovely name for a little girl. And then a stray thought skittered across her mind, startling her. She wondered what Stephen would have thought of their child's name, if he knew.

Why did it always come back to that, even now?

Stephen and Isabelle. Like two halves of the same whole. Even after so many years apart, how natural it felt to see him in her mind. How familiar. Thoughts of Scotland brought thoughts of everything else they had ever meant to one another—the key to a door, which, once unlocked, gave way to their childhood, here in San Francisco, and to what came afterward.

The deeper Isabelle had gone in this search for Glenna, the more she had reconnected with their early past. Her reality now was fast becoming an extended dream, filled with images and desires, tragedies. And, ultimately, resignation to what was meant to be. But in another place in time, like some warm and secret haven, safe inside the snug harbor of her soul, she was not a woman, nor a forbidden lover, but a child again. And so was Stephen. Two awkward youths sharing their dreams and their fears with no idea what fate, or God, had in store.

"Is there more?"

Isabelle could see from his sour expression that there was.

"I'm sorry, Mrs. Wescott, the rest isn't what we would have hoped."

"Your detective has given her my letter, then."

"Yes, ma'am, he has. And I'm sorry, but—"

She turned to face the grand bay window, holding very fast to what control she had left. Alice still touched her shoulder. "That's it then, isn't it? My daughter does not wish to see me."

"I'm sorry it has turned out this way for you," Greer offered awkwardly. "I know how much you had hoped."

The pain of disappointment pressed suddenly, fluidly, beneath that well-cultivated mask, the polite smile of a politician's wife that she'd had so many years to perfect. "You did what you could, I'm certain, Mr. Greer, and I do appreciate your efforts. I have only one further request."

"Anything that I can do."

"When your detective returns from Scotland, would you tell him that I would like briefly to meet with him?"

"Yes, of course, Mrs. Wescott."

"Thank you, Mr. Greer. My accountant will be forwarding your final payment in the morning."

He pressed his loose eyeglasses back up onto the bridge of his nose. "I just wish it could have ended differently for you, ma'am."

"Thank you," Isabelle said. "My sister will see you out. Good day."

Isabelle stood then and went to the bay window. She watched the traffic pass before her great old Victorian house, feeling unable to speak or even breathe. There was a steady stream of cars this time of day, and the mist up off of the bay was as thick as pea soup.

So now she knew, Isabelle tried to tell herself. *Glenna . . . Dr. McDowell.* Now could she close the book? Dear Lord, would she ever be able to do that?

"Belle, I am so sorry." Alice was being so kind, when she returned, and her tone was so sympathetic that it almost made the pain sharper. "I wish there were something I could say."

"Say you'll have a sherry with me."

"Of course."

Isabelle went across the room to the rosewood liquor caddy with three crystal decanters and glasses on top, and filled one for each of them. Alice sank into one of the soft, squashy chintz-covered sofas. "Do you want to talk about it?"

"I'm not certain what I want to do now. I didn't plan . . . I mean, I didn't think what I would want to do if she didn't want to see me. I suppose, under the circumstances, that was quite foolish, letting my hope get in the way like that."

"I think it is quite understandable."

Isabelle sank down beside Alice, not making a sound, pushing away the piercing sadness that was slowly overwhelming her. It surprised them both that Alice was the one who began to cry, mourning the loss of happiness her sister had so richly deserved and the hand her own selfishness had played in it.

Isabelle patted her sister's wrist. "That's not going to do anybody any good now, you know."

"I just really wanted it to work out for you," Alice softly sobbed, pulling a small white handkerchief from the pocket of her tight blue St. John Knit and dabbing her eyes.

"I know. So did I. But it's over now. I hired the best private detective agency in the country, and I got what I paid for. So that is that."

"Maybe you should go to Scotland, fight to see her, make her underst—"

"She has made her choice. I will respect that. . . . I must respect it."

Alice hung her head and daubed her eyes again. "Of course you're right," she said in a quivering tone. Then, except for the ticking clock, there was silence.

"Will you reconsider coming out to the vineyard with David and me for a few days? Getting away could really do you some good."

"Let me think about it?" Isabelle asked after a few moments. "I'll call you in the morning."

A smile dawned slowly on Alice's tangerine-painted lips. It was the closest she'd gotten yet to a yes. "Oh, it really would be splendid for you."

"I finally think you may be right."

"It would be such fun. We can eat chocolate, watch old movies, and have ourselves a good cry, like we did when we were kids."

Isabelle wrinkled her nose as they stood. "We never did that when we were kids."

"I know that. But I would have liked to."

"You know," Isabelle waited a moment and then forced up a little smile, "I think I would have, too."

More mist slipped across the sun and darkened the parlor

into shadows and all of the many different shades of gray. "I hope, if I decide to come, that the sun is shining out in Napa," Isabelle said with a little sigh as she glanced back outside. "Right now I could really do with a bit of that."

For a long time after Nathan Greer left, and after she managed to persuade Alice to leave as well, Isabelle stood alone in her lush little garden with the sounds of the traffic over on Vallejo Street steadily surrounding her. This place, so pleasantly overrun now with tangles of wisteria and that wonderful emerald ivy, was a great comfort. It was nothing like the grand garden she'd known as a girl in Scotland, at Willowbrae, with its reflecting pools, rows of emerald box, and the high yews, like grand green sentries, separating the garden and the long, crunchy gravel drive.

The sky had darkened quickly, and now was full of clouds, like giant silvery pillows scudding over the eaves. There were so many that they nearly blotted out the last of the sun, making San Francisco dark and even a little foreboding for so early in the day. It was fitting somehow, she thought, since it matched the mood of her heart.

She moved across the bricks, which were covered with a green, slippery moss, as an icy breeze swept up off the bay. A flock of seagulls came like a sudden snowstorm.

So this was to be the end of it. No final scene. No denouement. Her child, whom she had longed for, bled for, and hoped for for so many years, wanted nothing to do with her.

She was bundled up in her camel-hair cape, with a green and white Gucci scarf over her head and around her neck, Grace Kelly–style. Frank had liked her to wear scarves that way, with dark glasses; he thought it left an elegant impression. But after thirty years, it was simply now a habit.

She walked off the brick and across the path, her comfortable shoes crunching into the water-worn gravel as she gazed down at her precious roses, all buff and pink and mauve, like friends, sweet and fat, swaying slightly in the breeze. The

Cornelias, Penelopes, even the Reine de Violettes, turned up so proudly toward the sky and distant from the poor blood red geraniums, as if they were poor relations.

And as she took stock of them it occurred to Isabelle that she would have liked to share this with a little girl, her love of gardening . . . Like their shared interest in medicine.

What you wanted to do, my dear, was behave like an alley cat. So I simply treated you like one until you knew better. Isabelle shivered, shutting out her father's words. Why did they still come to her like this, even when he'd been dead for almost twenty years?

And it wasn't like that. It had never been like that. That sweet child who had been torn from her arms, still covered in their shared blood, wailing as if she knew what lay before her and fighting it, had not deserved the fate that lay ahead. Nor had she.

How sorry I am, my darling girl. How many things I should have liked to share with you. . . .

She bent down and took the secateurs from her pocket to snip a few of the Cornelias. She took the last three that had not already begun to die. There wouldn't be any more of these. Not until spring. She meant to put them in a vase at her bedside so that they were the first and the last thing she would see or smell. She needed something to cheer her. Isabelle sank heavily onto a gray stone bench, and the secateurs dropped onto the bricks as the memories steadily filled her like a fine old sherry, making her dizzy.

Suddenly, she almost wished she'd asked her sister for a couple of her precious Valiums before she'd gone. But the thought passed as quickly as it came, since there was nothing anyone could do, nothing anyone could give her for the piece of her heart that had been torn away. Hearts did not grow back. Sometimes they healed. Scarred over. Sometimes not. But her wound was there, still open and raw.

Vivid images danced across her mind as she gazed up into a sky that was like a broad canvas. . . . Blue eyes. Sweet, full, pale cheeks. Her father's dark hair. Sweet little rings she had seen for only a moment on top of that angel head. Those were the things she still remembered.

It was going to rain again. Her bones told her that. They ached so before a good rain. They were more reliable than the clouds. Frank used to say that. Dear Frank. Such a good husband he had been, even after the way her father had rail-roaded her into their marriage—after the way she had fought so against it. But Frank had never really had a chance with her whole heart, had he? Not after Stephen. *Oh, Stephen. So young back then, weren't we? Both so blissfully unaware of how we were about to change one another's lives.*

She hoped, after everything, that the years had been kind to him, wherever the road had led him after Glenfinnan. . . . Even though it had led him away from her. Lord, she thought with the smallest glimmer of a smile. Knowing Stephen, he was probably a monsignor by now.

The phone rang through the house an hour later. The sound was like thunder. Isabelle had gone upstairs to her bed need-ing to be alone and she had then found her way to the old dog-eared Bible she kept at her bedside. She always thought she should have bought a new one, but as in most things, she preferred the old. She ignored the loud ringing, held by the beauty of the words before her.

> *. . . Now we see in a mirror dimly, but then face to face.*
> *Now I only know in part; but then shall I understand fully . . .*

Ah, to know things fully! That passage from Corinthians had always been comforting, that her life one day would actually make sense to her, that she would know why things had gone the way they had. It was one of the things that had helped her survive the losses. And the loneliness. The sound of a phone ringing brought her slowly back from her thoughts. Willa had gone to the butcher. She'd have to answer it herself. Isabelle picked up the receiver.

"Hello?"

"May I please speak with Isabelle Wescott?" a small voice asked.

"This is Isabelle Wescott. To whom am I speaking?"

There was an interminably long pause. A prank call, she thought, angry to have been torn from her thoughts today of all days. Isabelle nearly hung up.

"My name . . . is Kate. Kate McDowell, Mrs. Wescott."

Was it possible? Could the Lord actually give something so dear when he had just taken something as profound as a child away? In shock, she could not force out anything beyond a single word. ". . . McDowell?"

"My mother is . . . Glenna McDowell. I believe that I'm your granddaughter, Mrs. Wescott."

7

◌◇◌ Isabelle and Kate

"Hello? Is anyone there?"

Kate was certain her heart was going to pound straight through her ribs as she forced herself to speak. "Mrs. Isabelle Wescott?"

Kate felt light-headed suddenly, even a little disoriented. *I can't go on with this! What a dreadful notion! This rates right up there with feedin' a diabetic man cake! What on earth was I thinkin'?*

She had prepared for all kinds of responses, but another prolonged silence had not been among them. It threw her off balance. "Mrs. Wescott?"

"Yes, I'm here. Your name is Kate, is it? I knew she'd had a child of her own, but they didn't tell me any more about you—" The words broke off, and she did not try to finish her sentence.

"Actually my name's Katherine Mary, but everyone calls me Kate."

"Well, it is a very lovely name."

"Thanks."

Again there was that same strained silence before the sentence sounded really complete. "I was under the impression that your mother did not wish to have any further contact with me."

"Callin' was my idea."

"I see. And does your mother know what you're doing?"

"Truthfully, no, ma'am. But I've thought about it a lot since your letter came with that American gentleman and I just felt like it was my right to know ye a bit if I wanted."

"Well, I suppose it is at that. I remember what it's like not to feel as if you have any rights."

Kate could hear a soft, rustling sound as if she were shifting in bed. She was sure that last comment had something to do with the child she had given up so many years before.

"So, was it all right that I called then, ma'am?" Kate asked with a tone of uncertainty.

"Oh, it was more than all right, my dear. But I'd really rather you called me Isabelle."

Kate felt herself smiling. She was feeling almost giddy now. And she knew that was a peculiar response. She suddenly wished she'd eaten more today; something to soak up all of that Scotch.

"So, you live in Arrochar with your mother and father?"

"Aye, ma'am . . . Isabelle, I mean. And next term I'll be startin' at university in Glasgow. At least I think I still will."

"That's wonderful," she said, and Kate could tell by her tone that she meant it.

"I have so many things I would like to ask you. My head is just so full of questions. As you may have guessed, I really didn't expect your call just now."

"I was no' sure I was goin' to call either." Kate managed a weak chuckle. "I can tell ye 'twas no' an easy thing."

"I can imagine. I'm sure this is going to cost you a fortune. Would you like me to call you right back and perhaps we could talk for a while?"

"No," Kate said quickly. "I mean, well, what I mean is that I'm a bit in transit at the moment . . . Not at home. The point is, actually . . . I wanted to tell ye that I'm comin' to the States tomorrow."

"*Where?* *I would drive anywhere, fly anywhere to meet you. I have only to ask me and I shall be there. It is the fantasy of my lifetime. At least part of it . . . Good Lord, don't push like that! I sound like my son Arthur. And pushing is the last thing she needs to hear!*

"Actually, I'm comin' to San Francisco."

Isabelle struggled to push down the note of surprise but it

bubbled up anyway. This was too much, this sort of good fortune, after so many years of waiting. Wondering. *Do I dare to ask? Could she possibly be ready, at last now, to know me as well?* "And will your mother be coming over with you?"

"No. Her parents, I mean the people who raised her, were killed some time ago, and she's finally gone home to make arrangements for their house and their personal effects."

Isabelle thought about asking Kate to convey her condolences for her. But, under the circumstances, that seemed rather trite, as if now, after so many lost years, Glenna would actually want something in the way of emotional support that she had to offer.

"I'm so sorry," she forced herself simply to say instead.

"It's all right. They weren't close, and, from what I heard, her father was no' a very nice man. My mother hadn't seen either of them since before I was born."

"I'm sorry to hear that as well." Isabelle leaned over and braced herself on the table. Truthfully, she was devastated to hear it. Her heart felt as heavy as lead, and she was suddenly very dizzy. The blood that rushed into her face and hands was very hot. *My dear, sweet crying little baby girl, with those beautiful blue eyes and her father's lovely dark hair, wasn't given up to caring people after she was torn from my arms. Not as Daddy promised me. There would be no reason for her not to see them for years if anything else were true! Good God in heaven, what sort of life was that sweet child given up to without me?*

Isabelle's thoughts were spinning almost out of control and she felt a sudden pain, sharp and searing, seize her heavy heart, as fresh and real as the night it all had happened. She took a deep breath, trying to still the ache. Is this what would keep happening if she met this girl, her granddaughter?

"Well, I'd very much like to meet you, if ye're thinkin' it might be all right," Kate said awkwardly into the silence.

"It would be more than all right. I'll clear my calendar. You have only to choose the place and the time." Isabelle was aware of the thin tone in her voice and how quickly her words were coming. It sounded, even to her, as if she were pushing again. But she very much wanted to get something agreed to before Kate had the opportunity to change her mind.

"Well . . ." Kate averred, "I'll be stayin' at a place called the Fairmont. I arrive tomorrow evenin', late, I think."

"You'll be quite tired from the long flight. How would Wednesday morning be? You'll feel more refreshed by then. You could come for lunch and that way we could have a nice long uninterrupted chat. I've a wonderful cook whose just dying to feed someone who'll appreciate all of her wonderful pastries and things."

"Your house? Well, I hadn't thought—"

Isabelle was quick to change her tack. "If you would be more comfortable I could come to your hotel. The Fairmont has a lovely dining room."

"No, your house would be fine."

"Good, then it's settled. I'll send a car for you at eleven."

"Oh, but I'm sure I can catch a taxi."

"I'd really *like* to send someone, if you wouldn't object. After we're through, he can show you a bit of the city, help you get your bearings for a bit of sight-seeing, if you have time to do that."

"'Twould be lovely, actually. Thanks, Isabelle."

"Believe me, child, it's only a fraction of what you deserve," she said.

Kate sank back into her seat on the airplane next to a little boy in a sweatshirt, blue jeans, and scuffed sneakers who had been sleeping since the plane had taken off, her mind still full of the conversation she'd just had on the pay phone in the terminal. She was glad she wasn't seated next to a talker as she opened her book. *Promise to a Child,* by Stephen Drake. She'd finally found a copy here in Glasgow at a book shop near the airport and this was the first opportunity she'd had to open it.

And I will be there for you always,
he said to the child.
But it came not in words.
The promise came from his eyes,
Bright blue like her own, Glenna's eyes . . .

Kate snapped the book shut and turned it over to the black-and-white author photograph on the back. That same handsome face from the Bull & Bear met her. He was not smiling. He didn't look like someone who smiled very often. Life had been so good to him. He was handsome. He was famous. And yet he looked like he had nothing at all in the world.

Whoever she was, she had really touched his life. From the sound of it, that Glenna had probably left him. Kate laid the book across her chest and closed her eyes, trying to imagine that kind of love, the kind someone would remember, write about. A forever love. It was so romantic. She opened the book of poetry again to "A Place in Time." It was the one he had read aloud that night at the Bull & Bear when she was certain she would come right out of her skin, and yet she had no idea why.

PART

3

But to see her was to love her,
Love but her, and love forever.

—Robert Burns

8

⟨◇⟩ Glenna and Father Buchanan

A tidal wave of emotion and memories flooded back to Glenna as the train clattered over the tracks toward Coatbridge. She hadn't returned to the dreary little suburb of Glasgow in years, and it was startling how little had really changed.

Rows and rows of red brick houses. White laundry hung from open windows beneath a brilliant blue cloudless sky. Black telephone lines looped from poles behind them. Her heart began to beat very fast. She wasn't ready for this. But then she never really would be. This working-class suburb was the place, through circumstance, she had been forced to call home.

Glenna took her overnight bag out from beneath her seat, the only luggage she'd brought, and headed toward the door. Father Buchanan waited for her on the platform, in his crisp black cassock and white collar. He stood out among the crowd, still reminding her of Bing Crosby in *Going My Way*.

He had always been one of the few bright spots in Coatbridge, the Catholic enclave ten miles from the city, and Glenna realized the moment she saw him that there was indeed one thing about the town she had missed.

He had aged. His white hair was thinner, his green eyes were a little less bright. But there was still that same unmistakable spark when he smiled, warming her right down to her toes.

She would have known him anywhere.

"'Tis grand to see ye, Glenna," he said as they embraced amid the other people who were coming and going in the cool springtime air. "It's been such a long time."

"'Tis good to see ye too, Father."

"I'm just sorry about the circumstances. But 'twas time ye came back."

"Aye, perhaps it was."

He picked up her bag and led her away from the platform and down a wide flight of steps to a parking lot stuffed with the cars of people who commuted into Glasgow. "I thought perhaps we could stop by the rectory for a while, give you time to adjust—"

"That's very kind of ye, really. But I think I'd better just go straight to the house. The sooner I attend to things there, the sooner I can get home to Aengus."

"As ye wish, lass."

They drove in silence down Dunbeth Road and out to Kirk Street, to the neighborhood where she had grown up. It was a dense warren of white stucco or red brick row houses, with neat stone steps and little black wrought-iron fences. So deceptively bland, so orderly, for the sort of fire so often ignited within those walls. Father Buchanan pulled up to the curb and shifted the beige Vauxhall into neutral. The engine idled as he looked over at Glenna.

"Should I come in with ye, then?"

"Thank ye, Father, but this is somethin' I believe I have to do on my own."

"We've spoken so little since your parents' passin', I have no' had a chance to tell ye that they did no' suffer. It was all very quick. I thought that might be some consolation to ye."

Why does that not surprise me? Of course not. They never really suffered much of anything in their lives, had they? Andrew and Jean Ferguson had always managed to escape that, too busy inflicting their own brand of anger, pain, and disappointment on me!

Glenna steeled herself against voicing that particular angry sentiment. It would have been useless at this point. And she couldn't bombard him with that, since it wasn't Father Buchanan's fault. Glenna had never found the courage to admit any of what had happened at home in her confessions.

After all, there were so many years when she had truly believed it was her fault. She was to blame for her father's anger. For her mother's apathy. So many horrible years when she had struggled to be good.

No, the closest she had ever come to confession was with that handsome stranger, Stephen something, wasn't it? Who had driven up beside her in his shiny silver car one summer afternoon when she had contemplated running away for good. That Andrew had found the card she'd been given and angrily tossed it into the fire had filled her with despair at the time. That card had felt very like a lifeline, a place for a powerless child to turn.

"Then say ye'll at least have supper with me. I know the best place for corned beef from here to Edinburgh. . . . 'Tis still your favorite, is it no'?"

Glenna's slow smile was one of surprise. "It has been years, Father Buchanan. Now, how d'ye recall a thing like that?"

"Oh, and how could I go and forget the way those lovely blue eyes o' yours used to light at the very thought. Besides, in truth, your ma, Jean, she used to talk about ye all the time. All o' the wee things about ye like that. She missed ye once ye left Coatbridge. I know your da did as well, but Andrew was just no' as able to talk about what he felt."

She pushed back the bolt of anger. It wasn't the old priest's fault. "Well, I'd be honored."

"Splendid," he smiled that big welcome grin of his that had always made her feel safe, loved. "Come by the rectory at half past six?"

"I'll be there."

Glenna opened the car door and looked up at the black lacquer door of 21 Kirk Street. Her heart lurched as she took her one small bag. "Ye're welcome to spend the night in the guest cottage next to the rectory, child. 'Tis small but clean, and it might be a better idea, considerin' all that's happened."

"Thank you," she said, closing the door and bending down to look back in through the window. "But I'm certain there'll be a lot o' papers and things to go through. I don't expect to get much sleep while I'm here."

The blinds had been drawn, and the house was very gray. The odor inside had gotten horribly musty. Glenna fought a shiver as she stood in the small foyer gazing in at the dim parlor. It was a cold, spartan room with furniture that hadn't been altered in forty years. A lime green 1950s sofa, a matching chair, two table lamps, and a simple oak desk. The only wall ornament was a small yellowed picture over the mantel of Jesus gazing heavenward with a piece of dried palm from a long ago Palm Sunday tucked into the corner of the frame. Glenna felt a searing rush of air enter her lungs as she glanced around. The sensation was panic.

There were so many things about this house that she'd forgotten until now. The tattered crimson Bible on the dining table. The little clay planter of red geraniums her mother had always kept on the kitchen windowsill. The old claw-foot tub upstairs, so convenient for dunking her in, head first, when she'd been unruly.

Things came back to her in painful little slices as she stood motionless, still holding her bag and the door key. Images. Memories. The sound of Andrew Ferguson's voice.

The wrath of Almighty God will surely be upon ye, for your actions, if I spare the rod now! Draw up your skirt! . . . I said draw it up, Glenna!

She squeezed her eyes and the overnight case fell from her fingertips and smacked onto the cold tile. She pressed a hand to her lips.

Don't fight me, Jean! She needs this. 'Tis for the child's own good!

Glenna remembered it all. Each excruciating moment. But the little girl who stood before her now, leaning over the sofa, tears raining down her freckled cheeks, her small buttocks bare, was someone else entirely.

He'd hit her again and again that day, until the skin broke, quoting from Proverbs with each stroke of his switch. *Foolishness is bound up in the heart of a child; the rod of discipline will remove it far from him. . . . Do not hold back discipline from the child; although you beat him with the rod he will not die. . . .*

She switched on a lamp on a table beside that same sofa. Light chased the hobgoblins of the past from her mind. Glenna stood there in the room a moment more. All of this would be given to charity. She'd leave it to Father Buchanan to know how to properly dispatch it all. She hadn't a single emotional attachment to anything here. Sad, she thought, that so many years here should have come to that.

She opened the fraying olive draperies and the window to let in the last vestiges of sunlight and the warm afternoon air. It was the first time in her life that Glenna could recall this room being filled with sunlight. Her father always kept the draperies closed, kept the rest of the world out.

Her stomach twisted as she sat down reluctantly at the small mahogany desk and picked up a plastic packet containing Andrew Ferguson's wallet and keys. It had a police label across the front of it. This was what he'd been carrying with him when he died, she thought. The same old brown wallet he'd had since she was a child and that same key ring with the silver Saint Christopher medal. To Glenna, this place, and these things were more than symbols.

Ye were the same predictable, pious, and sour man to the very end, weren't ye? Nothin' changed. Nothing about ye ever would have. . . .

Wanting, needing to get on with it, Glenna took the key ring and found the desk key. It was something she'd been forbidden to touch as a child. The third drawer down in that little gray metal box was where he had always kept his papers. Probably a will was contained there too. For a moment, her hand hung in midair, and she felt very cold. Alone and cold. The way she'd always felt here. Glenna didn't want a single thing from these people but the responsibility for handling it all still fell upon her.

As she knew it would be, the box was still there. She took

the key and slowly opened it. Beneath the open window she could hear children's laughter. A car passed by.

Glenna turned the little silver key until the lock clicked. A neat stack of letters, probably only four or five, lay alone in the box bound by a rubber band. They were addressed to Mr. Andrew Ferguson. There was no identifying name in the upper left corner of the envelope but the return address was in Glasgow. Glenna lifted the letters out and sank back against the desk chair. There was no will. Only a deed to the house and this curious stack of letters postmarked 1978. Her father didn't have any friends. She couldn't imagine who might have wanted to write to him.

She'd have done well with a glass of wine just now, but she could be well assured that there was none of that in this house. Glenna lifted the letters out of the box and carried them over to the chair where the light was better.

"Did ye know about this?"

The old oak front door to the rectory ushered in the butter yellow sunlight and the street noise, then slammed shut with a great thud. Glenna pushed past the stern housekeeper who'd answered the door. She found Father Buchanan and another priest having tea in the parlor, both wearing black short-sleeved shirts and slacks with their white tab collars removed. They came quickly to their feet in a room that was painted drab green, accented with a large picture of the Blessed Mother and another smaller one beside it of the Sacred Heart. The furniture around them was old, faded, and overstuffed. The two windows facing out onto Kildonan Street were covered with lace curtains over dingy beige shades; the old beige carpeting looked as if it had been down ten years too long.

"Come in, Glenna."

"Had ye any idea that, all along, they knew who my real father was?"

Her face was flushed and her blue eyes were bright with

anger and shock. She held the bundle of letters tightly in her clenched hand.

"Perhaps ye should sit down, child."

"I don't want to sit down! I want an answer! My God, they knew that there was someone else out there all o' that time who cared about me, and the Fergusons chose to keep it from me anyway?"

The other priest, a balding, gentle man with black horn-rimmed glasses, who had been reading the newspaper, stood and quietly left the room. Father Buchanan waited until he and Glenna were alone before he answered her.

"I'm no' certain that I know what' ye mean, Glenna. But perhaps if we—"

"Of course ye know! Andrew Ferguson was as pious a man as they come! And you were his priest! His confessor! And, I think, the only friend he had in the world! He confessed everythin' to ye to cleanse his miserable soul, didn't he now? Ye canno' honestly sit here and tell me he didn't! I had a right to know there was a man out there who was a wee bit more than *father unknown!*"

"Andrew never told me that ye knew ye were adopted."

"Oh, I knew! The bastard made sure that I never once thought o' myself as truly his!"

"Perhaps if ye tell me what the letters say, we can—"

"They're from him. Stephen Donnelly . . . my father!"

"I told Andrew I thought ye should be told," Father Buchanan finally said in a calm, even tone, one he'd used with his parishioners for over thirty years. "Ye were no' a child by then."

"So my real father *did* come here then? To Coatbridge?"

"Yes. He wanted to see to an arrangement with your . . . with Andrew."

"The letters made reference to money he was sending to me for medical school."

"Aye."

Glenna sank thunderstruck into the chair beside him. She spoke in a whisper, unable to find her voice. "The ol' bastard wanted the glory for himself. . . . He wanted me to believe he had scraped the money together for the grand and noble gesture of sending me to school as recompense . . . that somehow I should forgive him for all o' those bitter years. And me, fool child that I was, I wanted to believe that he might finally have come to love me enough. . . . God, how he lorded that over my head before I married Aengus. . . . How he said he was givin' up every last cent he had saved! "

"Andrew was no' a bad man, dear lass. Ye must believe that. Just, I think, misguided."

"I wonder, did ye know that, for years, he beat me? 'Folly is bound up in the heart of a child,' he'd say as he'd go after his switch."

Father Buchanan closed his eyes. "Dear Lord."

"That's what I said. Dear Lord, please help me. I pleaded more than once, when I was bloodied and cryin' from the pain. Please bring someone to save me from him. . . . But no one came. God wasn't there for me. The good Lord did no' ever seem to be there for me against Andrew Ferguson."

"I'm sorry, Glenna. I truly am. I had no idea at all."

"Ye've got to tell me what ye know about this man called Stephen Donnelly. I deserve at least that much, don't I?"

Father Buchanan took a measured breath and sank into the chair beside her. "He didno' tell Andrew anything about the circumstances of your birth when he was here, if that's what ye're meanin'. I gathered at the time that the two of them did no' get on particularly well. 'Twas a business arrangement, pure and simple."

"But this Stephen must have cared for me. The fact that he had a daughter must have meant somethin' to him if he was willin' to pay for my education."

"Aye, 'twould seem so."

"My mother . . . Jean, that is, always told me that they got me through the Carmelite convent on Mansion Street. The place is cloistered. How d'ye suppose he was able to find me, considerin' that?"

"That, I canno' say." He sighed, leaning back. "Perhaps he

had some sort o' connection to the Church. A payment here, a handshake there. Sadly, that sort o' thing happens even when adoptions are supposed to be confidential."

She thought: *This just cannot be happening. Not now. Not just after my birth mother found me.* . . . Glenna was beginning to believe that it was either a very grand coincidence or something that was eerily fated.

That old memory struggled to the surface of her mired thoughts again. She'd been walking along Warender Road, devastated and alone. A child. It was after that beating against the sofa where Andrew Ferguson had used the Bible against her, as much a weapon as his switch. And then suddenly there had been that man. Tall and handsome. Out of the blue. A stranger wanting to be her friend. A stranger named Stephen.

"It might have been him after all," she said softly, her eyes filling with tears.

"Who, lass?"

"A man I met once, a long time ago. I'd forgotten the name until now but I believe Stephen was it. He was full of such gentle kindness. . . . If it was the same Stephen, why wouldn't he have tried to take me away?"

There was no answer. Only silence. Glenna had never had a feeling quite like this, as if the floor had been pulled out quite suddenly from beneath her, and she was falling, unable to stop.

"'Tis so strange," she said, as she took the handkerchief Father Buchanan offered and then wiped her eyes. "One moment I'm happy and secure at last, leadin' a wonderful life away from here. And the next moment I am bein' hurled right into the eye of a cyclone."

"Our Lord does work in mysterious ways, Glenna, that I'll grant ye. But if I could tell ye anything, I would say to console yourself, not with the tests He places before ye but rather with the majesty of His presence in your life. It shall bring ye far more peace than questioning His will."

Her eyes were wide, still glistening with tears. "So what d'ye think I should do?"

"What d'ye want to do?"

"I hated them both for so long, my birth parents, for giving me up to the life that they did. For the longest time it seemed I had no room in my heart for anything but that."

"And now?"

"I wish I knew," she told him. "Suddenly, it just seems as if everything is changing."

So much was happening, and so quickly. Aengus had phoned to tell his wife that still there was no word from Kate. His sister, Janet, and her husband had tried all of the usual places. They had even sent their own son, Paddy, into Glasgow to see if he could find any clues as to where she might be staying. Then Aengus had listened to Glenna on the other end of the line, her voice strained, as she told him about what she had discovered in Coatbridge.

"Well, ye've no choice, then, do ye?" Aengus finally said.

"What'd ye mean?"

"Ye've got to try to find this man called Stephen Donnelly. If ye won't go to Isabelle Wescott for the answers to what ye've wondered all your life, then maybe he can help ye begin to put the pieces together."

"'Twould be impossible, even if I wanted to do it." Her voice was trembling. "The address on those letters is thirty years old."

"Will ye trust me about this?"

"Trust ye, how?"

"I've an idea," Aengus said. "A way to help ye find your father."

When he hung up the phone, Aengus lay back against the crisp white pile of pillows at the head of the oak bed he had made for his wife as a wedding gift. Yes, he knew her well. Sometimes better than she knew herself. He knew when his wife needed to be held and when she needed a gentle nudge. . . . Especially now, when what fate had in store for his dear Glenna Rose, and for her future, was as clear as this.

9

◈ Glenna and Mitch

There was someone standing at her hotel room door, his face obscured by the shadows, as Glenna got off the elevator and walked down the long corridor. She didn't realize until she was nearly there that it was Mitch Greyson.

Glenna's heart thundered in her chest, and, for the briefest of moments, she thought of turning around and getting back on that elevator. Everything about this said danger to her. But she just kept walking, gripping her room key until she could feel it digging into her palm, almost cutting her skin.

When she came upon him standing there, tall and commanding, with that slightly crooked smile, Glenna almost forgot to breathe. "What are *you* doin' here?"

Mitch bit back a smile. "Isn't the grandest greetin' I've ever gotten from a lady, but I guess, under the circumstances, it'll have to do."

"'Tis only that I'm surprised to see ye again."

"Not half so surprised as I was to get a call from your husband."

His name came out in a whisper. "Aengus?"

"He called my company's office in San Francisco. They tracked me down at the Glasgow airport, actually, just as I was boarding a plane to go back to the States. Said he wanted to hire me to help you find your birth father."

Glenna leaned back against the door feeling as if the wind had been knocked out of her. She waited a moment, trying to put the pieces together in her mind. "I figure he thought it would be easier for me than someone else since I found you for Mrs. Wescott," Mitch went on. "When you think about it, it's pretty natural, his callin' me."

Glenna steadied herself, opened the door. "'Tisn't that I do no' appreciate the idea. That I do, but—"

"But you'd rather work with a Scot."

"'Tisn't the problem, Mitch."

He leaned casually against the doorjamb, and Glenna's heart felt like a bird's wings flapping inside a cage. Since she had become an adult, she had worked very hard to gain total control of the things in her life. To keep them ordered. She had been very purposeful about constructing the life she had. The life she thought she wanted. It had been a response to having no power at all as a tormented child of the Fergusons. With Mitch Greyson, since the moment they had met, she had begun to feel that hard-won control ebbing.

"Look, Glenna." His voice deepened as he looked at her. "I'd really *like* to help you."

She glanced back into her hotel room, as if she could somehow run away from this. From him.

"If he's still here in Scotland, it really shouldn't be too difficult. Your husband told me on the phone that you have a name now. Donnelly, right?"

She walked silently over to the dresser and picked up one of the yellowed letters she had taken from the Fergusons, then she brought it back to Mitch. He looked down at the return address. "Well there now. That's promisin'. We've got two things to go on. That's more than I had when I was lookin' for you. Even if your father doesn't live there any longer, maybe someone'll remember him."

Looking up at Mitch, Glenna felt a strange sensation just then of letting go. It was something she couldn't remember ever feeling. "Perhaps ye should come in," she said softly.

They sat together on the floor of her hotel room, searching for clues, reading through the few letters the mysterious Stephen Donnelly had sent to the Fergusons. At first Glenna felt odd having Mitch go through them with her. But after they had talked about what must have happened, they ordered room service. Then Glenna drank a glass of white wine and eventually kicked off her shoes. She leaned against the foot of the bed, knees to her chest, and told Mitch about how it had been for her growing up. The confusion, the desperate desire to escape. Her anger at the two strangers who had given her over to that life. And he listened intently. As though it mattered to him.

"'Tis strange, readin' his letters, touchin' his words. . . ." She ran her fingers over one of the yellowed sheets of paper. "To know that he held this. 'Twas a time, these say, that he cared about me."

"Like your mama in San Francisco, I don't suppose he's ever stopped." His voice dropped. "A child isn't somethin' anyone with half a heart ever forgets."

Glenna looked at him. There was a strange silence as he met her gaze, then tried to take another swallow of beer to fill the void. But the bottle was empty.

"'Tis true enough. But sometimes they can pretty well tear that same heart in two if ye give them half a chance."

"Sounds as if you're talkin' about your daughter, not your mother, now."

Glenna nodded and took the last swallow of her wine.

"Troubles between mothers and daughters seem pretty normal for her age."

"Not of the drinkin' and runnin' away variety."

Mitch waited a moment. There was real pain in Glenna's expression.

"She's run away?"

"Again."

"I'm sorry, Glenna."

"Aye. So am I," she sighed. "The police do nothin' about it for at least forty-eight hours, since she's done it so many times lately and ended up sackin' out at a friend's nearby."

"But you still worry."

"That never stops. Not for a moment." Then a question came to her, and she looked at him. "Do ye have children, Mitch?"

"I wish I did," he answered honestly.

"I take it ye're no' married, then."

"I was once."

"I do believe she was a lucky girl."

"Believe me, *I* was the lucky one. And there's never a day that goes by that I don't think about her. And miss her. Miss the kids we never had. . . ." He stood then, and straightened his jeans. "But that, as they say, is ancient history, and it's late. Besides, I've got my work cut out for me."

"Tonight?"

He lifted his hand and tenderly brushed a stray hair back from her face. "You bet." He smiled. "After all, I've got a job to do. For starters, I've got to check out who's livin' at that address in Glasgow. If Stephen Donnelly is there, tomorrow oughta be a pretty big day for you." Then he took her hand and squeezed it gently. "So sleep well. I'll call you tomorrow, when I know somethin'."

After Mitch had gone and she had watched him walk back down the long corridor to the bank of elevators, Glenna went back inside her room and closed the door just as tears welled in her eyes. Then they overflowed.

She went into the bathroom, arms wrapped around her waist, and quietly sobbed as she turned on a very hot shower. She tore off her slacks and sweater and then stood beneath the stream, tears mixing with the tingly, almost scalding spray, as she cried into her hands. For the tiniest of moments tonight when Mitch had talked about himself, when she looked into his eyes, Glenna had actually allowed herself to forget her responsibilities. Promises that were deep and binding. She had listened to him with an interest that held a kind of caring. A dangerous kind.

She wanted control of her life again. She wanted to go back. Back to Aengus and that little white stone house with the dormer windows and the gray slate roof. Back to the safety of a bed she had slept in for more years than she could recall and a window out of which she looked onto gentle, rolling green farmland. Or did she? She wasn't a city girl.

And she wasn't free. But Aengus believed in her, trusted her.
And that was still enough.

Wasn't it?

He hadn't meant to reveal even that small part of himself.

Damn! That he might reveal the damning part of his past
. . . This was the first good job he'd found in over a year. And
he really did need the money. But it had slipped out,
nonetheless. Mitch ran a hand through his thick hair and
gazed down at the pile of bills he'd brought with him from
San Francisco. Bills that were overdue.

There was hardly anything left in his bank account. A
couple hundred dollars, maybe. The bills were mounting
into the thousands. And this had seemed like such an easy
job to do at first. He had trained with Nathan Greer. He
knew the routine. This job at least in part had been an
answer to his problems. He picked up the bills and tossed
them down again. Five thousand if the client, Mrs.
Wescott, was satisfied. Another two thousand for this sudden side job for Aengus McDowell. A little finessing.
Talking to a few people.

Easy enough for a man whose very life had been charmed
from birth. Until three years ago. Texas State All-American
running back two years in a row. At the top of his class as
well. The scholarships to Princeton. The residency at Johns
Hopkins. But then that was all before. A lifetime ago.

Before he'd become a murderer.

Mitch squeezed his eyes shut as if that act alone could blot
out the past three nightmarish years. A nightmare from
which it seemed he was never going to wake.

He glanced around the hotel room he'd taken in Glasgow,
done in the old Victorian style, with its peeling plaster and
filthy windows. It made him think of that cheap apartment
on Powell Street where, if you wanted, you could pay by the
week. The place he called home in San Francisco. By now he
should have been in one of those grand old mansions in

Pacific Heights. But for the way his life had turned out, he knew there was no one to blame but himself.

"I know who you are," Nathan Greer had said the first time they'd met, looking nothing like Mitch's image of a PI, with those coke-bottle eyeglasses and the miserable straining paunch. "And I need a blue-blooded boy like you to work for me. Someone who could slip into certain circles more easily than the others. Considering everything you've been through these past few years, I don't suppose there's a lot of other offers coming in just now."

It was just one job, Greer had said, a particular case he had in mind. But if things went well, there was no telling where that might lead. Mitch could not have known how this particular job, a dozen later than the first, would change his life and his heart, forever. *Sweet Glenna . . .* , he thought darkly. *Isabelle Wescott's is not the only heart you've broken without even knowing it.*

He sat hunched over a small table, elbows bracing him, in blue jeans, a white cotton undershirt, and his stocking feet. His boots, the Tony Lamas he hadn't been able to part with when he'd lost almost everything else, sat together neatly beside the door, as if they were waiting to walk him back into the life he used to have.

Through the paper-thin walls music bled from the room next door. Shrill and with no particular rhythm, it sounded, quite literally, as if someone were trying to charm a snake out of a basket.

It would have been so easy to kiss off Nathan's job and go home. Mama and Daddy would have taken him in. He wouldn't even have needed to ask. Christ, they still kept his old room with the football trophies on the dresser and his Charlie Daniels posters pinned to the walls, as if he had just gone down to Diego's for a burger and fries, not off to that hellhole for a two years.

Right now it was actually tempting. He pictured that huge old bathtub with the claw feet just down the hall from his room. How he would love to lie there, buck naked, feet hanging out the other end, soaking in scalding water filled to overflowing with those sweet scented bubbles Claudetta always liked to toss in.

Then she'd lumber upstairs, bring a Coke for him up to his room with a BLT, and he would lie across his old pine bed with a stack of magazines, at peace. Safe. Just like it used to be. *Fool! Those days are as gone as Livi is! Dead. Destroyed because of your arrogance. You can't bring 'em back anymore than you can her!*

Mitch picked up the warm bottle of beer by the neck and took a long swallow, for all the good it would do. No matter what it had cost him, he could not make himself turn away from Glenna. Once he had met her, spent time with her, he would never have been able to live with himself if he hadn't spent every legitimate moment with her he could.

From the first, she had reminded him of some delicate porcelain figurine, one with a cast-iron center hidden just beneath the surface. Someone who only looked like she would break, her reserved manner an image polished to perfection. But that fire blazing in her pale blue eyes gave her away to anyone who took the time to look. And he had looked. Glenna McDowell was a gem, as fine and rare as they came. Like Livi. God, was there really anyone left in the world like Livi? His wounded heart slammed against his ribs. He closed off the thought.

That god-awful music next door was really getting to him. He felt like pitching the beer bottle against the wall. He felt like hitting something. Someone. Wasn't that goddamn music ever going to stop?

Even though there wasn't a chance in hell for the two of them, Mitch was still glad he'd seen Glenna again tonight. And he was glad he was going to try to help her find some answers. *Glenna Rose.* He smiled at how stupid that sounded, the longing tone in it—even spoken in the privacy of his own mind.

It really was tragic. Someone had taken a newborn infant girl from a poor woman who clearly hadn't wanted to lose her. Not any more than he had wanted to lose Livi. But in the end, fate was always life's little tour guide, wasn't she? Always in control. And it was a wild ride if there ever was one.

◆　　　　◆　　　　◆

Glenna was still half-asleep as she reached over to answer the phone the next morning. "Aye?"

"We hit pay dirt. A man named Stephen does live at that address," Mitch said, jolting her awake. "Neighbor next door confirmed that he's been there for over thirty years."

"You must have been up half the night findin' that out."

"I never have needed much sleep."

She wanted to ask him why he'd gone to the trouble. But some part of her already knew the answer. This had become something more than a job to Mitch.

"Glenna, I know this will be a bit surprisin', but the man's last name is Drake. He's Stephen Drake, the poet." When she didn't respond he paused a moment. "You okay?"

"Aye, I'm fine."

"For my money, he and Stephen Donnelly are one and the same."

She raked the hair back from her face and wished desperately for a cup of very strong tea. "Is that possible?"

"Oh, darlin'," he said with a sedate chuckle, "I've learned the hard way that just about anything is possible."

Glenna's mouth was very dry and she felt her heart racing. "What do we do now, then?"

"I expect now we go to Glasgow."

"We?"

"Well, you don't expect me to leave with the job only half-finished, do you?" The tone of the question was good-natured. Mitch paused for a moment on the other end of the line. "Look, Glenna," he finally said. "I can guess what you're thinkin', but your husband hired me to find your birth father for you, and that's *all* that I intend to do. So I'm comin' out to get you and bring you back into the city, and that's that. I'm leavin' now, so I should be there in an hour."

For a moment, she closed her eyes. "I'll be waitin' for ye down in the lobby."

Chapter 10

∽◈∾ Glenna and Stephen

Glenna wasn't certain she could go through with it.

Or, for that matter, she wasn't actually certain that she wanted to, now that she was here. She stood with Mitch Greyson outside the brownstone townhouse for a long time, looking up at the gables and the dormers, beneath a cloudless sky, trying to imagine the man who lived inside.

Good Lord, those letters were so old. Could he actually still live here? Could Stephen Donnelly actually be the renowned poet, Stephen Drake? And why would he have changed his name? If it was the same man, what was he trying to hide?

A part of her honestly hoped none of this was true. Curiosity had drawn her here to Glasgow. But anger about it all had always been a far more powerful emotion.

She didn't want to despise him. After all, according to the letters, it was thanks to Stephen Donnelly that she was now a doctor, that she had found her way out of Coatbridge and to the safety of a life with Aengus.

But still, if he truly was her father, there had been a moment in time when he'd had the choice to acknowledge her as his own, back at a chance meeting on a country road. For whatever reason, he'd walked away from that chance, leaving her to fend for herself with the Fergusons.

I want you to remember that you have a friend. You can call me any time. . . . Drawing up those words, an echo now across time, made her soften to him. Perhaps his reasons for walking away were understandable. But in order to hear them, she needed to face him. She needed to force herself to climb those front steps and knock on the door.

Finally, Mitch reached over, took her hand and squeezed it. "You can do this, Glenna," he said with a gentle firmness.

She was still gazing up at the formidable-looking house. She realized only then that she was trembling. "Oh, I don't honestly know about that."

"Yes, you do."

The conviction in his voice made her look at him in surprise. Her own voice was low when she next spoke. It was almost impossible to hide the sadness in it. "I suppose ye'll be leavin' Scotland now that your job appears to be done."

"My flight leaves Glasgow in an hour."

They were still looking at one another. "Thank ye, Mitch," she said deeply. "For everythin'."

He forced a smile. Glenna was surprised that she felt like crying. "I was just doin' my job," Mitch said in a hoarse whisper, but she knew that wasn't true. His own eyes bore the truth. He was still holding her hand, gripping it tightly.

"Aye, well. Ye did it admirably."

He was close enough to plant a gentle kiss onto her lips. But he didn't.

"I really hate good-byes."

"Then let's no' say it."

His forced smile was fading. Mitch lifted a hand and touched her cheek. "Right or not, I'm goin' to think about you all the way back to San Francisco, you know."

"I find that I don't mind knowin' that."

He raked a hand through his hair then and turned to look out into the street. "I suppose I'd better go before it starts raining again."

Glenna drew her hand away from his and took a half step back, having heard the reluctance in his voice. Glad, even for this brief moment in both of their lives, that it had been there. "Have a safe flight, Mitch."

"Have a good life, Glenna," he said. "A healin', too. A lot of that, I have a feelin', is just up those stone steps."

◆   ◆   ◆

The new collection of poems was called "Remembering Love."

Stephen Drake sat in his dining room with Quentin, his butler and friend, as Barry and Helen Hardwick each read a copy for the first time. It was the first thing he'd written in more than four years, and he'd wanted the timing to be perfect. But now they'd eaten their brunch of steak pie and trifle, drunk their fair shares of Beaujolais, and the moment of truth had come. His old friends, the Hardwicks, were always the first ones, after Quentin, to read a new piece of work.

Helen, a stout woman with healthy pink cheeks, a slightly red nose, and short silver hair, was the first to look up, her tawny eyes glittering with tears. "These are brilliant, Stephen."

"Vintage Drake," her husband seconded, laying his copy back on the table.

"Precisely what I told him," Quentin said in his clipped British tenor.

Stephen smiled as he sipped the last of his wine, then reached down to pet the old black dog that lay sleeping at his feet. It had been as a favor to Barry Hardwick that he did his recent reading at their pub, the Bull & Bear. This big, kind-hearted man the locals called "the Bear" had always been, along with his wife, Helen, Stephen's greatest fan.

Barry had been the first to recognize something more on those ivory pages than the lament of yet another young man who had lost a love. Barry had believed in him and had helped him become the voice of an age. An icon. He had helped him become *Stephen Drake*. That was almost thirty years ago now, after he'd left the priesthood. After he'd buried his mother and had come back to Scotland. Where his new life had begun.

"You're biased, my friend," Stephen said.

"About your poetry, never," Barry replied.

"So then, are we ever to know if this first one here in the collection is about her? The mystery woman?" Helen asked, glancing up at the oil painting that hung over the polished mahogany sideboard.

They all looked up at the image of a very young woman, small and delicately boned, with lovely copper hair long around her shoulders and wide green eyes full of the innocence of youth. She had been painted in a garden as she sat on a white stone bench, grasping a small bunch of roses, with a strangely scruffy-looking black dog at her side.

The painting had hung there as long as any of them could remember but even after almost thirty years, Stephen had refused to name the woman or speak about the painting, and the great mystery had become something of a joke between them all. As he always did, Stephen demurred now by walking over to the silver coffee urn to pour himself another cup.

"Well, I don't see why you leave the ol' girl out here to taunt all of us if you never mean to talk about her," Helen said, her lower lip forming a little mock pout.

Quentin Marsh, tall, elegant, and English, with a clipped snowy beard as compensation for his baldness, stepped in smoothly. "That's simple enough," he said. "This room has the most wonderful light in the entire house coming in from the bay window. She really does look magnificent in here."

"Have you called your publisher yet?" Barry asked Stephen, changing the subject.

"Not yet. I wanted to get your take on them first."

"He'll be beside himself," Barry offered. "He's been after you to start writing again for how many years?"

"I wasn't ready before now."

"What changed, do you think?" Helen asked him.

"I don't know."

"Who the hell cares?" Barry chuckled. "The master is back!"

The truth was that Stephen had intentionally waited during the past four years. And after his recent reading at the Bull & Bear, he had intentionally begun again. Writing awakened in him all kinds of shadowy emotions involving the past. The outpouring of those first few years had made him famous and rich. It had also drained him. The remembering, the calling up of enough of the past to commit to paper, had been an exhausting search, and he had needed a break.

As it was, on several occasions this past week, he had found himself remembering very vividly, little things about when he and Isabelle were young. Before he'd taken his vows. Before Glenfinnan. He thought about her cool, even-toned voice. About her unshakable determination. And even about her body, beautiful, slim and lithe, with sheer apricot skin as fine as French silk. As he had written "Remembering Love," the title poem, the images had turned and turned in his mind from the most harmless moments of their child-hood together, to the most tumultuous fragments of what had begun between them in Scotland.

But it was the eighteen-year-old Isabelle immortalized over his sideboard in pastel oils and framed in a delicate gold filigree frame that he liked most to remember. As he dropped a lump of sugar into his coffee, Stephen glanced up at the image. He so loved that painting because the artist he'd com-missioned had captured Isabelle's essence, even from a faded black-and-white photograph. Her fragile side mixed with that incredible determination.

If Maureen Donnelly had only known what that photo-graph she'd given her son before he'd left San Francisco would come to mean to him. How he'd kept it beneath his pillow in those tormented years after Scotland. Before he'd given up the priesthood. Before he'd given Isabelle up entirely to Frank Wescott . . .

"Oh, Stephen, do listen to us, would you, when we're extolling your virtues," Helen said with a chuckle.

Quentin smiled as he settled his wineglass back down on the ivory lace tablecloth. "It goes completely against him. Understatement is a great virtue to the master. Just read his poetry!"

Ordinarily there would have been a snappy comeback. But Stephen hadn't heard anything they'd been saying. For a moment, the memories and images had completely taken him over.

Suddenly, he noticed Helen glancing out the dining room window that fronted Grayson Street. She was craning her neck to see something beyond the long lace curtains. "Do you believe it, she's still there," she said with a note of surprise, turning back to her husband and Quentin.

"Who?" Stephen asked.

"Well, if you'd heard a word I'd said this past quarter of an hour," she said with a grin, "you would know that there is a lovely dark-haired young woman who's been standing down on the street the entire time, looking very much as if she's trying to gather up the courage to knock on your door."

"Well?" asked Helen. "Do you know who she is?"

Stephen came away from the dining room window feeling as if he'd been struck suddenly, and very hard. He wouldn't have known her had it not been for her eyes, as brilliantly blue as his own, and suddenly, after all these years of wishing and hoping, she had finally come here. He sank into his chair unable for the shock of it to think what to do.

Taking one look at the way the blood had drained from Stephen's face, Quentin rose and went over to the window. He couldn't be certain, but he thought she looked very like the little girl in the photograph his dear old friend had kept all these years, the one he snapped himself in Coatbridge. Stephen's daughter.

"How about if we three take a nice long stroll to work off that lovely meal?" Quentin suggested, coming back to the table.

"I don't want to walk. Exercise is not a-tall good for the effects on a perfectly splendid bottle of Beaujolais," Barry said, leaning back comfortably in his chair.

"Dear, I don't believe that was a request Quentin was making."

Husband and wife exchanged a glance. "Oh."

Barry lifted himself from the chair and helped his wife with her sweater as Quentin looked back at Stephen. "Will you be all right?" he asked in a low voice.

"If she's who I think she is," he struggled to take a breath, "I'm not certain I will ever be all right again."

"Come," said Quentin. "We'll leave through the kitchen."

Stephen went slowly to the front door, then stood there motionless and waited for her to knock. Outside the open dining room window he could hear a sparrow trilling in the elm tree that would be shading the house so elegantly in another couple of months. He tried to think about those simple things to keep his mind and heart from spinning completely out of control.

A soft knock on the front door finally pierced the silence. It was so soft that he might not have heard it had he not been standing so close. Expecting it. He pulled the heavy oak door as his heart crashed into his chest, and looked out on a face he knew as well as Isabelle's, as well as his own. She looked so much like her mother that he could not quite catch his breath. Not the hair, perhaps, nor the eyes. But she was so much like Isabelle in the other ways that struck him first, that he felt as if he were moving back across time. Back to San Francisco.

"Stephen Donnelly?" she asked tentatively, not yet recognizing the face of the man who stood before her.

"Yes."

"I'm—"

"I know who you are, child," he breathed. "It's been a long time, Glenna Rose," Stephen said haltingly.

"Then you," Glenna paused as her voice caught in her throat, ". . . ye know who I am?"

"Yes. And I believe you know who *I* am," Stephen said, struggling not to falter or to give away in an instant what she might not yet know. She would have to tell him, or ask him, what she needed to, in her own time. "Won't you please come in?"

He closed the door behind her, and the house was very still again. They were standing in the shadowy foyer, all dark and paneled oak, as awkward with one another as children. Stephen had to fight with himself not to encircle her in his arms and pull her to him. Sensing this, Glenna took a step backward in her best navy coat dress and matching low-heeled pumps. She was holding her small Ferragamo hand-bag very close to her chest.

"You took a very long time in taking me up on my offer."

"Your offer?"

"The one I made to you when you were a little girl."

"So then it *was* you."

"Perhaps we'd be more comfortable in here," he said and he led her into his study, not wanting her to feel as formal or awkward as she might in his parlor.

"Please sit down," he said when she made no move to do so on her own. He could see that she was very nervous, this tension between them was making her quiver. "Might I offer you a cup of coffee? Or perhaps you prefer tea."

"I'd rather know if ye're my father," she said so directly that he was knocked off balance as firmly as if she'd struck him. How like Isabelle that was, he thought. She could cut so cleanly to the heart of the matter. His skin turned to goose-flesh, but he ignored it.

"Yes, I am," Stephen said.

Glenna blanched. "'Twas a grand mistake comin' here."

"Please! Don't go. . . ."

She stood there before him in a room that was dark and foreign. Glenna felt as if she had broken into a thousand tiny fragments of memory and pain, like the little glass chips in a kaleidoscope. Connected by time, yet separate. Images. Words. Missed chances. Moments in time. *'Tis for your own good. . . . Spare the rod and the child shall be spoiled. . . .* Two voices. Two fathers. *I'd like you to think you have a friend out there in the world, Glenna. . . .* She bolted toward the door. "I should not have come."

Glenna had almost reached the front door when he called out, "When we met so long ago, I truly believed that you were happy with the Fergusons."

She stopped and stood frozen in the small windowless foyer with her back still to him. His hand was pressed against his heart. "I swear it's true, Glenna. I had no idea at the time that it was anything more than typical childishness that had made you run away. But I gave you a way to reach me just in case I was wrong."

"Andrew Ferguson burned the card!"

"Oh, Lord."

She whirled around, her eyes lit by the wave of fury that had risen up from her soul, mixing with betrayal. "And what was your excuse for not claimin' me when I was born?"

Stephen stood in the aftermath of her question, shoulders slack, unable to give her what she wanted in a one- or two-line answer. "Life just isn't as simple as you'd like me to make it for you, Glenna."

"I'm no' askin' for simple. I'm askin' for the truth!"

"The truth is that I wasn't there for you or for your mother. I was a fool, and it cost me both of you!"

Your mother. The words somehow connected them all in a way for which Glenna wasn't prepared. Hot blood rushed into her face. She tried to steady herself, but all of her instincts told her to turn around, run, and never look back. For once in her life, her dear sweet Aengus had been wrong. Pursuing the past had been a dreadful idea.

The tall clock in the foyer chimed, shattering the stillness. "Now, will you stay a while and talk to me?" he asked her. "We've already come this far. Please, Glenna."

She still wanted to run, but something stopped her. Something beyond her control was happening. "I will stay," she finally said in a tremulous voice as she turned back to face him, "for one cup of tea."

"I can ask for no more than that."

Stephen's study was a small cozy room, she thought as she looked around. Two walls were lined with rich walnut book-cases and another wall was covered in a masculine tartan wallpaper. The window beside it was leaded, filtering a muted stream of sunlight that came in and cast white diamonds onto a big red leather easy chair. She drew near. Beside it was a small oak side table with two small photographs, each framed in silver. She flinched, recognizing the image in one of the frames.

It was a photograph of herself as a child with a tentative, awkward smile, dressed in pigtails and a pinafore, leaning against a shiny gray Bentley. *My God! He actually kept it all of these years? Not tucked away in some dusty photo album to be taken out when nostalgia got the better of him, but here, prominently, on a table in the center of his home!*

Her hardened heart began to soften slightly. The choking anger abated. Glenna felt as if she could almost breathe again. She picked up the photograph and stared at a miserable, frightened little girl who, that day, had tried very hard to smile. Glenna remembered her. Grieved for her still.

She set the frame back in its spot and saw the other photograph, also framed in silver, beside it. It was the image of two men with their arms around one another. The one with snowy white hair was much older than the other. Both of them were smiling broadly. *Priests*, she thought with a little burst of shock, recognizing the Mass vestments of one and the cassock and surplice of the other.

And then she recognized a face. *My God, My God! It cannot possibly be!* One man had changed a great deal, but there was no mistaking it. It was Stephen Donnelly, her father.

Glenna heard a roaring in her ears and once again her heart was crashing against her chest as if something had frightened her. She struggled to read the inscription.

> To my dearest Stephen, on your ordination day to the sacred priesthood. May you be as happy in your calling as I have been in mine.
>
> > with great love and pride
> > Father Keough

It was only then that she noticed, in a kind of haze of surprise, the other things dotting the room. Religious things. A large leather-bound Bible was on the small coffee table beside the red leather sofa, a lovely gold communion chalice on one of the bookshelves beneath a silver light, and a large wooden crucifix pressed against the tartan wallpaper. And then, a silver award on a black pedestal: *To Stephen Drake, Poet of an Age, 1979.*

She was holding the photograph, trembling, when he came back with the tea tray. One look and he knew what she had seen.

"Who are ye, really, then?" Glenna forced out the words as she looked into his searching blue eyes, eyes that mirrored her own.

Stephen set the tray down and then looked at her directly. *She wants the truth. She deserves the truth,* he thought. *After a lifetime on her own, now it is the best that I can give her.* "My name is Stephen Donnelly. I write under the pseudonym of Stephen Drake."

"You *are* him, then?"

"Yes."

She took a shaky breath. "And this? How do you explain this?" she asked, pointing to the photograph of him in priestly garb sitting on the side table.

"I think the inscription makes it fairly clear."

"You . . . are a priest, too?"

"I *was* a priest."

Glenna shook her head. "I canno' believe any o' this."

"You wanted the truth, and so now you have it," he said calmly, though inside he felt shattered, facing an expression full of such anger toward him.

"But why? . . . How?"

"Those questions do not come with easy answers. It was a very long time ago and the world was a different place."

"Not so different that I am unable to understand! Ye were a priest, ye got my mother pregnant, and ye left her so that she was forced to give me up!"

"Oh, my dear Glenna," he sighed, feeling the ache of over three decades and the weight of a stone across his heart. "If only it were that simple."

"Then tell me. Ye wanted me to stay, and so I am here. But ye must be after tellin' me how an American man goes from bein' a Catholic priest to becomin' one of Scotland's most famous poets, and gives away a love child in the process."

Stephen had waited for this, wanted this moment for a very long time. And yet now that it was here, he had no idea where to begin. He took a deep breath and tried to collect his thoughts. It was a good question, one he wasn't certain he had ever really answered for himself. Where had it begun, really?

Suddenly the images licked at the corners of his mind like a candle flame and they were new again. He could even hear himself and the shock in his voice. After a moment, he told Glenna the truth—about the chancellor of the diocese in Chicago. About the harsh reprimand, the one that had sent him to Scotland, and headlong toward his fate with Isabelle.

The angry expression on her face had faded after he stopped speaking. "So ye were sent here as punishment for tellin' the truth to a bishop?" Glenna asked as the first part of his story hung in the charged air between them.

"It was what they meant for it to be, I suppose. At the time it was devastating to me. But, looking back, it actually led me to the happiest time of my life."

"Because ye met my mother?"

"No. I knew Isabelle for a good many years before we both came to Scotland."

"Tell me," she softly bid him. "I want to know everything."

"You look surprised," Stephen said as he and Glenna sat now on the floor of his study with a half-empty bottle of Bordeaux and two glasses, the tall clock in the foyer tolling eight and the moon shining in across the polished mahogany and gold mesh bookcases. Beside them were both pairs of their shoes, one a set of navy-colored pumps, the other a set of slightly worn loafers. The whole story was out at last between them.

"Surprised only that ye actually told me all o' that," she said shakily.

He leveled his eyes on hers, those eyes that were so like his own. "You are my daughter, Glenna," he said. "You had a right to know how it was that you came into this world."

"But truthfully . . . I had no idea."

"How could you have?"

"So what ye're tellin' me, is that ye've had a deep, abidin' love for my real mother for most of your life, and even though ye have no' seen her for decades?"

"Yes."

"Then why on earth, in the face of that, did ye become a priest?"

Stephen took a breath. There was not an easy answer, but she deserved one nonetheless. "I suppose it began because I wanted to do something great with my life. To do something heroic, brave, and even difficult. The priesthood was the only thing that seemed hard enough. Total denial of all the passions . . . Rather humorous to admit that now, considering."

"Not humorous," Glenna said kindly. "When ye believed it so dearly once."

"Yes, I did. In the beginning, I believed that I wanted to be a priest because it fulfilled some need I had to do something selfless. The years in seminary were to test me and, if I survived it, I thought I would know it was what God wanted."

"But 'twas no', was it?"

"No. I believe now that I misread His will in that."

"Then the seminary helped ye to do it."

"No, sweet Glenna. I became a priest of my own volition. The misreading and the denial that went along with it were my own."

Glenna shook her head then reached over to stroke the old black dog sleeping across her calves. "This is not at all what I expected to find when I came here."

"I know."

Tears shimmered in her eyes that Glenna didn't want to cry. But it was no use. She was tired and emotionally spent. They fell onto her smooth cheeks in two long ribbons one after another.

"But you—What happened to *you* afterward? I mean, after ye went to claim Isabelle and ye discovered that the Maguires had so cruelly tricked ye, that she was no' in San Francisco like they'd told ye she was?"

"That was a very difficult time for me," Stephen said honestly, and she could see by the way his eyes narrowed slightly, the creases beside them deepening, as if he were pressing back a very sudden pain, that he was telling the truth. "I searched everywhere I could think of, borrowed money from my mother, from my friends . . . but I didn't learn for a good many years afterward that they had only gone and hidden out here in Glasgow. . . . The place where you were born."

Glenna almost couldn't bear to ask. It seemed so horribly wrong, what had happened to all of them. "And when ye finally did find Isabelle again it was too late?"

"Yes. It was too late. By then old Ross Maguire had won. His daughter was well on fate's course, heading her toward her destiny as a senator's wife."

Glenna pressed her face into her hands.

"There, now," Stephen said with a patient smile as he reached out and put a hand on her shoulder. "I didn't open up all of that ancient history to see tears in those beautiful blue eyes."

"I just really wanted to hate you when I came here. But I canno'."

"You mustn't be angry with Isabelle either. She was so young, and, believe me, her father was a very powerful force back then. If you were given up it was because he took you forcibly from her. No other reason than that."

"She wanted to meet me," Glenna confessed, and her voice cracked as she wiped her tears with a trembling index finger.

Stephen's voice rose a notch. "Isabelle knows where you are?"

"She sent a private detective to find me. He came to Arrochar with a handwritten letter from her. . . . but I told him to tell her a meeting was impossible."

His next words were a statement, not a question, but there wasn't the slightest hint of malice or reproach in it. "You believed it had been her choice to give you up."

"Aye. But my daughter did want to meet her, and so I . . . Oh—" She stopped speaking and looked up at him, her expression more open, eyes wide. "I have no' had time to tell ye with everythin' else, but ye have a granddaughter as well."

"Katherine Mary," he said calmly.

Glenna's lips parted in plain surprise. "Ye know about Katie?"

"Since this appears to be a day for confessions, yes," Stephen said. "Once I realized what a mistake I'd made, assuming you were happy back then, and the price we both paid for that, I stayed in Glasgow and promised myself I'd always be nearby if you or Aengus or Kate should ever need anything."

Glenna sank back onto her heels. "Ye were spyin' on me?"

"Not exactly. I have a gentleman who has been with me for years—his name is Quentin. He made several trips to Arrochar over the years and got to know the shopkeepers there. It's such a small town, it really didn't take much more than that."

He had been determined to tell her everything. How, after he had lost Isabelle for good, after she was married, he had taken an offer to study in Rome, extended to him while he'd been on the Ignatian retreat in Glasgow. So embittered had he been in those hazy days of pain and loss that he had gone to Italy intent on using God in the same way he believed he had been used. Stephen had known that there was a power-ful Vatican network in Rome, and he meant to use it to help him locate their child.

It had been difficult. In 1959, adoptions were even more

closed than they were now. But, as the saying went, he told her, all roads lead to Rome. And for one relentless American priest, they did. He made friends and connections there, all of which led him to Coatbridge. And finally to Glenna.

"I do believe I need another glass o' that wine," she said, exhaling a breath of air, like someone who'd just been hit very hard and was struggling to regain her footing.

"Not without some food."

"I'm no' really very hungry."

"We've been at all of this reminiscence business for hours," he said, his smile broadening, "and I'm quite starved. Won't you agree to indulge me at least by having a bite of something?"

Glenna followed him grudgingly out of the study, through the foyer and into the dining room that led to the kitchen. The sun was still setting through the tall windows and casting an explosion of gold and crimson against the wall. The light drew her eyes. Glenna stopped and looked up at the portrait that was highlighted now in a shimmer of filtered gold. Stephen was halfway through the swinging door when he saw her looking up at it.

"Is that her?"

Stephen came back and stood beside her, both of them gazing up at the image of the carefree young woman, caught in a moment in time, who bound them together from half a world away. "Yes," he said a little sadly. "That is Isabelle." He was silent for a moment as he looked up at the painting. "You know, I've never admitted that, nor spoken her name, to anyone here before. Oh, I'm sure Quentin assumed who she was, but he never asked. It just always seemed like my private little piece of her if I didn't tell anyone. I never felt I wanted to share that."

Glenna looked at him, a little surprised. "But ye chose not to hang it somewhere more private, like in your bedroom?"

"It may sound strange, or impossibly old-fashioned, but it just wouldn't have felt right to me. Not when she was another man's wife."

Glenna looked back up at the painting. "She certainly was beautiful."

"Yes, she was. And still is. . . . I've followed the events of her life as Mrs. Wescott through newspaper accounts over the years," he added haltingly.

Glenna sank back against the dining table still littered with teacups and cake plates from the luncheon, transfixed by the image of the stranger who was her mother. "This is all so curious," she said. "These connections . . . Ye knowin' all about me all o' these years . . . Me findin' out about ye just when Isabelle is tryin' to find me . . . Ye no' bein' the priest she once knew but *the* Stephen Drake . . ." Glenna turned to look at him. "Ye know, my daughter, my Katie, she went into Glasgow to hear ye read. The two o' ye were actually in the same room together not long ago."

Stephen's mind vaulted swiftly back to that evening, to the Bull & Bear, so crushed with denim and leather-clad students from the university who worshipped him almost like some sort of cult figure. His mind reassembled the room, thickly blue with cigarette smoke and laughter, and he remembered that one out-of-her-element face staring at him through the blue light.

"I saw her."

"Who?"

"Kate. I knew there was something, some spark, about her at the time. I just had no idea—" His words fell away and it was a moment before he could recapture his voice. "She's a lovely young woman, Glenna."

"Aye, on the outside. But she's a real firebrand if ye're lookin' a bit deeper."

They were gazing at one another through a pale pink light, touched with gold. It was a light growing dimmer by the moment as the sun set beyond the rest of the lovely houses all in an orderly row on the Landsdowne Crescent. It had begun to cast the room now in grays and shadows. "Isabelle's family always thought she was like that. Wild. Unpredictable. But, really, she was only curious about the world."

"It does sound like they'd have a fair bit in common, the two o' them."

Stephen smiled and studied her for a moment. "You know, I actually think you would feel that way yourself if you met. You have certainly got Isabelle's spirit."

She waited a moment. "Then ye think *I* am like her in some ways?"

"I think it runs through the three of you. You're small and delicate on the outside. Yet all three of you, it seems, have that grand, wonderfully strong core."

Glenna smiled at that. Then she followed him through a large butler's pantry and into the kitchen. It was a huge old-fashioned room with a big wooden butcher's block in the center, a mammoth old iron stove with copper pots hanging above it. Stephen fished in the cavernous refrigerator, extracting dish after dish covered over with plastic.

As he warmed some soup on the stove for her and poured her another glass of wine from a new bottle, he made himself a sandwich. Glenna watched, leaning against the butcher's block.

"Do ye ever wish ye could just see her again?"

Stephen looked up from the loaf of bread he had brought from a bin on the gray marble counter. She could see that the question had caught him by surprise. But he did not shrink from it. "With every sunrise that has come since Glenfinnan," he said with a sad smile.

"Then why don't you go to her, now that she's widowed?"

"Time is the greatest barrier there is, Glenna."

Thinking suddenly of Mitch, she said, "I would have said it was fear of the unknown."

Stephen set down the bread and picked up his wineglass. Why didn't wine ever seem to affect a person, he wondered, when you really needed it? He looked at her thoughtfully before he answered.

"Perhaps you're right. . . . To this day she doesn't know that her father sent me on a wild-goose chase back to San Francisco when she was pregnant so that he could spirit her away. She's had decades to think that I intentionally abandoned her, you, and any sense of duty I had to you both."

"But you told me you did finally find her *before* she married the senator. Why didn't you pull her aside and tell her the truth then?"

Why, indeed?

It had become the great question of Stephen Donnelly's life. There wasn't a day that he hadn't regretted what had happened to them. How God and circumstance had seemed to conspire to keep them apart. Not a day that he didn't regret having tried to be so damned noble when he'd finally found her back in San Francisco . . . on her wedding day.

What a shock that had been. Ross Maguire, that old bastard, had certainly worked with great speed. It wasn't even six full months after giving birth to one man's child that his daughter was set to stand at the altar with another. Stephen still remembered the wild elation he felt when his mother told him that, yes, Isabelle was there in San Francisco. It was all going to work out, he had thought with relief. He was finally going to be able to tell her that he was leaving the priesthood, as he should have told her back in Glenfinnan.

He had made mistakes, but it was all going to work out now. He wasn't meant to devote his life to God in that way. No, the Lord had put Isabelle in his path, and made them love one another so desperately, to show him that he could serve Him in another way. As husband and father. As a man who had truly come to know himself.

And then from so great a height, that horrific fall, like being dropped from an airplane without a parachute, when his mother had so happily told him how thrilled and amazed they all were that dear sweet Isabelle had actually landed the handsome young California congressman, Frank Wescott.

They were sitting at that white Formica kitchen table, each with a cup of coffee, and he realized that his mother had no idea at all what had happened in Scotland. The Maguires had kept their dark family secret from her after they'd all returned, and he knew then that they probably meant to go on doing that forever.

He had shivered in the silent aftermath of her happy news as the steam from the coffee coiled up and out of their cups. "Isn't that wonderful, Stephen? I've always said, if anyone deserves a marvelous life, it's dear little Isabelle. And she's grown into such a beauty. . . . Stephen, are you listening to me?"

"I'm sorry," he told her in a flat voice, the only one he could manage. "I guess I'm still just tired from the flight. It's a long way back from Scotland."

Maureen fixed her eyes on her son. "Is that all it really is?"

One heartbeat. Then two. "Of course."

"Well, good then. I, for one, am so glad you're home. And how curiously wonderful that you got here today of all days. The dear Lord certainly does work in mysterious ways. Oh, and I'm sure Isabelle would want you to come to the wedding if she'd known you were going to be home in time. In fact, it's a shame you can't perform the ceremony for them. Wouldn't that have been splendid?" she asked, beaming with that blissfully ignorant and trusting expression that could cut him to the core if he looked at her too long.

Lord, he felt sick. Like someone had pelted him in the stomach and then struck him, with the same force, over the head. He was dizzy, disoriented. Trying to think. It was all happening too fast. Just when he'd found Isabelle again, when he'd made his peace, he was about to lose her. This time for good. All he could think about was finding her and stealing her away. So he could explain how her father had connived to keep them apart.

How glad he was that Ross and Sunny Maguire both made it a practice not to set foot in the very plebeian domain of the kitchen. He was safe in here, at least for a while.

"Where is she, Mother?"

"Isabelle? Well, she's off getting ready for the big event by now, I expect. From what I understand, the congressman rented her a grand suite at one of the hotels so that she'd have a chance, this morning, to spend time with all of his family before the wedding. I heard Mrs. Maguire say last night that there are some of them in from Boston, New York, and even one uncle I think all the way from Paris."

"Which hotel?" He couldn't help it. Stephen's voice was very flat. He felt as if the very fragile hold he had on his emotions was about to be severed.

"Oh, Lord, I don't remember now. One of the fancy ones, of course."

"Think, Mother, can't you remember the name?"

"Leave her alone, Stephen."

The bitter twist in Alice's controlled voice came across the kitchen like a wave. Stephen and Maureen both looked up to see her standing there in her pale blue tea-length maid-of-honor gown and her dyed-to-match shoes.

"Would you leave us alone for a few minutes, Mother?" he asked as he stood and faced Alice, who was still standing in the arch of the kitchen door that led back into the dining room.

"Stephen," Maureen said, looking at her son, then over at Alice. A small frown of concern had begun to mar the soft roundness of her face. "What's going on here?"

"Please," he said in that same toneless voice. "Do as I ask."

When Maureen had gone out of the kitchen, Alice closed the door and then moved nearer. "You've got one hell of a lot of nerve showing up here now."

"You don't know the whole story, Alice."

She laughed at that. "I think I know enough, don't you? You came close to ruining my sister's life. How dare you come here, today of all days?"

"There's just a lot you don't know. A lot that is unfinished between us. You've got to tell me where she is."

"I don't have to do anything for you, Stephen." Her eyes were glistening with anger. "In fact, I'd say you're damn lucky I don't toss you out of this house myself. And the only reason I don't is that I respect your mother too much. Poor Maureen doesn't deserve the sort of heartache it would bring her to know the truth."

"You know, Alice," he said evenly. "I'd never taken you for someone who would judge without knowing all of the facts."

"And I'd never taken you, *Father Donnelly*, for someone who would seduce a childhood friend." Then her voice dropped a notch and suddenly held more pleading than bitterness as they looked at one another. "Let her go, Stephen. For God's sake, let her find some little bit of happiness now after all that you've put her through."

The tension crackled between them. It was a standoff. No matter what he said now by way of explanation, Alice was not about to tell him where Isabelle was, and he couldn't press his mother without arousing more suspicion. If he was going to find her, he was going to have to do it himself.

And he had done just that. Like a madman, he had gone from one of San Francisco's fine hotels to the next, The Fairmont, the St. Francis, then the Clift, all in hopes of finding Isabelle before it was too late. Stephen remembered it like it was yesterday, pulling into the circular drive of the Mark Hopkins, dashing from the old Nash his mother had kept for him, with the engine still running. If only he'd been wearing his Roman collar, perhaps then they wouldn't have been so reticent to tell a wild-eyed, desperate-looking young man whether or not a certain young woman was actually a guest there.

After trying the fourth hotel, the last elegant one in the city, he had sunk onto the curb out in front, slump-shouldered, beneath a sky pillowed with thick, steely rain clouds, and surrendered his face to his hands. It was impossible. The only thing left for him to do would be to go to the church, make a scene as she walked down the aisle and stop her marriage to a man she couldn't possibly love.

That was what he had intended even as he sprinted up the steps, through a fine mist of rain, to Saint Francis of Assisi, with the strains of the wedding march beginning just beyond the tall oak doors. Isabelle, he was thinking, couldn't possibly go through with it.

And then he opened the doors, slipped into the back of the church, and saw her. She was like an angel, he thought, all in white satin with her long veil trimmed in Belgian lace, as she took Frank Wescott's hand at the altar. Then both of them knelt solemnly and lowered their heads. And suddenly he knew he simply couldn't do it. If this was that little bit of happiness for her that Alice had said it was, who was he to snatch it away by coming back now? Now that their child was lost to them.

How could Isabelle ever look at him and not be reminded of that?

It all went racing through his mind in that excruciating split second when he had to speak or forever hold his peace. What sort of life could he offer a girl who had been raised with the best of everything? And he, about to become a former priest with no job and no money—and an excruciating memory to be reminded of every day of her life. Frank Wescott, on the other hand, was on the threshold of becoming a United States senator who could give her the world. He could also give her a fresh start.

Stephen had to let her go, he had decided as tears stung his eyes, then slowly rolled down his cheeks. *For Isabelle's sake. I must do this for her.* She deserved the best life had to offer, and he was never going to be able to give that to her.

"Good-bye, my heart," he had whispered to himself as Frank, so elegant in his expensive gray morning suit, the sun streaming in across his tan square face, had slipped the gold band onto her finger. As Stephen's heart tore in two. "Have the wonderfully rich life you deserve. That is the greatest gift my love can give to you."

And it all could have been yesterday for how much it still hurt to remember that day. Why hadn't he told Isabelle the truth? Glenna had asked. Why, indeed? Their daughter, that precious woman who would forever link them, was now standing in his kitchen, the question still suspended taut and thick between them.

"There is a passage in Corinthians," Stephen said softly.

"'Love is patient and kind; love is not jealous or boastful. . . . Love does not insist on its own way.' Do you know it?"

"'Love bears all things, believes all things, hopes all things, endures all things,'" she continued it. "Yes, I remember it well."

She watched the bright light in his eyes seem to dim a little with all of the recollections. "The answer to your question is that I couldn't tell Isabelle the truth that day because I loved her that much."

"And you still do."

"And I always will," Stephen said.

CHAPTER

II

❧ Stephen

He sat motionless, stony-faced, shoulders sagging, in his mahogany and red leather study. The sun was just rising, coming through the bank of windows in a flood of bold dusky rose and yellow light. But he didn't see it. As he had been for hours, Stephen was holding an empty coffee mug, gazing off at nothing. Seeing everything.

Isabelle. Glenfinnan. His life. That Victorian house on Nob Hill in which they had both grown up, she as the master's daughter, he as the housekeeper's son. Talking with Glenna had called up so much. Too much.

But that had been the risk, hadn't it, when he had agreed to open up a vein, and tell Glenna everything. And all of it had begun before last night anyway, hadn't it? Like a skein of yarn so intricately winding through his life—the evening at the Bull & Bear, with Kate, his own granddaughter, there listening to him—that had really begun bringing things back.

What great irony that it should have taken place at that particular spot, as a favor to his dearest friend. Barry, the man who had helped to bring about his new identity all those years ago, had played host to a granddaughter Stephen hadn't even recognized.

There was certainly no other way he would have agreed to an evening like that any longer, other than for Barry. Publicity and glad-handing wasn't what his poetry was about. Stephen despised the commercialism of tours and signings. But the intimate aspects, the reaction he got at a reading, he did very much enjoy. It was like food for a poet. According to Barry, the receipts had been good, too. The best in a year, his friend had said. And it had been nice to read the old poems again. The ones that had made him famous. The ones that had come from his heart. *His pain, and his heart.*

They were the same poems Barry had first heard one late night, a rainy awful night, the two of them alone in the back room of the Bull & Bear, amid crates of Glenlivet, long after Barry had closed the place. After coffee and Scotch, and then coffee again, Stephen had been drunk enough to read aloud one of the poems he carried with him in a satchel. "The Darkness of My Soul" was the first thing he had written after losing Isabelle. When Stephen had looked up from the final line, no one could have been more shocked to see tears in the old Bear's eyes.

"Ye've a God-given talent with that stuff, Donnelly. Ye've no choice but to share it. That's all there is to that." It had been a declaration, entirely nonnegotiable, as he mopped his wet gray eyes with a balled white handkerchief then blew his big red bulb of a nose.

"I can't put my name to it. It's too personal. . . . It would be a betrayal."

"Then change your name, man! A pen name. I know a lad over in the West End whose brother publishes experimental fiction and poetry."

Stephen had not been all that certain if it was the Glenlivet, the lateness of the hour, or sincerity talking. But he had still been too surprised by Barry's reaction to argue the point. That was due in part to the fact that Isabelle had once told him the very same thing about his poems—before he'd made that greatest of mistakes. And so it had begun.

Shortly afterward, Barry had put him in touch with the right people. More accurately, the Bear had become like a sledgehammer pounding the two parties together, artist and publisher, until the two actually began to fit. And through it all, Barry had let Stephen Donnelly crash in that same back room for over a month when there was no other place in the world for him to go. As he had slowly, inevitably, become Stephen Drake.

But even with the first taste of success, those had been dark days. Stephen had suffered it in a kind of haze of self-loathing and regret. That was also the year he had finally let go of Isabelle for good, having come back from Rome after using the Vatican network to help him find Glenna.

Quentin Marsh melted into the room just then, as if from the shadows, in a pale blue shirt, gray sweater vest, and slim gray slacks. "Good morning, sir."

"Hmm," Stephen replied wearily.

"So then. Do you want to talk about it?" Quentin asked in the silvery smooth voice that at times could be like music.

"Not yet, old friend. But soon."

"Well, in the meantime, you look as if you could do with a bit more of that coffee. At least let me fetch you some that's fresh."

Suddenly, Stephen was tired. So very tired. "Believe it or not, I finally think I can sleep for a while. I haven't actually even been to bed yet, I've been running on so much adrenaline. . . ."

"Tell me this at least, Stephen." Quentin's voice was low. "Was it her?"

They both knew he meant Glenna. "Yes."

"I'm glad for you then, no matter how it went. You deserved to see her again."

"No, Quentin. I *deserve* nothing. Last night was a gift."

Quentin smiled, but Stephen did not see it since he had laid his head back against the crimson leather and was closing his eyes. "Call if you need anything."

Stephen had foolishly wondered often before last night if Isabelle ever thought of their child through the years, or if she had ever tried to find her. Isabelle had gone on to have such an incredibly full and busy life. And she had other children. Three sons. One now, like his father, a U.S. senator. The *International Herald Tribune* had run stories about the philanthropic daughter of the late Ross Maguire and how her charm and determination had helped her husband, then their son, win their hotly contested Senate races.

It was so like Isabelle, that stalwart faith she put in those she loved. *All* those she loved. He wondered now, this morning, how he could ever have doubted the depth of what she must have felt for their daughter or the pain she must have endured at losing her.

As Stephen's mind began to give way to sleep, he could see her as she had been, so young and full of fire, with that tumble of rich copper hair. Her voice came at him swiftly, that sweet reedy soprano, as it had been the day he left San Francisco for the priesthood, full of such faith. The day when he'd chosen God over Isabelle . . . And oh, what a price he'd paid since then for listening to neither.

You were a great altar boy, Stephen, you were. You were the best-looking boy I ever saw dressed in a robe. But in your heart you're not a priest. You're a poet. You write the most beautiful poems. . . . You know it's all you've ever wanted to be. . . ."

"Damn." He gnarled a fist and pressed it into the arm of his chair, seeing her, feeling her as vividly as if it had been yesterday. "Why didn't I listen to the one person in the world who knew me better back then than I even knew myself?"

And even after all of the years, it had taken the sum of his strength not to go to her when he had first read she had been widowed. He had read the details of the senator's funeral: Isabelle in an appropriate black Chanel suit and a simple black pillbox hat with a slight veil, surrounded by her three sons. And her sister, Alice Hart, a woman he knew well. The funeral photograph the paper had printed had been useless, grainy and out of focus. Isabelle had appeared indecipherable, nothing more than a woman in black. Like any woman. Any widow. *Oh, but she was so much more than that.*

He couldn't help it. Stephen's mind had drifted out again on a sea of memories and images, setting sail for the possibility now before him. Now that Isabelle was free. Was it a sign? Could it be that the dear Lord should deign to look down favorably on him in this at last? Even after Stephen had betrayed him.

After he had betrayed Isabelle.

No. He knew it was still the only answer. No matter what Isabelle's circumstances had become, his actions all those years ago would forever be an impenetrable wall between them. How could she ever look at him and not see the child she'd given up?

"But, oh, my love," he murmured, "even so, the years have changed nothing inside of my heart."

His favorite poet, Christina Rossetti, once had written the words, *Come to me . . . in the speaking silence of a dream. . . .* Stephen remembered that now, now that he was tired, and he wanted just to sleep. To dream. And more than anything, he wanted to remember the little piece of heaven he had found, so fleetingly, that April with Isabelle . . . in that paradise to which he had never returned. Where the soft rush of the heather, tossed by the Highland breeze, echoed through his mind still, a heady, sweet song. In a green and lovely place called Glenfinnan.

CHAPTER

12

⬦❯ Isabelle and Mitch

In all, Isabelle left him waiting in her flower-filled parlor, with its Baccarat crystal vases brimming with freesias and long-stemmed white roses, for precisely ten minutes. During her own careful dressing ritual, she had decided to wear yellow because she looked the most vigorous in it. Her Yves Saint Laurent with the butter yellow jacket and matching skirt usually made her feel wonderful. Still, she was nervous about this meeting.

Mitchell Greyson was standing at the bay window with his back to her when she came in. He did not hear her at first, and she saw only his silhouette in the pale morning sun. Finally, hearing her, he turned around.

He was very handsome, tanned and fit. But he was very—how would Frank have said it? Western. A Texan. A cowboy. Albeit a prosperous one. That he was, from his turquoise and silver belt buckle to the black alligator boots. And in total, he was quite different from what she had expected.

"Mrs. Wescott," he said in a slow, deep drawl. Isabelle regained her composure. Moved forward, her hand extended politely, her chin lifted to the perfectly dignified tilt.

"I'm Mitch Greyson. Nathan said you'd asked to see me."

"A doctor who makes house calls. How ancient and lovely."

"I don't practice medicine anymore, Mrs. Wescott," he said with a smile, clearly surprised that she knew that important bit of truth about him. "I'm sure Nathan told you that, too."

"Yes, he did. I'm sorry, Dr. Greyson."

"And I'd just as soon you called me Mitch."

242

When he smiled, Isabelle noticed his teeth were white and straight. His smile lit his eyes, and she thought that he could have been one of those male models instead of someone trained to save lives or console wealthy widows. Nathan had only told her a bit about Mitch Greyson's background (and a guarded bit it had been) because just before she had signed the contract, Isabelle hadn't been certain she could trust a stranger with an errand so personal.

"So noted," she said.

She sank onto the sofa and he sat down beside her. Isabelle drew in a breath and tried to steel herself for the reason she had asked him to come. "You are the one who has seen her, then."

"Yes, ma'am. I've met your daughter."

She could not steady her heart. She wanted to. Tried to. But this was all really too much. Someone who had been so close, who had actually gazed upon that same beautiful face that had been torn away from her so many years ago. Isabelle clasped her hands together tightly as the memories and feelings skittered around inside her. She wanted, *needed* to do this.

"You may find me a foolish old woman, but somehow I thought that speaking with the man who had actually been able to see her, be with her, would be a comfort somehow."

"I'll tell you whatever I can."

"Tell me your impressions." Isabelle drew in another breath. She was still trembling. "For example, did you like her?"

Mitch swallowed hard. He had not expected that, nor how awkward he felt in answering. "Why, yes, ma'am, actually, I liked her quite a lot."

"What stood out to you the most?"

He shifted. The words came slowly at first, and with a hint of hesitation. "Well. She seemed to have a real strong sense of herself. Determination, I'd guess. Somethin' real deep down. Oh, and wit. She's clever with a phrase." He drew in a breath and ran a hand behind his neck, seeing Glenna in his mind, those few stolen moments between them, remembering the impossibility of what he had felt. "I liked that about her an awful lot."

"Yes, wit is a lovely quality in a young woman." Isabelle's smile was strained by her heart. "Did she seem happy? In her life, I mean? Did it look like a nice life she has now?"

"Scotland is a splendid country, Ma'am."

"Yes, it is at that."

"And Arrochar seemed a charmin' enough village. I really couldn't tell you about the rest, I'm afraid." Mitch had lied about that because somehow it seemed too personal. Something had happened between them. A spark of something that never could have happened if she had been completely happy in the life she had chosen. In the man she had chosen. But today was not about that. This long-awaited moment was about Isabelle and giving her something, anything, to go on now that she had lost a child for good.

"She's a very beautiful woman now," Mitch offered, hoping to give her some bit of that peace. "And I had the strong impression that she was as beautiful inside as out," he added.

Isabelle stood very suddenly and Mitch could see that perhaps she hadn't been quite as prepared to hear about Glenna as she thought she'd been. He could also see that their meeting was over. "I hope I haven't wasted too much of your time, asking you to come here."

He was still smiling, those lovely deep brown eyes rooted on her. "My daddy says that meetin' someone splendid is always worth the journey, Mrs. Wescott."

She nodded, feeling surprisingly gentle toward this doctor, this man who had laid eyes on her firstborn child. But she found it difficult at that moment to speak.

"Well, I expect I'll be goin', then."

"It means a great deal, your having come here."

What pain and disappointment there was in those words, he thought sadly, in spite of the perfectly proper delivery, because he had been able to give her so little. Mitch stood before her then and, almost as an afterthought, drew something from the inside pocket of his jacket. "I don't know if this'll be a comfort or not to you, ma'am. I really wouldn't want to make things worse, but I have a photograph of her, of your daughter. It's yours if you'd like."

He watched her fingers tremble as she reached out to take it. But Isabelle didn't look down at it. Perhaps, like his own thoughts of Glenna, this was simply too private for her to share here and now, with a stranger. There were tears pooled in her eyes when she looked up at him. "Thank you," she whispered.

"Will you be okay, ma'am?" he asked.

Isabelle straightened, struggling he thought to keep her dignity. "Yes. I think so, Dr. Greyson—Mitch—in time."

"Maybe you should get away for a while. Take a trip somewhere to get your bearings."

"My sister believes I need a trip to the country, to sit and listen to the clock tick, and watch her grapes grow."

He smiled again. A chuckle nearly escaped him as he leaned forward slightly. "And what do you believe you need, Mrs. Wescott?"

"I thought for a great many years that it was finding my daughter that I needed above all else. Now things are less certain."

"Maybe a few days at your sister's vineyard would be a nice compromise."

Isabelle felt herself softening further still in spite of the barrier her wounded heart had erected.

There was a small pause between them as Isabelle studied his kind face. "You're a nice young man."

His grin was lopsided. It might have seemed almost sly if he weren't so incredibly handsome. "That surprises you, does it?"

"What I mean is, I don't care for the kind of people doctors are, in general."

"Come to think of it," Mitch said, "neither do I."

"Medical school and the brutal training they endure seems to leach some of the humanity out of so many of them. But your patients really lost something special when you decided not to practice any longer," she said sincerely. "Tell me, Mitch, why did you chose to deprive them like that?"

"Oh, Mrs. Wescott, life is always so much more fun with a little mystery."

Isabelle's smile now was genuine. "Let me guess. Your daddy said that too."

"No, ma'am. Those happen to be my own words."

She walked with him out into the foyer and to the front door. "If you wouldn't think it was too forward of me, Mrs. Wescott, perhaps I could drop back by sometime. See how you're gettin' along."

Meaning it, she said, "That would be my great pleasure."

He smiled again, his rich brown eyes glinted at her above a smile that said he knew he could have the world by the tail, just for the asking. "I aim to make it a plan, then," Mitch said.

As Isabelle walked him to the front door and they said their good-byes, a long black limousine pulled up to the grand Victorian mansion and stopped. A moment later, a stout, uniformed driver withdrew and ran around to open the back door. As Mitch walked past he glanced inside, and there was no mistaking it. He had met her only briefly, but she had made an impression on him. Perhaps because of who she was. The passenger coming to see Isabelle Wescott, and a million miles from home, was Glenna's daughter, Kate.

CHAPTER
13

⬦ Kate and Isabelle

Kate peered out through the open limousine door and could not quite seem to catch her breath. Nervously, she smoothed her hair back from her face toward the herringbone clip that held it neatly at the nape of her neck. *This* was where Isabelle Wescott lived? Heaven above! This entire thing was all becoming like some sort of dream.

The driver held her elbow to help her out of the car, but after that she was on her own. She walked slowly up the stone steps, through a lush front garden, in her best blue-and-green plaid skirt, crisp white blouse, and navy blazer, to the black wrought-iron gate. A rush of fear mixed with anticipation shook her. Her heart was beating so forcefully that she could hear nothing else. *Don't be so foolish,* she told herself. *She wants ye to be here. She told ye to call her Isabelle. She sent a driver.*

It didn't make it any easier. The urge to turn around and run all the way back to the Fairmont Hotel was enormous. And then she saw the grand black lacquered front door standing open and a woman emerging. Kate was certain that it was her grandmother and that from this moment on there would be no turning back. Isabelle stood several steps above her in her smart yellow suit.

"Welcome," she said genuinely as Kate reached the top step, her heart now thundering in her ears.

"Thanks."

Isabelle extended her hand. Kate took it. Her own was shaking. For a moment, as they looked at one another, she felt how strange it was and yet how familiar. Bloodlines connected them. The direction their lives had taken did not. She recognized the strongly angled chin. The high cheekbones. A nose that was small and straight. They were all her mother's. The build as well. Small. Thin. Almost too thin. It was so startling to see these familiar features in a woman she had only just met. And then, as her mind whirled, Kate reminded herself. This was actually her grandmother.

"How was your flight?"

"Long," Kate said truthfully.

"Well, let's go inside, shall we?" Isabelle asked after a moment, and they both turned and moved into a foyer that very quickly took Kate's breath away.

She had never been in a house like this. Old and grand, all full of polished wood and crystal. A large glittering chandelier above them caught the light from the still-open door. The fragrance from a huge bouquet of freesias and white roses filled the house with sweet perfume.

"You look as if you could use a cup of tea," Isabelle said.

"'Twould be lovely," Kate replied gratefully as she followed her into the drawing room, which lay straight ahead beyond a curved arch. She could see even from the foyer that it was a cozy room to which she was being led, rather than something formidable. There were fat chintz-covered sofas, mahogany tables polished to a soft, warm glow, and topped with family photos in silver frames. The monstrous roaring in her ears quieted. Her heart slowed.

"I had no idea ye lived so grandly," Kate said as Isabelle poured two cups of tea from a silver urn that had already been set on the small rosewood table between the two sofas.

"It was my husband's home when I married him. A gift from his parents. I consider myself fortunate to have spent a great many happy years here."

Her husband, Kate thought as she took the tea cup and tried to drink from it without shaking. A man who, in all likelihood, was not her grandfather. There were so many questions that pushed at her like impatient children, ones she fought to keep silent. There would be time for that.

"Are you hungry?" Isabelle said, sounding suddenly a little

on edge herself. "May I offer you a pastry?" She indicated a little china plate filled with lovely things that under any other circumstances, Kate would have relished devouring. But just now she couldn't have eaten a bite if her life depended upon it.

"No, thanks."

The sudden silence which followed was strained. Kate heard a tall clock ticking away, a power lawnmower nearby. The far-off sound of a dog barking. And then, through it, she could hear her own heart again. What she wanted to say, the questions she wanted to ask, she knew her grandmother couldn't possibly be ready to answer.

"So, you live in Arrochar," Isabelle said, slicing into their discomfort. "I would much prefer hearing what *your* home is like."

"Well," she said thoughtfully, as she lifted the delicate china cup, "I've lived there all o' my life. My ma's made it nice enough, but it's much smaller, o' course . . . nothin' a-tall like this."

Isabelle's smile paled slightly when she felt a spark of guilt and then that irrepressible longing again. But then she would always feel that, wouldn't she? That lifelong anger at herself for all that her sons had. For all that her daughter had missed.

As if sensing Isabelle's discomfort, Kate set down her cup and met her grandmother's gaze directly. "My ma's quite content there in Arrochar, I'd not be meanin' to imply otherwise. 'Tis quite a small town. But she fancies that. She has her medical practice and all of her friends. And my father, of course. . . ."

Isabelle leaned forward, her posture impeccable, her hands clasped in her lap. "I find that there is so much I want to ask you, so much I want to know, but I don't want to push this. I want you to feel comfortable. And for now, I just want you to know how happy I am that you're here."

"Thanks. And ye can ask me what ye like. In exchange, I hope I'll be able to ask a few things myself."

"I don't expect that will be easy for either of us."

"No. But I suppose we both know I did no' come all the way from Scotland expectin' 'twould be easy."

Isabelle's tentative smile broadened. "You're a very lovely young woman, Kate."

"Well, ye might like to know that my mother does no' look like me a-tall. She actually looks quite like *you*. And everyone in Arrochar has always called her quite a beauty."

"That is lovely to hear." Still, Isabelle settled back against the chair, her face paling slightly. She hadn't expected to hear that. It was like a reward that Glenna should resemble her. A reward she did not deserve.

And of course she did not need to ask for the rest because, thanks to Mr. Greyson's photograph, she now had the answer for herself. Glenna had Stephen's dark hair, his exquisite blue eyes. The bittersweet shock of that, even now, still had not quite let her go.

"I'm sorry, Douglas," Willa firmly announced to the slim, copper-haired young man in jeans and a leather jacket standing before her, "but your mother has a guest in there with her just now and asked not to be disturbed."

"What do you mean, 'a guest'? We're late for our lunch reservation as it is."

Isabelle's youngest son, Douglas, dressed down as usual for their weekly lunch, stood in the foyer facing drawing room doors that surprisingly were closed to him. His mother's housekeeper stood like a huge unmoving rock before them, with her eyeglasses dangling from a chain around her neck and a dust cloth in her hand.

"Oh, don't tell me she's forgotten again, Willa."

"I'm afraid it does look that way, sir. She's had me see to brunch for two here today. I just assumed that you had rearranged your own outing with her."

"This is getting serious," Douglas said, taking a long, slightly uneven breath. "She forgot our standing lunch last week too. Well, who's she with? Do I know him?"

"Her, sir. It's a young woman she's with, but I'm afraid I wasn't introduced when she arrived. Pretty, though, and it sounded as if she had an accent."

"What do you mean, an accent?"

"Like from another country, sir. From what little I heard, she sounded Scottish."

"Are ye all right, Isabelle?" Kate asked when Isabelle continued to sit without speaking for several moments.

Glenna's connection to her father had, for an instant, felt quite like her undoing. But Isabelle Wescott excelled at keeping up appearances. "Yes, I'm fine, my dear. This is all just so difficult to comprehend somehow, you sitting here with me . . . my granddaughter . . . Glenna's own child."

Kate smiled. "I'm glad I'm here, too. I just wish my ma had come with me. I think she would have liked ye, in spite of—" She averted her eyes and did not finish her sentence.

"It's all right to talk about it, Kate. It's simply the truth, you know, what your mother feels for me. And I dare say, after all of these years, she has every right in the world to be angry and hurt."

"She believes that ye abandoned her."

"I suppose in a way I really did."

"But ye did no' want to. I canno' believe *that*."

"No, you're right," Isabelle said in an even tone, trying hard to ignore the sharp stab of guilt she always felt acknowledging that. "I didn't want to. But times were very different then. It is no excuse, mind you, but I was very young, and there were a great many factors working against my finding your mother afterward."

"I read the letter ye wrote to her. I hope ye do no' mind."

"No," Isabelle said softly, as she tried to smile. "I don't mind."

"You wrote that ye'd never stopped thinkin' about her all o' these years."

"Not for a moment."

"But ye've had other children since."

"It doesn't lessen what you feel for each of them, Kate . . . and your mother was very special to me because she was my first." *And because she was Stephen's child. . . .*

"The driver told me that your husband, I suppose he'd be my grandfather, right? That he was a famous politician here, but that he died a few weeks ago. I'm sorry I never got a chance to meet him, as well."

"Oh, my dear Kate," Isabelle sighed. "I too am sorry. He was a wonderful man. But I suppose you have a right to know that Frank Wescott was not your grandfather. That, however, is part of a very long story."

"I'd like to hear it, if ye'd be willin' to tell me."

Oh, I wonder, thought Isabelle weakly, *do I have the strength just now for a confession like that?*

His eyes twinkled, and an irrepressible little smirk crossed his face.

Douglas Wescott reached out and put an arm around Willa. Her body felt to him like a big downy pillow, so soft and warm and round. "Now you know, my dear old girl, that I'm going into that room to see my mother, don't you? And you aren't going to stop me."

"I can tell you only what she told me, Douglas. That she asked not to be disturbed. If you mean to go against that, I'll not be able to stop you."

"If it makes you feel any better," he chuckled as he gently waltzed her away from the door, "I'm sure she was thinking of my brothers when she made that particular pronouncement."

"Suit yourself," she said as he turned the handle.

Douglas found his mother sitting on one of her chintz-covered sofas facing a young girl whom he had never seen before. She wasn't beautiful in the classical sense, with that shock of copper hair and the smattering of freckles over milk white skin, but there was something about her that was striking, he thought. Actually, she looked just the slightest bit like him.

He moved forward quickly with a smile while Willa lingered at the half-open door. "Now what is all of this about you forgetting our luncheon again?"

Isabelle and Kate both moved quickly to their feet, but his mother's expression was the one that caught him. Her lips were parted, and her complexion was suddenly pale, as if she had been caught doing something, if not illegal, then at least terribly naughty. "I can see it did absolutely no good at all to say that I did not wish to be disturbed."

"Well, since I'm in, are we not to be introduced?" he said, quirking a little half smile.

In response, Kate looked at Isabelle. "Hi," he said, extending his hand. "I'm Douglas. Mrs. Wescott's youngest son. Her lunch date for today."

In spite of herself, Kate smiled at the sight of him in his chicly battered dark brown bomber jacket, faded jeans, and worn Gucci loafers. His nose and cheeks were pink from the morning air, and his unruly hair looked as if it hadn't been combed since yesterday.

"I'm sorry, darling," Isabelle said as her son and granddaughter shook hands, "I completely forgot that it was Wednesday."

"This must have been awfully important for you to have forgotten a meal with your favorite son."

"Douglas, this is Kate McDowell," his mother said in a curious tone that suddenly chilled him. He knew by the sound of her voice that this was not just any visitor.

His smile, in spite of that, was wide and welcoming. "Scottish, right?"

"Aye."

He looked back at Isabelle. "Your family owned a house in Scotland, didn't they, Mother?"

"Yes."

"What a coincidence." But even as he said it, Douglas could see that it was far more than that.

"It's not a coincidence, Douglas," Isabelle confirmed, and he could hear a tremble in her normal sturdy tone. "Kate is my granddaughter, Douglas. . . . She is also your niece."

"You're kidding, right?" he gulped, unable to hide his surprise behind any sort of tone of decorum. "You're not kidding."

"The truth is often difficult, darling." Her tone was as calm and measured as she could make it under the circumstances. "But I had a child before your brother Arthur. She was born in Scotland and was given up for adoption there. Kate is her child."

Douglas sank into a wing-back chair as Kate and Isabelle sat back down tentatively on the opposing chintz-covered sofas with the tea table between. No one said anything at all for several moments. "Who knows about this?"

"You're the first."

"Well, Dad must have known, right?"

"No, he didn't know, Douglas."

"My God, you kept a secret like that all of these years?"

"I didn't believe I had any choice. Your father's career was very important to him, and in the early years, he was working very hard to make a success of it. If he'd known about my child, and what she meant to me, he would have wanted to help me find her, and back then that would have destroyed his career."

Douglas ran a hand through his hair, trying to make sense of what he was hearing. "So Dad wasn't her father."

"No."

"Then who was?"

Isabelle exhaled a measured breath, looking a bit like a doe caught in the cross of someone's headlights. "I'd rather talk about your sister for a little while first, if you wouldn't mind. Kate here had just begun to tell me what a fine woman she'd become."

"A sister," he said just as the realization hit him. "I have a sister."

"My ma's name is Glenna," Kate tentatively offered when she saw just how startled he appeared.

"But why isn't *she* here, then? Isn't it usually the children who look for their birth parents?"

"It was my search, Douglas," Isabelle said.

"My ma's no' quite ready to come here. But I plan to tell her how kind and generous Isabelle has been, as soon as I go home."

Douglas crossed one knee over the other and shook his head. "I'm sorry for staring, but God, it's just such a shock."

"I know, darling, and I'm sorry about that. But I didn't feel that I could talk about it before now. You understand that, don't you?"

"I'm just really sorry you had to carry a burden like that by yourself all these years."

"Glenna, I think, has carried a good deal more."

Kate lowered her eyes for a moment when Douglas looked over at her. "Might ye tell me where I could freshen up a wee bit?" she said, and they all knew that she meant to give them a few moments alone.

After she was gone, Douglas sat down beside his mother. Tenderly, he took up her hand and pressed it to his lips. "Are you all right?"

"Truthfully, this has been the most difficult thing I've ever endured in my life, and I honestly might not have had the courage to go through with it if she hadn't come here."

"Hey now, gorgeous," he said with a sedate smile and that softly reassuring voice of his, as he held her hand. "I don't believe that for a moment. You're the most courageous woman I know."

"Once upon a time, that wasn't the case. No matter the excuses I could rely upon, I lost that young woman's mother. It was my fault. And the fate I set her toward, is something that I am only now beginning to imagine."

"Would I have known who her father was?"

"Do you remember Aunt Alice and I telling you about the young man, the housekeeper's son, who grew up in our house?"

"Yeah, Stephen, right? The one who went off to become a—" He leveled his pale green eyes on her, those eyes she so loved and trusted. "Mother, you can't mean her father was actually a Catholic priest?"

He could see that his question had hit her with the precision of a dart, and, in the face of that, he did not need to hear her reply. Douglas took one breath, and then another. *Please let me earn the trust she's had in me today, whatever it is that makes me so different from my brothers Colin and Arthur,* he was thinking. *Please let me soften what I say to her. . . .*

"You must have loved him an awful lot."

"He was my world for a very long time."

"What happened?"

"I always thought he would find me after I left Glenfinnan. But he never did."

She made it sound so simple now, but he knew that it had to have been anything but that. "Did he know there was a child?"

"He knew."

Kate returned at that moment and sat back down tentatively on the opposite sofa. "The two of you have a great deal to discuss," she said. "Perhaps I should just—"

"Now that you're here, don't go," Isabelle said quickly. "Not yet."

"No, please don't leave on my account, either," Douglas said, smiling. "After all, it appears that I suddenly have a new niece to get to know."

"'Tis generous to say, Mr. Wescott."

"My father was Mr. Wescott. My brother, Arthur, was the one to take over that mantle as soon as it became available," he said, smirking. "But I'd like very much if you would call me Douglas."

Kate nodded and gave him a small, careful smile. They didn't hear him come in just then, but as he slammed the door behind himself, everyone glanced up to see Arthur standing in the middle of the parlor, clearly drunk. His pale face looked stricken, as if he'd just received the worst piece of news in his life.

"Well, speak of the devil," Douglas said wryly.

"So, this is her, isn't it?" Arthur slurred as everyone came to their feet.

Isabelle's eldest son glared at Kate. His eyes were clear, cold, and gray. His face was handsome in a classic, business-man's sort of way, but overall it was a bit too bloated, which seemed to age him. Arthur was also balding prematurely, with only a little taupe-colored peninsula of hair remaining in front. But he didn't mind the loss, because it reminded people more of his father, especially the voters.

"Arthur, you're drunk," Isabelle declared with a scowl.

"Rip-roaring, as a matter of fact. It was the only way I could actually come here and face you after what I've found out." He moved slowly toward Kate, openly surveying her. "So you're the bastard's daughter."

"Arthur!" Isabelle gasped.

"Come on, Artie, there's no need to be—"

"Shut up, Douglas. You don't have a clue what's going on here."

"I know exactly what's going on here, and I at least have the good sense to act like an adult about it."

Arthur ignored his brother and turned his attention once again to Kate. "So you've come all the way from Scotland to meet my mother, have you?"

"Arthur Wescott, this is really quite enough!" Isabelle charged.

"Oh, Mother, no it's not. I haven't even begun to say what I came here to say. How could you hide something like this from your own family?"

"I don't know what you think you know, but—"

"I know everything, Mother. I've had your phone and Douglas's tapped since Dad died."

"Arthur Elliot Wescott!"

"I needed to make sure neither of you did anything to make yourselves a liability to me in the next election. So I know about your bastard child in Scotland. I know that now her daughter here thinks there might be something in it for her, you the widow of a famous politician, and so she's come halfway around the world to get what she believes she deserves!"

"Arthur, I am not going to stand here in my own home and listen to this a moment longer!" Isabelle said angrily. "You were not invited and you are not welcome now!"

"Oh, so now it's *my* fault simply because I've discovered your lies?"

"No. Now it is your fault for being so unbelievably boorish and cruel that, at this moment, I am ashamed to call you my son!"

Just then, Willa poked her head past the parlor doors. "Is there a problem, Mrs. Wescott?"

"My son here was just leaving, Willa. In the event that he has forgotten his way out as quickly as he has forgotten his manners, perhaps he could use a bit of guidance now in finding the door."

"Yes, ma'am."

"So, this is it?" he snarled. "*I* am to be cast out like bad company for discovering *your* sins?"

"No, Arthur. You are leaving because, quite honestly, I am ashamed of you. A mother's heart would like to attribute your behavior to the liberal amounts of alcohol you appear to have consumed, and to make allowances for that. If you wish to come back tomorrow, I will be glad to hear you out privately and to answer all of your questions then."

"We are going to talk about it *now!*"

"That is not going to happen, Artie," Douglas said calmly. "Go home and sleep it off."

"All of my life, I have respected you," he slurred again, a discordant flurry of tears suddenly filling his eyes. "You were always something fine and special. A person above reproach. Someone to look up to."

"Well, then, I am sorry to have disappointed you, Arthur," Isabelle said evenly. "I always tried to be a good mother. And I certainly tried to be a good wife. But, in the end, I suppose I was never really anything more than human. Nothing more than any of us."

◆　　　　　◆　　　　　◆

Isabelle lay alone in her bed against fresh white sheets, exhausted. It had been a difficult day, facing old demons and confronting a new granddaughter. Kate McDowell was lovely, with a spark of fire, everything a young woman should be. As weary as she felt, Isabelle wouldn't have changed their meeting. It was the dream of a lifetime. Part of one, anyway.

Arthur—well, Arthur had become his father's son. A junior senator now, he was as sure of himself and as smooth with a phrase as water on glass. Politics had fit him like a glove from the first. She understood Arthur because she was his mother, after all. But of her three sons, she felt the least connected to him. He had been her first child after Scotland, and she had not felt ready to be a mother. But she was a wife; compliance was a part of marriage. Motherhood was to follow like day after night, no matter how her heart still ached. Arthur had not been so much wanted as inevitable.

And she had not been the best mother to him. She blamed herself for that. He had leaned toward his father out of self-preservation. So much alike, they had naturally become close. So perhaps his fate would have befallen him anyway. But still, Isabelle had played her part in the downfall of her son's character. She knew that the secret she had carried would be almost impossible for a son like Arthur to ever fully understand.

Colin, her middle son, was in Paris and came home so rarely these days that he seemed almost a stranger to her. In many ways, she had asked for that from all of her sons. But Douglas, her youngest, the boy who called her "gorgeous" and meant it, surprisingly, was her greatest consolation now. Douglas, a child conceived at a time when she was so actively looking for her daughter and had secretly prayed that such "gifts from God" were behind her. Her body was tired even by then with the ones she had borne before him. So was her spirit for the nurturing he required.

Poor boy, with his pale copper hair, so like her own, and that sweet child's face, he had suffered too. Poor, sensitive boy, the bane of his tormented mother's young life. As if sensing her disinterest, needing her love all the more because there was less of it, he had become the willful son of the senator and his wife. Their embarrassment. Constantly in trouble by the age of ten, how Douglas had made it to this ripe old age (still a baby, really) and in one piece, no one was quite certain. Other than perhaps his friendship with Philip Danforth.

Friendship, she thought, rolling the euphemism around in her mind for only a moment, then releasing it like a captive bird. She had never been unable to think of it as anything more than something proper and completely respectable between the two young men. Her Douglas was sensitive. He had never gotten on particularly well with girls. It was natural. Expected. These friendships with men.

They went to lunch, they laughed and drank too much wine, the three of them, she and Douglas and his friend, Philip. They went shopping. Even to the theater. Of course she was lying to herself, and she knew it. But it was easier, somehow, she had decided, than the alternative. Whatever it was between them, and from time to time she still prayed God it really was only friendship, Philip Danforth had given her youngest son a welcome confidence. He had settled down. Lost the anger that had once been directed so vehemently at his father, a father in whose eyes he could never quite measure up.

Quite to her surprise, in the end, Douglas had become her favorite son. He was full of more zest, more life, than the other two, and with his adolescent trials behind him, she could see now that he was quite intent on living life to the fullest. And these days she adored his company.

Before he had gone home earlier, Douglas had embraced her heartily, kissed each of her cheeks and asked her if she would really be all right left alone. After she had assured him, Isabelle had studied him for a moment. "Thank you for being so kind to Kate today, darling," she had said.

"She's a sweet girl."

"Yes, I think so too. This all has to be very unsettling for her."

"And for you."

She had tried to put off his concern with a winsome smile. "I'm an old woman accustomed to dealing with life's rocky roads."

"That doesn't mean you can't use a soft shoulder and a willing ear from time to time."

They had embraced then, and Douglas had left the house assured that his mother was up to the recollections and explanations that they both knew lay ahead.

There was a soft rapping at her door that like a fine gold cord brought Isabelle's thoughts away from her son and back around to the moment. Kate poked her head around the half-open door. "Might I come in for a moment?"

"Please."

She moved tentatively into Isabelle's bedroom and sat on the very smallest corner of the bed when she was motioned to do so. Her hands lay softly clasped in her lap.

"I came to see how ye were."

"It has been a long day, my dear," Isabelle sighed, smiling. "Especially considering my eldest son's very convincing impression of Attila the Hun."

Kate laughed at that. They both laughed, and Isabelle took her hand and then squeezed it very tightly in her own. "I'm glad you wanted to see me."

Her voice went suddenly low and soft. "Ye're bein' so kind to me."

"That really should not come as much of a surprise, my dear Kate. You *are*, after all, my granddaughter."

There was the slightest pause as they looked at one another before Kate asked, "Will it be all right with your Arthur, do ye think?"

Isabelle smiled again and put her arm around Kate, bringing her close as she would have liked to have been able to do when she was a child. Surprisingly, Kate did not tense or pull away. There was something strangely natural about it for them both. A desire for the closeness that fate had denied them. "I suppose tomorrow I shall have to deal with both

Arthur and my middle son, Colin. I'm quite certain they will be plotting my punishment within the week."

"Your punishment?"

"They are my sons, and I love them," she said evenly. "But there are times now that I don't *like* either of them terribly much. But you didn't come up here tonight about that, did you, dear Kate?"

"I thought ye might fancy someone to talk with."

"About the past?"

"About whatever ye like."

"But you want to know what happened, don't you? It is why you have come all this way. To find out some small bit about your roots."

"I want to know about you."

"I've been dredging it all up so often lately," Isabelle sighed. "It hasn't been easy."

"My ma says that confession is good for the soul."

"And no one has more right to the truth than you and your mother."

Isabelle took a deep breath and lay her head back against the pillows, ready at last to tell the story, ready to hear herself speak Stephen's name, use the words to describe him, and what had happened to them, for the first time in so many years. There was safety here with her. Talking about Glenna. Kate's own mother . . . And Isabelle was glad that it was to beautiful Kate that she would speak them. *My sweet, sweet grandchild.*

Glenna picked up the phone in her hotel room, expecting it to be Stephen. They were meeting for breakfast and she was already late. But it wasn't Stephen. "Mitch Greyson rang me from back in the States," Aengus said.

Glenna sank onto the edge of the bed and felt suddenly breathless. Or panicked. Something foreign and unsettling was in the back of her throat. She had no idea what he would say next nor what she would say in return. The word came in a whisper. "Oh?"

"He's seen Katie."

Glenna gripped the phone hard. She had not expected that. "*Our* Katie?"

"He wanted us to know that she's safe but that she's in San Francisco."

"San Francisco?"

"Glenna love, she's with Isabelle Wescott."

Café Gondolfi, the Glasgow institution on Albion Street, wasn't fancy, but it was the best place for breakfast near the university, and it was within walking distance of Stephen's house on the Landsdowne Crescent. When they arrived, the place was filled with patrons and the aromas of coffee, cigarettes, pipe tobacco, and fresh newsprint. All around them, stuffed into wooden booths and a sprinkling of tables, were rumpled professors in their corduroy jackets and plaids, along with shaggy-haired graduate students and their textbooks, chattering, laughing, and drinking cups of thick, dark espresso. The clatter of plates and cups brought the sounds to a crescendo as they watched a couple leave and then moved toward their empty booth near the back.

A few minutes later, a waitress brought a pot of tea for Glenna and a whiskey coffee for Stephen, then, smiling like a schoolgirl herself, told them she'd be back to take their breakfast order. Glenna's gaze wandered to the table beside them. The couple was staring at them. A young woman in the booth beyond was whispering to her girlfriend and pointing.

"These people know who you are."

"It's just because it's the university crowd," Stephen said modestly, taking a sip of his drink. "I read near here not long ago."

"'Tis a wee bit more'n that. Ye'd think they were lookin' at a movie star or somethin'."

He leaned back in the booth, unfazed by the attention he was drawing. "I'd really rather talk about you, why you came back so early this morning. Let's say now it's your turn for confessions."

Glenna shifted, took a sip of tea and then settled her cup back in the saucer. "I was awake all night thinking about things. And I still canno' quite believe I'd come to feel this way, but I woke up actually thinkin' I'd like to see her after all."

"Give her a chance, Glenna. You'll not be sorry."

"I got a call this morning that Kate, my daughter Kate, has beat me to it."

"She's run away to San Francisco?"

"Apparently so."

Stephen's smile was slow and warm. "She certainly has her grandmother's spirit."

"Now I really do have to have this confrontation, I suppose, and go retrieve my child."

"Yes, I suppose now you do."

"Will you come with me?"

Even though he'd known it was coming, the question still hit him with a little smack, and he needed to take a breath to steady himself before he answered. "It's been too long."

"Was it no' Isabelle herself who once told ye to pay heed first to your heart?"

"Bright girl. You listen well."

She smiled back at him. "'Twas the story o' my own life. I heard every word."

"I don't know that she'd want to see me after all of this time."

Glenna's grin was suddenly lopsided. "Now ye don't truly believe that, do ye?"

"I know I hurt her deeply, not coming for her once I knew about the pregnancy."

"They say time heals all wounds. And ye did have a damned good reason."

"As quick with a retort as Ross Maguire ever thought of being," Stephen said, chuckling softly. "He'd have been pleased with a granddaughter like you."

"If only I had no' been his daughter's bastard."

The harshness of those words settled slowly as they were interrupted by a pretty young woman with long cocoa-colored hair standing beside the table in blue jeans and a black leather jacket. Her face was plain and freckled, and her lips were parted as she held up a book to Stephen. "Are ye no' Stephen Drake?" she asked with a quivering, high-pitched voice.

"I am."

She held out the book which, after a moment, he could see was a worn, leather-bound volume of his poetry. "I'm sorry to bother you, sir, but I was wonderin' . . . I've read every one of your poems. . . . I was hopin' that ye wouldn't mind signin' this for me."

Stephen smiled kindly at the girl, obviously a student, and took the book and pen from her trembling hands. "It would be my pleasure. What's your name?"

"Helen, sir, Mr. Drake."

Stephen wrote an inscription thoughtfully and neatly and then handed her back the book.

"Nothin' in the world has ever moved me like your words, Mr. Drake. I heard ye at the Bull & Bear when ye read there, and I've been filled with their meanin' every since."

"I'm glad they've touched you."

"My ma loves them too."

"You're kind to say so."

"I was wonderin', sir, 'tis been a long while. . . . Will ye be writin' anythin' new?"

"As a matter of fact, I've just recently completed a new collection of poems. I think you'll be able to find it sometime early next year."

Her face lit like a Fourth of July sparkler. "I'll be first in line! Thank ye, Mr. Drake. Thank ye indeed."

Glenna was smiling as the girl backed away from the table. "How long has it been since your last collection was published?"

"Almost four years." *Since the last time there was a major story and a photograph in the press about Isabelle and my heart and life were filled to brimming with memories and images of her.*

"What made you begin writing this time?"

"I'm not sure. Age. And nostalgia, maybe."

"And recollections about Isabelle?"

"There will always be that."

"Will ye no' at least think about coming to California with me? That way we could spend some more time together. And since my Katie is already there, it would give the two of you a chance to get to know one another, as well."

"What about Aengus?"

"His sister is with him. They're very close. But I do need to go home and check on him first, though. And to explain things."

"Do you suppose he'll want you to go that far?"

Glenna smiled, missing him. "He's the one who kept insistin' I find out the truth. Ye might say that my dear husband is the one who led me to you."

"Wise man." Stephen smiled.

"I owe him my life." And she meant that so deeply, no matter how her heart had betrayed her with her feelings for Mitch Greyson. "So will ye come with me?"

"I swore if I had the chance again, I'd never deny you anything. But this is one thing I can't give you, Glenna," Stephen said sadly. "I'm sorry, but I just can't."

CHAPTER

14

❦ Alice

Isabelle was surprised how glad she was to see Mitch the next day. She felt connected to him; he seemed to her to have somehow wound himself into the fabric of her new relationship with Kate, and even to Glenna.

And Mitch felt something for them. She was wise enough and old enough to have seen that in the first tentative moments of their meeting. What she had also seen, and what surprised her even more, was that so handsome and self-assured a man was hiding something profound. She wondered why he wasn't a doctor anymore. Why he had cut off that part of his life. But she knew only too well about secrets, and respecting them.

Isabelle was in the garden, clipping the dead beige leaves from her plants and tossing them into a wicker basket across her arm when she first saw Mitch Greyson again. She waved as he came up the stone steps in front of the house, and to the left of the small side garden, with strides that were youthful and full of purpose.

Isabelle stuffed the small gardening shears back in the pocket of her camel-hair cape as they came together beneath the same slate-colored, cloudless afternoon sky. She smiled up at him as if he were an old family friend.

"A mite cold today for gardenin', isn't it, Mrs. Wescott?"

"Never. Fresh air is the most marvelous tonic. Don't they teach you young people anything meaningful at those great and grand medical schools?"

"Not much about how to live a life, I'm afraid," he replied, smiling back at her, opening the iron gate, and coming across the small gravel path to the place where she was standing

267

among the clematis and the lavender. "Only how to save everybody else's. And, at that, they're not always so successful."

What an odd thing to say, Isabelle thought as she looked at him. He was wearing jeans again, a plain white shirt, tan corduroy blazer and those impressive Tony Lama boots. And she remembered more fully how handsome he was. Daylight made his hair look shinier, the color of fresh butterscotch.

"Is that so?" she smiled. "And where precisely did you say that abomination was allowed to take place?"

"I earned my medical degree at Harvard, ma'am."

"That's a very good school," she said, allowing herself to sound impressed.

"Yes, it is."

"But it is a terribly long way from Houston."

"A whole lot further than you can imagine," he said, and for the first time she heard his voice change distinctly. Those words were more serious, even a bit sad. And then it changed again when he added, "But San Francisco is home at the moment, and I'm right pleased about that."

"So tell me, Mitch: Why would such a young man leave his hometown and his family and come here alone?"

He hedged at the question, and Isabelle saw that it had made him uneasy. "Oh, I expect there are a lot of reasons."

"There are usually only two that matter to most men."

Her knowing tone made him smile. "And what might those be?"

"Women and grand secrets. Not necessarily in that order."

"It was both," he said, more directly than she had expected.

"I do like that honesty of yours."

She touched his hand briefly. Naturally. Then drew away again. He smiled too. "Well, ma'am, the feelin' is mutual."

They strolled like that up the second flight of stone steps that led into the house. Isabelle handed her cape and scarf to Willa, who was waiting at the door, her plump face full of suspicion. Disregarding that, Isabelle led Mitch into the salon.

They sat down on one of the sofas that faced the same grand piano on which Douglas had taken lessons and Frank had played so many Christmas carols. There was such history in this house. In this room.

"You know, I do believe you're lookin' better today," he said appraisingly.

"There is a certain strange peace in *knowing*."

"I'll hafta remember that."

A sudden silence fell as they smiled at one another. Mitch glanced at a small table beside the sofa, covered with photographs in expensive silver frames. The pictures were all of her three sons as boys. There was one in which all three of them, in adolescence, were standing in a park somewhere. Then three separate smaller images of each of them as very young children. They were the photographs she enjoyed most; remembering them as young innocents.

"Are these your other children?"

"Yes."

"Handsome boys," he smiled picking up the frame which bore the image of them together.

"Yes, they were. And they have become handsome men."

He set the frame back down, careful to settle it into precisely the same place.

It was another moment before Isabelle realized that Kate had come down the staircase toward them and that Mitch was staring quite openly at her as she drew near. "Mitch Greyson, may I present Kate McDowell, my granddaughter. She's here from Scotland for a bit of a vacation."

He extended his hand to her and smiled, but Isabelle could see something curiously strained between them. "It's a pleasure to see you again, Miss McDowell," he said, and Isabelle heard his voice change. It was still that smooth, sweet Texas drawl, but now there was something subtle, a tiny hitch in it. She looked at one of them, then the other.

"Ah, yes," Isabelle said. There was a moment's pause along with the realization. "You, my dear Kate, were there the day Mitch went to see your mother about me," Isabelle said a little sadly.

"Aye."

She looked at each of them again. But there was something more than that. Something had happened back in Arrochar. Hadn't she already known that? Before Isabelle could make sense of it, Willa came into the room.

"Have you forgotten your rescheduled luncheon appointment with Douglas and Philip is at noon, Mrs. Wescott?"

"Thank you, Willa. I suppose I did again, and they won't be pleased about it."

"Well, I do believe I'll be takin' that as my cue. But I did want to stop by and see how you were gettin' on."

Mitch stood, wanting suddenly to tell Kate that she had frightened her mother to death. Wanting to tell her that Glenna deserved better for the sacrifices she had lived through and that he had taken it upon himself to tell Glenna where her daughter had gone. But he held his tongue. No matter what he felt for Glenna, it was not his place. This was not his family.

"You know, Mitch, my sister is having a charity event out at her vineyard in the Napa Valley tomorrow afternoon and, since neither you nor Kate know a great many people here in California, perhaps you would consent to come as our escort. I think it would be nice for my granddaughter to see a familiar face besides my own."

Mitch smiled again, that handsome smile. "I'd be honored," he said.

Mitch propped the photograph of Glenna McDowell against the bowl of steadily rotting fruit on his kitchen table and gazed at it as his frozen Mexican dinner went cold. It was the same shot he had given to Isabelle Wescott but for some reason he had not been able to part with the original.

It wasn't that she looked particularly like Livi. But even in a photograph he could see that this woman had her essence. He couldn't believe he'd actually taken it out of the Wescott file at Tremont & Associates late last night. Brazen as a two-bit thief, he had been. But he'd thought of nothing except this face before him for days. Good Lord, now he'd not only spent time in prison, but he was ready for the nut farm as well!

He hadn't been with anyone that way in over two years. Looking back at her photograph, and the way he had obtained it, Mitch wondered if maybe deprivation was clouding his judgment, along with everything else.

Be that as it may, Glenna had such kind eyes. Bright, sunny eyes. The sort that said she could understand a man like him, who had done what he had done. A man who had paid the price he had paid.

"I can't do the surgery, Livi," he'd said. "I'm too close. It would be unethical."

"Then I won't have it."

"You've got to have it!"

"Only if *you* do it."

The memory gripped his heart and spread like long icy fingers. Mitch squeezed his eyes to blot out the sound of her voice. Three years? Or only a moment ago? *Doctor, I'm having a hard time picking up the pressure. . . . Oh damn! Doctor, we're losing her!*

Mitch took another swallow of lukewarm beer and gazed down again at the photograph, trying hard to see Glenna's image and not Livi's lifeless ivory face on that operating table.

She's gone, Dr. Greyson. You gave it your best shot. Let her go. . . . Greyson, for God's sake, she's gone!

He fiercely pushed away the echo and kept his eyes closed until it was gone completely. He hadn't called home once since he'd been paroled. He was just so ashamed. So sorry. Even the thought of hearing his mother's voice had been too hard to contemplate. God, what hopes they'd had for him. . . . What hopes he'd had for himself.

Mitch stared down at the phone, thinking of Glenna McDowell and how she had come into this life with Isabelle Wescott for a mother, a mother as kind and vivacious as his own. And Glenna had never had the benefit of knowing her. All of the things Isabelle had never been able to do for her daughter. The milestones of a child's life, which his own

mother had reveled in: helping him with his football uniform, filling out his college entrance forms so that he could
concentrate on taking Livi to the winter ball.

He picked up the receiver and slowly punched in the number he still knew by heart. It rang twice before he heard her
voice, sweet and thin, with that delicate Texas accent that took
him back to his childhood, and happier days, in a heartbeat.

"Hello?"

"Hi, Mama, it's Mitch."

At first there was nothing but the sound of silence. And
then the weeping.

"Aw, come on, Mama. Don't do that now. I just called . . .
because I wanted to see how you were."

She was sobbing into the phone, trying to speak, but his
mother was entirely incapable of saying a word. She had been
praying for this call since the day he'd walked out of jail.

It was a moment before she passed the phone. "Imogene,"
his father said, with a hand over the receiver, muffling his
words. "Settle yourself, now . . . Okay. Where are you, son?"

"I'm in San Francisco, Dad."

"What in hell ya doin' there, boy? Ya need money, son? Ya
want me to send you a plane ticket home? I can have one to
you in—"

"No, Dad. I don't need any money, thanks."

Mitch hadn't realized how difficult this would actually be.
Hearing both of them had brought back so much. It had
made him feel vulnerable again. Weakness was something he
had thought was impossible after state prison. A place he
never wanted to see again, but one he had not fought going
to. Penance, he had told himself repeatedly.

"I'm good, Dad," he lied when his father asked. "I'm gettin'
on with my life."

"Why don't you come home, Mitchell? Be where your
family is. People who love you instead of out there."

He squeezed his eyes shut again and took another breath.
"I don't think I'm ready for that just yet, Dad."

"Ready, hell!" His big, gruff baritone boomed over the

phone in protest. "All you gotta do is get on the next plane to Houston and I'll meet ya at the airport myself! You can be home in time for Claudetta's biscuits and gravy for breakfast. . . . Please, son. Your mama's missed you. I've missed you."

He took a deep breath, wanting to give them what they wanted. "I can't, Dad. Not yet."

His father's voice, in response, went lower still and Mitch heard it crack. "It wasn't your fault, what happened. You do know that, don't you, son?"

Mitch felt a sudden pain, sandpaper across his heart, and wished suddenly that he hadn't called. He could still hear his mother sobbing in the background, both of his parents knowing he was not yet ready to give them what they wanted and yet unable to accept the reality of that from their only son. "I'm just not ready to come home. It's just somethin' I have to work out for myself."

"Damn it, boy, it was an accident, what happened! Don't you know you paid your debt, if there ever was one?"

"I've gotta go, Dad. I just wanted to let you know I was all right."

"For God's sake, Mitchell, don't you go hangin' up now! Your mama needs to hear your voice again. She's been waitin' so long. You gotta talk to her."

It was a moment before she came back on the phone, and as she did, Mitch could feel her Southern frailty, and that gentility of hers, almost like a vapor through the phone line. She had always had that sort of presence. In a blink of his eyes, she was here with him. Surrounding him. That sweet-smelling honey-colored hair of hers that she always washed with camomile soap. Eyes wide and blue, and trusting. And that heart that was as full of love for him, and all of her children, as the whole state of Texas.

"Are you really all right, son?" she asked tearfully.

"Yes, Mama. Would you believe I actually like California?" he asked, trying to sound light, feeling anything but that. "And I've met some nice folks here."

"But it's not home, Mitch. Ya know that, don't you? I mean, good Lord, you're not plannin' to stay there, are you?"

"I'm not sure what I'm gonna do yet, Mama. At the moment, I'm takin' things one day at a time."

"You paid your debt, son," she said with a voice full of conviction. "Now why don't you just do like your daddy says and come on home? You got your room right here at the ranch and you don't have to see anybody you don't want to. We'll all see to that."

I'm not a boy who can run home to his mama! I've killed a person, the person I held most dear in the world, and I lost my own existence in the bargain! Things can't ever be the same for me . . . not ever again! "Mama, I'm gonna stay here in San Francisco a while to get my bearin's," he said in a measured tone instead. "But this ol' Texas boy's gonna come on back one day when I'm ready. You can bank on that."

"You promise?" she sniffled.

"Come on, Mama. You ever known me to lie to you?"

She chuckled weakly. "No, I never have."

"There, you see?"

"We just miss you so much around here."

It felt like he was suffocating. He couldn't breathe, and all he wanted to do was get off the phone. "I miss you too. Will you say hi to Arlene and Lucie for me?"

"Your sisters are gonna be furious they missed your call."

"I'll call again real soon."

"Give us a number, son, so we can reach you."

"I don't have a phone just now, Mama," he lied again. "I'm callin' from a pay phone at the moment. But I'll call y'all again when I get settled."

"Do you need money, son? If that's the problem, good Lord, let your Daddy wire you somethin'."

"It's not that, Mama. I'm just not settled anywhere yet."

"Are you workin', Mitch? I don't mean at medicine . . . I mean—"

His own voice dropped. "I know what you mean, Mama. I had a job for a while, but it was temporary. . . . Just wasn't my sorta thing. Listen, someone else wants to use the phone here. I gotta go."

"Oh, Mitchell, please don't hang up. Please—"

"I gotta go, Mama. I'll call again soon. Promise. Give everybody a kiss for me, now."

She was crying again. He knew that she wanted to keep him on the line, to hold him to her like she'd done when he was a boy. Pull him to her breast and make everything all right again. But they both knew it was far too late for that. "I love you, son."

"I love you too, Mama."

"Son?" It was his father again. "I just thought you should know that your mama's been goin' out to the cemetery once a week, puttin' fresh flowers on Livi's grave. . . . She thought you'd a wanted that, since you couldn't do it for yourself."

"Thanks for tellin' me, Dad."

Mitch hung up the phone and squeezed his eyes as he held onto the receiver. Thank God he had a party to go to later, or there was no telling what he might have gone and done. He was going out to Alice Hart's vineyard for a fund-raiser. With any luck, he would see Glenna's daughter. A visit with her and a little banter would certainly cheer him up.

Kate liked San Francisco.

It was a world away from the Scottish Highlands, more fast-paced and certainly more crowded. In just over a week, she had delighted in riding the cable cars from Union Square down to Fisherman's Wharf and in seeing the Golden Gate Bridge. She found it all spectacularly beautiful. And Douglas and his friend Philip could not have been kinder, going along with her and Isabelle, pointing out all of the sights, asking questions about her life back in Arrochar and seeming truly interested in the answers she gave.

After that first disastrous encounter, she hadn't seen Arthur again, though it didn't take much to realize that wasn't exactly poor fortune. Instead, the four of them had gone on picnics in that exquisitely beautiful place called Golden Gate Park, gone to the opera (which Kate had never done before), and taken a boat ride across the bay to Sausalito for lunch by the water. This afternoon, they were off to a fund-raiser at a place called Cielo Azul, a vineyard in the Napa Valley owned by Isabelle's sister, Alice, and her husband.

She still didn't know the entire story of her mother's conception and birth, other than that in her youth, Isabelle had fallen in love with a boy of whom her family disapproved, a boy she'd known as a child here in San Francisco. Kate still didn't understand how they had managed to meet up in Glenfinnan, of all places, or what had made him particularly undesirable to the Maguires, but she didn't feel right about pushing. Isabelle had been so generous about everything else. With a little time she was certain that the rest of the story would follow.

A knock at her hotel room door came precisely at four o'clock, and she knew it would be Isabelle. Kate closed her book without finishing the poem she had been reading, and went to answer the door.

"You look lovely," Isabelle said, glancing down at her hand. "I didn't know you enjoyed reading. I've a library full of wonderful novels if you'd like to borrow one."

She hadn't realized that she had brought it to the door with her. "'Tis a book o' poetry, actually."

An unexpected memory cropped up, and Isabelle felt close enough to Kate now to surrender a shred of confession. "I had a good friend who was a poet when I was a girl. Mind if I have a look?"

"Not a-tall. They're by a fellow called Stephen Drake."

Isabelle had heard of him, of course. He had been all the rage in Europe for years. But she had never quite been able to bring herself to read any of his work. It was just too close to home, another man named Stephen who wrote poetry, one who had actually been able to make a career out of his God-given gift. She opened the cover and thumbed through it until a page caught her eye. She saw that the poem there was called "Pieces of April."

> *I so often wonder what you remember*
> *of those pieces of April,*
> *moments more precious than jewels.*
> *I have forgotten nothing,*
> *the scent of your skin,*
> *the way you tasted,*
> *the way you looked at me the last*
> *time we saw each other,*
> *when you didn't want to go.*
> *Before I had a chance to tell you*
> *that it was you I had chosen . . .*
> *That it would always, always be you.*

Tears welled in her eyes, and Isabelle closed the book with a little snap, feeling suddenly weak. Light-headed. Her heart was pounding, and a vague sensation of nausea began to seep though her, but she wasn't certain why. This man was a stranger and yet his work touched her. . . . Who was she kidding? It had cut her to the core.

"I'm glad as pie to see that I'm no' the only one he affects that way," Kate laughed when she saw Isabelle's reaction. "I heard him at a poetry readin' in Glasgow, and his poems, and the way he read them, touched my heart so that I actually could no' stay in the same room. 'Twas the most curious thing."

That little sensation of nausea was crawling slowly up into Isabelle's throat, and she wasn't sure if she could bear to hear the answer. But Isabelle knew she was going to ask the question anyway. "What did he look like, this Stephen Drake?"

"Well, his photograph's right there on the—"

Suddenly, Douglas and Philip were pushing open the hotel room door and coming inside. Isabelle glanced up and saw them both laughing and looking happy, as if they'd just shared the most wonderful joke. "That's your idea of a minute, is it, Mother?"

"I'm sorry, boys. I made a little stop in the gift shop first."

"You really are incorrigible, Mrs. Wescott," Philip seconded with that winning, ski-instructor smile.

Then they each went around and took hold of one of her
arms like escorts. A tall blond man on one side, her copper-
haired son on the other. Douglas took the book of poetry
from her hand and tossed it back onto the bed, then kissed
her cheek. "See what you've driven us to, you gorgeous creature? Well, from now on, we're not letting you out of our
sight. We've come to escort you girls down personally or
we'll never get to the vineyard for a glass of Auntie's fabulous
new Sauvignon Blanc."

Isabelle glanced back at the book on Kate's bed. The side
with the author portrait was facing up, but she hadn't worn
her glasses, and now she couldn't see distances. All she could
see was a fuzzy gray image of a man, rather slim, with salt-
and-pepper hair.

She thought about asking Kate to bring it along, but
everything was moving so quickly and they were late as it
was. There would be time for that later. And anyway, coinci-
dences like that just simply did not happen.

Kate glanced at herself in the big wood-framed hallway mirror of Alice and David's vineyard home and felt a little jerk of
insecurity. It was mixed with the hope that she didn't look
too much like the poor relation from the country that she
saw reflected back at her. She wore a plain black skirt, ivory
blouse, and the little gold cross her parents had given her for
her fifteenth birthday.

Douglas had assured her, in that offhand, easy manner of
his, that tonight was distinctly casual, but by now Kate had
seen the sort of company Isabelle Wescott and her son kept.
And casual certainly was not the first word that came to
mind.

Why didn't this sort of thing come more naturally to her?
she wondered. Her mother always seemed at ease in these

situations. Why couldn't she be more like Glenna? She had long ago decided that particular part of the gene pool had positively eluded her at conception. The truth was that she really didn't want to be confronted with more people who would strain to understand her when she spoke and then smile and tell her what a charming accent she had when they really didn't mean it.

Kate drew in a breath, but Isabelle and her sister were hugging, Douglas was saying something to his uncle David about what a good year it had been for the grapes, and Philip and Mitch Greyson were standing behind. It was far too late to back out now, so Kate straightened her shoulders and forced out a smile.

"How lovely to see you, Kate," Alice said, extending her hands warmly.

"Thank ye for havin' me."

"That most certainly is our pleasure."

Kate looked over at Isabelle, who was beaming with what looked like pride.

"Well then," Alice said. "Most of the other guests have already arrived, and there is an incredible sunset this evening, so why don't you all just go on out to the terrace and make yourselves at home."

Sensing Kate's discomfort, Douglas extended his arm gallantly then gave her a little squeeze as he smiled down at his niece. "Shall we?" he said, looking through the foyer and out to the terrace where everyone had gathered. "Let's go knock 'em dead."

Isabelle then took Philip's arm in the same manner after that and the four of them moved through the grand living room, decorated in the Southwestern style. It was a marvelous room, with a vaulted, beamed ceiling, with red and blue Native American rugs on the walls and lots of colorful pottery dotting the furniture.

Mitch walked into the house behind them and followed them onto the terrace, taking particular note of each of them. Isabelle's son and his friend made Kate laugh, and when she did, Kate McDowell had a kind of innocence that made her breathtakingly pretty. She didn't look a great deal like her mother, though, he thought, remembering Glenna's incandescent loveliness. Kate did not have her mother's dark hair or limpid, ice-blue eyes, but she was pretty in a different way. Her square face bore a flawless, ruddy complexion, free of makeup or the need for any, and her hair, cut blunt just beneath her chin, was the striking color of burnished copper.

Thinking of Glenna and then looking at her daughter made him wonder (no, it made him hope) that she would one day find her way here to San Francisco and that somehow their paths would cross again. But he doubted that.

What an unbelievable irony, Mitch chuckled to himself, that he should be standing here like this beside her daughter right now. Why in hell hadn't Glenna been the one who'd been drawn here? That was how it should have been. He should be standing here in his best boots and his clean white shirt, preparing to charm the mother, not the daughter. Fate was always playing those kinds of tricks on people and then looking down from the heavens, he imagined, and having herself a good old laugh.

They all moved now through the open wall of wood-framed glass doors through which the pink and crimson sunset was bursting. Douglas squeezed Kate's arm again. "You'll do just fine," Mitch heard him whisper. "Remember, you're among friends here."

"Isabelle Wescott!"

A woman's thin, overly cultured soprano vaulted suddenly through the empty living room, meeting them as they stepped out onto the crowded terrace.

"Well, mostly among friends," Douglas amended.

"Who invited her?" Isabelle whispered to her sister as they linked arms and advanced.

"No one ever has to invite Beverly Kane. They say her broom has an antenna on board for where she's not wanted."

Isabelle glanced over at Kate and said a silent prayer.

Beverly Kane was an attractive, fiftyish woman, impeccably

dressed in a nautical theme, with white slacks, matching shoes and a navy and white blouse, who was coming forward with arms outstretched. "It's been ages," she gushed at Isabelle. "How in heaven's name *are* you?"

Isabelle smiled genuinely, but Kate could see a little piece of her was holding back, wary of the woman who embraced her. "Lovely to see you, Beverly."

"I'm so glad that you're getting out again. It really is the best medicine, you know."

"So Alice continually tells me."

"I know it took me at least a year after Winston died. But you really do have to get out. I hope now you will consent to join my committee at the club. You know perfectly well that we've been after you for months."

"I'll certainly consider it."

"Splendid." Then, as she looked over at Douglas, Kate saw a small wrinkle form between her perfectly arched dark brows. Her eyes narrowed slightly. "Hello, Douglas," she said, not acknowledging Philip who stood beside Isabelle's son.

"Mrs. Kane," Douglas said, with a nod.

"And who have we here?"

Douglas looked at Kate, along with Beverly and Isabelle. He then put a protective arm across her shoulder. "This is my niece, Kate McDowell."

Beverly Kane turned her widened eyes back to Isabelle. "Colin's daughter? Our esteemed Arthur certainly doesn't have any of those sort of skeletons in his closet."

"No, Beverly." Isabelle felt her heart skip a beat. The sensation was very strong, and for a moment she could not speak. ". . . Kate is my daughter's child."

"Your *daughter?*"

Kate's heart thumped against her rib cage, watching this. There was no mistaking it. She had created a scandal for her poor grandmother by coming here, and being a problem to anyone was really the very last thing in the world she wanted.

Kate fought a desperate urge to dash back through the living room and out of the house and keep running all the way back to the safety and security of tiny Arrochar. This was really all too much. But even if she did leave, how on earth would she go? You couldn't exactly find a cab way out here in the middle of a lot of rolling hills and grapevines, could you? *Bloody hell.*

Suddenly Douglas and Philip were forming a phalanx around Isabelle, closing in protectively. "Yes, I had a child before I married." She tried to keep her voice even. "She has been raised in Scotland."

"My, my." A jeweled finger sprang to Beverly Kane's chest. "Won't you just be the topic of conversation at the club next week."

"A child and granddaughter of whom I am immensely proud. *That* is what you can all talk about at your club next week. If you have an ounce of class, it will be nothing more than that."

"*You* lecturing *me* about class?" she chuckled bitterly as she glanced at Kate. "Rather a case of people in glass houses, wouldn't you say?"

Isabelle had turned to stone. "Leave it alone, Beverly."

"It's just rather humorous, the widow of San Francisco's leading archconservative with a love child just out of the closet the moment he's gone."

Douglas took a step forward. "My mother said that was enough."

"Anything about moderation coming from you, Douglas, seems quite banal."

As they continued to trade barbs, Kate bit her lower lip, slipped past the bar and dashed back into the house alone, looking for anywhere it was quiet. It was the first time since she'd left Scotland that she felt just maybe she had made a grand mistake running off as she'd done. She missed her father terribly. Even her mother. And she had actually begun to see that, as Glenna had tried to tell her for so long, the grass wasn't always greener on the other side just because sometimes it seemed that way from a distance.

What else, she wondered now, had her mother been right about?

◆   ◆   ◆

"Now, now. I'm not so sure a viper like that is worth any-body's tears."

She hadn't known anyone was standing there, or she never would have started crying. Kate brushed away her tears with the back of her hand and sat up straight on the edge of the bed. Mitch Greyson was leaning against the door-jamb, smiling and still holding his half-full glass of wine. After a moment, he moved forward, unclasped the little sil-ver button on his white Western shirt and drew a neatly folded handkerchief from the pocket.

"I feel like such a fool."

"Oh, I'd be a rich man if I had a dollar for every time I said *that* in my life."

Kate looked up and ran the handkerchief across her eyes as he sank down beside her. "Oh, come on, you?"

"That's not so hard to believe now, is it? Old man like me, long life like mine . . . lotsa chances to screw it up."

She chuckled at that, and sniffled. "Ye're no' old."

"Most of the time I feel near to a hundred and ten."

"I canno' easily imagine how anyone who looks like you do should feel anythin' but on top o' the world."

"Believe me, it happens," he shrugged.

"I just though' it'd be different here, that's all," she shook her head. "Ye canno' imagine how close I came to actually—" She looked up at him. Her eyes were wide again and sud-denly clear. Her chin was pushed up and those tears were suddenly pressed back by a clear spark of pride.

Mitch wasn't at all certain exactly why, but he knew he was going to ask her. All that was really certain in his mind just then when he looked at her was that he wasn't thinking about her mother at this moment, nor the fantasy that if their paths crossed again somehow it could be as it had been with Livi. What he was thinking about and concerned about was Kate. She had just looked so wounded sitting there beside him when the thought had first occurred to him, kind of like a little bird who'd fallen out of the nest before it was ready to fly. . . . And it had been such a long time since he'd been able to help anyone. Or since he'd really even wanted to.

"I do believe I've got a far better idea 'n that, darlin', if you're game."

"Like what?"

"How's your Texas two-step?"

"My what?"

He stood back up beside her, tall and lean, with that tawny tousle of hair melding elegantly with his deep brown eyes. "I know a little hole in the wall back in the city, called the Desperado, where the music and laughter rolls through the place just like Houston thunder in June. I'll wager you a truckload of forget-me-nots that by the time tomorrow mornin' rolls around you won't remember anyone named Beverly Kane."

Kate fought a smile she hadn't known she felt. "'Tis temptin', Mitch."

"Nothin' wrong with a little temptation, now is there? Long as it's legal."

"No, I don't suppose so."

"Good." His brown eyes sparkled. The smile widened. "That's real good. . . . So then, what d'you say?"

Kate knew she wasn't wearing the proper clothes (no boots or rhinestones) and she certainly wasn't managing all of the right steps (was it was two forward and one back, or the other way around?), but it didn't seem to matter much. The Desperado was packed, smoky and loud, and everyone was having a good time.

Kate had never danced so much in her life. And Mitch had been right. She had forgotten about Beverly Kane's cruel scene. Well, at least for the moment she wasn't thinking about it quite so much or feeling stupid anymore. Which, under the circumstances, she thought, was saying quite a lot.

Grinning from ear to ear, Mitch huddled next to her at the

tiny cocktail table, wedged in with all the others. He was holding a bottle of beer, but she noticed he hadn't drunk much of it.

"Havin' a good time?" he asked loudly enough to be heard over the music as he wiped the glistening dark hair back from his brow.

"Grand." She smiled back, and taking a sip of coffee and cream. "But ye really canno' hear yourself think in a place like this."

Mitch laughed. "Well now, I thought that was just the point!"

Kate knew that he was right, but she was more than a little glad when the band took a fifteen-minute break. "So," she said as the cocktail waitresses moved around taking more drink orders, "Isabelle says you're a doctor."

"Then it must be true."

"You didn't mention that to my ma back in Scotland."

"No, I didn't. But our meetin' was not about me."

Kate was uncomfortable talking about her mother and him. Mitch heard her slightly accusatory tone. She had clearly seen something when he had been in Arrochar, and this, he sensed, had been their entrée to that.

"Ye fancy her, don't ye?" Kate finally asked.

"Yes."

Mitch could see that she was taken aback by how quickly and calmly he had answered.

"Well, then. At least ye're direct."

"I don't really know any other way to be, Kate."

She looked back out at the dance floor. "Ye know my mother is married, don't ye?"

"I know."

"Ye wish she weren't then, is that it?"

Mitch took a swallow of beer. "But she is. And that is what's important. Remember, I left Scotland, and she stayed."

"I saw the way she looked at ye. 'Twas quite startlin' to me." Kate shifted in her seat. "In all my life, I've never seen her look that way at my da, nor anyone else. She's always been so busy, workin' for everyone. Always so selfless. I told her I did no' want to live my own life like that, full o' regrets, and longin' for what I never did."

"That was very direct of you."

"It took comin' here and meetin' Isabelle, I suppose, to realize that a lot of women end up makin' compromises. That my ma is no worse nor better than the rest."

"So then perhaps something good has actually come from your having run away?"

"Aye." Kate twisted her lips and leaned forward a little. The gold cross around her neck swung forward and glistened in the candlelight. "I did no' like ye at first, Mitch. But I believe now I've quite changed my mind. Ye're as quick as ye are handsome."

"Kate," he said deeply, "I am *not* a threat to your father."

She studied him for a moment, then said, "I was no' too nice to my ma about ye. In fact, I used ye as an excuse to leave Arrochar. I hurt her with that, I think."

"Don't wait too long to tell her that, hmm? Now," he said, smiling affably, "tell me about you."

"And ye thought ye were bored back at the vineyard?" she laughed.

It made Mitch laugh, too, and it was that nice, rich feeling, up from the soul. He hadn't laughed like that in such a long time. But what had there been to laugh about, really? He'd lost a wife, a career, and a portion of his life. He'd been walking around like someone out of *Night of the Living Dead* since then. Just going through the motions. But that wasn't living. Not by a long shot. A stray thought careened down suddenly from the place in his mind where he had hidden it. Maybe it was time finally to stop feeling sorry for himself. Maybe, just maybe, it was time to get on with his life.

The fifteen minutes went quickly, and the music began again. It was a toe-tapping kind of tune with a lot of gritty base and drums. "Wanna try this one?" he grinned.

Kate glanced over and saw several rows already formed on the dance floor. "I don't know how to do that!"

"Who cares?" he tipped his head back and chuckled. "It's fun! That's all that matters tonight anyway, right? All you have to do is follow my lead—and while you're doin' that, I'll try real hard not to step on your toes! Come on, now, let's dance!"

Napa Valley really was breathtaking in April.

Alice and Isabelle sat on the wide covered veranda of Cielo Azul, made cool by brick-colored Mexican pavers and a ceiling fan that whirred quietly above them, long after all of the guests had gone home and David had gone up to bed. They sat in green painted wicker furniture, both sipping the piña coladas that Antonio the butler made so splendidly. Each of them were still wearing their designer blue jeans and crisp Ralph Lauren white shirts; but Alice alone had kicked off her red and blue boots.

It had been a grand evening, except for that little problem with Beverly Kane. Even though Mitch had so gallantly spirited Kate away to safety, Isabelle couldn't help worrying about her. It must have been a dreadful thing to be so young and made to feel as if you had ulterior motives for something, especially when you were entitled to it, and more. How well she knew that every young woman's uncertain ego could use a white knight (especially one who looked like Mitch and had a sense of humor too), to ride up and rescue her, at least once in her lifetime.

"So are you never going to tell me about that dashing young man in your group this evening?" Alice asked.

Isabelle leveled her eyes on her sister. How like an open book she was, a rich meaty novel, one with a too-garish cover that didn't accurately describe the golden contents beneath. It seemed impossible to believe, but dear Alice actually believed that Isabelle had found a young suitor. It would have seemed more humorous if it weren't so incredibly preposterous. "He is the one who took my letter to Glenna."

Alice's painted and powdered face flushed. "He is a private detective?"

"At the moment that is how he makes his living. But there is a great deal of mystery to Mitch Greyson. In actuality, he *was* a practicing physician."

"Like Glenna. Now that is a curious coincidence."

"Yet for some mysterious reason he has chosen to set aside his Hippocratic oath. And tonight, watching him with Kate, I got the distinct impression that he took more than a passing interest in Glenna during his brief stay in Scotland. In truth, I think that's why he remains so interested in my welfare. Perhaps he thinks I may yet be some sort of conduit back to my daughter."

"Your daughter, and Stephen's," Alice reminded her in a nostalgic tone. She placed a finger to her chin a moment later. "Hmm . . . Stephen Donnelly. Now there was another gorgeous human being. . . . He must be nearly sixty by now."

"Just last month."

Alice shook her head. "Doesn't seem possible, does it?"

"Looking back," Isabelle sighed as she sipped the last of her drink. "There are a good many things about my life that don't seem possible."

"Do you ever wonder what became of him? After Glenfinnan, I mean?"

"I think about it more now than before Frank died. Until then I think I tried to put it out of my mind as much as I could."

"He was a spectacularly complex man, wasn't he? So handsome and so sort of unbelievably driven to make something of himself. . . .290

" Alice looked away from her sister and back out across the vineyard. "Did I ever tell you how I envied you and Stephen?"

"You're trying to make me laugh, are you?"

"I never had anything with either of my husbands close to what you had with him."

Isabelle looked at her. "I thought that you and David were blissfully happy."

"We are. But not passionately. Not like that."

"You never told me."

"You never asked. . . . What the two of you had was sweeping and all-consuming, and you had that childhood history that bonded you so completely. I really think Stephen loved you since you were children but he just didn't realize it until it was too late. If he had, I don't think he ever would have gone into the priesthood in the first place."

"Maybe not," Isabelle murmured, feeling a tiny dart of pain against her heart. "And I have always chosen to believe that, in the end, it was just harder to reconcile betraying God than it was betraying me."

"Still, what happened with you and Stephen was fated. I believe it would have happened anyway, Belle. In Scotland or somewhere else. . . . Lord, I envied the power of that."

Isabelle lay her head back against the scratchy wicker and closed her eyes. She loved the sound of the crickets. The peace. The feel of a quiet, still evening in a place like Napa Valley. She'd envied it too, what she'd had that once, in Glenfinnan and then never again.

"I suppose it's pointless to say this, Belle," Alice started. "But I always had this romantic notion for you, even after your wedding to Frank, when Stephen came home to find you, and I was so awful to him. That he would still leave the priesthood and come to sweep you up and carry you away."

Something snapped inside her as Isabelle lifted her head off of the chair and looked over at her sister. It felt brittle and very old. Isabelle breathed in and felt certain it had been her heart.

". . . *What* did you say?"

"You know, that old story about when Stephen came to—"

It was in the middle of the sentence, looking at the disbelief on Isabelle's shocked face, that Alice realized she had never told her about that day when Stephen had come into the Maguire kitchen trying desperately to find her before the wedding ceremony.

The silence crackled between them.

"Dear God . . ." Isabelle finally muttered, pressing two fingers against her lips. A rush of blood went to her face. She tried hard to right herself as the realization hit her completely, but she felt suddenly like a listing ship. Off balance. Sinking fast. Bailing out too many years of lies and misunderstandings to ever save the truth. *This truth.*

"It was all so long ago, Belle, and I really thought I'd told you. If I didn't it was only because—"

"You let me marry Frank *knowing* Stephen had come for me?"

Tears pooled in Alice's eyes at the horrendous gaffe she had just made, knowing that she could never take it back. Isabelle had gone very pale, and she could see her falter. But what could she do? The damage was already done. *Damn, why can't I ever learn to control my wretched mouth? David always says it's going to be the death of me, and right now I believe him!*

"I didn't want him to hurt you anymore," Alice managed to say, but she was almost whispering, as if she couldn't quite find her voice again, in the face of having destroyed so much. "You were so miserable when we got back to the States. I just thought—"

"I was miserable without *him*! You knew that!"

"He was a priest, for Lord's sake! Even if he was leaving the priesthood, he was still standing there in our kitchen as a man of God . . ."

Isabelle swallowed what tasted like acid. She couldn't quite catch her breath. "He told you that he was leaving the priesthood for me?"

"Yes! All right, yes! But you'd already given the baby up! The wedding was set! What kind of life could you have made after that?"

"*My* life! . . ." she sobbed, shaking her head. "Don't you see, that's just it! I could have had *my* life! Not the one Daddy had carved out for me! He told me Stephen had lost his nerve and had never come after me, and I . . . oh, oh . . . I believed him!"

"God, I'm sorry, Belle. I had no idea that I hadn't told you. I swear it. I really didn't know."

She tried to look at Alice, tried to focus, but it was like looking through a rain-splashed window. Colors. Shapes. A voice as familiar as her own . . . uttering words she did not want to believe. *How could it possibly be?. . .* And then the pain again of an undeniable truth reaching in and twisting her heart. Crushing it until she could not speak, or breathe . . . or feel anything else but that. That her life and Stephen's . . . and dear, dear Glenna's . . . would have been something so different, *if only . . .*

Suddenly the French door swung open onto the veranda. It was David, barefoot in red French silk pajamas, standing in a circle of butter yellow lamplight cast out from the living room. "What on earth is going on out here?"

Isabelle had forgotten to leave a light on upstairs, so by the time she returned from Cielo Azul it was very dark. It was also very late, after midnight, and she realized only as she started to climb the stairs that she was exhausted.

She'd told Alice it was all right about Stephen when she had seen how sorry she was, and Isabelle had just wanted her to stop crying and apologizing. But it wasn't really all right.

How could it ever be? The mere thought that once there had been a chance . . .

Alice's admission had unlocked that old Pandora's box, and beckoned her once again to look inside. When she did, Isabelle could see it all again so clearly. More clearly than she wanted to. The gentle farmlands of Glenfinnan laced with wind-bent trees, backed by mauve and lavender hills. Wild moors carpeted with pink thrift. Purple butterwort. That wonderful heather. The air crisp and full of the briny scent off of the lochs.

Figures abstract with time, as much as she could make them, were clear again. Sharp enough to reach out and touch. *Oh, Stephen, did you really come for me, after all? After all of the years of believing that you'd chosen God over me . . .*

She felt a sudden little glitch in her chest, and she gripped the top of the banister.

The words to that poem in Kate's hotel room came back to her then, tumbling over the memories until she could see them clearly too. They were words she'd never read before tonight, but somehow they were as familiar as an old friend.

> . . . *before I had a chance to tell you*
> *That it was you I had chosen.*
> *That it would always, always be you.*

"It cannot be," the pained whisper moved across her lips. "I will not believe that God could ever be so cruel."

Isabelle opened her bedroom door and flipped on the light, casting the place in pale gold and shadows. Then her heart leaped up and she grabbed her chest, startled to see someone sitting very still on the daybed across the room. Arthur. He sat slumped, with his legs crossed and something in his lap, though in the shadows she could not see what.

"A priest?" he said in a voice that was inflectionless and very hard. But she could see that his face was flushed. He had been drinking again. "Really, Mother."

Her own voice, when she finally answered, was equally stony. "What are you doing here, Arthur?"

"Did you really think I wouldn't find out the details of what Douglas knew? That boy is like putty. He told me everything. *God*, it makes me positively sick to know that you could have lived a lie like that with Dad!"

Isabelle took a step forward, feeling light-headed and queasy, not at all up to sparring. "Not that it is any business of yours, Arthur, but it all happened before I even knew your father," she said firmly. Then she took off her jacket and sank onto the edge of the bed to remove her shoes. Isabelle was trying very hard to stay calm and to sound calm, knowing how much he wanted to bait her into an argument.

They were closer now, she on the edge of her bed, he still on the daybed. And in the pale lamplight between them, now she could see that he was holding that very old bottle of My Sin. Her heart lurched, protectively this time, and he saw it, seized on it, and held the bottle up. "Ironic, don't you think?" he chuckled acidly. "That this should have been your choice of fragrance?"

"Give it to me, Arthur."

"They don't even make this stuff anymore, do they?"

"You heard me, Arthur. I said I want you to give it to me."

"My Sin . . . It really is disgusting that you would keep this old thing around all these years, like some sort of trophy or something. I remember this right there on your dressing table the whole time I was growing up. God, it was right under Dad's nose!"

She sprang to her feet and lunged at him, powered by a burst of indignation. The smell of gin on his breath made her feel even more ill, but she had to get him out of here. "I've had just about enough of this from you! You're a spoiled, insensitive man who doesn't know the first thing about what it is to really love or to be loved!"

"You can't mean . . ." His blue, bloodshot eyes narrowed. His voice went very deep and flat. "Where'd you get it, Mother?"

She turned away from the question. "Stop it, Arthur."

He rocketed to his feet and grabbed her shoulder with one hand. His fingers pinched her flesh as he jerked her back around. He was still holding up the bottle between them like some sort of weapon. "You didn't actually get this from him? From the priest, did you?"

She didn't respond, but he could see the truth written in her expression. Then, all of a sudden, he began to laugh, a haunting, evil sound. But she could see strangely, at the same time, that there were tears in his eyes glittering with something that looked like betrayal. "My great and virtuous mother . . . the woman who made me say my prayers every night, who sent me to bed more nights than I can recall without supper, just for swearing . . . who sat right beside my father and told me that sex was for marriage and only for marriage . . . that same woman, Jesus, screwing a priest?"

Isabelle pressed her hands to her ears. "I won't listen to this, Arthur!"

"Well, here's what I think of your damn sin!" he seethed and then, in a single wild instant, before she could stop him, thrust the old bottle, with all of its history and memories, against the fireplace hearth, shattering it like rain.

"Oh!" Her hand was against her mouth and tears rushed to her eyes as she let out a muffled cry. "Look what you've *done!*"

But he couldn't begin to know that, could he? He was nothing like her. He never had been. . . . Then very suddenly she felt the room begin to spin, and the queasiness swelled into a full-blown need to vomit. Arthur was looking at her in the silence now, but his face was all distorted, like an image in a carnival mirror . . . and suddenly, as she tried to take a step toward the safe haven of her bathroom, it felt like there was a very tight strap across her chest, cinching tighter every time she drew a breath.

She reached for her dressing table, something, anything to steady herself. The tightness became a stabbing. Sharp like a dagger. Thoughts and images whirled inside her head as she gasped for each searing breath. *Stephen . . . Kate . . . Glenna . . .*

Was this what it felt like to die?

How very curious that there wasn't any pain.

Isabelle's mind was whirling away from herself, as if she were a part of a sudden gust of autumn wind out at Alice's Napa vineyard, and the gold, flame red, and aubergine leaves were all her thoughts. And memories. Moments in time floating past her consciousness and then gently, softly, falling away. But the only ones Isabelle could seem to identify for more than a moment were the ones of Stephen. Then there were voices mixed in with the thoughts, Arthur's slightly nasal tenor, she realized, high and sharp, on the phone.

"Get a goddamn ambulance over here! I don't give a shit how busy you are tonight! You're talkin' to Senator Wescott here! Senator Arthur Wescott! Yeah, you do that!"

But even he didn't seem to upset her. Suddenly she was remembering that day when she and Stephen were children. Walking together up Market Street back toward Nob Hill.

"Remember now, we can't go palling around like this all the time."

"I know," Isabelle could hear herself saying.

"I mean, I really am too old for you."

"Okay."

"So, you want to read one of the new poems I wrote last night?" he had asked with a broad, dimpled smile as they reached the top of Nob Hill.

"Sure," she'd said happily, "but I'd rather read them all!"

Suddenly, things were whirling again, and this time she was being lifted up. *Give in to it . . . move toward the light . . .* a voice seemed to be telling her. It seemed so nice. So very nice. And peaceful. No more worries. No more regrets. *The light, move toward the light. . . .*

There had still been that little hope for so long, hadn't there? Something to hang on to. But now she would never again get to see Glenna, her sweet, beautiful child. . . . And she never would have a chance to discover what had actually become of Stephen.

Stephen was in the shower when the phone rang.

He dashed out of the bathroom, wrapping a towel around himself and stubbed his toe on the tip of the cherry armoire, and just managing to pick it up by the eighth ring. It was blessed six in the morning! Who on earth would have a reason to be calling at an unseemly hour like that?

"Oh, damn! Hello!"

"It's Glenna. I didno' mean to wake ye, I can—"

"No, no! don't hang up! I was just coming out of the shower and I'm still dripping wet. The blasted thing always rings when—"

She cut him off after that and he heard her sweet voice go

very stiff. Something was wrong. *Very wrong.* "Aengus just got a call from Kate in San Francisco."

"Oh, Lord." He sank onto the edge of his bed and a dart of alarm shot through him. "Is she all right? What's happened?"

"It's no' Kate, Stephen. . . . It's Isabelle. She's had a heart attack."

The whispered words came out like a plea. "God, no . . ."

"I'm leavin' on the next plane out."

"Is it bad?"

"They don't know anythin' yet, I'm afraid. Everyone has just gathered at the hospital waitin' for word. . . . So, now will you come with me? It might well be your last chance."

Stephen drew in a ragged breath, knowing suddenly, in that moment of sheer panic and searing pain brought by Glenna's words, no matter how many years, or how many continents there were to divide them, it would never really be over between them. And maybe just maybe, fate and God weren't entirely finished with them, after all.

"Yes, I will come," he said as the tears rolled slowly down the still-smooth plane of his aging face. "When does the flight leave?"

15

◈ Kate and Stephen

They all sat, quiet and sullen, on two long black leather couches, waiting for any word at all about Isabelle. Thumbing mindlessly through months-old ragged magazines and drinking cold coffee just for something to keep busy. Mitch and Kate. Douglas and Philip. Alice and David. Only Arthur stood alone outside of the waiting room, pacing the halls and whispering instructions to one of his aides, who had been summoned there and remained with Arthur's cellular phone.

It was midnight, and still no one was entirely certain what had happened. They knew only that Arthur had been with Isabelle when she was brought into the emergency room. And that he had told the doctor that there had been an argument.

Beyond the tiny and dim waiting room, the corridors were quiet except for the occasional call across the PA system for one particular doctor or another. After the first couple of hours, none of them even noticed the sounds.

Myocardial infarction, Douglas had just been told. Damage to the heart muscle. And the first forty-eight hours were crucial. Isabelle was in the coronary care unit, and, at the moment she was heavily sedated. She wasn't, the cardiologist had assured him, in any sort of pain. That, at least, was a blessing.

Mitch had sat with them, like a member of the family, holding Kate's hand at times, and going down to get coffee. It was nice to feel like a part of something again, he thought. It had been such a long time.

He began to doze, just after midnight, with Kate slumped onto his shoulder and the news playing, with the sound turned down, on a television in the corner. Then something woke him, and Mitch glanced up at two people, silhouettes at first, until they moved into the doorway and the dim lamp light. A man and a woman. And as they did, his heart squeezed. He was still so tired and full of sleep that it seemed like a dream. But it was real, he knew that. And he knew *her*.

Mitch bolted upright on the couch and watched Glenna McDowell step into the tiny waiting room and embrace her daughter, as Kate went to her with open arms. "I canno' quite believe ye've come," Kate said softly.

"In truth," Glenna said, "nor can I. How is she?"

"We still don't know much. But we're told she's restin' comfortably."

Mitch watched the man standing behind her. Tall. Quiet. Handsome in a mature sort of way, with salt-and-pepper hair and bright blue eyes. Eyes like Glenna's. The poet Stephen Drake. Her birth father. And Isabelle's forbidden lover. It had to be.

Lost loves, and what might have been, made him think not of Livi at this moment but of Glenna. His chest ached with anticipation and restraint as he gazed at her and came slowly to his feet. But he did not advance. This first moment with Glenna was not his. Instead, he watched as Kate introduced her to Douglas and then to Alice, her aunt.

"I never thought that I'd actually meet you. I'm just so happy. . . . And Belle . . ." Mitch heard Alice falter and then say, "Belle would have been so happy to see you here, Glenna."

When Alice began to cry, and David and Douglas sought to comfort her, Mitch drew in a breath, feeling as if he were about to jump headfirst into a very deep pool. He knew that he was going to move forward now finally and speak to Glenna again, this woman who had brought up so many things from inside him. A woman so evocative of depth and caring—and all of the special things that Livi had been.

From the moment she had entered the small room, his eyes had never shifted from her. Glenna was still so shockingly beautiful, even after a lengthy overseas flight, standing there now in a loose black sweater and black leggings, with her dark hair drawn back away from her face and sleekly knotted.

"Oh, Ma. You remember Dr. Greyson," Kate said, sensing him standing tall and straight behind her. "Although, come to think of it, ye did no' know he too was a doctor."

"Mitch," he corrected and drew Glenna's hand to his, feeling suddenly as if, like a jet airliner, he was on automatic pilot, pushing past the rush of blood and adrenaline he felt.

"He's been a good friend to me here, Ma. I'm afraid back home I misjudged him a bit."

Their eyes met then, their hands still joined. "So we meet again," she said in that soft, rich burr that filled his heart.

But before he could hope to even think of something clever to say to break the intensity he felt, Stephen Drake was stepping forward into the light and everything else seemed to stop. "Hello, Alice," Stephen said.

The intensity shifted.

Hearing this voice out of the past, they watched Isabelle's sister turn out of her husband's embrace, wipe her tears and draw forward. When she extended both of her hands, Stephen surrounded them with his own. "It is so good to see you again, Stephen," she said, each heartfelt word catching in her throat.

After another moment, he pulled her to his chest and they embraced deeply. And Alice was crying. "I don't know how a miracle like this happens after so many years," she sobbed. "But I'm so very glad you've come."

Mitch felt himself pull away just then, feeling a fool for ever thinking that a moment like this could have included him. He wasn't really a part of this family. And Glenna certainly had no idea who he really was. Hell, come to think of it, he wasn't so sure *he* knew the answer to that anymore either. Doctor. Private eye. Ex-con. *Murderer.*

It had been so long since he had known, since he'd really been Dr. Greyson and Livi's husband, that all of it seemed now like someone else's life. Mitch quietly left the small waiting room as Stephen and Alice continued to embrace and whisper things to one another, while everyone else—Kate, Douglas, David, and Philip—each a part of this very intricate puzzle, stood around them, and Glenna watched him walk away.

—"It's you," Kate said softly as Alice pulled away from Stephen and they both turned, with tear-brightened eyes, to look at her. "I knew there was somethin' about ye that night at the readin' in Glasgow. . . . But I had no idea a-tall you were . . ."

Stephen looked up as her words fell away, knowing her from the Bull & Bear. And because he saw now that she looked so much like Isabelle. Especially her lovely copper hair. Why hadn't he seen it that night? If only he had known. . . . Curious, how tightly knit their lives had been. So inextricably woven like some fine old tapestry: Isabelle, Glenna, Kate, himself, as if they had always lived their lives together. All of these little moments, through the years, each seemed now a part of a prelude for what was to become this very grand crescendo.

"Hello, Kate," Stephen smiled, moving forward and extending his hands.

Mitch poured himself a cup of coffee in the cafeteria, then poured one to take back up to Kate. Poor thing, she hadn't slept a bit since he'd brought her here straight from the hotel last night after Douglas had left that message about Isabelle. She had been such a rock for everybody, shuttling between Alice and Douglas to see how each was doing, and even taking messages out to Senator Wescott, who curiously refused to sit inside the waiting room with everyone else. In spite of how Glenna had worried back in Scotland, her daughter was learning some of life's hard lessons and growing up to be someone of whom her mother could be proud.

"Might I join ye for a cup o' that, Dr. Greyson?"

The sudden female voice behind him, so unexpected and yet so easily recognizable, hit him like an avalanche. Mitch did his best to stay calm as he pivoted around slowly and came face-to-face once again with Glenna.

"Why, sure," he managed to say casually, forcing the words up with that same automatic pilot response he had used with her before. "A little company would be right nice about now."

Without saying anything else, they took a table, a small Formica square set on a silver pedestal, that was over near the bank of windows. "So why did ye no' tell me ye were a doctor?" she asked, looking at him directly, her blue eyes glittering in the neon light.

Mitch shifted on the chair, feeling the weight of his desire for Glenna setting him off balance. Her brilliant, fathomless gaze held him powerfully. "Since I don't practice anymore, there really was nothin' to tell."

"Still, Mitch, I thought we did quite a bit o' sharin' back in Scotland."

He steepled his hands against his mouth. A muscle flexed in his jaw. "You're right."

They were both silent then for a moment, the poignant thread between them rich and strong enough to bear the quiet. "Did ye know Isabelle this well when ye came to me in Arrochar?" Glenna finally asked.

"No. But you were somethin' that seemed to bind the two of us when we met."

She smiled, and Mitch watched her expression soften. Glenna leaned back in the bright orange plastic chair. "So, what sort o' doctor were ye, then, Dr. Greyson?"

"A lousy one." He took a taste of his coffee, trying to look casual. But he couldn't. *Not with her.* "You know, Glenna, I really never thought I'd see you again."

She didn't respond, but as she looked at him, Mitch felt the power of their unspoken attraction. He thought of the brief moments they had shared, stuck together in his rented car half a world from here, the evening in her hotel room when together they had read those very private letters. Could it be, Mitch dared to wonder, that Glenna actually felt what he felt? That she could find the courage to give up a life with Aengus to be like this always, with him, after all?

Arthur swung inside the waiting room doorway and leaned against it.

"Look, whoever you are, I think we've had quite enough outsiders passing through here with their condolences for one day. This is a private family matter." His icy staccato voice tore across the small, dimly lit waiting room. He looked down at Alice, then at the stranger sitting beside her on one of the black vinyl sofas.

"Like it or not, Arthur, Stephen here is not an outsider."

"That would be pretty curious, since *I* have never seen him before in my life."

"Well, this may surprise you, dear boy," Alice said, "but you really don't know everything there is to know about your mother."

He glanced at Stephen then back at his aunt. "All right, then. Who in hell are you?"

"Arthur! I will not have you speak to Father Donnelly in that tone!"

The sudden, charged silence crackled like lightening. Stephen rose slowly to his feet and looked back at Alice. "It's just Stephen now. Remember, I left the priesthood many years ago."

"You've *got* to be kidding!" Arthur was shaking his head suddenly and laughing in disbelief. "You can't possibly mean that you're *the* priest! My mother's lover?"

"Oh, shut up, would you Arthur?" Douglas droned in exasperation. "This isn't the time or the place for that."

Arthur lunged for his brother and grabbed the collar of his shirt, twisting it and pulling him forward. "Listen, you little prick. Don't ever tell me to shut up! It's our mother who's in there dying now because of the heartache that hypocritical sonofabitch caused her almost forty years ago! And I have every right in the world to point it out!"

Arthur twisted the collar tighter against his throat and Douglas started to cough.

"Let him go," Philip said flatly as he took a commanding step nearer to Arthur. And it was very quickly apparent how much bigger—and stronger—he was than the junior senator from California. "Believe me, Arthur, I won't ask you twice."

"You don't give a damn about mother!" Douglas said, gagging. "All you care about is yourself and your precious political reputation! Now, you heard Philip, let go of me!"

Then, summoning more force than he had ever gathered and pressing it like gunpowder behind a lifetime's worth of anger toward a cruel elder brother, Douglas coiled his fist and landed a powerful blow to Arthur's jaw.

Arthur fell to his knees, gripping his face and moaning in agony. He gazed at Douglas with such unbridled shock that for a moment, he was actually speechless.

"And furthermore, if I find out that you had anything, and I do mean *anything,* to do with what happened to her last night, Artie . . . I swear to God, I'll do more than just deck you!"

"All right, both of you, that's quite enough!" Alice said, pressing Douglas back and doing her best to hide a smile of surprise.

A portly doctor in a white lab coat with a stethoscope around his neck appeared in the doorway just then, causing them all to freeze and turn around. "What is it, doctor?" David Hart asked.

"It's Mrs. Wescott. There's been a change in her condition."

4

Grow old along with me!
the best is yet to be. . . .

—Robert Browning

CHAPTER 16

◈ Isabelle and Stephen *Again*

He sat at her bedside trembling as he held her cool, limp hand.

Stephen had long ago given up praying that he would ever see her, or touch her, again. He wiped the tears away, but they only came back. It was just so bittersweet that when he was given another glimpse of Isabelle . . . it should be like this. Images kept playing through his mind as he looked at her lying there, so pale and so still. It was like a record he could not stop.

"Why don't I let you have a little time alone," Alice whispered.

"You don't need to do that."

"Oh, but I do." She tried to smile as she gently squeezed his shoulder. "Talk to her, Stephen. The doctor said that she's coming out of the medication and that hearing voices which are dear to her could actually help bring her all the way around at this point."

It was so different than he wanted it to be. The tubes, wires. The harsh odor of ammonia. A heart monitor blipping a shrill monotone. And yet all he could think of when he looked at her now was the copper-haired schoolgirl who had danced so awkwardly to that off-key tune at her prom, as she accidentally stepped on his toes. . . . The girl who had grieved for a stray dog that had roamed with her among the endless fields of heather and broom. . . .

The girl who once had loved him.

"Okay, Slugger," he said, low and awkwardly, as his voice began to break. "I think that's about enough of this. . . . I want you to open your eyes now. I want to hear you tell me, just like always, what a fool I was for not listening to you."

The monitor kept on, blip . . . blip . . . blip . . . as he wiped a hand broadly across his face. Isabelle did not move and his touch did nothing to rouse her. "Hey, now." His voice went lower. Gentler. "Is this any way to greet me after all this time?" Stephen tried to chuckle, but it wasn't the same without one of her snappy retorts. *God, how I've missed the way you could match me word for word. . . .*

Stephen squeezed her hand, then brought it to his lips, hoping that the strength of their connection alone could bring her back. But still she did not move. "Do you remember how you used to read all of my poems?" he softly asked. "For a long time, you were the *only* one I ever trusted enough to read them. . . . You always were my harshest critic, weren't you? And my greatest fan. . . . Well, would you believe I've been writing again? . . . Yeah, for a while now. I know, I know, you always knew it was what I was meant to do with my life, didn't you?"

He stroked the back of her hand tenderly and then leaned in a little nearer. "Well, I've got one of my favorites rolling around in my mind, that I've never had a chance to try out on you. . . ." He glanced down when he felt her seem to stir. "It was pretty successful a few years ago. But you're the only one I can *really* trust to tell me if it was any good at all. . . . Okay, here goes . . .

> I so often wonder what you remember
> of those pieces of April,
> moments more precious than jewels.
> I have forgotten nothing,
> the scent of your skin,
> the way you tasted,
> the way you looked at me the last time we saw each
> other when you didn't want to go . . .

Then, it happened so slowly that at first he didn't realize it. But when he looked down again, Stephen saw the eyes that he had not looked upon for such a long time, those beautiful moss green eyes he had seen so many times in his mind—and in his memories. And now, a miracle had happened, and they were gazing up, full of tears, at him.

"You wrote that. . . . I knew you wrote that. . . ."

"Shh," he said tenderly, reaching forward and brushing a hand across her cheek. "Don't try to talk."

The shock, the realization that they were actually here in this room together, was so great that for a moment, neither of them could speak again, nor even move. But Stephen was still holding her hand, and tears were suddenly raining down both of their faces. Time had stopped. Everything had stopped. Then he pressed her hand to his heart and finished the words to the poem he had shared with the world—the one that had made him famous, but which they both knew had been meant only for her.

> *Before I had a chance to tell you*
> *that it was you I had chosen . . .*
> *That it would always, always be you.*

"I came for you. I swear that I did."

It was much later, after Douglas and Alice had been told that Isabelle was conscious again and they had all come in to see for themselves. Arthur had taken their word about his mother's improvement and, with a very shiny purple bruise beginning to darken his jaw, had left the hospital. When Stephen and Isabelle were alone again, after the hospital staff had bent the visiting rules for Mrs. Wescott's very well known friend, who had signed autographs for all of them, he tried to tell her what she already knew.

Isabelle looked up at him, her eyes not tired at all from her ordeal, but bright with happiness. As he sat with her, she had tried to tell him, half a dozen times, that she finally knew everything—that Alice had confessed about his having come to Willowbrae and that her family had lied about her being back in the States. That she knew now too that he had come after her again the day of her wedding. But everything between them came in fits and starts. Their words tumbled over each other's, scrambling to be spoken. Begging to be heard. He started again just when she started. It made them both smile, and Stephen brought her hand to his lips.

"Oh, if I could take back the years . . ." He sighed. "The misery I have caused you."

"You gave me a great deal of happiness too."

"We gave *each other* Glenna." He squeezed her hand. "She's really such a beautiful young woman, Isabelle."

"Alice said she came to San Francisco with you."

"Yes, she did."

She closed her eyes for a moment and took a breath. "It's all going so fast. Too many good things all at once. I can barely think."

Stephen kissed her hand and then gently placed it back on her chest. "I have to tell you the truth about that, Isabelle. . . . I *want* to tell you," he said and her face grew very still as she listened.

He told her about studying at the Gregorian University in Rome after he'd left Glenfinnan. How he'd used the very effective Vatican network to try to find out what Ross Maguire had done with their child. Then he told her how a teacher of his there, an American Jesuit, had begun the process with a phone call to a fellow Jesuit in Glasgow who was tied to the Carmelite convent on the edge of town. Several calls, trips, dead ends, and many long years later, he'd finally found Glenna.

"I wish you had come for me too," she calmly said.

"You were married."

"I loved you."

"I was still a priest in the beginning, Isabelle, and I believed God had made His decision by giving you so swiftly to someone else."

This time, it was she who reached for his hand. "It happened the way it was meant to. . . . And so now you're here again." She ran her finger across the long blue vein in the back of his hand. "If this hadn't happened to me—do you suppose you ever would have come?"

"No."

"It hurts to hear that," she said. "But I know it's the truth."

And then Stephen told her how he had left the priesthood, finally, after he had found Glenna. How only then had he been able to let go of enough of the anger to begin writing his poetry again. How Barry had been there for him during those dark days, helping him find a new career. And eventually a new life, without her.

"So tell me about your wife."

"I'm not married, Isabelle."

The way he answered it made her ask, *"Never?"*

Stephen shook his head and then said very gently, "I couldn't. . . . For me, Glenfinnan and all of it never stopped feeling like yesterday. . . . It never stopped being real enough for me to believe I could love someone else the way they would have deserved."

She lifted her head after a moment and he saw the affirmation in her sparkling green eyes before she spoke the words. "I never stopped loving you, either," Isabelle said.

"I think I always knew that, which made thinking about someone else just that much more impossible."

She paused, drew in a breath, and then said very sadly, "I really ruined your life, didn't I?"

"You changed my life, Isabelle. That is something very different."

"But all the years you spent alone because of what happened between us."

"It hasn't been all that bad a life," he said, lying a little because he could not bear to make her feel that she was responsible for what had happened between them. "I have friends in Glasgow, a wonderful old house that I've renovated, and I have my poetry."

In the quiet that followed he could see that the past was rushing through her mind. "Oh, Stephen . . . how could we have lost so many years? Where did they all go?"

"They're gone forever, my darling." He leaned nearer to her. When he smiled, it was as brightly as she had always remembered. "But everything else is still there, the rest of our lives . . . just waiting for us to seize it."

Isabelle looked away from him, hesitating. "I've changed, Stephen. You've changed. We don't really even know each other anymore."

"I know your soul, my darling Isabelle, the real core of who you are. You cannot tell me that has changed."

"No, I suppose I can't."

"Well, I will go to my grave loving you."

"As I will go loving you."

Stephen bent his head then and very tenderly kissed her. When he drew back, Isabelle looked away again and squeezed her eyes shut. "How can you look at me here, like this with all of these tubes and wires, and want to do that?"

He sighed and reached for her hand again, taking it up in both of his. "Because you honestly look as lovely to me now, perhaps even more so, than you did the first moment I knew that I loved you."

"Well, they do say the eyesight is the first thing to go," she said with a note of self-mockery passing over the tenderness that had swelled and risen between them. Then her expression stilled. Isabelle's voice went lower. "I am no longer that pretty young girl, Stephen. I have more lines and wrinkles than I can count, and I am fast losing the battle with gravity, not to mention this graying hair of mine."

"As you can see, that is a battle to which I long ago surrendered," he laughed softly.

His answer made her laugh too. Then he paused. It was serious between them again as he pressed her hand to his mouth and kissed it deeply. "But none of that matters in the slightest. We have experience and life between us now. That is what those things are to me. Badges of living. Nothing more. I know it may take some time, but I don't want to lose this second chance between us, Isabelle. Tell me you don't want to either."

"When do you have to go back to Glasgow?"

"I will stay until you ask me to go."

"For now, would you just call up some more of your poems? I've really missed that."

A glimmer of sun through the slatted window blinds caught in Stephen's eyes and made the tears there sparkle. "You have an awfully lot of them to get caught up on."

Isabelle began to say something else. Then she stopped. There was no need for more words between them. The look in his eyes told her everything she needed to know, or ever would: that time, adversity, and even Ross Maguire had changed nothing between them.

"Are ye up to a visitor, then?"

Isabelle wasn't sleeping, but her eyes were closed when she heard the door click open and the sweet Scottish voice roll across her thoughts almost like music. Although it was a voice she had never heard, she knew who it was—who it had to be.

"Hello, Glenna," she said, and it was all she could manage to say, facing her daughter for the very first time, a beautiful young woman who was the very image of Stephen.

Glenna remained at the foot of her bed for an awkward moment, standing very still in a floral print skirt and rose-colored blouse. Then Isabelle sat up and adjusted the stiff white hospital bedding. "Would you like to sit down?"

"Thanks." She moved forward haltingly and sat rigidly in the chrome-and-vinyl guest chair beside Isabelle's bed. Glenna had put off coming in alone like this until the last possible moment. But it had been two days, and she had come to San Francisco for this confrontation, hadn't she? Hadn't she really been waiting a lifetime for it?

"How are ye feelin'?"

"A bit stronger. It's very kind of you to ask." She paused as their eyes met. Mother and daughter. Joined by blood, ancestry . . . but still strangers. Such very awkward strangers.

"Well," Isabelle said, breaking the silence again, "Stephen is right. You are a very lovely young woman."

"I think a father's supposed to say that."

"Well it's true, nonetheless. You're very like I always pictured you . . . So like him." *More like him than you will ever know, dear Glenna. That smile. The turn of your head . . . Eyes that light up the world and make all things seem possible when they are turned upon me . . .* "And so now you are here."

"Aye."

"And we're actually having a civilized conversation. I somehow did not expect that would happen when we met."

"'Tis just so difficult to be angry with all o' this goin' on."

"You *should* be angry. You have every right to despise me, you know."

"I do. I mean, I did . . . for quite a long time."

It surprised her that Isabelle smiled. "I'm glad," she said almost serenely.

"How d'ye mean?"

"Frankly, I don't deserve you being here now. I think we both know that."

Glenna considered that, then settled back a little in the chair. "The point is that while I'm no' so angry any longer . . . I don't feel much of anythin'. . . . 'Tis sad, really, what happened to us, but ye're a stranger to me." She hadn't meant to hurt her with that. But Glenna could see, by the little flicker of pain that darted across her face, that it had.

"I would give anything," Isabelle said more softly, "if that weren't true."

Glenna waited a moment to respond, wanting to be certain of what she felt. "I do believe I might, as well."

Quite suddenly, the corners of Isabelle's mouth lifted slightly. "Well, I suppose that's a start, isn't it? And when you're ready, I want you to feel that you can ask me anything."

Glenna waited a heartbeat, contemplating. *Ask her. You deserve to know, she was thinking. You have wondered for nearly your entire life and this is the woman who holds the key to so much.* "There is one thing that Stephen could no' tell me. . . . Somethin' I've always wanted to know."

"I will tell you anything that I can."

"How did ye do it . . . ?" The words came soft and unsure. Then suddenly they gained momentum. "I've had a child myself, and . . . I mean, how was it that ye actually parted with me when the moment came?"

She watched Isabelle's face change, slowly at first, then she went very pale, and Glenna could see that she had wounded her by asking. But Glenna had a right to know. How many nights had there been, when she was a child, that she had lain awake wondering how someone could have actually been so heartless to have given her away to people like the Fergusons. Then, when she'd given birth to Kate, the anger had intensified. She would have killed anyone who would have tried to take away *her* child.

The question still hung in the air like a dark, heavy cloud. Isabelle's eyes were filled with tears. She looked entirely bereft, and Glenna was sorry she had started this for how stricken Isabelle now seemed. But she couldn't take it back. It was there, plain and stark, between them both. *The past. The truth.*

"Very well, Glenna." Isabelle began. "I will tell you what no other living soul has ever heard me say—the thing I have tried so hard not to think about . . . for how I die a little more inside each time that I do. My own father tore you from my arms when you were no more than a few minutes old. . . . I can still hear myself lying in that bed, too weak to move . . . screaming, crying out for you, pleading with him. . . . I held out my arms to you . . . but he wouldn't listen. . . . He was just so angry and so damn certain that he knew what was best for my life."

More tears fell in crystalline ribbons. Then Isabelle sat up very rigidly in the bed, her words now high-pitched, desperate. ". . . And then you were gone and he wouldn't tell me where he had taken you. . . . I was young, Glenna. . . . I had no husband, no money of my own . . . and no power at all to fight him. . . . When I finally did have the money of my own to try to find you . . . I searched and searched. But it was too late."

Glenna moved a step nearer, hearing the rhythm of the heart monitor begin to rise. Knowing what it meant. She held up a warning hand. "Perhaps ye should no' upset yourself like—"

"Oh, I am so sorry! Horribly sorry. I have more regret in my heart for what happened to you than words can ever say!" She sobbed, struggling to catch her breath. Fighting to say what her daughter needed to hear without giving in to the darkest of her memories. "I will never, ever forgive myself for not finding a way, some way to come for you! And I will have to live with that for the rest of . . . my . . . life. . . ."

"Please, Isabelle—"

The heavy door swung open and a stout nurse in a white pants uniform rushed in with heavy-footed strides. "What on earth is going on in here? Mrs. Wescott, please! Lie back down!" She picked up Isabelle's wrist and then looked at her own watch to check her pulse. After a moment the nurse cast a little irritated glance behind her. "You have got to leave this room, miss! You've upset her terribly! That means *now!*"

Dr. Forman, Dr. Gerald Forman to CCU stat.

Glenna knew that the voice over the intercom out in the hall was calling the doctor here. She could see Isabelle fighting for breath, gasping like a fish suddenly out of water, tears still raining down her cheeks. Another nurse rushed in, and then an orderly. The room was quickly crowded with white-clad people hovering over her. But just as she turned away, Glenna caught one last glimpse of that pleading expression on Isabelle's face.

I am so very sorry. Glenna knew that was what she was trying to say. But they were still strangers, and she wondered now if anything was ever going to change that fact.

"Looks to me like maybe you could use this."

Startled by the sudden voice coming from beside her outside of the CCU, Glenna looked up and saw Mitch holding out a handkerchief, his mouth turned up in that slight, kind smile. Glenna tried to stop crying, but there were just too many years' worth of tears and anger, and she was just too tired of it all to push them back inside. She took the handkerchief and wiped her eyes. "I guess things didn't go too well with Isabelle."

"Not a brain surgeon, were ye?" Glenna's retort came before she realized what she had said or how horribly caustic it had sounded.

"No. Actually, I was an obstetrician."

The truth came out on a thread of bitterness. Glenna heard it and felt suddenly ashamed of herself. But right now she was bloody well tired of being the strong one. The stoic one. Aengus always called her as enduring as the Rannoch Moor. She was stable enough to have made it through a childhood as Andrew Ferguson's personal whipping post. Unyielding enough to have succeeded at medical school. Single-minded enough about living in safety and peace to have stayed in a passionless marriage.

"Well I'm certain ye were a fine obstetrician," she said more softly, more herself again.

"Actually, as I said earlier, I was lousy. I lost a patient several years ago, and I stopped practicing medicine all together."

Glenna looked up and wiped away the last tear that fell. "I'm sorry. I know what 'twould be meanin' to me if I were forced to give up my own practice."

I gave up a whole lot more than that, he was thinking. Mitch took her hand before she could object. "Come on, let's sit over here for a bit." When they were sitting together on the black vinyl bench in the corridor outside of Isabelle's room and she was shaking her head, he lowered his eyes thoughtfully and said, "Better?"

"I just don't feel anythin' in my heart for her."

"Now," his voice went lower, suddenly full of gentle understanding, "I figure those tears mean you feel *somethin'*."

"Aye," Glenna relented after a moment. "I feel sorry for her. She must have suffered an awfully lot all o' those years ago, havin' me taken away so brutally like that. 'Twas no' really her fault, I suppose. . . . But now, mother or no', she's still a stranger."

"Do you remember once I told you that relationships worth having sometimes take time?" She looked at him. The undercurrent of passion flared again between them. They both knew he meant something more than her relationship with Isabelle. After a moment, however, he spread his hands out on his blue-jeaned knees, locking his elbows and stubbornly pressed away the powerful sensation by smiling.

"You know, you do look as if you could do with a long walk somewhere lush and green and very quiet, right about now."

"This was a rather large city, the last time I looked."

"Trust me," he said. Then, hearing his own words, and their implications, Mitch added, "You *can* trust me."

"I already do," Glenna said softly.

Golden Gate Park, like a small forest inside the city, was bustling by the time the cab dropped them off at the entrance. People were picnicking, young girls in shorts and tank tops bicycled down the winding pathways that cut through the park, and tinny-sounding music from portable stereos floated in and out of the breezy spring air.

Glenna and Mitch walked slowly along a path bordered by lush green ferns and ivy. After a little while, Mitch bought her a soda and a hot dog with "the works" at a little cart, assuring her it was an American tradition. Then they sat on a freshly painted green park bench beneath a shady canopy of emerald branches, coppery pine needles beneath their shoes.

"It's lovely here."

"Didn't I tell you?"

She looked over at him and smiled. "Ye did indeed."

"I come here sometimes when I really just need to be alone with my thoughts," he said, looking up at the trees.

"I can see why ye would. Of course, 'tisn't the same as *really* bein' out in the country."

"You're right about that. In Texas, where I'm from, some of the open spaces are almost vast enough to blind you."

"I'm no expert in American geography, but are ye no' a long way from home?"

"Believe me, it's a world away."

She took a sip of the soda and then looked back at him. "So, Mitch Greyson, tell this girl here whose life is practically an open book to ye, why is it then that ye stopped bein' a doctor?"

He hadn't expected that, nor the sincerity with which she had asked. She had an honesty about her that was positively disarming. Of course he couldn't tell her. But for just a moment he actually considered unburdening himself of the whole ugly truth. It would have been the first time in two very long years that he would have spoken to anyone about Livi.

God, that would have felt wonderful, like taking off a very heavy coat in the middle of July. But he just couldn't risk seeing the expression of revulsion pass across her face that he knew would come if she knew the story. *Come on, you don't think she's ever lost a patient?* his mind asked him. *It happens to every doctor sooner or later. . . .* But it wasn't quite the same thing, was it, as being fool enough to treat your own wife? He doubted very seriously that dear Dr. McDowell, here before him, had any idea what it was to take a gamble like that.

And then to lose.

Why hadn't he insisted that Livi at least talk to Hal Davis? He was the best specialist in Texas, and Mitch knew damn right well, even to this day, that Hal could have convinced her that he was better equipped to do a delicate surgery like that. He had told Glenna he knew about regret. Oh, but most days, Mitch Greyson felt as if he had written the whole wretched book on it. "Come on," he said, taking her hand and drawing her suddenly back to her feet.

"Where are we goin' now?"

"Ever gone pedal boatin'?"

"What in heaven's name's that?"

"I'll take that as a no," he chuckled. Then Mitch pointed across the pond to a couple laughing and pedaling through the water in a small boat made of two pontoons, a seat, and pedals. "See there?"

"Och! I'd drown us both!"

"You'd have a ball. . . . and for a while, anyway, you might even laugh a little."

"Wait a minute," she said thoughtfully, reining him back in with a little tug of her hand. "Ye never did tell me why ye stopped bein' a doctor."

"Maybe after we do a bit of boatin'," he lied with a laugh. "I just might at that!"

Afterward, he took her to the Buena Vista bar and, after they called the hospital for the second time to check on Isabelle, Mitch bought Glenna a couple of their famous Irish coffees. He could have opted for some place a little more quiet, but this was a San Francisco landmark, he'd explained, and Mitch had actually gotten two stools at the bar (a sheer impossibility on Saturday afternoon). They'd laughed and watched incredulously the little sideshow as the busy bartender lined up twelve empty glasses before them, then filled each with a flourish, adding hot coffee to whiskey and a sugar cube with one long swipe of his hand.

They talked for almost two hours, pressed in among locals and tourists. Glenna told him about her meeting with Stephen, and Mitch told her about Houston. And they talked about other more inconsequential things as well, before either of them thought to look at their watches.

"Well," Mitch said with a little sigh. "I'd better be gettin' back to the hospital. I'd like to check in on Isabelle one last time today."

"Strange, isn't it? I expect it should be me who's sayin' that."

"Now, don't go bein' so hard on yourself, darlin'. You've only just met her. You need to give it time. It really does heal all wounds," he said. And then before his heart could beat again, he cringed at the sound of that and held onto his head with both hands. "Oh, Lord. I'm sputterin' platitudes now!"

Her eyes narrowed. "Did it work for ye?"

"Platitudes?"

"Time." Glenna said, leaning toward him on her elbow, her dark hair falling forward. Suddenly, she was close enough for him to catch the soft fragrance, just a trace of lilac perfume, even amid the odor of whiskey, cigarettes, and the sound of laughter. ". . . Did it help to heal whatever it was that broke your heart?"

The blood left his face in a hot rush. It was quite beyond his control. (Wasn't everything when he was with her?) She had that uncanny ability to catch him off guard, and she had from the first moment he'd seen her.

As Glenna looked at him now, her question hanging unanswered between them, he considered smiling slyly, leaning forward to meet her and then asking what made her think his heart had ever been broken. But Mitch thought better of it. That sort of sparring was beneath Glenna. And it was beneath *them*.

"No," he finally answered her honestly. "I wouldn't say time healed it, exactly. I don't expect that will ever happen. But on a positive note, I am managin' to get on with my life, which I couldn't so much as imagine a couple of years ago."

"That really is grand. " She shook her head. "I'm no' certain what I'd do if I ever lost Aengus."

"Your husband," he said, knowingly, and a little regretfully.

"My husband saved my life once, Mitch, a long time ago when I truly did no' believe there was any hope left for me in this world. I owe him everythin'. . . . Now he and Katie *are* my life."

Mitch picked up the bill that the bartender had just laid

before him, glanced at it, then reached for his wallet. "Well, I wouldn't mind meetin' him some time," he said, passing off the flicker of disappointment with that characteristic smile when he looked back at her. "Any man who could hold your heart for all those years has *got* to be somethin' extraordinary."

Glenna straightened as the bartender turned back from the cash register and laid down Mitch's change. Something important had just happened between them. She had given him a clue. What Nathan had speculated was true: Her marriage to Aengus McDowell was far more about duty than it was about love.

They stepped out onto busy Beach Street and waited for a cab. The breeze was blowing her hair back away from her face and keeping her skin that ruddy, just-washed color, when suddenly her bright blue eyes settled on his.

"There's one now," he said, tearing his eyes from hers to flag down a cab, because anything else he would say right now she most certainly would not have been ready to hear.

After they'd slipped inside and Mitch had told the driver, a dark-skinned, ebony-mustached man in a white turban, to take her to the Fairmont Hotel first and that he would be going back to Saint Francis Memorial, it grew achingly quiet between them.

The radio was on in the front seat, shrill sitar music, which sounded very like it was being broadcast directly out of Bombay.

As he struggled for just the right thing to say to bring back that easy sense of intimacy, Mitch suddenly became aware of how closely they were sitting to one another. Their shoulders met and his own thigh was touching hers. Realizing it, everything else became very vivid. He could still smell her perfume. The soft baby powder scent of her hair. Horns honking. That sitar music. His body growing extremely warm. He was aching with desire for her, a wild desire he did not dare to completely reveal.

"I wanted to thank ye for bein' so kind to my Katie,"

Glenna suddenly said, as if she'd sensed the intensity too and was seeking to escape it with a comment that had nothing to do with them. "She told me all about ye takin' her dancin' that night when she was so upset about the rudeness of Isabelle's society friend. It really was kind o' ye."

Maybe it was the time they'd spent together, or those velvet hammers they served at the Buena Vista, but suddenly he was possessed enough by the power of his feelings for her, and the sense that she felt a spark of something too, to reach for her. Then, surprising even himself, after he had touched the back of her hand, he let his own come to a rest there. It was more a friendly gesture than a sexual one, the way he cupped his larger hand over her smaller one, then gave it a little squeeze. He hadn't meant for it to happen, but there was raw power even in that. Something undeniable.

"Your daughter is wonderful company," he said, leaning nearer, his voice rough and deep. "Believe me, kindness had nothin' to do with it."

Mitch struggled not to bite off the tip of his own tongue with expletives when the driver pulled sharply into the drive of the Fairmont Hotel. They'd only been in the cab for a few moments, hadn't they? Was it possible that the ride, and this precious moment, was already at an end? How much he would have liked to ask that turbaned driver to go anywhere he liked, as long as he didn't stop. But before Mitch could utter another word, Glenna pulled her hand very casually from beneath his and the doorman opened his car door. *Double dog damn!*

That old Texas term from his childhood bubbled up and surprised him. He hadn't thought of that, or felt it, in years. A remnant of youth and innocence long ago lost. Or so he had believed. Until he'd met Glenna. It was curious, he considered, that she hadn't torn her hand away nor berated him for reaching for her in the first place. There was so much against it, against *them,* but could that little fragment of something he kept seeing mean that somehow there was actually hope?

Knowing full well that he might never know the answer, Mitch reluctantly stepped out of the cab and waited for Glenna to scoot across the torn cocoa-colored seat and join him on the curb. "Thank ye, Mitch, truly, for a wonderful afternoon."

His smile broadened in the shadow of hers. "Thank you for joinin' me. You were a real sport about the pedal boatin'."

"'Twas fun."

"Life is full of those sorts of surprises."

He caught her eye again just as her smile began to fade and she looked suddenly very serious. "Perhaps I'll be seein' ye at the hospital tomorrow, then?"

"I do hope you'll decide to try again with your mother. Isabelle really is one splendid lady. I think you both deserve another chance."

"Well, you've certainly given me somethin' to ponder," Glenna said. "And that alone is a great gift."

It'd be an honor to think that I could give you anything at all that you valued, Mitch thought. But he didn't say it. Instead, he just leaned over and pressed a chaste kiss onto her cheek. "Sleep well," he said and then smiled at her for another moment before he turned and got back into the cab.

Alone in her hotel room, Glenna tried to catch her breath. Suddenly, she needed desperately to phone Arrochar, to hear Aengus's deep, reedy voice and the assurance she knew it would bring. *'Tis the life I've always wanted,* she stubbornly told herself as she went to the edge of the bed beside the small putty-colored telephone in her hotel room. *'Tis the life I still want now. . . . Oh, God, isn't it?*

"'Tis good to hear your voice, love," he said. But it surprised Glenna to hear how far away he sounded.

"How are ye, Aengus?"

"I'm fine here. Janet is a good enough nurse. But you, how is it with Isabelle?"

"She's improvin'. Stephen was by her side when she came out o' the coma."

"And how did it go for the two of ye when ye met?"

Glenna hesitated a moment before she answered. "No' so well, I'm afraid."

"What happened?"

"Oh, there's just been so much goin' on here, and we really have no' had a proper chance to mete it all out."

Aengus laughed, and the sound she knew so well quickly warmed her. The distance between them filled very quickly and she felt as if they were suddenly in the same room. "Glenna, love. 'Tis no' the whole truth ye're tellin' ol' Aengus, is it?"

"I just was no' quite prepared for her answers, that's all."

"I don't suppose ye ever can be ready for a thing like that. 'Tis like swimmin', ye just have to hold your nose and dive on in. Ye grow accustomed to it soon enough."

"Aye . . . I just didn't fancy the feel o' this particular pond very much."

"Oh, dear Glenna, always such a clever lass . . . I wish I knew what perfect thing to say to bring ye the laughter ye bring to me."

"I miss ye, Aengus," Glenna said, meaning it. "I want to come home."

"Now, don't go closin' your heart off to what ye might be findin' there, Glenna Rose," he said after another silence. "When ye least expect it, life has such a splendid way o' surprisin' ye."

Life is full of surprises. Isn't that what Mitch Greyson had said, as well? She shivered and gripped the phone tighter. It was like someone was trying to tell her something that she didn't want to hear. "I don't want surprises, Aengus McDowell. I want *you.* Just like always."

"Oh, now, ye know well, Glenna lass, that *always* is no' possible with a man my age," He took a labored breath. She could hear it even through the phone line. It made her heart ache as if someone had just cut a very small, sharp hole into it. That was the way it always felt when she even considered the possibility of losing him. Her touchstone.

"And besides, ye've had this ol' lion for ages. Perhaps 'tis time now for a new chapter in the splendid life o' Glenna Rose McDowell."

"Damn it, Aengus! Ye're no' goin' to die! I told ye that before I left! Now I won't be hearin' that sort o' thing on the phone like this!"

There was a long silence on the line before he said, "We both know the good Lord has his own time for things such as that."

"Well, I've fought him on that score more than once and won, Aengus McDowell, and I mean to go on doin' him battle for ye as long as I can!"

"See your mother again, Glenna," he said, changing the subject with that firm kind of insistence that called up for her the days when they first had married, when he had been so like the father she had craved. Secure, kind, patient. All of the things she had never had as a child. "Talk to her, lass. . . . and let her talk to you."

"I miss ye," she said again, aching a little for the security he brought to her life.

"My sister's fine company. And ye'll be home soon enough."

"As soon as I can."

"Good night, then, Glenna love."

"Good night, Aengus."

Mitch turned the key and went into his dark apartment. He had forgotten this morning to close the window by the kitchen table, and it was freezing. It felt like the north wind was blowing in past the threadbare white kitchen curtains he kept meaning to replace.

He tossed the mail, two circulars and a telephone bill, onto the nicked Formica table and went to take a beer from his refrigerator. His head was swimming with thoughts of Glenna and from the Irish coffees, but he wouldn't be able to sleep if he didn't sit, watch some mindless comedy, and drink a beer. It was the only way he knew to chase away those relentless thoughts of Livi that reared up at him in the darkness. When he was alone and vulnerable.

He twisted off the cap and tossed it in the brown trash bag by the sink just as someone knocked on the door. Who in hell could that possibly be? It was after ten. And besides, there wasn't a soul in San Francisco who knew where he lived. Except, of course, Nathan Greer at Tremont & Associates. But he felt reasonably certain that it wouldn't be him trekking down to this neighborhood.

Mitch set his beer down and opened the door. Oscar Middleman, the thin, gray-haired manager of the Benson Arms Apartments, stood there in his blue plaid shirt, sagging mohair sweater, and horn-rimmed glasses, holding up a large box wrapped in brown shipping paper. "This came for you today. I signed for it. Hope that was okay."

"Sure. Thanks," Mitch smiled.

He could see the old man, a widower after forty-two years, in his worn moccasin slippers and thick black socks, straining to look inside a young man's apartment where there was very little coming and going and never any telltale noise. For a lonely man like that, Mitch thought a little sadly, the curiosity must have been killing him.

"Well, thanks," he said again. "Good night."

"Oh. Sure. Well, good night, then."

As Mitch closed the door, he saw then that the package had come from Houston. It was his mother's writing on the label. His heart lurched a little. She had never been the sort to send him cookies or cakes, so it wasn't anything harmless like that. *Damn,* he thought. *Why did I ever give in and give them the address?*

He had done that in a moment of weakness. A second call to his father. In case of emergency, he had said. But was that all it had been? They loved him so dearly, his family. They wanted the best for him.

Still, something told him to wait until morning to open the package before him. After having spent so much of the

day at Saint Francis Memorial, and having spent the afternoon with the very-married woman of his dreams, he wasn't
at all certain he was up to whatever it could be.

He picked up the beer again and took a long swallow as
he gazed down at the box, contemplating. He hadn't closed
the window all the way, but suddenly he was very warm
and the chilly breeze actually felt good.

Oh, what the hell.

He tore back the brown paper and pulled apart the seams
of the box. Right on top of a lot of crumpled paper was a
note in his mother's smooth, careful handwriting.

My dearest son,
Your father and I weren't certain of how to tell you this
because we don't want to do anything at all that might
upset you. You sounded so much better the last time we
spoke. But we agreed that you had the right to know that
your house finally sold (to a young couple relocating from
Dallas with three adorable children). Your father took care
of the entire sale and made you a nice little profit. In the
meanwhile, there were a few things that we thought of stor-
ing for you but then I thought that maybe you would like to
have them with you. I know how much they always meant
to you and we thought maybe you had been wondering
what became of them. If you want to send them back to us
for safekeeping, we'll gladly do it for you. We'll do what-
ever you like. And please, Mitchell, please think again
about coming home. I know what you said, about needing
to start a new life away from Olivia's memory, but a visit,
at least that, would mean a great deal to your father. It
would mean a lot to us both.
Love Always,
Mother & Dad

Enclosed with it was a check for a thousand dollars, which
he knew they had meant for airfare. God, he missed them.
The ranch where he had grown up, big and white and sprawl-

ing with its smart ginger-colored trim. Evenings out on the porch so quiet that the silence was almost like a dull roar. And the peace of mind it brought just to be in Texas. *Home.*

But Texas was Livi's home too. And her parents' home as well. It was where he and Olivia Chase had married, bought a house. Papered a baby's room. Planted a garden. Where he had been accused by her grieving parents of her murder. Where he had spent two years in prison for involuntary manslaughter because he had refused to take the plea bargain offered to him. Penance. Yes, that. He had deserved to suffer.

Mitch cringed, closed his eyes for a moment, then pulled the stiff packing paper out of the box. Wound in bubble wrap was their silver-framed wedding photograph. Her sweet face staring up at him again suddenly, smiling, happy, the whole future before them. As if he had only to reach out and touch her to make her real again.

You bloody quack! You goddamn charlatan! How could you have operated on your own wife? Where did you get a deadly ego like that?

Had that been Lester Chase's voice, he wondered now . . . or his own?

Mitch reached into the box again. Inside a small velvet jewelry pouch were their two platinum wedding bands. In the end, her father had refused to let her be buried wearing it, and Mitch was just too blighted by sorrow to fight him.

"Now will you wear a ring if I buy you one?" Livi had asked. "I don't want you to have one that just sits around in a jewelry drawer gatherin' dust."

He reached inside the box again. His framed medical degrees. One from Harvard. The other from his residency at Cornell. Livi had had them done up professionally that first Christmas for him. "Don't hide 'em away, honey. Be proud of what you've accomplished. Be proud of what you are. . . . You're a fine doctor. . . . and I surely am proud of you."

Tears dripped onto the degree, pooling on the glass as Mitch gazed down at them, fragments, symbols of his life. *I can't go back. . . . Not to any of it.*

Using every ounce of strength he had inside, Mitch stood and went into the small, dim kitchen with the peeling yellow paint and old curve-top refrigerator that never worked right. Carefully, he took the wedding photo from its sculptured silver frame and the diplomas from their matching matted black wood. He tossed them into the sink and lit a match. His heart wrenched.

The flame grew, feeding on the ivory vellum emblazoned with the university's gold stamp. *Doctor of Medicine . . .* From there it spread quickly, reaching out with searing gold fingers, devouring the part of his wedding portrait with him first. Black tuxedo. Brightly smiling. The world on a string. *With this ring, I thee wed . . .* Livi next. So radiant. Her white Villanova gown, the powdery pink roses and green ferns cascading from her joined hands. Mahogany-colored hair swept up in white Belgian lace . . . *gone, gone . . . all of it gone.*

When it was over, Mitch wiped a hand across his eyes and called a cab.

"Where to, buddy?"

"Golden Gate Bridge," he flatly said.

The cab idled behind him, the cabbie cursing and angry for having had to stop, here of all places. "Hey, buddy," he complained, chomping on a stale, flattened stub of a cigar, craning around on a short stub of a neck to look at him. "Don't you know this is a suicide mecca for every lovelorn idiot who sobs his way to San Francisco?" If a cop saw them like this, especially after midnight, he was sure to get a ticket. Maybe worse. "Let me take you somewhere else. Anywhere else . . ."

Mitch gave him a twenty to ignore his fears, then walked alone out across the great iron expanse of bridge. The icy midnight wind whipped through his light shirt, battering his clothes and hair. But somehow he didn't feel it. He didn't hear the cars racing by, nor did he see the glare of their bright headlights coming at him from both directions.

He stood against the railing quietly for a moment, looking down into the great obsidian water below as if he were looking into eternity. Fitting, he thought.

After a while, Mitch plucked the two platinum wedding rings from the front pocket of his jeans. He held Livi's up, then kissed it. It was like saying good-bye to her all over again. The wrenching pain of a forever loss.

He put them both in the palm of his hand and clenched his fist. Eternally, he remembered her saying. He held their rings like that for a little while, his closed fist pressed against his chest. And then very swiftly and purposefully he reached out across the railing . . . opened his hand . . . and let the dream go.

Glenna stood in the dimly lit waiting room outside Isabelle's new private room, drinking a cup of cold coffee she really didn't want from a styrofoam cup. At least it was something to help her hands stop shaking. *Anything to avoid Isabelle,* her conscience said, *the woman who wants so much more from me than I am ready to give.* Glenna still wanted to put this off. But now she had to face this lifelong emptiness, this bottomless pit of questions that might finally be answered.

She had to try again to get to know her birth mother. She had to try to bridge this gap of years, and anger, that was keeping her from really feeling complete.

"Well, well, well . . . So what do *you* want?"

Glenna pivoted around, startled by the man's booming question. It was so early in the morning she was certain there'd be no one else here yet to see her. Damn. "Ye must be Arthur, then."

"At least you have enough breeding to know who I am. I will say that for you."

"It's your reputation that precedes you, Senator. My daughter told me all about ye."

"A *glib* gold digger?" he snapped bitterly, then rolled his eyes. "Terrific."

"What are ye meanin' to imply?"

He stiffened in his crisp navy pinstripe suit and took two bold steps toward her. "How much?"

"I do no' want your money, Senator!"

He cocked a bushy brow. "My mother's, then?"

"Ye may well be a respected politician, but ye're also a very vulgar man."

"Oh, come now. You certainly did not travel halfway around the world simply to check up on the health of a complete stranger."

She had met people like this before. First at medical school, tired, frustrated old doctors overstaying their welcome in the profession. Then later, in Arrochar, before she had been truly accepted. Oh! That she, of all people, should be thought a gold digger! Wasn't that the ultimate irony, when she had worked all of her life for everything she'd gotten! Glenna leveled her eyes with his. It was the only way to deal with people like Arthur Wescott. Straight on. And never let them see your fear.

"That *stranger*, Senator, is my mother every bit as much as she is yours."

"That might be true but for one crucial little fact."

"Aye, and what might that be?"

"*I* am her acknowledged firstborn. The one she kept. You, on the other hand, are nothing but her dirty little secret."

"My, my . . . What do you suppose those constituents of yours would think if they heard you talkin' like that? Damn, but you have a foul mouth for a man of the people."

Glenna whirled suddenly at the sound of Mitch's smooth-as-silk Texas drawl. "Well, either way, Senator Wescott, I'd strongly suggest you don't say another word to the lady if you can't say anythin' nice at all." He was leaning against the doorjamb, arms and ankles casually crossed.

"Who the devil are you to talk to me like that? Another of my mother's *friends,* like the good Father Donnelly? Or are you just another bastard child she's hidden away in her closet all these years?"

Mitch moved forward, the heels of his Tony Lama boots tapping on the bare, ammonia-scented floor. His smile was self-assured as he surveyed the senator. "That's right. I'm a friend. A real good friend. And I'd advise you to be more polite when you're speakin' to a lady. Especially when I'm around."

"Look." Arthur lowered his voice as if he had only just considered that there might be someone listening. "My family is not without a certain amount of influence in this community, and I believe I have an obligation to protect that. It's nothing personal, Miss—"

"*Doctor* McDowell, if ye please," Glenna angrily corrected him.

Suddenly, as they eyed one another combatively, a gray-haired nurse poked her head around the corner. "Mrs. Wescott is awake, Senator," she said. "You can go in now."

Arthur turned around when he reached the door. "We're not finished with this," he said.

"Now, why doesn't that surprise me?" Glenna shot back. If she'd had a cup of hot coffee in her hand instead of one that was cold, she'd have thrown it at him.

When Arthur left the waiting room, Glenna blanched, her fragile mask of confidence falling away. Tears fell as Mitch wrapped his arms around her.

"Ooh! He's every bit as foul as Katie said he was!"

"Well now, darlin', that bein' so, he's not worth a single one of those teardrops stainin' your pretty face."

It would have been so easy for him to kiss her just then. He thought about taking this chance, a chance, at the least, to taste those full, tawny lips that he had studied so longingly since they first met. But he couldn't do it. When it came right down to it, Glenna wasn't a woman to be taken advantage of. . . .

Glenna was a woman to love for a lifetime.

Mitch felt his heart catch as her tears wet his neck. He thought it was the most blissful sensation he'd felt for a very,

very long time. Finally, forcefully, he gripped her shoulders and pressed her back just enough for her to see his face. He wiped her tears with his own fingers. Then he held her face in both hands.

"Whatever Arthur Wescott is, you're every bit his match."

She shook her head. "I don't know about that."

"Well, I do. Now, when he's finished in there," Mitch insisted, "you go ahead into that room yourself, with your head high, just like this, *knowin'* that you have every right in the world to be there."

"I don't know, Mitch." She tried to look away, but he wouldn't let her. "It's all just so much more awkward bein' here than I had even imagined."

"Then you just push right through it, you hear?" They both heard someone walking quickly out in the corridor. Mitch glanced over and saw that it was Arthur, already leaving his mother's room.

After he had passed, Mitch looked back at her. "You came here because you wanted to get to know your mother, didn't you? Well, you just march right in there and let her know what a splendid woman you've become in spite of the obstacles life has tossed your way."

Glenna's smile was tentative as she cocked her head. "Are ye always so wise concernin' matters o' the heart?"

"I think today might only be the second time in my life. Now get goin'. Don't lose another minute, you hear?"

She took a step away from him, then turned back. Her face was shining, strangely incandescent, in the light and shadows cast into the dim waiting room from the fluorescent lights in the corridor. "Ye really *are* a fine man, Mitch Greyson."

His grin was slow and warm, only slightly devilish. It was his heart's best defense. "Heck, darlin', that's just an old rumor I started."

He didn't move as she rounded the corner and went out of his sight. Mitch wanted to linger for another moment where they had been, where he could still almost feel her pressed against him. Even needing him a little. Yes, he thought, remembering what he had just told her about matters of the heart. He had been smart twice in his life. *Once when I married Livi . . . And the moment, back in Scotland, when I fell in love with you.*

Glenna poked her head around the corner tentatively.

The nurse was in the middle of checking Isabelle's pulse. This room was nicer than CCU had been, she thought, hanging back a little until the nurse was done. It was private and fairly large by hospital standards, and there was a veritable flower store of bouquets on every table and tray.

The morning sun was coming in through the slatted blinds casting Isabelle in ribbons of light and shadow, and she was no longer wearing one of those atrocious green hospital gowns but her own shrimp-colored peignoir. *She does look better,* Glenna thought with a bit of surprise, then feeling a strange unexpected glimmer of tenderness lighting up from that dark place deep inside her. *If I were a bettin' Scot, as Aengus always used to say, I'd wager she's goin' to be just fine. . . .*

"Are ye up for another try at things?"

Isabelle glanced up as the nurse fluffed her bedding and pillows. Seeing Glenna, Isabelle's eyes widened. "Absolutely."

She moved into the room a few steps further, remembering Mitch's words and pushing past the little rush of insecurity. "I was hopin' we might take a little time to try again to search for some common ground at least."

"It has been my dream," Isabelle said, struggling to keep her voice from catching with emotion. "Will you sit down with me, then?"

"We could be at this for a while," Glenna gently warned, her lips turning up just ever so slightly at the corners.

She could see Isabelle perk up and her eyes widen even more. Then suddenly she was smiling. "Well, I'm not going anywhere in the near future, am I, Mrs. Hudson?" she asked, glancing up at the stout old woman who looked somewhat more like a drill sergeant than anybody's nurse.

"No, ma'am, not for a while."

Glenna and Isabelle both smiled, tentatively at first, then more broadly. "Mrs. Hudson," Isabelle said as the nurse collected her tray of little paper cups that had held Isabelle's morning dose of medication and was preparing to leave. "Do you suppose an old senator's widow could pull a string or two with you to bring two cups of tea?"

Mrs. Hudson frowned endearingly. She was Isabelle's favorite. "I'm afraid there's to be nothing more stimulating for you than a little prune juice, Mrs. Wescott."

"Spoilsport," Isabelle said with a little pouty smile. "Then would you bring a cup of tea for Dr. McDowell and a prune juice cocktail for me?"

"I'll see what I can do," she said, heading briskly for the door, her heavy white support hose swishing as she walked. "But only for you, Mrs. Wescott, and *only* this once."

CHAPTER

17

◈◈◈ Glenna and Mitch *Beginnings*

"Mother, you have *got* to slow down! You've only been out of the hospital since yesterday!" Douglas pleaded as he followed Isabelle around her flower-filled drawing room, the sun pouring in through the bay window like shimmery golden waves. "Oh, I give up." He rolled his eyes. "Stephen, maybe *you* can reason with her."

Stephen Donnelly looked up from a copy of the *San Francisco Chronicle* as he sat cross-legged on the blue chintz sofa. "Not on your life," he said with a crooked smile. "You're on your own doing battle with *this* particular iron-willed lady."

"I'm fine. Both of you," she said, her slim face wreathed in a calm, happy smile. "Besides, being here with my family, *all* of my family, really is the best medicine."

"'Tis so romantic," said Kate. "How this all has turned out."

"I think it is, too," Isabelle said, her voice quaking with sudden emotion as she glanced over at Stephen.

Glenna looked at her father as he came to his feet and then went to the sofa to sit beside Isabelle. He was looking at her with an expression full of enough love to make Glenna want to weep. This thing between them, *her parents*, she thought, was something very powerful and very rare. It made her sad that she had missed that in her own life. And now, because of Mitch Greyson, she had begun to get a sense for herself what it was she had sacrificed all of this time for security.

"Come on, Katie, Douglas," Glenna said thoughtfully, wanting to give Isabelle and Stephen some time alone. "Let's go and see if that lovely housekeeper has any more of her wonderful lemonade."

337

◆   ◆   ◆

When they were alone, Stephen put his arm around Isabelle. "There are so many things I don't know about your life anymore, when once I thought I knew everything," he said. "There is much we have yet to learn, my darling. But we have the rest of our lives for catching up."

Isabelle turned away from him, but Stephen was not deterred. "I expect this is as good a time as any to talk about this. Something has come up back in Glasgow. I need to get back, Isabelle," he said tentatively. "The Bear, I told you about him—"

"The gentleman who owns the coffee house."

"Right. Well, in my absence, Barry and my publisher have arranged a couple more readings for me in Glasgow. And I had forgotten until he phoned last evening that I had agreed to it."

They had been dancing around it for days. But Isabelle knew what he was going to say, because even with the great heavy veil of time between them, she still *knew* Stephen.

"You know that I want to marry you, Isabelle," he said, taking her hands after he'd led her to the sofa and made her sit beside him. "I want us to have the life we should have had all those years ago."

"We've been all through this," she sighed. "We're different people. We have different interests, different friends . . . different lives."

"So do all couples. In the beginning. Look at Glenna and Mitch. They've got a river of problems ahead. But they love each other."

"Oh, dear. Do you think so?"

He smiled softly. "Have you any doubt when they look at one another?"

Isabelle smiled too, knowing he was right. "It's sad, really, what's ahead of her about all of that."

"We each have our trials to pass through. Thankfully, ours are over at last."

"We're not children anymore, Stephen. People our ages get set in their ways."

"Oh, come now, my darling Isabelle." He chucked her tenderly beneath the chin. "You know I don't believe that for a moment about you. You are as vibrant and spirited as you were the day I met you."

"Certainly as stubborn, I expect."

He leaned closer and took up her hands again. "Marry me, Isabelle."

"I need time to think."

"I've done nothing *but* think since the moment I knew that you were going to survive this. *Please.*" He squeezed her hands lightly, then said in a deep, velvety voice, "Don't let's waste any more time. Say you'll come back to Glasgow with me."

"What about my family? The house?"

"Your family will always be welcome. And I'm not trying to tell you what to do, but, since you asked, maybe you could think about leasing this wonderful old place out to Douglas and Philip. It would be well cared for, you *know* that. And that way you wouldn't entirely be giving it up."

"But what am I to do in Glasgow? I wouldn't know a single soul there besides you."

"What do you really do here in San Francisco since Frank died?" he asked in a kind, not at all an accusatory, tone.

"I love you," she said softly. "You know that I do. But giving up a life is not so easy as all that. I have commitments here. Obligations. People depending on me."

He brought her hands to his lips and kissed each of them in turn. "And where does Isabelle fit in with all of that? Do you just get lost helping everyone else out, being there for everyone else but yourself?"

"You make it sound so bleak."

"I'm trying to convince you that we belong together."

"You're doing an admirable job of it. But I just can't decide right this moment. Right now I have to worry about Glenna, see if I can be a help to her. She's married and about to embark on a dangerous course with Mitch. I can feel it."

"It reminds you of us, doesn't it?"

Isabelle looked at him. "I suppose it does."

"And was there anything that could have stopped our fate back then?"

"Nothing," she agreed, and pressed a gentle kiss onto his cheek.

"I owe ye a grand apology, Ma." Kate leaned against the kitchen counter with her glass of lemonade as she looked across the kitchen at Glenna. "'Twas wrong o' me to run away again. To frighten ye as I did."

Glenna held her breath. It was difficult to believe what she was hearing, no matter how she had yearned for it.

"I've learned a lot about myself, bein' here. And I've learned a bit about *you*, as well. I was tough on ye, Ma. Pigheaded. I guess I'm learnin' now, because of Isabelle, I think, that women have to make hard choices sometimes. The point is, I always thought ye just chose the life ye had in Arrochar because 'twas the easiest way. That ye worked so hard to avoid really livin'."

"'Tis partly true, I think," Glenna said haltingly, her eyes locked with her daughter's.

"But there was always a lot more to it, wasn't there?"

"Aye. That is also true enough."

"I want ye to be happy, Ma." They were gazing at one another, mother and daughter, the years and the conflict melting away. "Whatever that ends up meanin'."

Glenna's eyes suddenly filled with tears. Her words came with a hint of warning. "A lot has happened to me lately, Katie."

"I know, Ma."

"I honestly don't know what the future is goin' to bring."

"'Tis all right. I love ye. And so, ye know, does Da."

It was beautiful in Isabelle's gazebo, blocked from the cool wind by its thick, twisting wisteria and white, stenciled ginger-bread wood. Glenna left the kitchen alone after her conversation with Kate, and sat down on the white wrought-iron bench. She took a sip from the glass of lemonade she had brought with her and looked out across the bay.

This trip to San Francisco had been an odyssey of sorts. It had not been just a trip of discovery for her and her birth mother but for her and her own daughter, as well.

She and Kate were spending time together, sharing again, and enjoying one another's company. It was what she had wanted so desperately—for them to reconnect. And here in this place that seemed so full of surprises, they had.

A part of Glenna actually hated to leave San Francisco. It was that same part that had been missing for most of her life—and which she had found here, so unexpectedly, in this place and in these people. It was like that last stubborn piece of a jigsaw puzzle, one you can't quite bring yourself to put away until it's completed. *Now, finally, the last piece was in place.*

She did need to get home to Aengus. She'd promised him she would be back by week's end. And she wanted to go. The guilt over the forbidden things she felt for Mitch made going home that much more urgent. It simply could not be between them.

Maybe if they had met in another time, in another way . . .

But that was an exercise in futility, wasn't it?

Then why, in the face of that, she wondered now, had she been allowing both of them to walk along the very fringes of temptation for days now? Not just back in Scotland, but here as well.

Why had she allowed herself to go pedal boating with him in the park. Then, after her run-in with Arthur, why had she gone with Mitch again, to that same Western bar to which he had taken Kate?

Glenna had relented, after Kate had urged her on, and she had even danced with Mitch. Lord help her, but she had reveled in the feel of his taut, slightly sweaty body pressed close to hers as they moved in a slow two-step rhythm to a song, quite unbelievably called "I Was Meant to Be with You." It was like fate's cruel jest that somehow it had played just then, the slowest, saddest song she had ever heard.

Oh, the way he had smelled, like leather and denim mixed potently with just a hint of tangy musk. So hard and raw, as the lights softly changed from dusty blue to gold. And when a tear had escaped her eye at the futility of what she had begun to feel, he had reached up and ever so gently brushed it away with the back of his hand, never losing his step or that firm, strong way he moved as he held her. But it was more than attraction. That alone would have been easy enough to negate.

It was also just so easy to talk with him about things. Especially awkward things, feelings, about Isabelle. Glenna seemed to be able to tell Mitch things she couldn't even imagine telling Aengus—about the way she felt about Stephen, about the way she felt getting to know the woman who had given her up.

"Well, far as I know, you can't reclaim the past, darlin'," he had said that night when they'd stepped outside of the Desperado for a breath of air. "But you can damn sure claim your future."

Glenna took a sip of the slightly sour lemonade to cauterize the sharp memory of desire as her mind crossed back to how another evening, two nights ago now, had ended.

She had thought it was so safe, going out again like that with Kate and Douglas and Philip. They'd all had such a good time at the Desperado. But she had been lying to herself. She had wanted to see Mitch again, be with him. That time, the evening had been *her* idea.

They had all gone over to Sausalito to the same restaurant where Isabelle and Douglas had taken Kate. And they had sat at a table by the water sipping those icy margaritas and watching the sun set. It was breathtaking, she remembered. Then, as Kate and Philip had lagged behind while Douglas made a phone call to his mother, she and Mitch had walked down to the landing to wait for the next boat to take them back across the bay.

It had been cold and very dark, and she had begun to shiver as they gazed out at the distant lights of San Francisco. And then it had happened.

Mitch had kissed her.

It was so sweet and yet so sensual, as she had tasted his lips, opening her mouth and her heart, as if she were giving in to forbidden fruit, wanting to taste fully this foreign and dangerous pleasure, just this once in her life. And then there had been that still, small voice taunting her as she felt her lips pressed beneath his, *Give in*, it said. . . . *For once in your life, just let it happen.* . . .

But her face had been stricken as she'd brought two fingers to her lips—a place that still burned with their kiss. "I can no' . . . " she had sighed

"You can't or you won't?"

"I'm married, Mitch."

"What's between us has nothin' to do with what is waitin' for you back in Scotland."

"There is nothin' between us."

He had leveled his eyes until they met and held hers, bright in their sincerity. "Now, you know that's not true, don't you?"

"Why are ye doin' this?"

He sighed and held her face up in his warm and powerful hands. "I actually promised myself I wouldn't ever tell you what I was feelin'. Even though I've wanted to since the moment we met."

"I think that would have been for the best."

Mitch let go of her then and looked back out across the bay. "I lost my wife a few years ago. . . . " he confessed and she heard the pain in each slow and deliberate word. "Livi was the most important thing in the world to me. God, I loved that woman. And when she died, I can't begin to describe what it felt like—what it was like to be without her." She saw a muscle tense in his jaw, and he did not look at her again as he went on, suddenly pressed to unburden himself to her. "A part of me was actually dead too. . . . I felt old and very dark, and I really wanted to be the one who had died instead of her."

"Why are you tellin' me this, Mitch?"

"Because I trust you. I never thought I'd say that to another human bein'. . . . And because I believed that I could never feel for anyone that spark, that wild, all-consumin' passion that I felt for her."

"'Tis a rare gift, I think, to have that with someone."

"And rarely ever does it happen twice in a lifetime."

Her heart rocked in her chest. "Please, say no more."

"I'm in love with you, Glenna."

"No." She had turned away, but he held her shoulders squarely. The wind was tossing her hair and throwing it back like a dark satiny, raven-colored sail, making her shiver, almost as much as the warmth of his touch. The words hadn't come as a surprise, but somehow hearing them made them seem more real. That much more dangerous. "Please, Mitch," she pleaded in a pained whisper. "Say nothin' more."

And so he hadn't. Instead, his mouth had come down on hers again, parting her lips in another powerful, sensual kiss. What a warm trail he had blazed, moving down her throat touching her in a way that . . .

"Hello, Glenna."

She was jolted back to the present at lightning speed by the sound of Mitch's smooth drawl, suddenly in front of her in Isabelle's gazebo. When she glanced up, she saw him, tall and commanding, standing there in the sunlight.

She pushed away the memory of his touch and came to her feet. But her legs suddenly felt like butter on a July afternoon. "How did ye know I was down here?"

"Isabelle told me." There was something different about his voice. A hitch. An odd kind of strain. "Why didn't you tell me that you were leaving for Scotland with Stephen tomorrow?"

"After last night, I thought 'twould be best if I just quietly slipped away," she said haltingly, trying desperately to mean it.

"Certainly not best for me."

He took a step nearer until they were almost as close to one another as they had been when they were dancing. She was certainly close enough to see the hurt in his eyes. Glenna felt suddenly very lost and very alone. *I don't want to let go of what I feel for him,* she was thinking as he looked at her, his sincerity stabbing at her like a blunt-edged knife. *But I canno' leave Aengus.*

Caring for two men and believing she couldn't really give herself fully to either of them had made her feel strangely empty and very adrift with no shore or touchstone anywhere in sight. "Mitch, this is an impossible situation."

"Do you love me?" He cocked his head, seeking those eyes of hers which were cast down to avoid him.

"I canno' answer that and save my marriage."

He waited a moment but he did not take his eyes from hers. "Then I won't ask you again for an answer."

She turned away from him for a moment, feeling as if she were being torn in two. Glenna had seen, by the expression on his face—the steady gaze, the way that hint of disappointment flickered in his eyes, that he had known what she was going to say. But, for him, this was just something that was meant to be said between them.

She waited a moment, her heart beating very fast and making her think she'd drunk those Irish coffees instead of lemonade. She was thinking, in this awkward little silence, that he was about to suggest the alternative. An affair. Wasn't that what people did who were attracted to one another but knew that they were like those proverbial ships passing in the night?

She prepared for the suggestion, lines racing through her mind, things that she could say in response. She would have to wax indignant and go very quickly back up to Isabelle's house. Because that was what she did. The right thing. Always the right thing.

But Mitch didn't ask. He just stood there in the cool, glinting sunlight, looking more handsome and more desirable than any man she had ever seen.

On top of everything, he was going to be a gentleman now.

When the last thing she should have done was draw nearer to him, Glenna ran a hand along the line of his jaw. So strong. So firm. Yet there was still that sadness behind his smile, the smile he always tried to show to the rest of the world. She wondered if that was still because of the wife he had lost, and how long it took—if you ever really got over losing someone with whom you had shared a part of your life.

They were so close, she suddenly realized, a breath away. He wanted to kiss her again. And she wanted him too, very much. As they touched, desire grew within her. It was a powerful force drawing her nearer, easing the fear. Pressing into its place a warm, numbing sensation that would make it all right, for a while, to have that with him again.

Then, just as Mitch pulled her forcefully into his arms, Glenna caught a glimpse of four people drawing toward them. She moved away from Mitch quickly when she saw that it was Isabelle, Douglas, Arthur, and Stephen.

"All right, Mother, now ask him to leave," Arthur commanded.

"Maybe there is a plausible explanation for all of this," Isabelle said. "Let's just hear him out."

"My sources found his picture in the newspaper and a follow-up story about his trial. What more do you need than that?"

"Mitch is my friend," Isabelle said evenly.

"Thanks to your utter lack of judgment yet again," Arthur cruelly quipped.

"One more shot like that," Stephen intervened, "and I will throw you out of here personally."

Glenna took a small step forward. "Might I be askin' what's goin' on?"

"This has nothing to do with you," Arthur said. "Why don't you just go on back up to the house with your daughter while my mother and I have a word with the doctor here."

Glenna studied Arthur. "I'd like to stay, if ye would no' mind."

"Suit yourself." He shrugged. "But I don't imagine you will like what you hear."

Glenna glanced again at Mitch, whose expression was strangely calm, as if he already knew what they were going to say.

"How could you pass yourself off to my mother as someone of good moral standing after what you've done?" Arthur charged, his hands going very sharply onto his hips.

Mitch's tone was very low, but not at all defensive. Senator Wescott had discovered the truth. "I made it very clear to Mrs. Wescott that I didn't practice medicine any longer."

"But you didn't tell her the *whole* truth, did you?"

"All right, Arthur, that's quite enough," Isabelle intervened.

"Perhaps I am guilty of the error of omission, and for that I apologize."

"Well, I'd say you are guilty of a far sight more than that!"

"Arthur," Stephen warned, pressing an iron hand onto his shoulder. "Your spies also said that the case was heard by an appeals court and Dr. Greyson was finally acquitted of the charges. Didn't you just tell us that as well?"

"Charges?" Glenna mouthed, feeling suddenly sick and even a little betrayed by a man to whom she felt she had nearly bared her soul.

"Charges that he murdered his wife!"

"You . . . killed Livi?" Glenna breathed, feeling her head like a balloon with too much air, about to explode.

In the wake of her question, everyone looked at him. But Mitch leveled his eyes on Glenna, and only on her. "Yes."

"Well, I just don't believe it. It's as simple as that," Isabelle took a stand as she gazed appraisingly at Mitch and shook her head. "I'm something of an expert on knowing that things are very often not as they seem."

"My wife is dead. Her death was *my* responsibility. I accept that," he said almost a little too cavalierly, and Glenna felt as if her heart was suddenly being squeezed very hard.

"Well, I would like to hear the story," Isabelle said.

"I am guilty, as your son says. I suspect that's about all there is to say."

"But you were acquitted."

"Doesn't mean I didn't do it," Mitch said.

It was evening now, very late. Glenna knew that much because she felt so achingly tired. But she had no idea what time it was. All she knew for certain was that she was glad that Mitch was here with her and that they were walking the streets of San Francisco, like any other couple. Alone. Anonymous. Quiet in the knowledge of how what had happened had drawn them even closer together.

Mitch's admission had not driven Glenna away, as he had feared. Rather, it had deepened her feelings for him. It made her feel that she was not the only one with a complex and painful past.

He had been there for her since Arrochar. Oh, that kind way of his, how it could wrap itself around your heart. Gentle as a whisper and yet strong as an ancient redwood. And now, tonight, her heart urged her to be here, this time for him.

"You know," he said, pulling her from her thoughts, "we've been walkin' around like this for hours. These hills take stamina. You must be starved."

"Oh, I'm no' hungry, Mitch. Besides, I expect I'd fall asleep in my soup."

"Well, I'm not the world's greatest chef, I'll admit, but I do make a pretty mean pasta Bolognese and I've got a first class pinot grigio just gathering dust in my kitchen. You could come home with me, put up your feet and catch a few winks while I'm puttin' everything together."

Glenna's smile was slow and grateful. "Thank ye Mitch. But I do no' think 'twould be such a good idea."

"Look," he said, pivoting around to face her as they came to yet another street corner. "You need a good home-cooked meal, and I promise not to try anything objectionable."

She felt something catch inside her. Objectionable? Could anything about him ever be that? He was like a knight in shining armor whenever she really needed him to be there. The truth was that she was famished. She hadn't eaten anything all day but a few hors d'oeuvres.

"It does sound lovely," she recanted, weakening at the temptation to be alone with him for a just a little while longer.

"I'm gonna warn you, it's not the Ritz, my place."

"I'm sure it's every bit as charmin' as you are."

"Come with me?"

They linked hands then, as naturally as if they had been doing it all of their lives, and Glenna wondered if it was actually possible, that being with someone could make you happy and sad at the very same time. The way she felt now. With Mitch. Worse than that, she still had no idea how on earth she was going to get on that plane and walk away from him tomorrow.

Glenna drew in a breath as he opened the door.

Mitch hadn't been kidding when he'd warned her about his apartment. She never would have imagined (not in her wildest dreams) that Mitch would live in a place like this, small and boxy with no pictures on the grim beige walls. Little furniture and no green plants. The surroundings didn't suit him in the least. Nothing about it spoke of the man she had come to know. This place, with no soul and no history, was certainly not where he was meant to be.

"Make yourself at home," he said, flicking on a little table light and then stepping back into the kitchen as he raked a hand through his hair. "Now where'd I put that wine?"

Glenna sank onto the edge of the worn gold-and-green easy chair. Her eyes searched the small, Spartan living room for any sign of homeyness. Photographs. Knickknacks. Mementos. There was nothing.

She heard the cork pop and then, a moment later, he was coming toward her with a glass filled with white wine. She took a grateful sip and then said, "This is no' exactly how I pictured your home, ye know."

"I know," he smiled. "And you're the only person in the world who has ever been here to tell me so. It's awful, I know. Early shabby, I like to call it. But—well, window dressin' doesn't matter, in reality, much, does it? It's what's inside that matters. Now, I promised you some time to relax, and a good meal, and so you shall have it. Put your feet up and make yourself comfortable while I get to work."

But when Mitch went back into the small kitchen, she didn't relax. Instead, Glenna followed him, holding her wine and sinking slowly onto one of the two wrought-iron barstools separating the kitchen from the small living area.

He turned his back to her and was fishing out things from the refrigerator as she took several sips of the wine. It was surprisingly good, and she hadn't realized how keyed up she had gotten until she began to unwind.

"So, why are ye livin' somewhere like this when ye could be anywhere ye wanted?"

"Because I *can't* be where I want to be, darlin'," Mitch said looking up from a glass container of dry pasta and a handful of tomatoes that he tossed onto the counter before he turned back to the open refrigerator. "Ye can't bring back the past, no matter how much you want to sometimes. I'm learnin' *that* the hard way."

As he put a pot of water on the stove and flicked on the burner, Glenna turned and went over to the little Formica table and two chairs. In the shadows, she saw a photograph of a woman and, even though it was obscured by a wooden bowl with two apples and a browning banana, her heart sharply twisted.

Could it be a photograph of Livi? Glenna was curious to see the kind of woman who could capture Mitch's heart. She focused in a bit more closely. Then a little knot of shock hit her. *It canno' be. . . .* Glenna moved a step nearer as Mitch turned back to the refrigerator and opened it again.

Something was drumming in her ears as she picked up the

photograph and saw, quite unmistakably, that the image on his kitchen table . . . was not Livi. It was a photograph of her! Glenna could see that it had been taken in Scotland. She was going into the cottage, wearing her best dressy suit. The day she'd come back from London. *But how on earth could Mitch Greyson . . . Why would he . . .*

"Shit," he breathed as, seeing her, he dropped a handful of onions into the sink. "Now, it's not what you're thinkin'. If you'll just let me tell you—"

Glenna pivoted around without saying anything and headed in bold strides back toward the front door. "Wait a minute!" he said charging after her.

"I've got to get out o' here!"

"You can't! . . . I mean—" His face had a suddenly stricken expression bordering on desperation as he seized her shoulders and jerked her back around. ". . . I mean, please, don't leave. Let me explain the photograph."

"Were ye . . . spyin' on me, then, Mitch Greyson? Is that how ye got this thing?"

"No!"

Then he led her back to the table and showed her the photograph he had taken of her for Tremont & Associates, and then, against everything he knew was right, kept. And he told her how the image of the incandescent woman before him could not compare to the flesh-and-blood woman he had come to respect, to know. And to love.

"It's part of Tremont's policy, photographing people for clients. In case things don't go right, at least they have the memento. As for me, when I got to know you, to *love* you—" His words fell away and it was a moment before he finished them. "Well, anyway, Isabelle now has the only other copy."

The wild pounding in Glenna's chest slowed.

"I know it sounds crazy, but the day I met you, right from the first moment, something happened to me, Glenna." He raked a hand through his hair. "God, I wish I knew how to explain it. I still don't know exactly what it was. I mean, I knew from the beginning that you weren't free. But all I know is that I stopped thinking that my life was over. I looked at your face and for some reason it made me think of Livi."

"Your wife."

"Promise you won't laugh?"

"I would no' laugh."

"It seemed to me you remindin' me so much of her was a sign from her to get on with things, that there was another woman out there to love. . . . if I just forgave myself a little."

She turned her head to the side, but Mitch brought it back around with the power of his thumb and forefinger. "This is dangerous territory we're headin' into, Mitch," Glenna said softly, her voice breaking.

"I know."

"I'm afraid."

"So am I." He waited a moment; steadying himself beneath her fragile gaze. "I guess it was the real reason I wanted you to come here with me tonight. The truth is that I haven't been able to go home to Texas since it happened. . . . It's like, if I'm not there, I'm not the same man capable of what I did. Here, I've been someone else, this glib, carefree carica-ture of myself. But after I met you, Glenna, I started seein' that I haven't just been runnin' away from Texas . . . but I've been tryin' to hide from myself."

He took a breath, then waited a moment before he spoke again. "I felt that if I could bring you *here,* of all places, if I could be real about myself with at least one other human bein', I'd have a chance of really gettin' on with my life, once and for all."

His fingers tightened slightly on her delicate jaw.

"I know it won't change anything for us," he said deeply. "But once I got to know you, it just seemed really important to me that you understand what happened, that you really *know* me, this crazy Texan who's in love with you."

"Ye don't need to be doin' that for my sake, Mitch."

"Yes, I do," he said softly, with an expression of pure pain in his eyes. "Because tomorrow you're goin' back to Scotland

and I really can't stomach the idea that you'll go home only knowin' a part of things."

And so, as they sat together on the old threadbare sixties sofa with the nicked dowel legs, Mitch held her hand and told her about Olivia. He told her everything about how he had loved her. And how she had died when he had gone ahead and done a surgery that he knew only too well should never, ever have been done by a family member.

As he spoke, in halting starts and stops, all of the things he'd been trying to shut out for two long years flared in his mind. Flashes. Scenes. Images of Livi, slim and long-legged, with her shoulder-length brown hair that glimmered like polished teak . . .

"It's not a normal pregnancy, Livi. It's called an ectopic pregnancy."

"Speak English, will you, Greyson," his wife had said. She was always calling him that, even after they were married. He remembered now that it had actually become something of an endearment, a kind of lover's little joke between them. "Tell me what's wrong with the baby."

But even that horrible encounter, where they had cried together and given up hope of the child they both had wanted so desperately, was not as bad as letting her talk him into doing the risky surgery himself. *What an idiot you were! A self-aggrandizing idiot to ever have believed you could—*

In the intense silence, Mitch pulled in a breath and Glenna saw something dark pass across his face. Then saw him struggle to push it away, and she was swept with a sudden tenderness for him.

"Now that's no' truly killin' your wife," she said softly as the words lay like a fresh spring rain, newly fallen and cleansing, between them. "'Twas a risky surgery. I'm no' an expert in gynecology but even *I* know that. 'Twas nothin' more than a horrible accident."

"Call it what you like, darlin', I was responsible for her dyin', just the same."

Glenna took his hand and then held it as firm and sure

as if that connection alone was the thing that would save him from drowning in his own bottomless well of self-recrimination. "No' long ago, Aengus puts the same sort o' faith in me. . . ." she confessed. "And the same pressure. I should have seen him to a hospital, but I ended up carin' for him myself at home. So I understand what it must have been like for ye to be pulled by your loyalty to her. 'Twas what she wanted."

"I still went to prison for killing her. Can you understand that, too?" His voice went suddenly low and sharp as he looked at her squarely. "I am exactly what Arthur Wescott says. In the state of Texas, I am a murderer, Glenna."

It was so awful, that this big, tenderhearted man beside her had ever been forced to suffer a day's punishment for that. Glenna was quite certain that living with Livi's death would be punishment enough.

"'Tis just so hard to believe when she was your wife."

"Not hard to believe at all, really. Especially when her father hired the best lawyers in Texas. Then the DA got involved and they built this case, sayin' that I had killed her purposely to collect her life insurance policy. The ironic thing was that Livi had taken out this whoppin' big thing on herself when she'd found out she was pregnant. I guess it was supposed to be a surprise, because, I swear to God, Glenna, she never told me. . . ." He struggled with each word, and she waited patiently for him to speak them. ". . . Would you believe, I found out about it with the rest of the jury and the rest of Texas right in the middle of open court?"

"Oh, Mitch." Glenna pressed her fingers against her lips.

"My lawyer told me that he'd never seen such an impressive case of circumstantial evidence mounted against someone who had once been so respected in the community. He really didn't know how to fight it. Thing was, they could counter the life insurance policy since I never even tried to collect on it. But what they couldn't fight was that I *did* know better than to operate on my own wife, and by the time the prosecutor was through puttin' me through the meat grinder, the jury knew it too. In the end, he said my best hope was a plea bargain. . . . Livi's daddy really wanted to go for the jugular. . . . but in the end they settled on manslaughter even without me agreeing to somethin' less. I couldn't do that. I served two years in prison. That much I wouldn't argue away."

She was still holding his hand tightly and looking up at him.

Mitch raked a hand through his hair again and drew in a difficult breath. "Funny, you know, two years in that hellhole wasn't as bad as livin' with the knowledge that I am, and always will be, responsible for Livi's death. That's a life sentence that can't ever be overturned."

He gulped back sudden tears when his own pronouncement registered deeply within him. Glenna saw his struggle to rein in his emotions, and she was swept with a new wave of sudden tenderness for him.

She moved a step nearer then, her lips gently brushing his cheek. Consolation. Then it was suddenly something more as it became a soft, gentle kiss. As it grew quickly more urgent, she opened her lips to him and felt a surge of dark pleasure, wanting him.

Wanting this.

Glenna closed her eyes for a moment. Then finally she spoke, and her words came with a little sigh. "If only things were different."

"They can be. We can make them different."

"We live on opposite sides of the world. And I think ye know I could never leave Arrochar. The people there have come to depend on me."

"People like Aengus?"

"Yes," she said, "like Aengus."

Mitch kissed her again, his lips moving so gently against hers. Then he pulled away, cupping her face in his hands. "I want to tell you one thing before tomorrow comes and you go back to your life and the responsibility there."

She waited.

"Now, I know that I haven't done the best job convincin' you that, at the moment, I'm a stellar catch or anything—"

"I think we were both a little wounded when we met one another."

Mitch smiled in silent agreement.

"This time we've spent," she said, "has been a healin', and I—" The rest of the words died on Glenna's lips. What was the point, she thought, of telling him how she felt now? When it wasn't going to—when it *couldn't* change a thing.

"Well, if you ever wake up one mornin' and decide what you have there in Scotland isn't what you want anymore—"

She could feel tears suddenly stinging the backs of her own eyes. A collage of images and feelings came at her. So many of them were bits and pieces of her life with Aengus and Kate. How she had become a part of the fabric of Arrochar. "I won't," she said shakily.

No matter how much I want to, I canno' possibly.

"But if you did, and it was all aboveboard and straight-forward-like—because I know that's the only way it could ever be for you—I'd want you to know that I'll be here."

Glenna tipped her head slightly as her eyes shined. "What are ye sayin'?"

"I'm sayin' that I don't fall in love every day, Glenna Rose McDowell. And I won't be fallin' out of it any time soon, either."

Was this actually possible? Could it be that he truly *had* fallen in love with her, and that love was deep enough for him to simply let her go?

Oh, why had she had to meet this wonderful and complex man now when there was simply no possibility of a future with him? When Aengus was old and sick—when he needed her more than ever. It was the same question she had been asking herself for days. But she never got any answers.

It didn't seem possible, but she had fallen in love with him, too.

It was just so unfair to fall so deeply in love with someone and yet be faced with the fact that you couldn't be together. She and Mitch were meant for one another now, just as Isabelle and Stephen once had been. But fate stood in their way just as powerfully as it had for her parents, all those years before.

Glenna touched Mitch's arm, only a touch, but it was enough to revive that powerfully passionate sensation between them. She watched the same sad smile resurface on his handsome face.

"Why do I feel as if I've lived a lifetime with you?" she asked in a voice that came just above a whisper. It was in that moment when they were close, when she could feel his warm breath on her face, smelling ever so lightly of pinot grigio, just before he kissed her again.

A deep and powerful ache coursed through Glenna as their lips met. It was a kind of longing she had never even been able to imagine before this moment. As if she had never in her life felt anything more wonderful or more excruciating.

How Isabelle had felt so long for Stephen.

"What is it ye want from me, then?"

His voice was low and husky, slightly out of breath. "What I want is to make love to you, Glenna."

"Oh, Mitch, I—"

He held up his hand. "I said I *want* to. More than anything in this world, actually. But you mean that world to me now, and I won't be the one to ask you to go against your commitment to Aengus."

Glenna felt as if she were on an emotional rack, that her heart was still in the process of being torn very slowly and painfully into two halves. Tomorrow she would leave San Francisco and Mitch, perhaps forever. The reality of that now was almost unbearable. But for this moment in time, this old and battered apartment could be like an island, a place where time could be stopped, merely for the asking, couldn't it? A place where she could have just a small jewel of the happiness she had only just begun to feel, to take back with her to Arrochar. To take out and look at sometimes like a special gift, some little piece of this magnificent, enigmatic man. How strange the parallels had become between them and the impossible love her parents had known.

"I want to tell ye," she said softly, and for a moment her voice caught. "I want you to know . . . that I love ye, as well."

A silence fell between them, then deepened. There was only the far-off sound of a police helicopter circling overhead and the steady whir of cars passing by down on Larkin Street. The tiny living room seemed to be whirling around them, then steadily closing out everything, like a cyclone, where at the center, where they were now, everything was perfectly still. Glenna was struggling to hold on to her composure in the midst of that, when what she wanted to do right now more than anything was to lie against him and cry.

If only . . .

Did he sense that? she wondered when he took her hands, drew her back to her feet, and led her into the small bedroom behind the kitchen. Glenna did not know what was going to happen, but she did not object. It was like completing the chapter of a book, their chapter, and knowing you couldn't bear to put the book away until you did.

The room was dark and sparsely furnished, with only a bed and thrift store dresser, but the curtains were open, along with the window, drawing in a lovely fresh evening breeze.

"Just lie with me for a while," Mitch bade her. "It is all that I will ask."

As Mitch looked at her, she saw his eyes glitter with desire. But he did not press her to give any more of herself than she was able. Nor would he. She knew that. Trusted it completely. Because he loved her. He brought her into his arms and she settled against him. They did not speak for a time. They just lay there breathing in rhythm with one another.

This was a kind of intimacy all their own, a nearness deeper almost than making love. It was something that could be private between them. And, that, she knew, it would remain. The little jewel of time she'd thought about, dreamed about, for days now, was theirs. Lying on his still-made-up bed, hours later, wound together, talking, laughing at times, and sharing little jokes as lovers do, Glenna knew in her heart that this was as close as she would ever be to cheating on Aengus. There wasn't going to be anything more. Not tonight.

Yet she felt strangely at peace in her decision to be here, as if some part of her belonged like this with Mitch. And somehow even this place didn't matter. It had at first when they had come through the door and she had been shocked at the simplicity and downright meagerness of where he chose to live. But then, as he told her about Livi, and all that he had lost when she died, Glenna understood that Mitch was giving her a great gift. He was making himself vulnerable again by bringing her here—sharing almost more deeply of himself in that than if they had taken that final step, and gone on to become lovers.

It was strange but, just as she had said before, Glenna felt she'd known Mitch all of her life. And how long had it been really? A week? A few days? But matters of the heart didn't operate on time clocks. Wasn't that what Stephen had told her his friend Father Keough had always said? Well, that too was as true for her now as it had been for Stephen and Isabelle.

When she glanced at the little alarm clock on his bedside table, she was shocked to see that it was almost five-thirty. It felt like only a moment since he first had touched her, and now it was time for her to go.

She shouldn't cry, she knew, but she could feel the tears stinging the backs of her eyes anyway. When Glenna sat up, Mitch did not hold her back. He knew what destiny lay before them. And he understood.

He simply lay there watching her for a little while longer. She felt him trying to memorize the exact shape of her face, the shades of her hair, the color of her eyes. She knew that he was trying very hard to hold those images that would sustain a man who had fallen deeply in love with the right woman.

At the wrong time.

Glenna sat on the side of the bed and slipped her heels back on in the grainy, silver first morning light. Each movement was painful because it took her a little more closely toward good-bye.

Realizing that, she began to cry, softly, silently. Missing him so much already.

Mitch came and sat beside her on the edge of the bed and brushed the tears from her cheek. "Remember what I said now, will you?" he softly asked. "Anytime you need me . . . "

"I won't," she quietly sobbed. "I can no'."

"Don't feel guilty about this. Promise me, hmm?" He placed a finger beneath her chin and turned her face toward his. "You were a perfect lady . . . and, like I said on a night that now seems a lifetime ago to me, too . . . Aengus is one lucky man."

An image of Aengus flitted across her mind, then died. There would be time on the flight back to think about him. About the guilt for almost having been unfaithful. *For having wanted to be.*

Mitch called her a cab because she did not want him to see her back to hotel. Leaving him here, she said, would be difficult enough. They stood at his open front door as a yellow cab honked twice down in the parking lot below. It was very cold, and the mist was almost as heavy as rain.

Mitch wound one of his Pendleton flannel shirts around her shoulders since she hadn't worn a jacket. Then he brought it together, gently, at her throat.

She wanted to tell him again not to wait for her. To get on with his life. Tears were streaming down her cheeks. And they were shining in his eyes, too, making them seem deep and fathomless. Like something magical. But Glenna faltered. She couldn't bring the words in her throat up across her lips. Because the truth was, she didn't want him to get on with his life. To love someone else. Selfishly, she wanted to believe that maybe somehow, someday—

"Well, I suppose by this time tomorrow you'll be havin' a proper cup of good English tea and things will about be gettin' back to normal," Mitch said, his voice breaking slightly.

"Perhaps I'll be takin' a bit o' tea." She tried to smile through her tears. "But things will never seem normal to me again. Not after lovin' *you*, Mitch Greyson."

Then, without telling him good-bye, knowing that she could not bear to, Glenna turned away and walked very quickly down the outside flight of stairs.

When she reached the bottom, she saw an old man gazing at her from behind a kitchen curtain in another of the apartments, and she fought a teary smile. She remembered what Mitch had said about his landlord. Well, this certainly would give the old widowed gentleman something to wonder about, she thought, trying hard not to feel so sad.

The cabbie, a squatty little man with greasy dark hair, a cigarette hanging from the corner of his mouth, and dry sweat stains beneath his short-sleeved white shirt, held open the backseat door for her. She was leaving. She must. But had anything necessary ever hurt so badly? Glenna wondered as she turned one last time and glanced back up at the second-floor landing where Mitch still stood, and would remain, she knew, until the cab pulled away.

She lifted her hand to wave to him, then stopped. If she didn't say good-bye, she thought, then maybe it wouldn't really be over between them. Maybe, just maybe, one day, they might still have a tomorrow.

"Well, I suppose you could call this the moment of reckoning," Stephen said as he rolled over beneath Isabelle's crisp white sheets and pressed a kiss onto her cheek.

Isabelle waited a moment before she opened her eyes. She would have liked to pretend she was asleep. She would have liked to put off for a little while longer that which she had known would have to come . . . to have reveled just a little longer in this their own private splendor. But she could feel the morning sun flooding in across the bed in long, gold streamers, and now he wanted a decision. But, God, how wonderful it was to have him here with her again, just to *be*, with no past, and no future looming fatefully before them.

They had not made love since she had been released from the hospital. But last night, it was as if all of the years between them had been dissolved.

Stephen had followed her upstairs then, in the dimly lit house, and they had gone together silently into one of the guest rooms. Not the room she had shared with Frank. For Isabelle, that would have been too much of a betrayal.

Making love with Stephen last night had been so different, so wanton and free, she thought now, without the dark specter of her father or the priesthood between them. And yet so much about it had been the same as it had felt back in Glenfinnan. The intensity and a passion that quickly overwhelmed them both was there again.

Just as it always would be.

Her mind, still swimming up from a sleepy haze, wound back to Stephen poised over her, his body still nearly as firm and slim as when they were young, his hair still full but now lushly peppered with silver. How she did love the solid feel of him, that raw, trembling bulk of a man whom she had loved since the beginning of time. . . . *And the desperate way he wanted her.*

The memories of what they had done together, here in this bed, made Isabelle suddenly blush. How many years had it been since she had felt that hot rush upon her face? Oh, and elsewhere!

He had been tentative at first. Unsure. Then impatience had overwhelmed him as he'd fumbled with the brass buttons on her cream silk blouse. But that was to be expected, she had thought, as his firm, warm fingers had played over the curve of her cheek, and then down the gentle slope of her bare shoulders, setting her ablaze with desire. He had waited for her all of these years, Stephen had so unbelievably confessed. Never had he given his heart nor any other precious part of himself away, because he had already done that long ago with Isabelle Maguire. In a place called Glenfinnan.

Now Stephen, the one great love of her life, was offering a miracle to her. And this time there was no one, no force against them, to keep her from taking it. Finally, she opened her eyes, and when she did, he kissed her. Tenderly at first, then as firmly as last night, and Isabelle felt that same heat, like a warm glow, begin to rise up and spread from very deep within her. Isabelle sighed and looked at him poised above her.

Stephen ran a finger from her breastbone down between the little cleft her breasts made. "Well?" he asked. "Have you an answer for me now?"

Mercifully, before she could respond, he leaned down and kissed her again, this time passionately. *How I could just stay like this with you forever,* Isabelle was thinking. *So safe here in your arms. So blissfully content. But that is not the real world for me. Someday, I hope. But not yet.*

Stephen touched her then, his fingertips playing over the surface of her skin, blazing that same scorching trail that excited her, and reassured her that yes, after so many years of longing, he really was real—and he was actually here with her.

"Oh, Stephen, my darling Stephen," she whispered as he lowered himself gently onto her once again. She buried her face against his throat, drinking in that sweetly intoxicating musk of his skin and the age-old comfort of his nearness. "First, make love to me again. . . ."

The limousine Stephen had ordered was waiting out on Buchanan Street to take them to the airport. The bags were safely stowed in the shiny black trunk. Now all that was left were the good-byes. Stephen and Kate walked out into the honey-colored morning sun of the rose garden to give Glenna what she had asked for. A moment with Isabelle.

The two women, mother and daughter, tentative friends, stood in the foyer just beyond the open front door. "I wanted to thank you," Glenna said.

"What on earth do you have to thank *me* for?"

Her voice went slightly lower. "For trying to find me all of those years . . . for wanting to find me even now, when I didn't want to find you."

"We have a ways yet to go, don't we?"

Glenna smiled. "But I believe now that we'll get there."

"Oh, I do hope, more than anything in the world, that that's true."

Glenna glanced beyond Isabelle then, into the cozy parlor with its chintz furniture, blue-papered walls, and that wonderful grand piano. But there was something else. Something new. On the mantel, framed in sterling silver, between the potted topiaries, was that same photograph of herself that Glenna had seen last night at Mitch's apartment. A detective's photo set out with the same care and pride as a family portrait, because it was the only one that Isabelle had. Glenna was overcome with a tender affection for this woman she had so wanted to despise but couldn't. A woman she was just beginning to come to know. Glenna moved from the foyer into the parlor, drawing nearer to her own image, the giant wall between them crumbling yet a little more all the time.

"I hope you don't mind," Isabelle said, seeing what Glenna saw, and following her.

"I only wish it could have been a better picture."

Glenna looked back at her and Isabelle smiled. "I think it is an exquisite picture."

When she did not turn away from it nor move to leave, Isabelle took another step forward until they were standing very close. "You don't want to leave San Francisco, do you?"

Glenna wrapped her arms around her waist, wondering for the briefest of moments what it might have been like, through the years, to have had a mother like Isabelle to confide in. Someone who sensed when something was wrong and cared enough to ask. How very different her life might well have been. "It's just so hard," Glenna said softly, deciding to confess it.

"It's Mitch Greyson who's holding your heart here, isn't it?"

She hesitated, but only for a moment. "How d'ye know that?"

"It wasn't all that difficult to figure out," Isabelle's kind smile broadened. "You had to be in the same room only once with the two of you to know that there was something very special there."

"I shouldn't love him," Glenna confessed with a painful sigh, "but I do."

"That is a feeling I know very well."

Glenna looked up, remembering how things had been for her mother and Stephen, all that they had endured to be together. . . . Kindred spirits suddenly, she and Isabelle? After everything, was it actually possible? Life had such a curious way of surprising you, didn't it? The last thing in the world she expected was to feel some connection to Isabelle Wescott beyond their blood. Yet here it was. Shining brightly and unexpected before them both.

"Would it be too much if I asked ye to look in on him from time to time? He's gettin' his life back in order finally, I think, but it's goin' to take him a bit of doin'."

"I'd be happy to do that. Mitch Greyson has very quickly become one of my favorite people."

"Even after what your son accused him of, and without knowin' the whole story?"

"Oh, my dear child," Isabelle smiled. "I learned a long time ago not to judge others by what they *seem* to be, but by what I can see in them for myself. Surely the story of my life has shown you that. And what I see in Mitch, what I have always seen, is a very fine man. A survivor."

And he was that. In fact, Mitch had already told Isabelle what he had confided in Glenna last night: that he had left Tremont & Associates and had embarked on a new chapter of his life. He was beginning a medical hotline, a referral service to physicians for people who needed to find a new doctor. It wasn't practicing anymore, he had told them both, but it was his way of keeping his hand in the field he once had loved so dearly and a way to reconcile with, not run away from, the past.

After talking alone for a few moments, Glenna and Isabelle walked together, their hands gently linked, back out into the sunlight where everyone stood beside the limousine waiting for them. Mothers and daughters. What was it about that bond, Glenna wondered as she looked back at Isabelle, not wanting to say good-bye. It was something so complex, delicate as silk and yet, at the same time, as enduring as a mighty stone. She had it with Katie, that fearsome need to be connected. To stay connected, against all odds. And now, like a great unexpected gift, she had the beginnings of that now, with Isabelle.

Suddenly a gray BMW screeched to a halt behind the limousine and Arthur Wescott shot out of the driver's seat. Seeing the suitcases on the sidewalk, he dashed toward his mother. "For God's sake, Mother, you can't be going off with him now!"

Isabelle drew in a breath. Finally, after a very long time, this was her life. She had control of her destiny, and she meant to seize it.

"Yes, Arthur, I *am* doing just that. In a few weeks, after I have settled my affairs, I am going to Scotland with Stephen, but we are *not* getting married. At least not for the moment. We have to get to know each other again, and I expect that will take time."

"Well, you're certainly *not* going to live with him, I hope!"

"I will be staying at Stephen's home in Glasgow indefinitely, yes, Arthur. And if you have any problem with that, any problem at all, I suggest that you keep it to yourself."

"But what about your life here? Your friends, Douglas, Colin? Me?"

"My life here was very much tied up in your father, Arthur," she said calmly as Stephen, Kate, and Glenna came up beside her. "Now that he's gone, a great deal of that is gone, too. As for Douglas, well, I am very pleased to know that he has Philip. And you, of course . . . well, you have the Senate, at least for another term, don't you?"

"That's rather trite, coming from you."

"Arthur, frankly, I am getting too old to coddle you. I have wasted over half of my life worrying about other people, and I don't plan to do it for one more day. Now, I hope that you will grow accustomed to the idea of my splendid fortune in finding Stephen again. But whether you do or do not is not going to change things."

He rocked back on his heels.

"Oh, don't pout, Arthur. You don't wear it at all well."

"I just don't want you making a fool of yourself, that's all."

"Well, most likely, I will be too far away for anyone you know to hear about it if I do."

Stephen stifled a smile as Isabelle reached up, after a moment, and ran a hand along the curve of Arthur's face. "I love you, son," she said. "But now it's my turn."

"Take care of yourself," Isabelle said, as she moved away from Arthur and across the sidewalk to Glenna.

"Ye do the same." Glenna took her mother's hands. "And I'm happy to hear that the two of you will have each other at last."

"By the end of next month," Isabelle confirmed with a smile. "Wild horses couldn't keep me away from him now."

Glenna climbed into the back seat, and as she watched her parents embrace, she felt a little tug at her heart. Theirs was a love that was deep and abiding. As rare as jewels. To have survived what they had, and now this. The reward for so many years of longing. Of waiting. Of enduring.

Glenna looked away, giving them their moment. But not all love stories had happy endings, she remembered, thinking of Mitch and Livi. Of Mitch and herself. She ached to be with him. A part of her always would. It was that corner of her soul she had given up to him last night—that piece of herself that would remain here, with him, forever, that hurt so now. But going back to Aengus for now was what was right. It was what she had to do. And her regret, if she had one, was only in not being the two people her divided heart had made her.

"Shall we drive past Golden Gate Park on our way out?" Stephen asked as he slid into the seat beside her and pulled the door.

Glenna turned to him, her blue eyes shining, mirroring his. "'Twould be lovely, I think," she smiled through her tears.

Stephen took her hand and gently squeezed it as the driver started the car. "It's going to be all right, you know."

Oh, how desperately she did want to believe that. But right now, the gaping hole in her heart, a wound that seemed to deepen with every beat, was only making her dread all the longing that lay ahead.

"Perhaps we could drive through the park for a bit," Glenna said in a voice choked by a tiny sob. Thinking of Mitch. Wanting to hold onto what small vestiges she had of him.

Yet knowing, somewhere in that little corner of her heart that now belonged to him, that the beginning of their forevers still lay out there, like the vast, heather-clad, mauve-tinted moors she had told him about. That it was only a matter of time.

"I believe I'd like to watch the pedal boaters, and those carefree lads on Rollerblades one last time, if ye would no' mind too much."

America's #1 Bestselling Female Writer

Janet Dailey

Over 300 million copies of her books have been sold, in 98 countries!

NOTORIOUS
In rugged northern Nevada, Eden Rossiter fights to protect her family's ranch. But Eden's strong will weakens when a handsome stranger takes up her cause and captures her heart.
"The novel succeeds on the strength of Dailey's well-paced plot and emotion-packed ending."—*Publishers Weekly*

ILLUSIONS
The glitz and glamour of Colorado ski country is the setting for this spellbinding story about a beautiful security expert, Delaney Wescott, who is drawn into a high-profile murder case while protecting a handsome movie idol.

And a must-have for the millions of Janet Dailey fans...
THE JANET DAILEY COMPANION
by Sonja Massie and Martin H. Greenberg
A comprehensive guide to the life and the novels of Janet Dailey, one of the world's bestselling authors. Includes in-depth interviews and profiles of many of her books.